Darrell listened to the secretary's footsteps echo in the stairwell, and when the sound died away, he said aloud to the empty room, "O-kay, then." Exactly what he needed. Move half way across the country and run into another damn ghost. His gaze swept the small office and took in the widow's walk, remembering the shadowy figure at the railing and the prickle on his neck. He inspected the entire office for paranormal evidence. He saw nothing, of course. Still, there was someone or something there, he sensed it.

Ambling over to the picture window, he took in the expansive scene, white posts and railing of the widow's walk up close and the water of the Chesapeake shining emerald beyond. He could get used to this view.

He'd take the job and...deal with the rest, if it came.

He strolled over to the door. Something drew his attention, and twisting around, he glanced back into the office. A draft of cold air struck him. He shivered again.

He turned to go but couldn't. His shoes were glued to the floor. No, it felt like two huge hands held his ankles and wouldn't let him leave. He pulled on both legs. He stared down at his legs but saw only the smooth cuffs of his dress pants and his black Oxfords.

Ugly memories resurfaced, as if it were yesterday. His uncle's ghost using him as a conduit. The death of two friends. The crippling of his brother.

Blood on the Chesapeake

by

Randy Overbeck

The Haunted Shores Mysteries

This is a work of fiction. Names, characters, places, and incidents are either the product of the author's imagination or are used fictitiously, and any resemblance to actual persons living or dead, business establishments, events, or locales, is entirely coincidental.

Blood on the Chesapeake

Cover Art by *Debbie Taylor*

The Wild Rose Press, Inc.
PO Box 708
Adams Basin, NY 14410-0708
Visit us at www.thewildrosepress.com

Publishing History
First Mainstream Fantasy Rose Edition, 2019
Print ISBN 978-1-5092-2328-2
Digital ISBN 978-1-5092-2329-9

The Haunted Shores Mysteries
Published in the United States of America

Author's Note

This novel is a work of fiction. With the exception of Dr. Martin Luther King, Jr., all characters are products of the author's imagination and are used fictitiously. While several locations on the Eastern Shore are of course actual towns and places, the town of Wilshire, Maryland, and the incidents which occur there in the narrative, are entirely fictional. The civil rights activities, depicted in this narrative, did in fact occur as described, though the author took some license as to place and date. All other elements of the story are completely fictional.

Acknowledgement

While writing is certainly a solitary venture, I did not make this journey alone. First, I would not have accomplished this without the support of my wife and family. Next, my beta-readers were crucial in providing input to fashion the narrative and tweak the story, even as it was evolving. In similar fashion, I have gained much from reading and learning from the works of great fiction writers such as Zoe Sharp, William Kent Krueger, James Benn, and Hank Phillippi Ryan. The opportunity to meet such gifted authors and learn from them at writing conferences was indeed transformative. Most critical to making this novel a reality is the Dayton Tuesday Writers Group, a group of dedicated, unselfish individual authors who gave me hours of advice, criticism, and suggestions to make my writing the best it could be. Finally, I'd like to thank two talented editors who lent their talents to sharpen my story and strengthen my writing, Jaden Terrell and Dianne Rich.

Hardly alone in this adventure. I doubt I could have achieved this if my life had not been blessed by the individuals above.

Chapter 1
August 1998
The Eastern Shore of the Chesapeake Bay

"You see that widow's walk up there, with the white railing and the cupola in the center? That's where they say he died."

The high school secretary, one Mrs. Harriet Sinclair, stood beside Darrell Henshaw on the cracked asphalt parking lot, her small, blue-veined hand pointing up to the third floor.

Darrell's gaze crawled up the two floors of traditional red brick and landed on the white fencing of the widow's walk. He'd noticed the unusual feature of the building when he arrived for the job interview two hours earlier.

Harriett's high voice continued. "Years ago, a student, some poor young black kid took his life up there. Some history, huh?"

Surprised, Darrell looked at the secretary, who kept her gaze focused on the top floor. *She was serious.*

Then Darrell returned his glance to the widow's walk. The brass-topped cupola shone green in the morning sun and below it, a bare-chested, young black man leaned against the fence, his hands dark smudges on the white railing. The youth stared down and met Darrell's gaze. Even though Darrell couldn't read the features on the face three floors up, he was mesmerized.

Somehow, an overwhelming sense of sorrow and regret seemed to emanate from the young man, and for an instant, Darrell felt it pierce him. The hairs on the back of his neck stood on edge. He shivered and stared, unable to look away. The figure at the fence shimmered and then disappeared.

Oh, God, no. Not again.

He turned to ask Harriet, but she rattled on about some of the less morbid history of the school. "That walk is famous, all right. There was the great piglet race up there and the famous protest streamers on the walk…"

Darrell stopped listening. He hadn't felt that…that sensation for years. Ten years. A decade earlier, he'd had a confrontation with another ghost. One that ended in death. It still haunted him.

Then, something Harriet said registered. "That window up there to the right, that'll be your office."

He struggled to find his voice. "My office?"

"Yep. At least, if Mr. Douglass likes what he hears when he calls your references." She winked at him, one gray eyebrow curling like an albino caterpillar. "Our athletic office isn't much, only a tiny space, but it's got the best view in the building. I thought you might appreciate the vantage point better from down here."

He got the job? He couldn't believe it. After thirty-seven resumes, eighteen phone calls, four failed interviews, he'd done it. And just in time, too.

He stared open-mouthed at the building, trying to keep his exhilaration under wraps, and then remembered the shimmering image of the young black man and realized the job may come with some *extras*. He was not thrilled about any extras, but he *really* needed the job. Before he had time to think about it, Harriet was off.

For the next forty minutes, she took Darrell on a non-stop tour of the empty high school, leading him past dueling trophy cases—one for sports, one for band—through run-down classrooms, and into a dilapidated gym with collapsing bleachers. Twice he paused, seeing an award or painting hanging crooked, and reached out to straighten it. He stopped himself and then had to hurry to catch up.

Harriet charged ahead, short legs pumping like pistons, while she regaled him with more stories about the old high school. Darrell was hardly able to catch his breath. At her pace, he felt like he'd done a 5K, zigzagging through hallways and up and down creaking stairs. They finished by climbing two flights of stairs to arrive at the athletic office.

As they reached the top step, a door in the hall slammed shut. Darrell jerked. He glanced over to his escort, who hadn't even flinched. Instead, the school secretary asked, as if reminded of something, "Mr. Henshaw, uh, do you believe in…uh, ghosts?"

Darrell's mouth went dry. *She didn't just ask that.*

"What?" he managed.

Harriet shrugged, the collar of her gray dress almost touching the lowest locks of silver hair. "I simply asked if you were superstitious. You know, if you believe in ghosts?" She strolled over, turned the handle, and pulled open the door.

Darrell fought not to go pale. Could she possibly know about the ghost back home? He fumbled for an answer. "Uh, no more than most, I think. Why?"

Standing at the door, she lowered her glance, as if

examining her black flats. "Well, uh, some folks say the school is haunted. Ghost of that student who committed suicide I was telling you about. They say his spirit likes to prowl the hallways at night, 'specially up here on the third floor."

Darrell remembered the figure staring down at him from the railing and the prickling hairs on his neck. He studied Harriet. She *was* serious.

But when her gaze lifted, the secretary smile was back in place. "What do you expect? It's an old school. Bound to hold a few skeletons, right?"

Harriet stepped inside the office, burying the subject as abruptly as she raised it. She led him in, and Darrell watched as dust mites rose and danced on a wave. The cramped space was small, eight by twelve maybe, with a worn, blue couch under the broad window and a standard gray metal desk and file cabinet on the wall opposite. A lone, wooden bookcase stood facing the door, barren and sad-looking, its shelves sagging.

She moved to the window, pointing, "Great view of the widow's walk from here, too."

Several questions pummeled his brain—about what happened on the walk, about the kid who died—but he needed this job, so he didn't ask.

She plowed on. "I got to get back to my desk. Mr. Douglass will need a few more minutes. If you want to get the feel of the place, you can hang out here if you like, but make sure you're back in his office in about fifteen minutes." Two brisk steps took her to the door.

Darrell thought of one question he figured it'd be safe to ask. "Harriet, you mentioned I was the last name on Principal Douglass' list of candidates. How come?"

She turned and grinned. "Maybe I shouldn't have told you. The answer's simple, though. None of the rest of the candidates were *Yankees*." She waved a hand. "Anyway, you must've made quite an impression, 'specially for a Yankee. Not many get the fifty-cent tour. Enjoyed showing ya around. I'm a good judge of character, and I think you'll do fine."

"Thanks, Harriet, for the tour and all the background. And the vote of confidence."

"I'll see you downstairs in a bit." Her leg pistons chugged, and she disappeared through the open doorway.

Darrell listened to her footsteps echo in the stairwell, and when the sound died away, he said aloud to the empty room, "O-kay, then." Exactly what he needed. Move half way across the country and run into another damn ghost. His gaze swept the small office and took in the widow's walk, remembering the shadowy figure at the railing and the tingle on his neck. He inspected the entire office for paranormal evidence. He saw nothing, of course. Still, there was someone or something there—he sensed it.

Ambling over to the picture window, he took in the expansive scene, white posts and railing of the widow's walk up close—with no young black man there—and the water of the Chesapeake shining emerald beyond. He could get used to this view.

He'd take the job and...deal with the rest, if it came.

He strolled over to the door. Something drew his attention and twisting around, he glanced back into the office. A draft of cold air struck him. He shivered again.

He turned to go but couldn't. His shoes were *glued* to the floor. No, it felt like two huge hands held his ankles and wouldn't let him leave. He pulled on both legs. He stared down at his legs but saw only the smooth cuffs of his dress pants and his black Oxfords.

Ugly memories resurfaced, as if it were yesterday. His uncle's ghost using him as a conduit. The death of two friends. The crippling of his brother. *Oh, hell, not again.*

Sweat dripped down the side of Darrell's face, and he blurted out the only thing he could think of. "I haven't even been hired yet," he said in a harsh whisper. "And won't be, unless I get back down there to see the principal."

The grip on his ankles released. He opened the door, stepped through, and slammed it. In seconds, he hit the stairs, taking them two at a time.

Chapter 2

It was the students' first day, and Darrell wanted to be there before anyone else. In the misty dawn, he stood facing the old Wilshire High School building, watching twelve mirrored suns in the ancient windows. He took a deep breath and released it. What a sight.

Over the past month, while he got his football team ready for the season and his classroom ready for teaching, he'd struck a bargain with himself. He would put his haunted childhood and cheating fiancée behind him and focus on the students, *his* students. When nothing more had happened after he felt the stranglehold on his ankles, he'd almost convinced himself he'd imagined the whole thing. Almost.

Examining the school, he reminded himself, this, this was what he really loved—connecting with teens, breaking through their shells, and helping them appreciate the history of their incredible country.

He studied the building—now, his building—fifty feet across the pockmarked parking lot. The old building's two sets of six domed windows perched beneath ornate white trim at the roof line. Once a proud building, years of winds and rain off the Chesapeake had pelted the surface into submission until the mortar wept and strips of the gray, aged cement dangled out like emaciated snakes. The new high school planned for next year would open none too soon.

"You're here awfully early, kid. Who you trying to impress?" called a voice from across the lot.

Darrell lowered his gaze and caught the broad grin of Al McClure, band director. A slim five-foot-eight, the guy bounded across the cracked asphalt to where Darrell stood. Al reached up and clasped Darrell on the shoulder.

"Couldn't sleep, huh?" Al asked, his face bright, his blue eyes bloodshot behind brown-framed glasses. "First day jitters?"

Darrell nodded.

"Good sign. Means you're excited...or scared." Al released his hold. "Look, twenty-seven years now and I'm here at the crack of dawn."

Darrell had met Al on his second day, and though a generation apart, the two men hit it off immediately. During a month of football practices and marching band camp before the school year began, Al had been glad to answer Darrell's many questions. But Al also delighted in taking every opportunity to needle him.

Standing there, Al asked, "Hey kid, you know why you play two halves of a football game?"

"Why?"

"So the crowd's ready for the real entertainment. The band halftime show." Al laughed, and Darrell couldn't help but chuckle, a little more relaxed.

Al asked, "Now, ready to head in to meet those not-so-anxious faces?"

"Almost. Trying to take it all in." Darrell squinted at the top of the school building, arm shielding his eyes against the multiple suns' reflections.

Al asked, "Hey, did you hear about the guy who stayed up all night to see where the sun went? Then it dawned on him."

"I get it." Darrell grinned, without shifting his gaze.

Atop the small third floor stood the crown of the old school building, a thirteenth domed window, a shorter version of the dozen below. The same one Darrell had studied for the first time more than a month ago, when Harriet pointed it out. When he saw the figure and sensed *it*. Even though he'd been in the office, his office, almost every day since and been on the widow's walk several times, the sensation had not returned. That was fine with him. He'd had enough of a "spiritual encounter" when he was a teen. He wasn't looking for another.

Then, as if his thoughts had summoned something, someone, Darrell saw a figure in his office window, a large, bare torso of a black man. The same one he'd seen on the day of his interview? His neck hairs started to prickle again. He glanced over to his friend and then back up. The sun rose a degree, igniting that window pane and incinerating the image. When Darrell adjusted his arm to see again, the top window was empty.

"Did you see that?" he asked Al.

"What?"

"I saw somebody in my office. Black kid. A student, maybe?"

"Can't be." Al pushed his glasses up his nose and peered at the top floor. "No kids allowed in the building yet. Probably Jesse Stewart, head custodian. You know, he gets here early."

Custodian with his shirt off?

Darrell concentrated on the building. Beside the empty top window sat the widow's walk, surrounded on all sides with a railing fence of elaborate, carved white trim. An octagonal copper cupola, supported by four white corner posts, covered the walk. The walk was large, he'd found when he walked out there, probably twelve feet on a side, with room for several jostling adolescents. He'd never seen anything like it on a school building.

Al marched across the parking lot, hollering back over his shoulder, "The students'll be here before you know it."

"Mornin' Mr. McClure," called a short, wiry black man, who fell in step beside Al.

Al turned and smiled. "Morning, Jesse." The two disappeared together through the wooden double doors.

Darrell hustled to catch up and then pulled up short. Jesse? He shot another look at the window in his office—empty. It couldn't have been Jesse. The hairs on his neck stood on end again. *Oh, shit.* He brushed hand across his neck, shaking his head, and hurried inside.

****

Before his students arrived, Darrell tried to dismiss what he'd seen and calm his jittery nerves by setting out the essentials on his desk—class lists, textbooks, seating charts, gradebook—in a reassuring, rectangular arrangement. Then, he decided he wasn't happy with his chosen array, so he repositioned each, twice. Shaking his head, he reached to rearrange them again.

Leave them where they are, he thought. It won't matter to the teens. He stared at the almost "perfect" arrangement and remembered a time when he didn't have to set everything into perfect order. When he didn't feel the compulsion to control every part of life possible. When it was okay to let life happen. Before the first ghost.

Breathing slowly, he focused again on his players and his other students. That's why he was here he told himself again. These kids needed him, even if they didn't yet know it.

A few minutes later, he faced his first period class, arms crossed, as the students settled in, jostling in the uncomfortable desks and messing up the perfectly straight rows he'd taken pains to organize yesterday. These teens didn't look eager to learn history or... anything else. Like adolescents everywhere, most appeared to wear their indifference like a badge of honor.

Principal Douglass had warned him. Most of his students were poor, and their body language screamed alienation and resentment. Instead of the designer clothes he'd seen in some of his classes in Michigan, most wore weathered tees with sayings like "Just do it" and "My other car is a Porsche" above cheap stirrup pants and ripped denim.

To start off, he completed the required first-day ritual—attendance, rules and regulations, lunch arrangements—but the students took little heed. Only his story of coming to Wilshire elicited any response. A skinny, black youth in an oversized FUBU tee shirt called out, "Dude, how dumb do ya have to be to leave the big city and come to this shit hole nothin' of a town to teach?"

Amid the laughter, Darrell chose not to confront the student yet. He'd learned the ones who act out first often need the most help. "Oh, I decided I needed a change. And Chesapeake Bay is one of the most beautiful places in the country." And, he thought, I needed to get away from my ex.

With not much time left, Darrell wanted to get something memorable into their first day's class and decided to start with a lesson that might nudge them a bit. He turned his back to the class, always a tricky proposition with teens, and wrote on the scarred blackboard, "American History." Then right below it, he scrawled, "The difference between being free or slave, being here or not." He turned and stared at the students.

Another male black student, this one near the front, large with a shaved head, grumbled, "What's a pasty white face like you know about slavery?"

A white girl in the second row with short black hair and multiple studs and earrings challenged, "Who cares what a bunch of white guys did back in the day, anyway?" She drew a round of "yeahs" from the other kids.

Well, at least, he moved their indifference dial a little.

Darrell felt a trickle of sweat crease his hairline. "You should…unless you want to be *losers*." Though their careful, bored postures barely altered, he could see the response in their eyes. Disagreement, defiance. He figured *that* got their attention.

He continued, "History is written by the victors. And unless you want to be losers, you need to know the lessons of history…and learn from them. Instead of starting at the beginning with *a bunch of white guys from back in the day*," he stopped, glancing at the studded girl. "I thought we'd start with one of the most pivotal Supreme Court cases ever, 'Brown vs. Board of

Education.' "

He grabbed another piece of chalk and scribbled the five words on the board.

"You've probably heard of it. The case in 1954 which banned segregation in schools and changed public education in America. It established all students, black or white, are entitled to the same quality education. We'll talk about how that decision affected public schools all across this country, even right here in Wilshire."

The bare-headed teen who had made the earlier challenge shifted in his seat. Darrell could now see he was tall, well over six feet, with a gang tattoo on the student's neck that pulsed in the overhead fluorescent light. This kid reminded Darrell of the apparition on the walk and in the window—tall, big black guy.

The teen said, "That's great, Teach, but maybe *you* ought to learn the history of Wilshire first?"

Darrell shot a quick glance at his seating chart and found the student's name. "Tyler?" The student gave a slight nod. "What history did you have in mind?"

Tyler checked the classroom clock and rose in his seat, eyes now level with his teacher. "I mean real history, not the stuff they feed the tourists. Like the real history behind our school ghost."

The gaze of every student turned from Tyler to Darrell and back to Tyler, who smirked as the bell rang, clamoring and emptying the room.

Chapter 3

The stadium horn blared a long, mournful blast, and the loudspeaker barked, "Well, the Wilshire Pirates lose their first game of 1998 in a squeaker, 20-17. On behalf of the Pirates and from all of us at Williams Stadium, thanks for coming and drive home safely."

Darrell followed his players across the field, curved helmets bobbing in a long white stream in front of him, as they exchanged hand slaps with their opponents. Pogo, his new brown and white pug, weaved between his legs, managing twice to almost trip him. After finding the pug at the animal shelter, Darrell had brought it along to the first practice. The players adopted the pooch, and Pogo became the unofficial team mascot, running up and down the sidelines during practices and now, games. While Darrell stopped to chat with the Cambridge coach, Pogo squatted at his feet, tongue lolling to one side and tail flopping back and forth like a furry metronome. Congratulations exchanged, coach and dog trotted back across the field and Al, his band uniform still crisp, strode over.

"Good game," called Al.

"Thanks." Darrell was proud of his kids, even if they didn't win.

"Your guys gave the spectators something to watch...besides our half-time show, that is." Al glanced around conspiratorially and grinned at Darrell. "You know what you really need though?"

"What?"

"You need to talk to the Wilshire ghost and convince him to play on our defensive line." Al chortled.

Darrell didn't laugh. "What are you talking about?"

Al put his hand on Darrell's shoulder, still grinning. "You know, the school ghost who likes to roam around the third floor. He's so big, he'd scare the hell out of them."

"Wha-a-at? What do you know about a ghost?" Darrell's eyes got wide, and his breath caught in his chest.

"Relax, kid. I'm only pulling your chain. I know you heard the stories by now." Al slapped Darrell on the back and bent down, petting the pug. "Hey, what are you guys doin' later?"

Darrell exhaled, glad to change the subject. "Hitting the showers and heading home, I guess."

"No way. You're comin' over to our house. We're all getting together and having a few beers. You've earned them. And my Sara made some of her great football chili."

After his first game, his first loss as a head coach, Darrell wasn't sure he wanted anyone else dissecting his failures. "I don't know. I'm pretty bushed."

"Ah, come on over for a bit. It's a Wilshire tradition," Al said. "Win or lose, *usually lose*, we have the coaches and wives over for a little R and R."

Darrell shrugged. He was hungry, anyway. "Okay. For a little while, I guess."

"Besides, somebody'll be there we want ya to meet."

The way Al said it made Darrell nervous. "Thanks, Al, but I'm not really interested in meeting anyone." When he thought of his last *someone*, it still stung.

"Trust me on this, you'll want to meet *her*." With a wink, the band leader headed off toward the field house, hurrying to catch the trailing sousaphone player.

Darrell crouched down and petted his canine companion, rubbing the smooth fur behind his neck. "What do you think, Pogo? Al wants me to meet a *friend*. Didn't we swear off girls?"

The pug lifted his head, two black, sorrowful eyes staring up. Darrell said, "That's what I thought."

He glanced across the field and saw his principal approaching, accompanied by two men dressed in full business attire. Partway down the chain-link fence, they stopped and spoke with a larger, pear-shaped, uniformed man with a wide-brimmed "Smokey" hat. The men exchanged warm handshakes with the cop and headed his way. Watching them approach, Darrell was reminded of Tyler's grumble the other day in class, "*The Man* is always out to get ya."

Darrell wondered if Tyler was right. Was his principal coming over to chide him on his first failure as a Wilshire coach? The guy'd probably blame it on Darrell's Yankee roots. He'd brought it up often enough. Watching Jeb Douglass approach, Darrell was struck by how much the principal looked like Icabod Crane—tall, willowy, crooked nose, wire-rimmed spectacles.

"Coach Henshaw, I got a few people for ya to meet," said Principal Douglass. "This is our Board President, William—"

"Bud Williams. Everyone calls me Bud," broke in

the first man, tall and broad shouldered, with a privileged bearing and hard olive eyes. His crop of short hair may have once been brown or auburn, but had migrated to gray. He wore a tight smile with perfect white teeth and extended his hand, his handshake solid, grip a little too firm.

Board president? Oh, this was going to be great. Darrell rubbed his hand behind his back. Now, he really wished he'd been able to pull out a win. "That would be Williams, as in Williams Stadium?"

"Named for my grandfather, William Williams the First," announced the board president. His words were crisp, clipped. He crossed his arms in front of him.

"And soon-to-be new Williams High School," added the principal, one finger pushing his bifocals over the bump on the bridge of his nose. "The Williams family has done more for this school than anyone else. He and his bank have donated a great deal of money for the new building, and the board decided to name it after the Williams."

Darrell thought, the real boss. Who practically owns the school. He studied Williams and noticed a small crescent scar on his right chin. He tried not to stare.

"Back in the day," Douglass said, "Bud here tore up this field. Some kinda quarterback. Set all these school records. Won his share of trophies along the way."

"I've seen your name on the trophies in the case. Impressed." Darrell remembered reading the plaques— *Athlete of the Year. League MVP. State Championship Team Captain*. Oh, great. Rich *and* knew enough football to criticize Darrell's every move. "You don't happen to have any sons you've been hiding away, do you?"

"I am afraid not. I have two *daughters*, twelve and sixteen. One in your American history class," said Williams.

"Carrie Williams." Darrell recalled the sharp-dressed redhead. "Third period."

"And speakin' of football," said the principal, indicating the shorter man next to him, with a fireplug of a body encased in a tight-fitting gray suit. "This here is Dr. Trevor Remington, best surgeon in town, another great school supporter and also one of the finest to wear the Pirate uniform. In the '60s, played the other side of the ball, tackled anythin' that moved."

The squat physician extended a pudgy hand. Darrell shook it, thinking the fat fingers would make delicate surgery a little cumbersome. The man had black hair, cut short, and a small black goatee covering his chin.

With a smile that started at his mouth, but never reached his hazel eyes, Remington said, "Jeb said he wasn't sure about you when he hired you."

Super, two former football stars and hyper critics, both "great school supporters." Just what he needed. Darrell fought to hide his anxiety and kept his smile fixed.

Remington continued, "But he said he likes what he sees so far. I can see why. That's some of the best football I've witnessed from our kids in years."

Darrell relaxed a bit but didn't let down his guard. "We still didn't win it. You don't get any points for nearly winning."

Remington dropped the handshake. "Still. You

should've seen these kids last year. They've come a long way in a few weeks."

"They're young, but they're learning." Darrell shot a glance toward the locker room.

The shorter man placed a fleshy palm on Darrell's arm. "Bud and I have come to pretty much every home game. For more than twenty years, we'd shake our heads in disgust. Your kids played hard tonight, at least. Makes me think there may be hope for Pirate football again. Can't wait to see what they can do the rest of the season."

"We'll do our best," Darrell said. No pressure, though, right? Certainly no unrealistic expectations or anything. No, of course not.

"If your team needs anything, anything at all," Williams said, "simply notify Dr. Remington or myself, and we will do what we can to accommodate you."

"Really?" Darrell was so surprised he didn't know what to say. "Well, nothing comes to mind right now, but I'll keep your offer in mind. I'm sure we'll come up with something."

He noticed Douglass scowling at him, his thin frame standing right behind the other two, probably because Darrell wasn't excited *enough* about the offer, so he said, "Oh, thanks for the offer. It's great to meet you, Bud and Trevor. Now, I better get in there and give my players a few inspiring words."

He threw a small salute and jogged toward the locker rooms, Pogo trotting alongside him. Feeling their stares at his back, Darrell picked his way across the field, being careful not to step on the chalk stripe at the thirty-yard line. And the twenty-yard line *and* the ten-yard line.

Anything the team needed, huh? he thought as he made his way toward the fieldhouse. Anything? Our own set of Santas, huh? Lots of coaches would kill for such benefactors, but something, something nagged at him. The offer sounded really good.

Almost too good to be true.

He wondered what strings were attached to it.

Chapter 4

The excitement of the game ebbed and Darrell's adrenalin drained away along with the water as he showered. Yawning, he wavered, contemplating the smooth, freshly made bed in his apartment. But he had promised Al, so he decided he'd make a brief appearance at the McClure's, fill up on chili and beer, and head back home.

Then, he met *her*.

The chili was served up by Al's wife, Sara, who wore her blonde hair cut short, pageboy style, and a sunny, yellow tee shirt with the words "Maryland is for Crabs." The dish was as good as promised and filled the crowded family room with a delightful odor of cooked beef and spices, as well as animated conversations. Darrell enjoyed the food so much, he dribbled some, to his horror, on the front of his bright yellow polo.

The stain looked huge, dark brown against the clean, pristine yellow, and practically screamed at him. Embarrassed, he dabbed at it with a napkin, which of course only made it worse. *Shit.* He glanced around, worried everyone would stare at it. You're overreacting, he told himself. Two deep breaths in, out. It was only a small stain, about the size of his fingertip. He shot another glance around. They don't care.

After downing two bottles of a local beer Sara favored, Dogfish Head, he was able to forget about it.

21

He relaxed a bit and even laughed at the ribbing he took from the gang for his "football foibles."

Around midnight, Darrell rose to leave.

Al kicked back the recliner, cranking the lever and lifting argyle-stocking feet in the air. "No can do, at least not yet. I told you there was someone we want you to meet."

"I'm pretty wiped out," Darrell said, with an anxious look at his stained shirt. "I don't really feel like meeting anyone." His sloppiness would've driven Carmen, his ex, nuts. "Darrell, why don't you change that shirt?" she'd ask. Darrell hardly needed to be reminded. He drew the last of the beer. He'd had enough "someones" to last him a while.

The doorbell sounded, and Sara called from the kitchen, "Don't get up, you lazy slugs. I'll get it." In a few seconds, she reappeared at the family room door with a stunning, tall, twenty-something redhead. Her hair was tied in a ponytail and pulled back from a near perfect, oval face. She had graceful features, a long, slim neck and a sprinkling of reddish-brown freckles that, rather than distract from her beauty, accentuated it. And two of the most gorgeous green eyes he'd ever seen. He realized Sara was saying something and pulled his gaze from the young woman beside her.

"Darrell, this is Erin. She works as a nurse in OB with me at Chesapeake and just got off her shift. Erin, this is Darrell, who I told you about."

Deep green eyes crinkling, Erin smiled and extended her hand. "Hey, Darrell," she said in a voice both breathy and tired. "Erin Caveny."

"She's a local," Sara said. "Family goes back a couple generations on the Bay."

"You betcha." Erin raised her right fist in a weary Pirate salute. "Wilshire Class of '91. Go, Pirates."

Despite his resolve to swear off women, Darrell couldn't keep from staring. "Uh, it's great to meet another local. Um, someone who's native. I mean, someone whose family is local to the Bay." His cheeks reddened. God, he sounded so lame.

"Family's been here since the late 1800s," she said.

"You must be tired after being on your feet all night." Darrell recovered and led her to his chair. "Here, have a seat." He enjoyed watching her move across the family room. When she settled into the chair, he noticed how her slim hips and ample breasts tugged at her scrubs in all the right places. She didn't look *anything* like Carmen.

"Can we get you a drink?" Al asked.

Erin said, "I'd love a Dogfish Head beer, and I was promised some of Sara's great chili. I'm famished."

"Coming right up." Al disappeared into the kitchen with Sara.

The other coaches and wives stood and made their excuses, calling their thanks as they went out the door. The only two left in the room, Darrell and Erin glanced at each other, and, after a bit they both started talking at once, then stopped. Darrell chuckled, and Erin released a delighted giggle. A minute later, Al delivered the chili and beer and backed through the swinging door, leaving them alone again.

Darrell thought the whole thing would be awkward. He figured he'd be tongue-tied or even make a fool of himself. But as the two of them sat before the hissing blaze, Erin made it easy. She went first, and they simply talked. About Wilshire, about football, about nursing. She even asked about his students. Much to his surprise, Darrell found being with her comfortable. He glanced down and noticed again the stain on his shirt and placed a hand over it. He'd forgotten all about it. Unbelievable—he wasn't even embarrassed.

He probably would've chatted with her all night, but Erin claimed exhaustion. An hour later, he held open her car door and she said, "I'm so glad Sara talked me into coming by tonight." The touch of her fingers lingered on his. "It'd be nice to get together tomorrow night."

"Sounds good. I've got your number," Darrell said, and she made the "call me" sign through the window of the Jeep. He nodded, and she smiled back.

A really nice smile. The rest of her wasn't bad either.

Her taillights disappeared in the dark like the dying red embers of the fire they had watched. Then, as exhaustion from the days' events battled with the thrill of meeting Erin, he crossed to his Corolla and inhaled the nighttime smells of the Bay. As he sniffed the aromas of fish, kelp, and brackish water, he was reminded how lucky he was to be here—teaching, coaching, and living on the Eastern Shore. And now, Erin. Maybe, one more reason to love the area.

Inside his apartment, he undressed, folded each piece of clothing carefully, and laid them on their appropriate piles in his laundry basket. He flipped off the lights and collapsed into bed. Beside him, Pogo burrowed into his blanket and settled down with a few whimpers. Within a minute, Darrell succumbed to sleep, savoring the details of his late-night encounter with Erin.

Sometime after, the dream began, reels of sputtering film projected inside his head. From the first, it felt different, more ethereal. His hairs started to prickle, but Darrell's consciousness was so diluted by alcohol, weariness, and the intoxication of meeting Erin, he didn't notice. Instead, he surrendered to the strange vision.

The image of auburn hair coalesced before him and shimmered in the reflection of a single light bulb, as she turned away, laughing. The scent of a strong floral cologne in the air, he leaned over and caressed her neck, running his lips down her graceful throat. He kissed the sprinkling of freckles, the taste of her skin slightly salty. Beside him, her hand materialized and guided his down her naked body, her long, beautiful fingers the becoming perfect escort.

From somewhere, music floated in, three finger snaps followed by the bouncing sound of guitar, drums, and harmonized voices. The song tugged at his hazy memory, but he couldn't call up the title. One of the oldies his dad liked to listen to, he thought, but couldn't be sure. He glanced across the room and could've sworn he saw a 45 spinning on an old turntable, the needle balancing on the black plastic. The record played on and, four chords later, it hit him, like an inspiration. "My Girl."

His gaze drifted down, and he noticed, in the dim light of the room, his hand looked large and strangely dark, black almost. Before he had time to think about it, she giggled, and he glanced back up. Her laugh sounded different, and he moved to turn her face toward him, but her features went hazy.

"Yip. Yip, yip."

Wet tongue slobber across his face jerked Darrell back to consciousness. He sat up in bed and sent Pogo scampering to the floor.

"Thanks, boy, I think." Darrell stared around the room. The murky features of his apartment emerged in low light. He was alone. No girl. No sound other than the panting of the pug, the dog's black eyes fixed on him.

"I'm okay." Darrell reached his hand out, and Pogo tongued it. "It was only a dream. One weird dream." Darrell grabbed a wipe from the box he kept close and cleaned off his face and hand. He'd only met Erin tonight, and he didn't usually dream like that. Not that he minded it.

The bedside clock read 3:13. He stared at the three numbers, sensing there was *something* about the time, but his tired brain simply couldn't process it. "3:13," he said aloud.

Chapter 5

"I can't believe I didn't see that, Pogo," Darrell said, staring at the TV in front of his desk. "Look. Jake, our QB, telegraphed his pass, right before he threw it. See that? No wonder he got picked off." He stopped and hit the *rewind* button on the VCR and then watched the action replay, this time in slow motion. "I think *you* could've intercepted that ball, boy."

Darrell went through the game tape four times, taking time to analyze every play and review every call. He was stunned he had amassed six pages of detailed notes. The guys had fared pretty well for their first game of the year, but he figured, if they kept losing, there wouldn't be many more kudos from Williams and Remington. They *had* to get better. No pressure, though. Yeah, right.

He smiled to himself and shook his head. Still, he loved working with these kids and thought he was making a difference. And he especially enjoyed watching game film like this in his office, window open, sound off. Thankfully, there'd been no more visitations up here the past six weeks, though, when he thought about it, he could still feel the iron grip around his ankles.

He stretched. The quiet murmur of the waves against the shore cloaked the office. His gaze migrated to the picture window, and he examined the widow's walk with its four corner posts and green brass cupola. He stared beyond it at the incredible blue-green of the Bay and then glanced back at his office.

He was embarrassed. Six weeks in and he still hadn't unpacked everything. Not like him. The final three boxes sat in a neat stack in the corner. He needed to get them emptied and organized. At least, the bookcase no longer looked barren. He'd stacked a few books on the top shelf and reserved the middle shelf for the NBA basketball autographed by Michael Jordan, which gleamed as if it had just bounced off the court.

Darrell yawned. After the crazy dream last night, he'd tried to sleep but found any real slumber elusive. Was the dream about Erin? That didn't seem quite right, though she was the only redhead he'd met recently. Now, in the light of day, he realized the dream had seemed so real he didn't know what to make of it.

The appearances in this window, the presence here in the office, now that crazy dream. He didn't know how, but he felt—or rather sensed—they were all connected. Somehow.

He checked his watch, surprised to find he'd been at this for almost three hours.

From the second desk drawer, he grabbed and tossed a doggie treat. Pogo caught it in midair, and in two seconds it disappeared with loud, gulping sounds. Darrell reached into the third drawer and pulled out a package of cheese crackers and a white napkin. He unfolded the napkin and laid it out on the blotter. Then, his thumb and index finger carefully tore the cellophane off the package, making sure to keep any stray crumbs over the napkin. He ate the snack and when he finished, he pulled up the napkin by the four corners, rolled it all into a tight ball, and laid it in the trash can.

"Okay, boy, what do you say we take a look at those Easton Bulldogs?" He glanced down at his pug, who stared back, tail slapping the floor. "No, they're not that kind of bulldogs."

Darrell inserted the videotape and settled down to watch their next opponents. He tried to concentrate, but after a few minutes, weariness overcame him. Partway through the first quarter of the game, his eyelids heavy, he drifted off.

Pogo's bark woke him with a start. Darrell heard the yip but, looking around, couldn't see the pug. Thunder boomed. He looked out the window. Under a dark sky, a fierce storm sent rain against the pane, drops running down the window, turning the glass translucent, and spilling onto the back of the TV.

Atop the desk, his leg muscles had grown numb, and Darrell struggled to pull them off and onto the floor. He hobbled over to close the window and turned to see the dog. Pogo stood stiff, staring up at the TV, rear backed almost against the desk, little tail straight up.

Darrell tugged the ancient window down. "What's the matter, boy?"

He studied the room, searching for anything out of place. Found nothing awry. Bookshelf, boxes, doorway—all undisturbed and empty. No one around. Out of instinct, he glanced down at his ankles. He lifted them off the floor, one at a time. Nothing. To be sure, he went to the door and scanned the hallway.

No one.

Returning, he noticed the pug hadn't budged, still focused on the television. The TV image had frozen, little more than a gray fuzzy blur, and Darrell figured he must've bumped the *pause* button on the remote earlier.

"Did you see something, Pogo?"

He rubbed the dog behind his head, but the pug didn't react. Instead, Pogo growled and pointed his snout at the TV. Darrell grabbed the remote and hit *play*.

No miniature players scurried across the football field. In their place, a bare torso of a large black youth filled the screen, eyes blazing. His mouth moved, but no words came out. The young man looked immense. The powerful sinews in his arms and his bare chest seemed to bulge out through the screen.

Darrell glanced from the TV to the dog. "You see that, boy?" The pug yipped once but stood rigid, riveted. "Of course, you do. You saw it first, didn't you?"

When he looked back, Darrell could have sworn the young black man stared straight at him, could *see* him. The man's lips moved as if he was trying to say something, but Darrell couldn't hear anything. Then he realized he had the sound off and reached for the remote again without taking his eyes off the screen. He noticed two wet trails of sweat roll down the youth's chest and appear to drip onto the black plastic frame beneath the screen. Darrell told himself the rain must have gotten onto the front of the television, somehow— even though it was facing away from the window. Puzzled, he approached the TV and touched his index finger to the plastic. It came away wet. He brought his finger to his lips and tasted the slightly salty moisture. He reached to touch the second stream, and the image evaporated, dissolving into a gray haze.

Darrell shuddered, the hairs on his neck prickling. *What the hell.* He glanced down at his ankles.

A second later, the small uniformed players reappeared, scurrying across the dark gray turf. For a few moments Darrell watched, confused. Then anxious. Then dreading.

Apprehension gnawing at him, he hit the *stop* button and then *rewind*. From the whirl of the tape in the VCR, he guessed he'd gone back far enough and punched *stop*, then *play*. When he did, the players scurried around. He let the tape roll on, eyes fixed on the picture. The teams went through one snap, then another, then a third. Then he saw the play he had watched right after...after what? The quarterback keeper around left tackle, like he'd seen before.

He must've misjudged. Darrell tried five more times to locate the spot on the tape with the black youth, rewinding and replaying, but each time he stopped and hit *play*, he found only football footage.

"If you weren't here, I would've sworn I dreamt the whole thing." He glanced at the pug. "But you saw it too, didn't you?"

Pogo barked once and panted, his tongue dripping onto the threadbare, gray carpet.

"Maybe we're both going crazy, huh?" But he knew he wasn't. Just like the last time. His uncle—or rather his uncle's ghost—had tried to tell him, tried to warn him. But what connection did he have to this ghost? *Why is this happening again?*

The phone bleated, and Darrell jerked. Grabbing up the handset, he glanced outside and noticed the storm had moved on, the sky now a stunning palette of reds, yellows, and blues. "Hello?"

"Darrell? It's Erin." Still thinking about the image on the video, he didn't respond right away, and she added, "From last night?"

"Yeah, oh, hi Erin," he managed. Smooth move, Romeo.

"Is it okay if I called? I called your apartment and didn't get you. You told me to try this number. You okay?"

"Yeah, I'm fine. Studying some game tapes and lost track of time. Your timing's perfect, though. I was ready to pull the plug for today anyway." He glanced at his watch. 4:35? How long was he out? He finished the Wilshire game tape around one and started—

He remembered Erin on the line. "Man, I let the time get away from me. I was going to call you this afternoon. You want to grab something to eat?"

"I'm sorry, but I can't," Erin said. "That's why I was calling. I'd love to go out with you tonight, but I promised my parents I'd take them to dinner. Tonight's their anniversary. Set this up weeks ago and forgot about it last night."

Was she blowing him off? Darrell worked to keep the disappointment out of his voice. "I, I think that's a great thing to do for your folks. How about tomorrow? Breakfast maybe?"

"Hum. Sounds good, but I'll do you one better. How 'bout we go for a run first thing in the morning and then grab a bite?"

Yes. "You're on. When and where?"

"Eight sharp. We can start at the gazebo in the park," Erin said.

"Great, I'll see you there. Go show your folks a fun

night." When he hung up the phone, he noticed his fingers left wet prints on the handset.

Chapter 6

Sunday morning Darrell awoke nervous and anxious, ready to run. The eerie dream with the naked girl and the oldie song didn't return Saturday night, but he couldn't get the strange vision from the videotape off his mind. The black youth with piercing, sorrowful eyes. It was *there* on the tape or VCR or whatever. He knew it, even though he couldn't find it again.

And, he *knew* it was all connected to the ghost, but he had no idea what it meant. It couldn't be good.

So, he was really glad for this morning run. He needed the distraction, and jogging usually did it for him. The physical exertion and accelerated heart rate would take over and help clear his head. When he ran flat out, legs pumping and lungs heaving, he could jettison his baggage, at least for a while, and forget about controlling the world. He could simply let it fly by.

And this morning, he had a special reason to savor the experience. *As long as you don't blow it, Romeo.*

He dressed in gray gym shorts and tee shirt—his third choice this morning—and arrived early at the park gazebo. The sun had been up for more than an hour, and he stared at the glowing ball carving a golden swath across the blue-green waters of the Bay. The tide already out, the waves lapped at the shore a few yards away and made quiet, gurgling sounds, sending the subtle brackish odor into the air.

"Wicked beautiful, isn't it?" said a quiet voice behind him.

He tried a fake Irish brogue. "Well, Erin Caveny. Top of the morning to ya."

Erin chuckled. He definitely liked her laugh.

As a football coach, Darrell worked to keep himself in shape, but he had nothing on her. The morning sun lit up her lean body, encased in a top with horizontal stripes of vivid pink, purple, and blue. Pink running shorts completed the outfit, exposing long, toned legs.

Erin came over beside him and using the gazebo rail for leverage began her stretching routine. He glanced from her to the Bay.

"This is stunning. Nothing like this view up in Ann Arbor." He eyed her. "By the way, the scenery up close isn't bad either."

She grinned.

For a few minutes, they stretched side by side in quiet while Darrell stole glimpses. She'd pulled her red hair back into a ponytail again, her rusty freckles prominent. Her green eyes sparkled like the shimmering water of the Chesapeake.

Studying Erin, he couldn't help but compare her to Carmen. Though his ex was pretty and cute in her own way, she was nothing like Erin. Carmen was short and busty and looked good in, and out, of a bikini, but she was hardly athletic. Her idea of exercise was bar hopping. Darrell's foot slipped off the step.

Erin asked, "You okay?"

He felt his face grow red. "Fine." He turned away from her, bent his elbow, and extended his arm behind his head. "Nearly finished. How about you?"

"Almost. A few more." She sat and bent over each leg, leaning her torso close to the concrete.

Man, she has *some* kind of flexibility. He conjured up images of Erin making moves Carmen could never do, then fought to rein in his libido. It was only a run.

When she relaxed her posture and stood, he took it as his cue. "Okay, this is your show. Do you have a regular route?"

"A'course. How far do you want to go?"

Darrell didn't want to look like a slouch. "About three miles, twenty minutes or so. How 'bout you?"

"Awrighta. Enough to get the blood going, but not enough to wipe you out." She pointed. "Let's do an easy run along the shore here to the marina, up Shore Road, and back into town on Water Street."

"Sounds great."

"When we're finished, we can grab a bite at Ben's. Right around the corner...and they don't mind if you're a little—"

"Winded?"

She smiled. "Okay, let's say that."

Yeah, nice smile. "Lead the way." Nice other parts, too.

She turned and smirked at him. "Try to keep up."

She led him along the sand, her sleek legs taking graceful strides, as Darrell hustled to catch her. Even though he had a few inches on her—he guessed she was about five eight—she had a long, smooth gait, and he had his hands full staying up with her. They ran the shore first, its surface soft, and they left matching pairs of shoe prints in the smooth sand. When they came to the marina, the path narrowed and Darrell let her lead, following a few steps behind. She wound her way around the dock and gestured to some boat hands on the crafts bobbing gently on the water. They waved back and one called her name.

Off the walkway, she headed for Shore Road and, this early Sunday morning with almost no traffic, they ran side by side on the asphalt. The road took them past rustic cottages and large, clapboard houses, many with white picket fences enclosing gardens of fall color.

Darrell gasped a little and said, "I see why you chose this route."

"Best way to enjoy the beauty around here." She didn't even appear winded.

About a mile farther on, they came to Wilshire High and Darrell managed enough breath to point out his classroom. She nodded but never broke stride. They jogged through the building parking lot and had to dodge plate-size potholes. Darrell peered up at his office window. He half expected to spy the mysterious figure he'd seen there, but the old building appeared dark and desolate. A thought struck him. He realized even though he'd not been able to make out the face of the figure he'd seen twice here, the rest—large muscled black man, bare-chested—matched what he'd seen on the VCR tape. That rattled him, and he slowed a bit. Then he saw Erin pull farther ahead and pushed his legs harder.

When they returned to the road, they heard the purr of a car engine, and both runners edged to the side of the asphalt, craning their heads at the sound. A town police cruiser, a "black and white" that was actually brown and tan, rolled up behind and came even. Darrell glanced inside to see a man with a clean-shaven head and a small goatee. He had a rotund body encased in a gray police uniform. On the seat beside him lay a wide-brimmed, "Smokey" hat. He figured it was the same cop he'd seen at the game Friday night. When the window slid down, Darrell caught a whiff of cigar smoke.

"Hey, Erin," called the driver. "You're looking good, as always. Can't say the same about the character next to you, though."

"Hey, back at you, Officer Brown," Erin said, without breaking stride. "This is Darrell Henshaw, new teacher at Wilshire High."

"New *football* coach, right," the cop said, his "i" a little long. He kept the car at the same pace as the joggers. "Saw you at the game. Tough loss Friday."

Darrell nodded and Erin asked, "Out early keeping Wilshire safe?"

"You know me. Protect and serve. Protect and serve." Brown buzzed the window back up. The car headed down the road and turned onto a side street.

Not sure he had enough breath to form a coherent sentence, Darrell shot a questioning glance at Erin.

She said, "Ah, Mom and Dad know him pretty well. Graduated a few years ahead of them at Wilshire, sometime in the sixties. Fought and was wounded in Vietnam and came back here. Became a cop."

Erin hooked a left onto Water Street, which ran down the center of town, and accelerated.

This was an easy run? Maybe he'd been suckered. She was some runner.

As if she read his thoughts, Erin upped her tempo still more, and Darrell could've sworn he saw her wiggle her butt at him. He enjoyed the flirtation and the view, but didn't want to be shown up and sped up to run alongside her. The scenery on Water Street flowed by, much the same as Shore Drive, with residences of different sizes, from quaint weekend bungalows to two-story Victorian mansions. Many sported intricately carved wooden railings and ornate, stained glass windows, but only half the homes appeared occupied. Darrell remembered learning many were summer or weekend homes for the wealthy who wanted to escape the city.

Not many of his kids lived along here.

A stooped, black man shambled down the steps of a tiny, run down bungalow and picked up a newspaper off a cracked sidewalk. When the man smiled, brilliant white teeth floated in a narrow, brown face. Darrell recognized him and saluted. "That's Jesse. Head custodian at the high school," he managed between quick breaths.

Erin nodded. "Yeah. Jesse Stewart. Was there when I went to school."

Then it dawned on Darrell why Jesse stood out on the run. During the whole three miles, his was the only black face they'd seen. Another of Tyler's comments in class echoed in his head. "Nothing but rich white dudes by the shore."

They ran past another huge white colonial, this one with a massive set of pillars in front and a second story balcony that stretched across the front. It sat on the largest plot of land they passed on the run.

Erin said, "That's the Jameson place. Back in the early 1800s, they owned a lot more land. Supposed to have had twenty slaves."

Darrell glanced over at the huge mansion which

looked empty, deserted, and gloomy.

They passed a few businesses intermixed with homes along the road, their shingles and marquees out of place among the older houses. As Darrell and Erin passed one business, Maryland Third National Bank, he recognized Bud Williams, dressed in a gray suit, coming out of the building, money bag in hand. Darrell waved, and Williams gestured back. Beside him, Erin gave a small nod and, after they had passed, released a grunt. Before Darrell could ask, she turned it up again, and he had to hurry to keep up. A little farther on, they reached the park, jogging past two waterfront restaurants. Erin slowed to a walk.

"Usually start my cool down around here," she said, with only the slightest breath.

Heaving, Darrell reduced his pace. "Whew. Sounds good."

They trotted into the park entrance and slowed on the cinder path as they neared the gazebo. Once there, both runners repeated their stretching routines. Waiting for his heart rate to return to normal, Darrell extended his limbs and stole another glance at his jogging partner. He thought Erin chose a spot to give him a great picture of her slim, cute butt, but maybe that was his libido talking. Still, he appreciated the view.

Erin saw him staring and grinned back. She fingered the hair band and undid the pony tail, shaking her head and releasing the long red strands. Her actions set Darrell's heart racing again, driving energy to a different part of his anatomy. He ogled the glistening colors of her top and shorts, now lit up by sun and moisture.

Wonder what she looks like under those?

Chapter 7

Five minutes later, they were seated at an outside table at Ben's-by-the-Water, reviewing the menu. The scent of bacon made Darrell's stomach growl, and he hoped Erin didn't notice it. They ordered with her advice—an egg white omelet with mushroom and onions for her and a meat lovers omelet for him—and relaxed with their coffee, the pungent aroma wafting from their cups.

"How did the big celebration go last night?" Darrell asked.

"Big celebration?" She blushed, reddening her cheeks even more. "Oh, you mean dinner with Mom and Dad. *Wick-ed.* Took 'em to Latitudes 38 over at Oxford. One of dad's favorites. Been there yet?"

"Oxford, yes. Latitudes 38, no."

"We should go sometime."

"I'd like that." He took a sip of coffee and set the cup down, making sure it sat precisely in the center of the saucer. "You said your dad works here in Wilshire? What's he do?"

"Dad works on the water. Always has. Like his dad and granddad. Done a little bit of everything, from crabbing to fishing. Right now runs a charter, taking tourists on sailing trips around the bay. *The Second Wind.* We ran past his boat."

"Which one?"

"The first sloop. Tall, handsome, gray-haired guy, polishing the rail," she said.

Darrell remembered the man calling Erin's name. "That is some boat."

"Yeah. Dad's real proud of it. Keeps it sparkling." Her gaze slid from Darrell to the inlet where a craft glided by, its white sail billowing with the breeze. She pointed with her cup. "You ever sail?"

"No. I've never had the chance. Love to learn."

"Maybe I'll teach you." She grinned.

He noticed she did that often, at least around him. Watching Erin's face beaming across from him, he was reminded Carmen seldom smiled like that. Oh, his ex could be happy and even silly, especially after she had a few drinks, but he couldn't remember her grinning at him like this, like she was happy just to be with him. He smiled back at Erin.

The young waitress came and set their orders down, refilling their coffees. Starved from the run, Darrell found the food quite good. Erin ate with as much gusto as she ran, and he liked that about her. Darrell's gaze went from her face to her brilliant top, where a few beads of perspiration clung to the fabric, as if they didn't want to let go of her breasts. Catching him staring, Erin made her eyebrows dance and giggled between bites. Darrell returned his attention to his omelet, cutting the egg dish into ten near-perfect square bites.

Erin said, "Your turn. What brings a born-and-bred Yankee like you to our fair shores?"

"Well, I wanted to be head coach, either football or basketball. Here, I get to do both."

"Must've been lots of places closer where you

could've gotten a coaching job. This is how many hours from your folks, eight?"

"More like ten," Darrell said.

"Okay, then, tell." She set down her fork and did a come hither gesture with her fingers. "What brought you to our little corner of the world?"

He didn't really want to talk about this but figured he had to get it over with. Besides, he wasn't going to lie to her. He finished a small bite and dabbed at his mouth. "In Ann Arbor, I was engaged and…well, it didn't work out. I decided I needed to get away."

"Lemme guess. Commitment issues?"

He squirmed in his chair. He saw where she was going and wanted to head her off.

"It wasn't me." His fingers fiddled with his utensils. He rearranged the knife, fork, and spoon into exactly parallel positions.

"She got cold feet?"

He met her gaze and felt his face reddening. "Naw, her feet were plenty warm. The problem was other parts of her body were friggin' hot. With others."

"Oh. Sorry." Erin blushed this time.

Darrell didn't want to make her feel any worse. "That's all right. Better now, than later." He sipped his coffee. "Besides, if she hadn't, I wouldn't have come here to the Bay." He glanced out at the shimmering water. "And I wouldn't have been able to take such a great Sunday morning run with such stunning company. Who pretty much kicked my butt."

"Goin' to have to learn to keep up."

Darrell had another small bite and let his glance wander around the cozy restaurant, which was filling up. He saw a few older couples in suits and dresses, probably from church. A few families with small kids filed in, along with other couples in their twenties and thirties like Erin and him. He noticed, as he scanned the diners around him, not one black face in the crowd. He was about to mention this to Erin when a waiter brought a party past them. After they were past, he asked, "Wasn't that Bud Williams, board president?"

Erin nodded. Sipped her coffee.

"Is that his wife with him?"

Erin's eyes came up over the rim of her cup. Nodded again.

"I don't know what the protocol is. Do you think I should go over and say hello?"

Erin stared into her coffee. "Don't know. Don't care. Do what you want."

Her smile had disappeared. "Erin, what is it?"

"Nothing." Her gaze stayed on the cup she grasped with both hands.

"I noticed your reaction when we passed him and now, here. You don't much like Bud Williams."

"Good guess."

"Fill me in. You must have your reasons."

Erin glared at the Williams, as two other diners came up and greeted the couple. She turned back. "Mom used to work for him. She's an administrative assistant, a really great one. Can run a whole office. Used to work as *Bud's* second at the bank until..." She stabbed a bite of egg white.

"Until what?"

She nibbled and swallowed. "Let's simply say, the Williams think they're better than everyone else. Treat the rest of the world as hired help."

Darrell didn't know what to say, so he waited and

glanced over at the Williams table. "I met him for the first time after the game Friday night. Told me what a great game the kids played." When Erin didn't respond, he said, "He and some guy named Remington—"

"Trevor Remington, big friend of Bud."

"Anyway, the two of them offered to get me anything I want for the football team."

"What'd you say?" Erin stared at Darrell.

"I said I couldn't think of anything yet."

Her gaze made a quick dart to the table at the other end of the deck and then met Darrell's again. "Be careful. Any *gift* from Bud Williams is more likely to be a Trojan horse."

She rose, plunked her napkin down, and headed out the way they came in. Darrell jumped up, grabbed a few bills from his wallet, and threw them on the table.

Chapter 8

"Saw you and that fine young lady joggin' past yesterday," Jesse Stewart said, as Darrell exited his classroom. The short custodian stood next to the open door and set the half-filled garbage bag on the floor, expelling the odor of almost empty Doritos bags. Beneath wispy black hair, two brown eyes searched the empty hallway and he grinned. "Don't tell the missus, but that was a really nice way for an old man to wake up." His words ended in a wheezy chuckle.

"That'd be Erin Caveny."

The custodian's grin widened. "So that was little Erin. 'Member her in school. Grown into quite a creature, that one. Certainly classed up your running act."

"Can't argue with you there."

Jesse's eyes scanned the corridor a second time. Darrell followed his gaze and didn't see anyone. The custodian licked his lips and wiped his forehead. "Say, Coach." Another furtive glance around. "Heard you was asking about our resident ghost. I wanted—"

"Oh, there you are," called Al from the top of the stairs. "Been waiting for you to head to lunch." He ambled over. "Hi, Jesse."

"Hey, Mr. McClure." Jesse gave a slight shake of his head at Darrell. He picked up his trash bag and, turning to head down the hall, hollered over his shoulder. "I'll talk to ya later, Mr. Henshaw."

"Well?" Al put one arm around Darrell in a conspiratorial hug.

Darrell's mind was still on what Jesse wanted to say about the ghost. He glanced at Al's face and realized his friend was waiting for an answer. "Well, what?"

"How'd it go with Erin? I simply want the guy's side." Darrell didn't say anything. "Okay, okay, smile if you got any." Al smirked, his eyebrows doing the crazy Groucho Marx thing. "Come on. Ya got to give me something. I'm an old married man."

Darrell shook his head but couldn't help but chuckle.

"I knew it. I knew it." Al nodded twice. "I told Sara you guys would hit it off."

"We had a nice time. With those long legs, she can run. I had all I could do to keep up with her, though the view from behind wasn't bad."

Al's eyes widened. "She does have nice legs, and I bet they can do more than run. You'd better be careful. You know what Confucius say? 'Man who date tall girl get bust in mouth.' "

Darrell clapped him on the shoulder, the sound echoing down the corridor. "I think it's 'short man who date tall girl' and I doubt it's Confucius." They headed toward the cafeteria. "Anyway, Erin seems great. We had a nice morning run along the shore and through town. I thought we were hitting it off pretty well and then something strange happened."

Darrell stopped outside *The Wilshire Café*. He glanced around to make sure no one else could hear and then told Al of Erin's reaction to Bud Williams.

"Oh." Al surveyed the lunchroom and reached for the door handle. "There's some bad blood between the Williams and the Cavenys. Erin's mom used to work for Bud."

"Erin told me that."

"The rumor is Bud promised to promote Erin's mom but wanted more *benefits* than she was willing to give. If you get my drift."

"I do." No wonder Erin was so angry with Williams. Darrell hoped he hadn't screwed it up with her.

"I'd tread softly around that, if I was you." Al pulled open the door and a cacophony of student voices rushed out.

The steaming homemade chicken and noodles tempted them, and they queued into the line, making their selections. Al, two steps ahead, was already at the cash register, wallet in hand, when Darrell heard his name.

"Mr. Henshaw?"

Darrell glanced up to see a young woman, her face a chocolate brown, with a cap of short black hair. Large coffee eyes stared at him and then darted around the serving room. She was so short, she could have been mistaken for one of the students, but her eyes seemed older and worried. A single bead of perspiration dripped across her forehead. He searched her anxious features but couldn't remember seeing her behind the serving line before.

She held out a bowl of fruit, but her hand trembled a bit. "You, uh, you're definitely going to want to try some fresh fruit." She pushed the bowl across the glass shelf. "Cut it myself. Watermelon and cantaloupe." She smiled nervously and then glanced around again.

Darrell mumbled, "Thanks." When he grabbed the dish, he felt something underneath.

"Anytime *soon*, Coach," Al called at the end of the line.

Darrell hurried and fumbled with his wallet. While the cashier counted out his change, his fingers probed under the fruit dish and came out with a small, folded sheet of paper. He looked back at the server, whose eyes got wide, and she moved her head from side to side. He glanced around, but no one seemed to notice.

"Darrell, sometime this century?" Al barked.

With a quick nod, Darrell stuffed the paper in his shirt pocket and followed Al into the Teachers' Lunchroom. The door closed behind them, reducing the adolescent noise to a low rumble. From the machine, Al grabbed a diet cola and Darrell a water.

"This diet would taste so much better with some rum in it," Al said.

"Yeah, but then we'd have to cart you home," said Molly McQuire. "And somebody who doesn't know a piccolo from a saxophone would have to try to teach music."

A twenty-five-year Wilshire instructor, Molly served as the dame of the English department, as well as department chair. She looked the part, complete with a short, stocky build, black hair cut above her shoulders, and black-framed glasses on a chain around her neck. Darrell liked her and was glad she agreed to partner with him on the senior projects.

Across from Molly, Principal Jeb Douglass peered through his wire bifocals and called in a croaky voice, "Besides, I might have to fire ya. Then, who'd teach those crazy kids to do a halftime show?"

Al grinned. "It's nice to be irreplaceable."

Darrell and Al squeezed into the long table up front, scissoring their legs around the bench, and busied themselves with their lunches. The small room was full, the other teachers in knots of conversation. Darrell studied the assembled group and noted almost all the faces were white. The only exception was Wilt Byerson, a black teacher from Baltimore who taught low level math.

After a bit, Molly broke the silence. "Hey, Coach. I forgot to ask how you like your office. Have you been out on the walk much?"

Darrell slurped a noodle and wiped his mouth. "The place may be tiny, but it's got a great view. I stood out on the perch and watched the sun set behind the building last night. Quite a sight." He folded his napkin. "Harriet said there've been some great student pranks out there."

"Oh yeah," Molly said. "My favorite was '73, my first year here. Monday of senior week, remember, Jeb?"

A few chuckles ran through the small group.

"Hard to forget that sight." Douglass exchanged grins with Molly.

"That's because you stood there and stared at them for ten minutes," Molly said. "What were you then, twenty-five?"

"Twenty-six," Douglass said, a faraway sound to his voice.

Molly said, "Well, it was spring of '73 and the Women's Lib movement was in full tilt."

Douglass took up the tale. "The week before, some

of the female students had put up signs around the school. Ya know, signs that read 'Equal pay for equal work' and 'Pass the ERA.' Anyway, Andrews—he was principal then—was *not* happy, and that Friday had all the Women's Lib posters taken down."

Darrell said, "Let me guess, the students used the widow's walk to make a statement."

Molly laughed. "When we arrived at school the next Monday and looked up, we saw about fifty bras flapping in the wind off the bay."

Douglass said, "Quite a sight. All these different sizes, a lot of white along with colors all flutterin' in the breeze. And Andrews was furious. I thought he was going to have a coronary."

"And to make matters worse," added Molly, "someone had called the TV station from Baltimore, and they sent a reporter and camera crew to capture the protest. I think it was even picked up by the network."

Douglass jumped back in. "Andrews ran up the two flights of stairs and squeezed out onto the walk and started pullin' the bras off. With half the school watching and the news crew filming, he grabbed those bras, yellin' like a madman." Douglass' bony arms did an impression of yanking phantom bras. "Remember the one bra strap got caught on the crack in the railing, and Andrews couldn't get it unhooked." The teachers laughed again.

Byerson chuckled, his large belly bouncing. He said, "Yeah, going to miss that widow's walk next year. Nothing like it in the new building, hey, Jeb?"

Douglass slid his long, pencil legs from under the table. "Nope, no 'affectations,' the board decided."

"Maybe that'll be enough to dissuade our resident

ghost from moving to the new building." Byerson smirked, running a calloused hand through his short hair.

"Okay, guys, okay," said Darrell. "What's the story about this ghost?" He hoped his question didn't sound desperate.

Byerson grinned. "Why, Darrell? Has our resident ghost been bothering you up in the tower?"

"No," Darrell said, a little too quickly. "I mean Harriet mentioned the ghost and a couple of other—"

"Nobody knows for sure," Douglass cut him off. "It's only a story. Supposed to be the ghost of a black student who died here in the sixties. In more than twenty-five years in this building, I've never seen him." He moved from the back of the room and stood next to Darrell, the principal's tall frame over him like a gaunt scarecrow. The fluorescent light reflected off the principal's bare forehead.

"How'd he die?" Darrell asked.

"Before my time," Douglas said.

The way he said it, Darrell figured there was more—or at least, Douglass knew more than he was saying—but before Darrell could ask, the bell rang, cutting off all conversation.

One by one, the teachers hustled out the door. Darrell waited until he was last, then carried his dishes over and stacked each in its proper space. He glanced around. He was alone. He pulled out the paper he stuck in his pocket and read the note.

I'm part of the Black Underground. We heard you were asking about the Wilshire ghost. If you'd want to know the real story about him, meet me tonight, 10:00 by the dumpster behind the school. Tell no one. —Ruby

Chapter 9

"Okay, I'm here. Behind the school. By the dumpster. In the dark," Darrell whispered to no one in particular. Because there was no one here. And it was creeping him out.

What was he doing here? All because a girl he didn't know had information about a ghost? A ghost he'd decided *not* to have anything to do with? And how did she know he was asking about the ghost? He'd only raised the question with two other teachers. Besides, what was this black underground?

Still, he sensed something was coming. He feared the ghost would not leave him alone, and he wanted to be ready. He didn't want to make the mistake he had with the first ghost.

He stood there, silent, and listened for footsteps, for anything. The only sounds he could hear were the murmur of the waves lapping at the shore a few hundred yards away. Behind him, Wilshire High School loomed like a squat giant, huddled in shadows, the lights in two upstairs rooms looking like blazing eyes.

His final period class and another punishing football practice had consumed the next four hours after lunch. In the locker room, he took a long shower, allowing the harsh jets to soothe his aches and bruises from practice, until the hot water ran out. His mind conjured possible revelations the young girl might share.

First, the appearances in the office window and the shadowy image on the video, both of a large black youth. Then, today, Douglass confirms the ghost is supposed to be a black teen. Now, this Ruby wants to share the truth *about the ghost. This cannot be good.*

This afternoon, he'd gone back to the cafeteria during his planning period, but his messenger had already left for the day. He learned she'd been a sub but couldn't find anyone who even knew her last name.

After he showered and dressed, he sat in his office and, trying to focus his mind on something else, viewed the video of the Bulldogs for a third time. Didn't see the image again. Stomach in knots, he couldn't eat. He started a cola, but bile bit back in his throat and he couldn't finish it. He pushed it away and stared out his window, watching the crimson light leak out of the sky, replaced with the blue blackness of the dark over water.

At 9:50 he locked up his office. The building seemed empty, dark and sheltering secrets. He made his way down the two floors and half expected to confront the ghost on the shadowy stairs.

"Coach Henshaw?"

He jerked around to see Jesse Stewart, his diminutive figure half hidden behind a massive trash bag. "Jesus, Jesse, you scared me to death."

"Better me than the ghost," the custodian's tinny voice called. "Hey, you got a moment?"

Darrell glanced down at his watch and then his gaze darted outside. He shoved one hand into his pocket and felt the note. *Tell no one.*

"Not tonight, Jesse." He released a long breath. "I'm pretty beat. Can we do it later—"

"Sure. Sure." The custodian's teeth flashed in the weak light. "Can ya get the door for me?"

Darrell propped the door open as the older man stumbled down the three steps to the dumpster and heaved the plastic sack into the container. Releasing the door, Darrell exited as Jesse re-entered, calling, "Night, Coach."

"Night, Jesse."

That was twenty minutes ago. Darrell checked the luminous face of his digital watch, again. 10:16. Still, no Ruby. He glanced around. The call of a loon out on the shore echoed across the water and was answered with the lonely hoot of a land-bound owl. With no stars out and no lights on behind the building, darkness blanketed the area, objects casting amorphous, blackened shadows. Darrell had grabbed a flashlight from his office, but its feeble beam cast only a small, pale circle on the ground. The odors of high school—pencil shavings, printing ink, spoiled food—flowed from the dumpster nearby. Surrounded by the darkness and the stinking garbage, his condition threatened to swamp him. His anxiety ticked up. He fought it with three slow breaths.

I can do this. Breath. *I can do this.* Breath. Why *am I doing this?* Breath.

He wet his lips and retrieved the note, now crumpled, from his pocket. He aimed the flashlight. His hand trembled. The words shimmered.

I'm part of the Black Underground. We heard you were asking about the Wilshire ghost. If you'd want to know the real story about him, meet me tonight, 10:00 by the dumpster behind the school. Tell no one. —Ruby

What or who was the Black Underground, he wondered again and what did they know about the ghost? A car crawling around the corner of the building interrupted his thoughts. Tires crunched gravel. Darrell released a breath. He turned as the headlights lit him up. He raised his arm to shield his eyes.

"Is that you, Coach?"

The male timbre of the voice froze him. Officer Brown. Darrell's stomach dropped.

"You okay?" Brown asked, his voice phlegmy.

Darrell jammed the note back in his pocket. His mind raced, fumbling for an explanation. "I'm, uh, fine," Darrell said, a little too loud.

"What you doin' out here?"

God, what was he going to tell the cop? *Tell no one.*

"Aw, well, uh, you're not going to believe this, but my grade book came up missing, and I didn't notice it till tonight after practice," Darrell improvised. He felt his face redden and was glad for the darkness. "I feel really stupid but thought maybe it made it into the trash and got dropped off here."

"You need any help?" Brown called and coughed twice.

"A little light maybe." Darrell waved the flashlight in his hand. "This thing isn't worth much."

Brown swiveled the car's spotlight as Darrell turned around to face the dumpster. He took a step and looked down. His shoe landed on another small, torn sheet of paper. With a furtive glance back at the car—he was relieved to see the officer kept his ample bottom on the seat—he snatched up the scrap and shoved it into his pocket.

While the cop watched, Darrell fought his compulsion and spent a few minutes pretending to rummage in the dumpster. He tried not to inhale the fumes of rotten produce and didn't touch anything, the toe of his shoe moving a few things around. After what he figured was enough time, he announced it wasn't worth it and he'd replace the gradebook if he needed to. He thanked Brown. The cruiser eased around the building and back onto the road. Darrell released a long breath. He hustled over to his own car. When he reached the parking lot, his gaze darted over one shoulder, then the other. The dark almost suffocated him, and he tried three deep breaths, again. He was alone—at least as far as he could see.

God, that was too damn close. Stupid. Why was he doing this?

He waited until he was inside the car, windows up and turned on the interior lamp. He pulled the second note out of his pocket and, holding it under the beam, read the few scribbled words.

Sorry, there watching. Couldn't take the chance. Members of the Underground believe there is a diary hidden in your office. Find it and you'll understand.—R

What the hell? What diary?

Darrell sat there, unable to move, feeling his paranoia rise along with the hairs on his neck.

Tell no one.

Chapter 10

"Pi-rates! Pi-rates! Pi-rates!" Packed together shoulder to shoulder in the locker room, all forty-seven members of the football team chanted in unison, stomping their cleats on the concrete floor.

Twenty minutes earlier, they had completed one of biggest upsets in Wilshire High School history, to the delight of their amazed fans. The Pirates had beaten the bigger, faster team from rival Easton. They'd been high-fiving and shoulder-pounding ever since.

"Nobody expected us to win," yelled Seth Hart, junior wide receiver, "but when Jason threw me that bullet, I was off to the races. It was wick-ed!" He glanced over at Jason Thompson, the quarterback, who grinned back, as he slid off his grass-stained pants with small tears in both knees.

Stripped to the waist, Seth climbed onto a bench in the center of the small room, cleats clicking atop the scarred wooden plank. His lean, dark-skinned physique and stringy black hair dripped sweat onto the wood, and he raised his hand, fist clenched, in a Pirate salute. He howled and the rest of the team picked up the baying, the sounds of "Ah-hoo, ah-hoo!" rocking the entire locker room. Even Pogo got into the act with one "Yip."

Darrell studied the students and a grin broke across his face. It *was* funny. He loved watching them celebrating like this. They earned it. After a bit, he said, "Okay, okay, guys. You did an incredible job out there tonight. I'm really proud of you. Hey, you've made the whole town of Wilshire proud."

The changes Darrell put in, based on the game tape—they double teamed Easton's star receiver and blitzed every three or four plays—had worked well. Better than he expected, really. "Seth *is* right. Good work tonight between you and Jason, but if George didn't hit his block,"—he clapped the small, chunky lineman on the shoulder—"Seth's run would've been for all of three yards, not fifty-three. In fact, everyone did their part tonight."

This brought another chorus of rousing cheers.

"Coach Henshaw?" called out a raspy voice from the doorway, and coach and players turned to see Principal Douglass. "Mind if we crash this party? I got a couple of VIPs who want to congratulate the boys."

Darrell said, "Sure, Mr. Douglass." Then he glanced from the principal to his players. Seth caught the look and scampered off the bench.

Douglass entered followed by three men, two in gray suits and a third in a black turtleneck. Darrell recognized the first two, but not the third, a slim, almost emaciated figure with thinning brown hair, bloodshot blue eyes, and a pair of oversized ears. Douglass made the introductions.

"I'm sure you boys know Mr. Williams, our board president, and Dr. Remington. Some of you probably even know Mr. Jeff Jefferson. What you might not know is they're the three biggest fans of Pirate football. They got something they want to tell you." Douglass moved aside, and the tallest of the visitors stepped forward.

Williams said, "Fine performance tonight." His glance moved around the room until he found the quarterback and receiver. "In fact, Jason and Seth, the way you young men connected, you brought back memories for the two of us."

Jeff Jefferson took a tentative step forward, slightly off-balance. The board president wrapped one arm around the shoulder of the smaller man, as if afraid he might fall over.

Douglass said, "In case you boys don't know it, the young Mr. Williams and Mr. Jefferson set school records for completed passes back in the sixties. You might've noticed a few of their trophies in our case."

"For perhaps the first time in years," Williams said, "it is possible Pirate football *might* have a duo who could challenge a few of our records. What do you think, Jeff?"

"Mebbe, maaa-bbe," Jefferson slurred.

In his few conversations with him, Darrell noticed Williams' speech sounded formal, almost stilted and couldn't decide if it was part of his formal upbringing or an affectation.

"And the defense held up their end as well," said Remington.

"Anyway, you boys played so effectively, we decided *you* need a new look," Williams continued and glanced back at Douglass, who gave a slight nod. "Dr. Remington and I have agreed to purchase new uniforms for the whole team, and Mr. Jefferson,"—he squeezed the shoulder he held—"the master salesman here, will be responsible for all the details."

"Sh-should be here in t-t-two weeks," Jefferson

stammered, sporting a vacuous grin.

Seth asked, "What will they look like?"

Williams examined the black student and narrowed his olive eyes but didn't speak right away. For a few seconds, the room took on an uncomfortable silence. Maybe, Seth had crossed some invisible line.

After a beat, the board president smiled. "That, son, is a fine question. The uniforms will be designed in classic Pirate colors, of course, black with gold lettering. Is that not so, Jeff?"

"R-r-right oh," Jefferson said.

Another brief silence followed and then the principal said, "The school is mighty grateful for your generous gift." He scowled at Darrell.

"Yes. This is…uh, quite unexpected," Darrell said.

"But long overdue." Remington pointed one pudgy finger at the player next to him, whose uniform had been ripped and repaired several times.

"How 'bout we thank these men for their generosity," Douglass said and began clapping. All the players joined him, adding whistles and catcalls.

"Okay, that is enough," Williams commanded and flicked a piece of dust off his tailored suit. "You young men have earned them. Continue your hard work. Your families and girlfriends are waiting for you, so we will take our leave. Coach Henshaw is correct. The town is proud of you. We will be looking for another great performance each week."

Remington strode over to Darrell and extended a hand. "Fine game, Coach."

Darrell grasped the offered hand. "Thanks, but they did the work."

Williams nodded and led the visitors out. Douglass

shot one last look at Darrell before he disappeared through the opening. When the large metal door creaked shut, all the students' eyes turned toward their coach.

Darrell said, "Well, isn't that something? New uniforms." He shook his head, smiling. "I guess now we'll have to keep playing well enough to deserve them." He looked around the room. "Okay, get yourself cleaned up, so you can go celebrate."

The players headed for their lockers, and Darrell said, "Hey, just because you won tonight, don't leave this place a pigsty. What do I always tell you?"

All forty-seven students recited in unison, "Your mother doesn't work here. Clean up after yourself."

"You got it. See you for practice Monday." Darrell headed into the coaches' shower room next door. He sat on his own bench, savoring the victory and the looks on his players' faces.

The noises next door dwindled, and he found even the great Pirate upset couldn't hold his attention. His thoughts returned to the two enigmatic notes from Ruby. As he moved through the lunch line all week, he had searched for the pretty, young black face behind the counter but hadn't seen her. He inquired, but the rest of the cooks said she was a sub and had only worked the one day.

Still, he heeded Ruby's note, and when he could grab a few minutes, he searched his office for a diary. Came up empty, of course.

Now, Williams came bearing gifts.

As he stood under the spray, he thought about the donation from Williams and Remington, and the silent scold from Douglass. He should be thrilled, but... He hoped it wasn't simply because Williams and Remington had gone around him, bestowing new uniforms for the players—which they needed by the way—without consulting him.

But he also recalled Erin's warning, "Trojan horse."

God, he hoped she'd be at the McClures' tonight.

When Darrell stepped out of the shower, Al popped in and said he was heading over to the house to help his wife. "Sara said she thought Erin might stop by for a few minutes when she got off shift." His eyebrows did the darting movement atop his glasses, and he added, "Maybe you'll get lucky tonight."

Darrell threw the deodorant at him.

Their parting Sunday had been a bit awkward, and Darrell had wanted to reach out to Erin all week but was afraid. Besides, with the two of them working opposite schedules, Darrell seven to seven and Erin three till eleven, there wasn't time to connect. At least, that's what he told himself. He took extra time in front of the mirror, fussing with the gel in his hair. He buttoned and unbuttoned the collar on his polo.

By the time Darrell returned to the team locker room, the place was empty, a few lights still on, casting uneven shadows. He was glad to see his players heeded his words. The dirty uniforms were in the bin where they belonged and only two soiled, mismatched socks lay on the floor. If possible, the stench drifting from the overloaded bin made the room even more rank.

He bent down to pick up the two stray socks and heard it. "Damn, one of the guys left a shower on."

He tossed the socks into the bin and headed around the corner. A shroud of darkness cloaked the shower room. Diffused light filtered in from the hallway. When Darrell peered in, he stopped short. "Oh. I didn't know anyone was still here."

A tall, black student stood under the pulsing shower head, his back to Darrell, the top of his head a bare two inches below the spray.

"Seth, is that you?" Darrell asked. "Is everything okay?"

Darrell stared at the figure. He could tell, even in the dim light, it wasn't the junior receiver. He could only see the figure's backside, but the torso was larger and his skin looked even darker than Seth's. Powerful arms and shoulders twisted under the spray, drops bouncing off bulging biceps. Water poured down the student's back and splashed onto the floor.

"Are you okay?" Darrell called. The young man didn't move. Darrell froze. He told himself the student, with the shower pounding in his ears, maybe couldn't hear him. Then the hairs on his neck prickled.

Darrell stepped around the corner and flipped all four light switches, bathing the entire area in blinding white. He took the two steps back and poked his head around the corner. He gaped into the shower room.

It was empty.

The third shower on the right was on, water surging down and running into the drain. The sound thundered in the enclosed space. Rust streaks scarred the concrete block walls and pulsed under the bright light. Darrell walked across the room and turned off the faucet. The room was plunged into silence as the last of the water gurgled into the drain.

"Is anyone here?" His voice echoed through the empty locker complex.

He stared at the third shower, trying to confirm his...hallucination? Darrell exited the shower room and flipped off the light switches. Then he couldn't help himself. He stepped back and glanced into the darkened room, expecting to see...something. Shaken, he held his breath.

Everything was dark.

Chapter 11

The next day, Saturday afternoon, Darrell stood at the end of slip number twenty-eight. Alone. He glanced at his Pulsar digital watch, again. 4:43. Erin had said to be here at 4:30, and of course, he'd arrived early. Twenty minutes early. He shifted his weight from foot to foot and scanned the rippling, blue-green waters, using his left arm to shield his eyes from the bright sun. He didn't see them. He fiddled with the top two buttons of his shirt and then stopped.

Leave them alone and watch for her.

Other than two small pleasure sloops bouncing on the waves at the west horizon, the waters appeared empty. The day had warmed, and the slight breeze off the water made for a delightful September afternoon, with temps in the seventies.

He hoped he got it right, didn't screw this up. He'd been so preoccupied with the figure in the shower last night, maybe he got the slip number wrong. Or the time. Or both. God, he hoped she didn't think he stood her up.

****

When he'd arrived at the McClures', his colleagues saluted him with cheers and drinks, which helped him to forget, briefly, about the latest apparition. The smell of soup again warmed the cozy family room where the whole gang gathered. They were in a celebratory mood, drinking to the man of the hour.

Then Erin stepped through the doorway, the flaming red hair loose on her shoulders framing a weary smile. Darrell forgot everything else.

She really seemed glad to see him. Him?

But when she said, "Hey, Darrell," he could hear the exhausted devastation in her words. As she took off her raincoat, his eyes widened at the sight. Her nurse's smock—this one white with a blaze of flowers scattered across the front—was splattered with jagged red splotches, making the blooms appear drenched in blood.

Darrell glanced from the scrubs to her tired eyes. "Tough day?"

She nodded, came over, and sat next to him on the couch. "Yeah, they called me down to ER. Had an eight-car pile-up on 333 with some really terrible injuries." She shook her head slowly, as if the movement pained her, and looked down at the smock. "Tried to stem a gash in an artery of this tiny two-year-old." A tear squeezed out her right eye and rolled down her cheek. "He didn't make it."

"I'm so sorry." Darrell held her hand tightly.

"I know it's part of the job, but I don't think I'll ever get used to it."

"You're not supposed to get used to it," said Sara, coming in from the kitchen. "Can I get you anything?"

"Thanks, no. Couldn't eat anything now," Erin said.

Darrell said, "Look, I was going to ask to take you out tonight, but if you're too wiped out, I understand."

"Thanks. Right now, I don't think I'd be any fun. Need to go home and crash." She placed her head in her hands. "But I'd love to get together, so I have a proposition for you."

Darrell smirked. "I love propositions."

Erin rolled her eyes but allowed a weak grin. "After the chaos died down tonight, I called Dad during my break. He's got a charter tomorrow, so I asked him if I could use the boat after. He said sure, if I help with the charter. Supposed to be a gorgeous day. What do you say to a sail on the Chesapeake, about 4:30?"

"Sounds great."

"Okay, then, you bring something to eat, and I'll give you your first sailing lessons."

Erin rose, leaning on Darrell's shoulder. "See you at the end of slip twenty-eight at 4:30. I'm going home to have a good cry and then sleep. I'll be better tomorrow, I promise."

****

Now, here it was Saturday, and there was no sign of Erin or the sailboat. Darrell stole another glance at his watch. 4:48. He wiped his brow with his arm, and he realized he was sweating, even though a steady wind blew off the water.

He prayed he wasn't about to be stood up or dumped. Again.

He strode the length of the pier, the old wooden boards creaking under his weight and the picnic basket heavy in his hand. As he'd never sailed before, he wasn't sure what to wear, so he'd chosen a nice pair of jeans and tan golf shirt. White sneakers sans socks completed the outfit, and he brought a windbreaker.

His gaze searched the parking lot again, to be sure. Erin's shining, red Jeep sat in the third spot. When his pacing brought him back the length of the thirty-foot pier, he rested his hands on the rubber bumpers. He stared out again and spied the two white and gold sails billowing in the breeze.

"Thank God," he said and exhaled a long breath, his loud release of air sounding like the swish of the water.

The craft grew larger, moving silently across the water. Its front triangular sail, white with a broad gold stripe around the edge, ballooned with the wind, propelling the boat at a surprising clip. As the sailboat glided across the water, a lithe figure, clad in a white top and shorts with blazing red tresses flying behind her, stepped to the bow. She waved, and he felt his whole body respond. He watched as she lowered the sails and used the engine to ease the boat in.

"Ahoy, there," Erin called out, "can you catch our lines?"

"Aye, aye." He set the basket down and grabbed hold of the thrown rope, the hemp rough against his fingers. He fastened it to one of the pilings, then repeated the process with a second. She tugged on the lines, and the sailboat came to a stop with a pop, the fenders tucked against the dock.

"And that'll be the end of today's cruise on the beautiful Chesapeake," a deep voice said from inside the cockpit. A white-haired man with a suntanned forehead emerged, and then used a hand to help a middle-aged couple step up. Standing farther aft, Erin held their arms and guided them. Darrell extended a final hand to help them climb out of the swaying boat and onto the dock.

The couple thanked their hosts, nodded at Darrell, and staggered toward the parking lot, obviously trying to get their land legs back. Erin followed them out of the boat.

"So, *this* must be Darrell," called the man, as he stepped onto the wooden planks and extended his hand. "Sean Caveny." His grip was strong, his hand calloused, and he was tall with broad shoulders—Darrell could see where Erin got her height—and had powerful forearms.

"Darrell Henshaw, but you already know that." Darrell pointed to the sailboat. "Beautiful craft."

"Isn't she?" Sean put an arm around Erin. "Almost as beautiful as this one."

Erin blushed and smacked him on the shoulder.

"No argument from me," Darrell said.

Sean leaned in and gave his daughter a peck on the cheek. "I'll leave *Second Wind* to you then. Don't stay out too late. Forecasts calling for a storm later."

"Thanks, Dad. See you tonight," Erin said. As her father strode up the pier to the parking lot, she nudged the basket on the dock with her toe. "Got anything good in there?"

Chapter 12

After climbing aboard and casting off, Erin took only a few minutes to move the sloop away from the dock using the diesel engine, the motor a quiet gurgle, and eased it into the center of the channel. There, she showed him how to use the rigging—or she taught him, the halyards—to hoist the sails and the wind did the rest. Since he confessed to being "not the best swimmer," Darrell grabbed the life vest she offered and wrapped it tightly around his body. He felt a little safer.

"You turn this—we call it 'the helm'—to control the rudder and steer the boat," she said. "You want to try it? It's easy." She gestured to the wooden steering wheel with eight cylindrical posts rotating around as spokes.

"Aw, not just yet." Darrell re-checked the Velcro straps on his life vest. He caught the same excitement in her voice he'd heard from teachers who love their subject. From himself, in fact.

As she glided the sloop into open water, he noticed her strong, athletic arms beneath a sleeveless, white top with a ribbed blue neckline. She stood confident at the helm, red hair fluttering in the breeze, gaze behind green sunglasses, and tongue in the corner of her mouth. She leaned into her work, her toned legs braced against the floorboards.

Studying Erin, he found himself comparing her

with his ex again. Carmen was the kind of girl who loved to be taken care of and pampered. She thrived on Darrell's attentions, which he'd lavished on her. And she loved the attentions of others too, he realized. Erin, on the other hand, seemed quite able to take care of herself. He realized she was a little headstrong. He remembered her visceral reaction to Williams. But after Carmen, Darrell thought he might like "a little headstrong." He grinned at her.

Erin glanced over and saw Darrell watching her. She grinned back. Her gaze returned to the horizon as the boat slipped through the channel. The sailboat's motion generated little sound, the only noises the wavelets slushing on either side. Gusts of wind filled the two triangle sails and flapped the four-square Maryland flag at the rear.

Darrell studied the shores on both sides. Along the rock-strewn shoreline, charming Cape Cods with Adirondack chairs in front competed with two-story Colonials, wearing white clapboard siding and green sloped roofs like their best Sunday suits. The view looked like some picture postcard, almost too perfect and he said as much to Erin.

From her position at the wheel, she glanced at the properties along the shore. "Being out here on the water gives you a different perspective. The owners work to keep their places looking like something out of *Southern Living*, but don't let appearances fool you." She pointed left or to port as she already taught him. "See that third house there, the one with only one Adirondack chair?"

Darrell followed her arm and nodded.

"Well, the reason there's only one chair is because

he killed his wife…though they could never prove it. Got a *lot* of money. He said he was the only one going to get to enjoy that view."

"Okay." His pulse quickened, and he tried to cover it by returning his attention to the shoreline. Each property had its own slip that extended out into the water, some piers about twenty feet long and others jutting out nearly one-hundred-fifty feet, almost into the center of the channel. He shot a questioning glance at Erin.

She said, "The Bay is so shallow in places, some boats have to be docked that far out. More than eighty percent of the Bay is only six feet deep or less. It varies a lot out here and you gotta know where to steer, so you don't get hung up." She pointed to a buoy floating out in the middle of the channel. "Less than four feet there."

A few minutes later, when they were settled into the center of the Bay, Erin set a rope around the wheel and took Darrell's hand. She led him past the sails to the front of the boat, or as she called it, "the forecastle." They sat together up front, and he tried to enjoy her and the slight rocking motion of the craft. It was not easy. He tightened the Velcro strap on his vest and shot a glance into the water.

"This sailboat is quite something. Is it new?" he asked to cover his anxiety.

"Hardly. Six years ago, my dad found this boat rusted and abandoned in a boatyard upriver. He bought it. Completely rebuilt the diesel engine and restored the outside. Took him almost two years and most of his savings." Erin's face lit up, as she spoke of her dad's accomplishment.

"*Second Wind* is an Irwin Citation 34 built in 1979, some thirty-four feet long with a beam a little over eleven feet," she explained like a proud salesperson. She pointed to where they were sitting. "That's the width of the boat at the widest part, helps keep her stable on the water. Kinda important."

Darrell struggled to fight his anxiety but could tell she was excited. He wanted to like what she liked. He tried, "How does it work? I mean sail?"

While Darrell still held on, she pointed to the high mast. "She has two sails. The smaller one in front is called the jib, the larger one behind, the mainsail. The mainsail catches more wind and propels us. The jib helps us maneuver."

As if it were listening, an extra gust of wind filled the mainsail and the sloop sped forward, bouncing twice across the waves. Darrell's eyes got wide, and he tightened his grip on the rail, his knuckles turning white. With his other hand, he checked the straps on his life vest. The movement didn't even faze Erin. She placed a hand on his arm, her touch warm and assuring.

"I'll teach you more later." Erin pointed back to the basket on the floorboards, the red-and-white checkered cloth hiding its contents. "Anything in there for a starving girl?"

"Sure, let's eat."

The boat rocked, and Erin had to guide him back to the aft deck where they sat on the cushioned bench. He opened the picnic basket and brought out some sliced cheese and crackers and cold chicken cut into bite-sized pieces. Next, he pulled out small bunches of red grapes. He laid out all the food in careful rows, not touching, atop the wicker basket lid and added utensils to the precise display. Then, he withdrew a bottle of wine and, pulling the cork, poured the Pinot Grigio into two plastic cups, careful not to spill any. He handed her one, and they both took a sip.

"Quite the feast. You did all this?" she asked.

He was thrilled. "With expert help, I must admit. Chef Pierre at the Old Stone Inn put it together for me."

"Looks great."

As they ate and drank, she moved her sunglasses to the top of her head. The boat glided almost silently across the Bay now. The gorgeous surroundings and quiet sounds of wind and water urged them to whispers. When he went to slide his arm around Erin, the bulky life vest got in the way. He thought, for a moment, about removing it so he could get closer but then dismissed the idea. He also wanted to live. He stretched an arm around her shoulder as best he could and asked about her night.

Instead of answering, she said, "Nursing *is* me. What I was destined to do, I think." She told him she went to nursing school at Maryland State, and after she got out, they were hiring at Chesapeake and she got the job in OB, working with Sara. "Best job in the hospital...usually."

She nibbled on a cracker with cheese. "Sorry about last night," she mumbled between bites. "The little boy's death...hit me so hard. Felt so helpless. When I got home, all I did was cry."

She took another small bite. "Anyway, I feel better today. Spending time with my dad is a plus. Besides, it's hard to feel too down when you're out on the Bay like this."

Darrell stared at the slightly ruffled surface of the

water. He felt safe with her. "Out here with you, I agree." He set down his drink and brushed one red curl off her cheek. "I'm glad you care so much about your patients. I bet it makes you a great nurse. It's one thing I like about you."

"One thing?" She gave him a crooked grin. The sunlight reflected off the waves and lit up the sprinkling of freckles on her face.

"One of many."

They sat there, gazes locked, faces a few inches apart, the boat rocking in the swells of the water. As the sloop bobbed, they had to move in tandem to keep their closeness, and for a minute, neither spoke, both swaying in the strange, quiet dance on the water. A small wave splashed against the starboard side, causing them to tilt left. Darrell leaned in a little farther and kissed Erin, his fingers caressing her cheek. She returned the kiss, raising her hand to his shoulder, and for a bit, they lingered there, enjoying the hypnotic embrace of the Bay. Out in the middle of the wider channel, the *Second Wind* was the only boat in sight, as if they were completely alone on the water.

A rogue wave slammed the port side, breaking them apart. Darrell dropped his hand to the bench, his eyes wide at the sudden motion. Erin chuckled and used her hand to steady him. "Some sailor." Her hand on his leg felt warm.

He grabbed his glass and took another drink. Steadier, he placed his arm back around her shoulders, and they sat together, watching the Bay and the sky. The sun, now an almost red-orange ball, hung still a good way over the horizon, as if some giant hand suspended it there for them. She leaned her head into his, and their bodies moved together in the rhythmic sway of the waves. A lone gull flew in lazy circles high above them, its dark outline like some elongated Batman symbol on the water below.

After a bit, she turned to face him. "Okay, your turn. Why you'd decide to become a teacher?"

Her question made Darrell's anxiety spike. He remembered her lithe athletic form and thought she was probably a cool jock back then. What if she thought he was some kind of weird school geek? He really wanted her to like him the way he was, though, so he took the chance.

"Well, as long as I can remember, I wanted to be a teacher. I know I'm not like most guys. I liked learning, the studying and the research. It came easy for me, and I had a few great teachers early on. The history part came later, when I had this great local history teacher named Mr. Simpson. Got me fascinated in the stories about things that had happened right there in our town."

He shook his head. "The problem is, so many kids have been ruined by what we put them through in school. You know, kids say history is their *least* favorite subject. Too many dumb teachers simply make them memorize dates and battles."

"Exactly what my history teachers at Wilshire had us do."

"See. That's what I want to change."

"And I hear you're a pretty good football coach, according to some of the nurses."

On safe ground again, he grinned. "I do love working with young athletes."

She chuckled. "Hey, since I have the winning coach alone out here, I want an exclusive interview.

Want to hear all about this earth-shattering win last night."

He filled her in on the high points, ending with the game-winning pass in the end zone with time running out.

"Everyone must've have been delirious. Easton's been our nemesis forever." She took another small bite of the chicken, following it with a bit more wine. "Don't think the Pirates have beaten the Bulldogs since my sophomore year."

"How many decades ago was that?" He smirked.

She slapped him on the shoulder. "*Very* funny. Would've been fall of eighty-eight, ten years ago."

The boat rocked gently, the rigging creaking. Darrell selected a slice of cheese and a cracker—both perfectly square—and made a sandwich, which he offered it to her. She took it. He asked, "Can I ask you a question about when you were a student at Wilshire?"

"Sure. Shoot."

She nibbled around the edge of the cracker sandwich, and Darrell noticed it was no longer square. That bothered him, but he focused on his question. "Did you hear anything about the high school being haunted when you went there?"

She giggled. "That's a funny question."

"I know, but on the day of my interview, Harriet mentioned the school had its own ghost."

"Loved Harriet when I went to Wilshire, but she can be a little…" She rolled her eyes.

"Yeah, but since then, I've had a few other teachers say something about it. Even told me I needed to talk the ghost into joining the football team."

"Don't pay attention to them." She finished the

cheese, then sipped and replaced her cup in the holder, her glance drifting from the ship's wheel to the waters ahead.

He said, "This week when I asked about the ghost at lunch, Douglass said he was supposed to be some kid who died in the sixties."

Erin's gaze was on the two sails, as if she were inspecting them. She didn't respond. She pulled a grape from the bunch and brought it to her mouth, the purple fruit disappearing between her red lips. She nibbled in silence. The air between them froze.

He might've blown it. Still, he pressed, "I wondered if you'd heard anything about it when you were a student."

She turned to face him. "Sure. Heard about the ghost when I was in school. Kids like to talk about that kind of thing, especially to scare the younger kids."

"Do you remember any of the details?"

She gestured to the calm expanse of water around them. "We're out here alone together, and *you* want to ask about a ghost. Why all the questions about our resident phantom?"

He knew he sounded a little weird, but he was in this far, so he plunged ahead. "I'll explain in a minute. For now, could you humor me?"

Erin stared across the water. "Well, supposed to be the spirit of a black student who stalks the halls at night."

"How'd he die?"

"One story is he committed suicide, but nobody knows."

The boat bobbed again. Darrell almost spilled his wine, but Erin seemed unruffled. He drank a little more and asked, "How did he commit suicide?"

"That's where the story gets a little murky. Kids loved to tell some scary ghost tale but never said much about *how* he died." She turned to look at Darrell.

He was making her uncomfortable. When she didn't say more at first, he was sure he'd blown it. Then, Erin said quickly, "He was said to have hanged himself, completely naked, from the railing along the widow's walk by your office. Teachers came in, found his body dangling there in the morning."

"Jesus." The word was out before Darrell realized it. "Must've been some sight. I'm beginning to see why the story gets a little...what'd you say? Murky. Why'd he do it?"

"Who knows?" She slid her sunglasses back down, rose from her chair, and went to the helm. She released the rope and steered the boat to starboard into the wind, until the sails filled with the breeze. "Back in the sixties, the Bay area was big into civil rights protests."

"Really?"

"We weren't Birmingham or Selma, but my folks told me things were pretty tense 'round here. Anyway, supposed to be about the time those three students from the north went down to register blacks to vote in Mississippi and got killed." She waved her hands. "I dunno. Talk was, the guy was depressed."

"He hanged himself naked? Must've been some depression," Darrell said.

Erin got the sloop positioned into the wind and reattached the rope, holding the helm in place again. She returned to the seat beside Darrell.

"Okay. Humored you enough. Why all the questions about the Wilshire High ghost?"

Darrell swallowed, the lump large in his throat. He took a leap of faith. "I think I've seen him."

Chapter 13

Now that Darrell was here, he didn't know what to say. He feared he'd sound like a raving idiot. He hadn't thought this thing out.

Still, while the sailboat bobbed on the waters, Erin sat across from him, glasses off again and eyes fixed on him. And she waited. So he talked and she listened, the details of his "encounters" coming easily.

He started off with his "sighting" of a large black figure in the window of his office, twice, the day he was hired *and* the first day of school. Then he told her about the "presence" in his office and the iron grip on his ankles.

She said nothing, only stared at him. Darrell studied her face. Did she think he was crazy? He couldn't tell and his insides churned, but he was in too deep now. Finally, he described the image of the black figure on the videotape. Which he couldn't find a second time.

"You could've simply been dreaming," were her first words.

"I realize that, but Pogo saw it too." God, he sounded desperate. He was desperate. Whatever *this* was about, he didn't want to be in it alone. "You believe me?" he asked, his voice a little squeaky.

Erin didn't say anything else at first. Instead, she jumped up, went to the pilot's wheel, and undid the strap. Adjusting the jib, she turned the helm to steer the craft to port and spoke without looking at him. "There are more things in heaven and earth, Darrell, than are dreamt of in your playbook." Her eyes stayed focused forward. "Learned everything in life doesn't have a rational explanation. Seen plenty of strange things out here on the water."

Thank God, she didn't think he was crazy.

Darrell could see now what had drawn her attention. He got to his feet and stood next to her. Up ahead, forward as she said, a large, gray storm cloud hung over the water, and he could make out streams of rain cascading down

As she adjusted the sails to move the sloop out of the path of the oncoming storm, she explained weather on the Bay can change quickly. "We better head back."

With a hard turn of the helm, she executed another maneuver—which she called tacking— turning the boat into the wind. The boom swung all the way across the boat, and Darrell had to duck to get out of the way. The sailboat leaned over the water, hard to the right, and the surface loomed close. He stared, terrified, until the sails filled with air and the boat tilted back up and accelerated. Erin grinned. "That's keeling. Most exciting maneuver on the water."

"Certainly was." He was simply glad he hadn't wet himself.

As the boat bounced on the waves, he stayed on his feet next to her, though he had to use the console to keep himself steady. Erin maneuvered the sailboat back into the channel. The wind picked up, whipping up waves with larger whitecaps and stretching the sails, the rigging creaking with the strain.

She saw him standing beside her and said, "Here, you try."

Before he realized what was happening, she ushered him behind the wheel and placed both his hands on the helm, keeping her hands on his arms. The wood of the wheel felt smooth and worn and almost comfortable. Her hands around his arms felt even better, and she stood close behind him, their bodies touching. He was conscious of the very nice pressure of her breasts against him. And here he was, stuffed inside a stretched life vest, actually steering a sailboat. *He* was steering the boat. Life was good.

He released a long breath and breathed in the Bay air rushing past. His glance went from the swells around the boat to over his shoulder at Erin. The wind sent the strands of her red hair dancing in crazy motions around her face, and she smiled at him.

"You're doing great. Now cut it to the right a little. That's it. Nice job." His heart leaped at her praise.

The sailboat cut smoothly across the froth. The swish and slap of the waves and the billowing of the sailcloth serenaded them as they stood, bodies together, and Darrell even caught a hint of the herbal shampoo she'd used. Twice, Darrell glanced back behind them and saw the storm chasing them into port. Erin seemed unconcerned and left him in charge for a while, one reassuring hand on his arm.

About halfway to port, she took the wheel back, and Darrell was both relieved and disappointed. She steered and adjusted the sails, all the while providing him with a running, maritime commentary. He drank in her teaching, learning all he could about sailing. Seeing her in charge, strong arms commanding the boat, he was mesmerized, and his fascination now replaced his anxiety. And she'd let him navigate. He could never imagine Carmen doing any of this.

Darrell was thrilled to have been able to share his secret. And she hadn't laughed at him. But he didn't get the chance to tell Erin about the naked figure in the locker room shower or Ruby's note. And he didn't get to do some of the other things he had planned.

The kiss was great though, and at least he didn't blow it.

Once she used the diesel engine to place them in the berth, it took only a few minutes to tie up the boat, drop the sails, and attach the necessary covers. As they dashed up the pier, the rain followed them, the drops pelting the waters and the wood beneath them. She clicked the lock on her car door and jumped in. He shut the door. She started the engine and lowered the window. When Darrell leaned in to kiss her, the rain caught up and sent a shower down his back, drenching his shirt. He gave her a quick peck and hollered he'd had a great time and would call for next week.

"Off both Saturday and Sunday next weekend," she yelled as she raised the window to keep the rain out.

"Count on it."

Holding the windbreaker over his head, he ran across the small parking lot. He yanked open his car door, tossed the picnic basket on the passenger seat, and jumped in. He watched Erin drive her Jeep up the driveway and shot a quick glance back toward the dock. A small, young black woman stood at the end of the pier. She stared at him, rain streaming down her black curls and her petite face.

He couldn't believe his eyes. "Ruby?" he yelled,

his words drowned in the storm.

He got out and started to run to the dock when thunder exploded. A streak of lighting ripped the sky into two jagged halves. As if on command, the shower turned into an unrelenting torrent, water hammering him like liquid BBs. He leapt back into his seat. He got the engine started and turned on the wipers. Peered out toward the dock. The rain fell in a deluge against the wooden slats and into the water. His gaze swept back and forth.

There was no one on the pier.

Chapter 14

Darrell told himself he must have imagined it. How could it have been Ruby? She couldn't have simply disappeared.

He'd sat there for long minutes, peering into the rain and seeing no one. After a while, he returned to his apartment, stripped, and carefully stowed the soaked clothes in a black plastic bag. He showered, and the water from the showerhead reminded him of the gentle spray off the Bay…and the taste of wine on Erin's lips. The thought of her made him hard, so he turned the water to cold, and when he could stand it no longer, shut off the faucet, and toweled off.

He didn't want to think about Ruby and tried to focus on something else. Sitting on his bed in pressed pajama bottoms, he watched a tape of next week's opponent, the Mariners, the sound off. As the storm raged outside, the reflection of the lightning etched ragged slashes across the football field on the TV screen. The pounding of thunder and the pinging of rain against the window and metal siding were the only noises in the bedroom. He concentrated on the rival team, paying close attention to formations and searching for weaknesses, all while he took neat, careful notes. Pogo snored on the floor at his feet, and no strange grainy images appeared in the video. He yawned. Having never sailed before, he was surprised how tired he was, and when he could keep his eyes open no longer, he turned off the VCR, hit the lights, and collapsed.

As he slid off to sleep, Ruby and her cryptic notes creeped into his consciousness, but he deliberately conjured up a different image. Erin's beautiful, long hands on the pilot's wheel, red hair flying wildly in the wind. Savoring the memory, he succumbed to the embrace of slumber, and somewhere in the middle of the night, the dream crept back.

It began again with the familiar chords of the same song, "My Girl," voices, guitar, and static floating across the apartment. *She* was there, lying next to him, and they kissed. Eyes closed, he inhaled the scents of her—sea, perspiration, and a floral cologne—and thought how lucky he was to have found this woman. At first, they exchanged tender, emotional kisses, like on the boat earlier. Then, their kissing became more urgent, their tongues searching desperately for each other. He opened his eyes to enjoy watching her like he had on the sloop, but she broke off the kiss and leaned into him, her head buried in his neck. Her slender fingers wrapped around his arms, which looked almost *black*. Her long legs lay against his, and his loins responded.

The dream had the same feeling as the earlier one, both ethereal and strangely real. All this was really happening? He tried to recall when Erin came over to his apartment—when he was watching the tapes? He couldn't remember. Not that he was complaining.

Another bolt of lightning sent a brief flash across the room and ignited a few strands of damp red hair clinging to her cheeks, and some freckles on her neck and shoulder. The light vanished as quickly as it came, and they were plunged again into darkness. Hardly a disadvantage. He felt her hand slide inside the waistband of his pajama bottoms, her nimble fingers lightly brushing his skin, as she undid the tie. *Oh, God.*

Darrell had so enjoyed his time with Erin, and he had done some fantasizing about her, but this? *Something* was off. He couldn't figure out what it was, and she wasn't making rational thought any easier. He felt her lean in more, her nipples two very nice pressure points on his chest. Her hand slid a little farther. He groaned and closed his eyes again.

Then, it was all gone—the touch of her lips, the press of her body against his. Darrell opened his eyes and saw...nothing. Shadows blanketed the room, the only faint light from the clock radio on the bedside table. He heard sounds from the doorway. Another flash of lightning lit the room. He saw her tall, lithe, naked body in the doorframe. He started to call out and stopped himself. Was that *Erin*? The girl looked...younger.

The darkness returned. He felt a hard yank on his ankle and he landed, butt first, on the floor. Pogo growled, and he realized it was the dog's grip on his foot. He struggled to get up and reached over to switch on the lamp on the bedside table.

He stood up, his chest now drenched in sweat. He searched the room. He was alone. No girl. No oldies song. In fact, no sound other than the panting of his pug beside his bed and the pelting of the rain outside. He glanced down and noticed the waistband of his pajama bottoms were untied, the flaps open. He pulled the two strings and tied them together in a perfect bow.

"Thanks, Pogo, I think." He felt his heart racing. "It was only a dream. *One hell* of a strange dream."

He fought to control his breathing and calm his heart rate. Darrell glanced around. The dim features of his apartment emerged slowly in the low light. The bedside clock read 3:13. *Again?*

"What the hell is going on?" he said to his pug partner, who only stared back. Apparently, Pogo had no answer, and Darrell realized neither did he.

Chapter 15

Early Monday evening, Darrell stood on the edge of the widow's walk, alone. He looked toward the Bay and noticed the sun had dropped across the sky and disappeared behind the trees on the other shore, sketching red and gold streaks across the water. His hand gripped the rail, knuckles white, and he edged carefully across the square space. He lingered there and faced the Bay, drinking in the vista and inhaling the scent.

This was where it happened? At least, the young man died looking at an incredible sight.

He tried to picture the naked body of a large black student hanging from the rail. How desperate do you have to be to hang yourself? Between his trouble with women, ghosts, and his OCD, Darrell had his own share of problems, but hanging himself? He shuddered and closed his eyes.

His fingers fumbled on the wooden rail. Here, in the middle, he found the railing wobbled, as if it had been cracked and never fixed. Where the wood fence piece met the center support, it still held together, barely, and the crack was only noticeable up close. While his left hand gripped a sturdier piece, Darrell stared down at the rickety length of white wood in his right, wondering if *this* was where the black student hanged himself, all those years ago. Then, a giant weariness flooded over him, drawing him back inside to his desk.

He'd spent much of the day before, Sunday, examining every space in his small office, from floor to ceiling, looking for a diary. He came up empty. He searched the walls, the bookcase, the sofa. Nada. Like some detective in a noir novel, he'd pulled out each desk drawer and examined the undersides and cavities behind, but found nothing. Frustrated, he went over to his battered, brown briefcase, pulled out Ruby's two notes, and reread them, if only to prove to himself he hadn't imagined the whole thing.

He finally gave up and got all his boxes unpacked. He even tacked up his framed diploma on the paneled wall next to the calendar. As usual, the top of his desk was clean, displaying only one picture in the precise center of the back edge. Darrell studied his graduation photo, the one with his brother. Craig's arm wrapped around his shoulders, and both flashed wide smiles. There was no evidence of Craig's limp. For the hundredth time, Darrell offered his older brother a silent apology. If he had to do it over, he would've done things so differently. He'd sighed and decided to get back to his *real* life.

He had made it to Monday, but *it* had been a killer.

He'd spent the day prepping his seniors for their research project, teaching the basics on how to use primary sources. He hoped the project would show them the real, human side of history. He thought he was making progress with them. Maybe not interest yet, but the students' demeanors had lost their angry, bored façade. It wasn't much, but it was enough.

The weather had turned unseasonably warm, full

tilt Indian summer, and during football practice, the temperature never dropped below eighty-five degrees. With every player suited up, they were all sweating in minutes. He had to send the guys for water after every other drill. And of course, he had to keep up with them, so by the end, he was drenched and exhausted too.

So here he sat, slumped at his office desk after seven at night. The temperature had cooled a bit in the last hour, and the open window delivered a small breeze, carrying the aroma off the water.

He checked out the bookshelf, hoping for inspiration, now that he had unpacked and stacked a few more titles on the shelves. But he was too drained to even get up and open any of them.

Pogo emitted a small growl.

"What is it, boy?"

The pug, on all fours, stared at the open office door.

"Is somebody there?" Darrell called out to the hallway.

No answer.

Pogo remained frozen in place, eyes and snout focused on the doorway. Darrell got up and stumbled over to the door. He stuck his head into the corridor and looked both ways. Nothing. He walked down to the hall window for another look at the widow's walk. Nothing there, either.

When he came back into the office, he said, "Pogo, I don't need you growling at things that aren't there."

The pug seemed satisfied with his master's inspection and resumed his accustomed position, snuggled into the small, woven rug in front of the desk. Darrell returned and collapsed again in his chair.

Reaching into a drawer, he pulled out a doggie treat and tossed it over his desk. He heard Pogo catch and swallow it, and Darrell smiled.

He pulled out his notebook and re-read the plays he'd scripted for this week's game. When he came to his fifth entry, he felt the hairs on the back of his neck rise. He forgot about the game.

He craned his neck to look down at the pug. Now, Pogo lay motionless, tongue lolling out the side of his mouth. Darrell's right hand moved to his neck and fingered the hairs. He shook his head. The sensation lingered.

Something, a slight motion in his peripheral vision, drew his attention. His souvenir basketball rolled out of its wooden stand and off the middle shelf. It bounced onto the floor next to Pogo. The pug jumped to his feet as the ball rolled around the edge of the frayed rug and across the worn linoleum. The basketball stopped beside the leather briefcase, bumping against the paneling.

Darrell stared at the gleaming basketball, and then his gaze swept the rest of the office. The hairs on his neck still prickled. He glanced outside at the widow's walk in the setting sun. Nothing.

"Is anyone there?" he yelled again. His voice echoed back at him.

He got up and walked over, leaning down to pick up the ball. Pogo moved alongside him, the small body rigid with tension again. The dog stuck his snout next to the ball, blocking his owner's view. Darrell shoved the pug aside and reached for the basketball. And saw it.

The ball lay at the foot of the wall, the leather panel with the autograph facing up. He picked it up with both hands. Held the basketball frozen in midair. The familiar, scribbled signature of Michael Jordan was *gone*. Instead, a different name stared back, scrawled in black across the leather—*Oscar Robertson*.

Darrell yanked his hands away as if they were stung. The ball bounced twice on the floor. The boings echoed loud in the small room. Pogo trotted after the ball, and Darrell's gaze darted around the office.

"What the hell?" He stepped over to the door and glanced both ways in the hallway. "Okay, this is not *funny*," he hollered. His heart hammered in his chest.

He peered again at the different name and then at the pug, who sniffed the ball. "You see it too. Don't you, boy?"

Pogo gave another tiny yip.

He picked the ball up again and fingered the neat script, certain the ink would rub off and blacken his fingertips, but his skin came away clean. He stared at the name, anxious, then angry. *Oscar Robertson.*

He held the basketball between his index fingers and spun it around, watching the manufacturer's name and the NBA logo fly by. He stopped it at the oversized autograph. It still read *Oscar Robertson.* He was not dreaming.

Maybe this was a prank, something Al would do. But his hairs did not relax.

Darrell hefted the ball in one hand, convincing himself it was real, and then walked back to the bookshelf. Using both hands, he placed it into the stand, the altered autograph facing out. Then he walked around the desk, slumped down, and laid his head atop his notebook.

"I think I've had enough for one day, Pogo. How

about you?"

The pug gave no response.

"Okay, let's head to the showers." Darrell got up and grabbed his keys out of the center drawer. Sticking the key in the ancient lock, he shot a glance again back at the bookcase. The bright orange basketball still perched where he set it, but the trademark name, not the autograph, faced out.

What the hell? Man, was he tired. He could've sworn he'd set the ball down, autograph out.

Darrell strode over and turned the ball so the autograph faced front again. His hands jumped back from the touch of the leather like an electric shock hit them. He stared.

Michael Jordan.

Chapter 16

The young black student stood in front of Darrell's desk, large, powerful arms crossed in front of his chest and gang tattoo pulsing on his neck. Darrell let Tyler wait. The clang of the final bell faded away, and the sounds of students shuffling down the corridors filtered through the open doorway. Darrell continued making careful checkmarks on the next test and glanced up from time to time.

The student slid into a slouch. As he stretched his neck from side to side, the light from the fluorescent fixture reflected off his shaved, brown head. "Can we get on with this, man?" he asked.

"Tyler, I'm ready to listen if you have an explanation."

Darrell thought he'd made some progress with the sullen student in the last few weeks. Tyler had even started volunteering a few answers in class. Nothing earth-shaking, but not resentful silence anymore. Now, he caught him cheating. Darrell glanced from his dress shirt and tie to Tyler's fashion tee and worn jeans. Two different worlds.

Maybe he wasn't making as much difference as he thought.

Darrell finished grading the test and set it on the finished pile. He picked up the papers and stacked them against the edge of the desk, aligning the corners and arranging the stack into a precise, neat formation. "When I get to yours and Damien's, I'm going to know. I saw you guys passing answers."

Tyler shifted from foot to foot. "We weren't passin' no answers."

"Ah, here it is." Darrell grabbed the next test, the name "Tyler Carroll" scribbled in the upper right-hand corner. "Might as well come clean, 'cause I'm going to know in a minute." He dangled the paper.

The student leaned forward, both palms on the desk, the large muscles in his upper arms taut, his breath warm and sour. He lowered his face so it was inches away from Darrell. "We weren't cheatin'."

Darrell leaned across the desk toward the student. "Okay, humor me. I saw you and Damien passing something during the test. If they weren't answers, what'd you pass?"

"Ya wouldn't understand, Mr. H. You old and you white."

"That's lame, Tyler. You got to give me something. If you do, maybe I can cut you loose." Darrell glanced at his watch and figured he had another seven minutes before he had to be at practice. He waited out the student.

Tyler straightened up, his tall figure looming over the metal desk. "Hell, Damien don't even care 'bout your stupid test. It was jus' a note about Felissa." When Darrell didn't respond, he added, "Ya know, the wicked chick in the second row with the big—"

"I know who Felissa is," Darrell cut him off.

"Dudn't matter. You won't believe me anyway." Tyler shrugged. "Nobody cares about us blacks around here."

"Don't play the race card with me." Darrell replaced the test on the stack. "There are plenty of teachers who care about you and the rest of the black students. Mr. McClure, Mrs. McQuire—

Tyler interrupted him. "Lemme ask you a question. How many dark faces do you see in the teachers' lounge?"

Darrell shifted in his seat. "There's Mr. Byerson and Mrs. Greene and…"

Tyler unleased a little laugh. "Yeah, remedial math and home ec. See a pattern here? And whitey keep saying everything's all right."

Darrell started to respond but stopped himself. He really liked the shore town, but he'd picked up on several racial innuendos by the townspeople. Subtle, but there. At school, he'd overheard teachers saying things like, "You know you can't expect *those* kids to do well. Look at where they live, who their parents are." They might hide their prejudice behind a professional veneer, but it still leaked out.

Could he have been quicker to assume these two boys were cheating because they were black?

His thoughts were derailed by Tyler's next words. "It's jus' like the Wilshire ghost."

"What did you say?"

"I said, you wouldn't understand…jus' like the ghost."

"What's the ghost have to do with this?" Darrell asked.

"Heard you was asking about the Wilshire ghost." Tyler leaned away from the desk and folded his arms in front of him. "White people don't *really* want to know the truth about the ghost."

"Because we're white? Come on. You got to do better than that." Darrell clicked his pen several times, then realized he was doing it and stopped himself. When Tyler didn't respond, he added, "Tell you what. Give me a few answers, and you can get out of here, for now."

Tyler shifted on his feet. "What about the test?"

"I'll grade it and let you know tomorrow. If there's no evidence of cheating between you and Damien, you're clear. Okay?" Tyler nodded and Darrell asked, "What do you know about the Black Underground?"

Darrell saw recognition flash in the young man's eyes, but Tyler turned away and said, "Never heard of it." He glanced toward the door.

"Uh-hum." Darrell stared at him, but the student refused to meet his eyes. Darrell remembered Ruby's words on the note. *Tell no one.* "Okay then, what can you tell me about the Wilshire ghost?"

Tyler looked at him sideways, the barb wire tatt on his neck gleaming again. "Lemme ask you a question. Ya ever heard of any kid—white or black—strippin' off all his clothes *before* he hanged himself? As if."

Darrell thought for a moment and shook his head. "No. I guess not."

"Hell, no. Weren't no *suicide*." The student grunted. "We done now?"

"Yeah, sure." Tyler headed out, and when the student was past the last row, Darrell asked, "Why do people say he committed suicide then?"

"'Cause easier for whitey to take." Tyler slipped through the door and closed it behind him.

Darrell glanced at his watch. He had less than four minutes before he had to start practice. He was turning the key in the ancient lock, the ring jangling, when he heard his name. Darrell looked behind and saw Jesse Stewart, half bent over a wide broom, wobbling down the hallway. The custodian lifted one calloused hand in greeting.

"You got a minute to talk?" asked Jesse, his voice tinny in the enclosed space.

"That's all I got." Darrell pointed to his watch. "I've got to be out on the field in a few minutes."

"Okay, well, this won't take long." The scrawny black man cast a glance down both directions and dropped his voice. "Heard you've been asking 'bout our school ghost."

Darrell asked, "What do *you* know about the ghost?"

"You work at night, ya see things." The custodian nodded, the thinning black hairs on his head swirling.

Darrell fixed his gaze on the custodian. "What'd you see?"

"Well, some won't believe this—"

"Coach? There you are," yelled a student half-dressed in football gear. As he ran down the length of the hall, his shoulder pads flapped in motion to his hurried steps, the slapping echoing down the corridor. He pulled up. "You better come right away, Coach. Damian cut himself, right on his forehead. He's bleeding pretty bad."

"Okay, John, have Dan put a compress on it, and I'll be right there. Step on it." Darrell watched the kid disappear down the stairway and turned back to the old custodian. "Looks like I better get down there. I want to hear what you got to tell me. Let's finish this later."

Darrell started to leave, but Jesse grabbed his arm

with one bony hand. The strength of the older man's grip surprised Darrell.

"For now, I'm telling you to watch yourself," whispered Jesse, his voice stern. "Some people ain't goin' like you asking questions about the Wilshire ghost. Don't want you openin' old wounds."

"What old wounds?" Now Darrell searched the corridor for eavesdroppers. "Do you know anything about the Black Underground?"

The student, back at the top of the stairs, hollered, "Coach, we can't stop the bleeding. We need you now."

The custodian released Darrell's arm and scurried away in the opposite direction.

Darrell called after him, "Thanks for the heads up. Let's talk more later." He headed down the hallway, rubbing the spot where Jesse had hung on. *As if for dear life.*

Chapter 17

Another grueling practice—no more bloody casualties—kept Darrell's mind occupied and away from any paranoid tendencies. Until after the athletes left and Al came in.

"Seen any great ghosts lately?" Al said and laughed.

Darrell couldn't get Jesse's warning out of his head and said, "Not funny."

"Not, huh?" Al slapped a hand on his friend's shoulder and grinned. "Then how about this? You know what they call an almanac of famous ghosts? The Boo's Who's."

Darrell turned and headed into the hallway. Al hurried alongside. "No? Well then, what do you call a ghost's mother and father? Well, trans-parents, of course." His booming laugh resounded down the corridor.

Darrell stopped and stared at his friend. "Right now, not funny, Al."

"Not even a little?" Al held up his index finger and thumb a half inch apart.

"Okay, maybe a little," Darrell said, unable to keep from chuckling. Between his bad puns and the occasional prank, Al always made him smile. "But the prank last night with the basketball in my office, not funny. Scared the hell out of me." He shook his head.

"Love to know how you did it, though."

Al's grin disappeared. "What are you talking about, kid?"

"You know, the bit with rolling the ball off my shelf. How you changed the autograph on my basketball, right in front of me. Pretty slick stuff."

Patting his thinning hair back in place, Al said, "I'd love to take credit for all the wrinkles life throws your way, but I don't know what the hell you're talking about."

So Darrell explained about the basketball incident and when he finished, Al asked, "This ever happen before?"

"No, but other things like this image…"

"Hold that thought." Al shot a furtive look around. "Let's head over to Nick's for the rest of this conversation where we won't be overheard." Without another word, Al hurried down the hall, Darrell a step behind, recalling Jesse's warning.

They took their own cars, driving along Shore Road, on much the same route he and Erin had run more than a week ago. Along the beach, Darrell noticed large, angry whitecaps on the waves. Then, they turned and headed inland, to the rougher part of town. In ten minutes, they were ensconced in a corner booth at Nick's, away from the other patrons, both with a Dogfish Head beer in hand.

"Okay, tell me the rest, kid," Al said, his cheeks red and his eyes wide behind his brown plastic frames.

Darrell's gaze searched the bar. The few other patrons sat away from them, absorbed in their drinks or focused on the TV. Glad to have a sympathetic ear, he explained about the visions or apparitions between pulls on his beer. He filled Al in on the figure in the window, the image on the tape, the black kid in the shower. He also told him about his sense of being watched and Pogo's reaction. After another furtive glance around the bar, Darrell finished with Jesse's warning this afternoon. He decided not to mention Ruby and her notes, at least not yet. And he didn't think Al was the right person to ask about the Black Underground. *Tell no one.*

While he was talking, Darrell had used a handkerchief to wipe up the moisture ring his bottle left on the wooded tabletop. He hadn't even realized it. He looked down and stopped himself. He stuffed the cloth back in his pocket.

"Jesse said some won't like you asking questions about the ghost, huh?" Al said, taking another pull on his beer. "Anything else?"

"Isn't that enough?" Darrell clanged his bottle down on the wooden table and then glanced around to see if anyone noticed. They hadn't. "Am I going crazy?"

"Well, let's face it, you have to be a little crazy to teach teenagers. And then, you throw in coaching them. Well?" He clicked the top of the bottle to his temple.

"Al, that's not what I'm talking about."

"I know, kid. Naw, I don't think you're crazy, any more than me, but I'd listen to Jesse. He's been around here a long time, and he knows this place pretty well."

"That makes me feel great." Darrell took a long drink of the Dogfish Head beer. He might need another.

"Kid, I don't know how you do it."

"What?"

"Well, I've been here twenty-five years and only

heard bits of gossip about our local ghost. You've been here, what? Two months and you're stirring up all this ghost stuff."

"I didn't ask for any of this." Darrell's voice got indignant...and loud. He shot another glance around Nick's.

"Relax. I didn't say you did, but I think there's somebody you need to meet. Right now." He threw a few bills on the table and slid out of the booth.

Darrell hurried after him. "Where we going?"

The band leader headed out the door, turned a quick right, and started down the sidewalk. Even though Al was shorter, when he adopted his quick marching band stride, he could move, and Darrell had to hurry to stay even.

"Two blocks down. Don't tell me the *kid* can't keep up." He shot a glance across, grin showing, legs still pumping.

Darrell grabbed his friend's shoulder, making him halt. "You didn't answer my question. Where are we going?" Darrell panted once and noticed Al wasn't the least bit winded.

"You need to get yourself in better shape, kid."

"Gimme a break. I just finished a full day of classes and a couple of hours of football practice."

Darrell noted where they were, somewhere outside of the commercial district. No storefronts, no neon signs in the windows. Little activity, besides the drunk in the doorway they passed and the homeless man lying in the cardboard box across the street. Where were they, six or eight blocks from the shore? You'd never know it. Darrell had driven by this section of Wilshire before, but had never *been* here. He wondered how many of his students lived nearby. And what color their skin was.

Low rent apartment buildings fronted the sidewalk, three ugly floors squatting shoulder to shoulder like cramped brothers squeezed into too tight a space. The stench of rotten garbage flowed out from an alley they passed and one discarded, white plastic grocery bag clung to a porch light like a desperate wraith. Cigarette butts, pop cans, and empty liquor bottles lay scattered across the sidewalk, as if the buildings had vomited them onto the concrete.

"Where are you taking me?" Darrell asked, glancing around.

"We're going to see somebody I think may be able to help. She's in the next block. What's the matter, kid? Don't you trust me?" Without waiting for an answer, Al started again, and Darrell hustled to catch up.

Darrell's paranoia went on full alert. His head swiveled, checking in all directions. He wet his lips, still tasting the tang of the beer. In a doorway of an apartment across the street, he spied a short, young black woman with a petite face, bundled in a dark overcoat.

He called, "Ruby, wait." The woman didn't move. He turned and pointed. "Al, you see her?"

Al, who had been searching for building numbers, turned and glanced across the street. He gave a little wave. "Cute. Good looking."

Darrell started to cross the street. "I need to talk to her."

Al grabbed Darrell's arm. "Sorry, lover boy. Keep your libido in check, at least till we get upstairs." He grinned and pointed at the second door, "169" in faded brass numbers on the old, scarred wood. "We're here."

Chapter 18

Al pushed the door open and gestured *after you.* A quick glance at the building across told Darrell the woman had disappeared again. Sighing, he stepped through. Two apartment doors stood inside on the first floor to the right, with black plastic letters A and B at eye level, and a set of stairs led off to the left. Al bounded up the steps and Darrell, scrutinizing the surroundings, followed. The stairs were old and decaying, the boards creaking under each footfall. The wooden rail bordering the steps was cracked in two places and several of the white wooded slats wobbled when Darrell grabbed them.

On the second landing, one light bulb had been shattered, while a second created only dingy shadows. The gray paint peeled away from the wall in places and jagged splotches of brown stains were strewn across the drywall like some grotesque Rorschach test. Water stains marked the ceiling over the door to C, strips of plaster drooping overhead like suspended white tears. Darrell sniffed the odor of urine from above and cringed.

Al moved to apartment D and knocked on the hollow wooden door, which bore a two-inch hole a third of the way up.

About where someone would kick it.

He turned to Darrell. "Usually, you're supposed to

have an appointment, but since we were in the neighborhood, I thought we'd take a chance."

"An appointment? For what?"

Al opened his mouth to answer, but a female voice called from deep inside. "I'm a little busy at the moment." Breath. "Almost finished. Ya need to wait." Grunt.

"We'll wait," Al called and turned toward Darrell. "I thought it being a weekday and early enough in the evening, she wouldn't be busy. Never can tell." He smirked and shrugged.

Darrell's thumb jabbed at the door. "Is *she* who you want me to meet?"

Another grunt from inside and a man's voice called out, "Yes. Yes. Oh, yes!"

Darrell couldn't believe it. Had Al dragged him to a... "Is she...? This isn't..."

The sound of a dead bolt sliding inside stopped Darrell mid-sentence, as the door swung open. An attractive young woman stood framed in the opening, dressed in a short plaid, wrap-around skirt and a blue cut-off top, revealing a flat expanse of stomach punctuated by a small diamond belly-button stud. She broke out a broad smile. "Mr. McClure."

"Uh-um." A male voice came from inside and an older man stepped into the space—near sixty, Darrell thought. The man wore a navy pin-striped suit, very crumpled, a red tie thrown around his neck. "See you next week," he said, as he tucked in a half-buttoned white shirt, zipped up his suit pants, and stepped into the hallway.

"Same bat-time, same bat-channel," said the woman. Strands of her long brown hair fell around her small, heart-shaped face and the rest was tied into a ponytail. A blue and red scarf that matched the skirt hung around her neck.

Al stepped inside the apartment and Darrell, not at all sure, followed. The mingled aromas of incense, perfume, and sweat assaulted him as he crossed the threshold.

What had Al gotten him into?

The young woman shut the door behind them, slid the dead bolt again, and turned. "Mr. McClure," she repeated and wrapped both arms around Al in an amorous hug, leaning in close and tight.

After a bit, Al used both hands to extricate himself and hold her at arms' length, looking her in the eyes. "Darrell, this is Natalia Pavlenco, a former member of the marching Pirates."

"Not to mention, proud Wilshire graduate of '89 and cheerleader extraordinaire," she said. One foot in front and the other behind and both arms held high, she struck a familiar cheerleading position and pumped imaginary pom-poms.

As she posed, Darrell couldn't help but notice large, generous breasts, which bounced in the blue top—with no bra. It was hard not to appreciate the view, but he tried to concentrate on her face. She had shining brown eyes under heavy green eye shadow, a cute nose, and small, perky, scarlet lips. Darrell guessed she was in her late twenties.

Al said, "Natalia, this is Darrell Henshaw, a teaching colleague of mine from Wilshire."

Natalia came out of her pose and extended a hand. "And what do you teach, Mr. Henshaw?" Her voice became low...and sexy.

Darrell took the offered hand and found it warm, the skin smooth. When he spoke, his voice cracked. "History."

She didn't release his hand, warm chocolate eyes staring up at him. "If I'd had a history teacher like you when I was at Wilshire, maybe I would've paid more attention." Still holding Darrell's hand, she turned toward Al. "Are you here to take advantage of my professional services?" She smirked. "I'll give you a special discount for a double."

Al flashed a lopsided grin. "Shame on you, Ms. Pavlenco. You know I'm a happily married man...and want to stay married."

"I know, but you can't blame a girl for trying." She released Darrell's hand, and he felt immediate relief and disappointment.

Natalia moved to a round mirror beside the door. Studying her face in the glass, she took her time puckering her lips and reapplying bright red lipstick. "Okay, then, how can I help you?"

"My colleague here has need of your...professional services," Al said, smiling.

"Well, yum." She turned from the mirror. Her attention on Darrell, she sidled next to him and eyed him from head to toe. "Why didn't you say so?"

Darrell felt his face redden and turned toward Al. "Now, wait a minute..."

"No, Natalia," Al broke in. "Not that kind of service. Your *other* professional service."

"Oh, damn." All the innuendo leaked out of her voice. "Come over to the table then."

She walked over by the bed and extinguished the light, then sashayed across the apartment. All the while,

Darrell studied her and took in the rest of the place.

The apartment was small, a queen bed with ruffled pink sheets and a nightstand with a TV on the right. A tiny kitchenette complete with a soiled stove and mini refrigerator filled the left side of the space, the aroma of stale take-out mixing with the other odors. Beside the appliances, a tower of dirty dishes sprouted from the tarnished white sink and looked ready to topple like a child's uneven construction of blocks. The blinds over the single window were pulled shut, and the only illumination now came from several candles, the lights from the wicks flickering with every movement in the cramped space.

Natalia settled into one of the chairs at the small table. When Darrell stayed by the door, she gestured to the other remaining chair. "Come, sit, Mr. Henshaw," she said, her voice still low and sultry. "I promise I won't bite."

His paranoia raging, Darrell glanced back at the door and then at Al, who gave a quick wave. While he edged his way across the room, Darrell fingered the top button on his wrinkled dress shirt, making sure it was buttoned. He pulled out the vacant chair, sat, and watched Natalia as she adopted a new persona and seemed to age before his eyes. She pulled the scarf from her neck and used it as a bandana around her forehead. Her features seemed to harden, her eyes narrowing, and her mouth becoming a single slash.

Natalia extended both arms across the table, palms up. "Give me your hands."

Darrell shot another glance at Al, who said, "I have it on good authority Natalia is a fine medium…among other things." He grinned. "If anyone can help you sort out this ghost thing, it'll be her."

Darrell's gaze returned to the woman. "You, a medium? But I thought—"

"My family migrated here from New Orleans," Natalia said. "It is in the bloodlines. My grandmother and mother had the second sight and now, so do I." She looked around the apartment. "But there's not a lot of call for the services of a medium in Wilshire, so I've developed...other professional services." She flashed a sardonic smile. "A girl's got to live."

She motioned with her hands, palms up again, her voice serious. "Now your hands, Darrell Henshaw?"

Al said, "That's my cue to go. Natalia, thank you. Darrell, I'll see you at school tomorrow."

Jeez, Al was going to leave him here alone.

Before Darrell could verbalize any objection, Al slipped the deadbolt and stepped through the door, shutting it as he left. Darrell's collar suddenly felt tight, and his hand went to it. But he didn't undo the top shirt button. He took one more desperate look around the apartment and returned his stare to the strange, voluptuous woman.

Oh, hell.

He placed his hands in her warm, smooth palms.

Chapter 19

Amazed, Darrell felt his own hands begin to tingle. Natalia closed her eyes and tilted her head back. Her slender fingers tightened around his hands. Streaks of warmth raced across his skin. Darrell squirmed in her grip, turned, and looked toward the closed apartment door and then back at Natalia. "Al's a great guy and everything, but I don't know about this. How am I supposed to believe *you* can help me?"

Natalia said, "You had a close encounter with the spirit world, a number of years ago, many miles from here."

"What? What are you talking about?"

"When you vere a child," she said, without opening her eyes, her voice now a deep, creamy tenor, taking on a slight Slavic accent. "No... I can see you vere not a child. Older. You met with a spirit in your thirteenth year of life. I see...someone of your blood who had passed over. A relative reached across the curtain of death."

How could she know that? He tried a bluster. "I don't know what you're talking about."

"You did not heed the spirit's warning."

Darrell couldn't believe what he was hearing. He blurted, "What? I was, I was thirteen...and confused."

"Did the spirit give you a warning?"

Darrell hesitated. "Yes."

"But you ignored it?"

Darrell stared at her. Even though the woman's eyes remained shut, he felt like she could peer inside him, see his heart hammering inside his chest. Bile bubbled up in his throat. He licked his lips. He needed another drink. "I was only a kid and didn't know what to do."

She gave a slow nod. "And vhat lesson did you draw from this encounter?" The medium's voice took on a different tone, now older, somber like a tired teacher.

To never tell anyone what he'd seen. "Lesson?" he managed.

Natalia opened her eyes and stared at him, hard brown eyes boring into him. "Surely, you have learned you ignore such spirits at your peril, and the peril of those around you. Consequences followed from your inaction. You realize that every time you look at Craig."

Craig? How could she possibly know about his brother?

Her hands turned around his, rotating her fingers around his palms. Another wave surged through his skin, sending burning streaks up his arms. The feeling was so intense, Darrell expected to see hot oil crawling up his skin. Powerful scorching sensations seemed to emanate from her fingers. He stared, but saw nothing.

She said, "But I sense you have sought me out for a different reason."

He watched as she rolled her eyes back inside her head, white orbs replacing the dark brown irises. Her voice, this time, sounded like it came from farther away. "Here in Wilshire, you have had a second encounter...vith another spirit."

"Yes."

"This spirit is not someone known to you." She squeezed his hands again. "I see...the essence of a young man...a large black youth."

"Yes," Darrell said again, no longer concerned with how she knew these things, only relieved she did.

"Tell me what you have encountered, and I vill interpret."

So, there in the darkened apartment, wrapped in the aroma of vanilla and human perspiration, Darrell talked. In hushed, urgent tones, he told this sultry, exotic woman about the apparitions and about his visions and dreams of the ghost, while flickering candle flames made the shadows of their figures sway.

Her hands never released their grip on his, but halfway through his narrative, her eyes returned to normal, and her intent gaze focused on his again. When he finished, the words spilling out of him like water from a burst dam, she said nothing at first.

Unable to bear the silence, he said, "Tell me. What's going on?"

Rather than answer, she asked, "Has the spirit found a way to communicate with you yet?"

"What do mean, communicate?"

"Has he spoken to you? Left messages for you? You know, like your uncle did when you were young."

"N-n-no..." Darrell started, flashing on the autograph scrawled on the basketball. "I don't think so."

"Hu-um." She paused, still holding Darrell's gaze.

"Why me?"

"Vhat is it you ask?"

"Why me? Why is this spirit haunting me? I mean, I'm new to the shore, only been here two months." Darrell jerked his head back toward the door. "Al's been here for twenty years, and he said he's never seen the...the...the spirit. Why me?"

For the first time since they sat down, Natalia smiled. "I have great affection for Alan McClure, but he is not sensitive to the spirit world. The spirit must sense you are. You are indeed blessed."

"Blessed?" Darrell barked. "I thought I was seeing things. Maybe going crazy."

"You may well be seeing things, Darrell Henshaw, but that does not mean you are going crazy."

Darrell felt himself connected to this curious woman in ways beyond the physical. This woman was a stranger. He did not know her, should not be willing to trust her, but he did. He wanted her help.

"Do you know about the...Black Underground?" he got out. And waited. For thirty seconds, Natalia said nothing and only stared at him. Perhaps deciding what to say?

"I have heard of them, whispers from some...clients. They are secret group formed to fight racism on the Bay," she said, her eyes checking for listeners in the walls of the small apartment. "Vhy do you ask? Are they connected to the ghost?"

"Secret group to fight racism, um." Suddenly Darrell wasn't sure he should've asked and glanced toward the door as if expecting Ruby to appear. *Tell no one.* "I don't know. Maybe. What am *I* supposed to do about the ghost? What does the spirit want?"

She lifted her arms and gave his hands a gentle squeeze, as if by assessing the energy flowing between them she might discern an answer. She closed her eyes again. "It is not clear. I sense this spirit has walked the earth for some time. Do you know how many years have elapsed since his passing?"

"I don't know. Supposed to have died sometime in the sixties."

She tugged on both hands. Sent another hot spike through them. "I cannot yet see what he vants, but I can tell you this much. If a spirit still walks the earth, he cannot rest. He must have some unfinished business with this world."

"What unfinished business? What does that have to do with me?"

"The spirit believes there is something he needs to do. I sense he needs *your* help to conclude his business. Only then, can he find peace and cross over."

"Oh, lucky me." Darrell gave a sarcastic laugh.

"But there is more." Natalia yanked on his hands again, drawing his attention back. Her eyes were wide, the white now making the pupils tiny. When she spoke, her voice was low, breathy, scared even. "You must be very careful. I see a shroud of malevolence surrounding this spirit."

"Malevolence? Like evil?" Darrell snapped. "You mean an evil spirit, like a poltergeist?" His throat had gone dry. He tried to lick his lips. No saliva.

"I am not sure. The malevolence has cloaked itself, and the sight is not clear on this. This evil has slumbered a long time, but it is still there, lurking. It waits and will not hesitate to kill. Be careful *you* do not fall victim."

Chapter 20

A black kid who didn't commit suicide. A spirit who had some unfinished business. Some unnamed *malevolence*?

Inside Darrell's head, these thoughts chased each other like whirling, haunted phantoms as he headed down the stairs and back across the littered sidewalk. With her admonition, Natalia had released his hands and risen. She untied the bandanna from her head and re-tied it around her neck, taking time to lay out the fabric. She explained she was expecting her next client in a few minutes, and then extended her palm. "Fifty dollars, please." The amount surprised him, but he realized he had little choice and paid her.

When Darrell made it to the door, he turned. He noticed Natalia had transformed herself, once again, into the seductive working girl. All the mysterious aura lifted like a curtain.

"Come back again, and I'll be happy to show you my *other* talents. They are far more pleasant and, I've been told, considerable." One hand holding his, she placed a business card in his palm, her touch igniting his skin again. "Call me anytime."

"Okay…thanks." He stuffed the card in a pocket and let himself out.

When he stepped outside, Darrell found the sunlight had fled, the area enveloped in darkness punctured by only a few feeble streetlights. Along with the twilight, a heavy fog had crept in from the Bay, casting a strange haze to the surroundings.

Was Mother Nature conspiring with the spirit world?

He searched the street opposite, where he had seen Ruby, but the sidewalk was empty. Of course.

He glanced back up at Natalia's apartment, his palms still pulsing with the warmth her touch ignited. He stared at them and rubbed them together. His eyes on the ground, he tried to count the sidewalk blocks, anything to keep his mind off the escalating fear, but he stumbled over the uneven pavement.

His gaze swept the sidewalk in both directions and landed on the drunk in the next block where they had left him earlier, still asleep in the doorway. Across the street, the collapsed cardboard still held the gray, lumpy figure he'd seen before, the box leaning into the sidewalk. His eyes half on the concrete at his feet and half on where he was headed, Darrell navigated his way back to Nick's.

As he searched the street in the darkness, trying to remember where he'd parked, he felt it. This time the hairs on his arms stood up, as if charged with electricity. Darrell had never been afraid before, well, not since he was a kid anyway, but a palpable fear grabbed him now, two steely hands gripping his heart.

Someone was watching.

He stopped and turned his head slowly. He examined the shadows up and down the street, each one cloaked in the spreading fog. Found nothing.

He tried to convince himself it was only his imagination, galloping wildly after being released by

Natalia's tales of spirits and lurking evil. This sensation—like a premonition, he realized—was not what he'd experienced in his office. Earlier, in the school, he had the unsettling feeling of not being alone. He had felt uneasy, but never threatened. This presence felt menacing, ugly. No. He remembered Natalia's word, malevolent. He scanned his surroundings but could locate no threat.

There was little movement on the street. Ahead of him, country music wilted out the door of Nick's when a patron staggered through the opening. As he watched, the man stumbled across the street and vomited onto the sidewalk, the stink carried on the wind. Darrell felt the bile rise in his throat and choked it back.

At least, he'd made it back to the bar.

Several cars sat on the street, their interiors dark and hulking. His gaze scrutinized each one but found nothing, no movement, no shadows, at least none he could see in the creeping fog. A wave of exhaustion competed with his rising anxiety. Darrell racked his brain to remember where he'd parked.

"When we got here, I followed Al in," he said out loud, "and we parked on that side street." Pointing to the intersecting road, he read the British-style street sign, "Westminster Alley." He hurried in that direction. The foreboding, the sensation followed him. He glanced over his shoulder. Couldn't find anything out of place, but the hairs on his arm still prickled. He forced himself to move.

He found his car snug against the curb, fifth down the row. Thank God. He released his breath. Hurrying, he fumbled with his keys and dropped them onto the cement. Their collision sent tinkling sounds down the shadowed street. As he bent down to pick them up, he felt *it* again. From his crouched position, his gaze darted across and down the darkened street, trying to make out some menace in the shifting fog. Nothing. He grabbed up his keys. He unlocked and opened his car door. He slid in quickly. The door shut with a satisfying thud.

He started the engine and checked the street for cars. His mind racing, he pulled away from the curb.

He decided he needed to uncover whatever he could about this ghost. Maybe find out something about the Black Underground. About this black kid who *didn't* commit suicide, about this shroud of evil...and maybe find that diary. He rolled down the street and then caught sight of a figure ahead on the sidewalk. He slammed on the brakes.

A petite, black woman stepped from a darkened doorway into a streetlight. She turned and spoke to two other figures, deeper in the shadows, two men, Darrell thought. The weak light cast an eerie glow over her features in the fog. Same small nose, same mahogany-colored skin, same brown eyes, at least he thought so. He lowered his window. "Ruby?"

The young black woman stepped to the end of the sidewalk.

"Boy, am I glad to see you," Darrell said through the open car window.

As he watched, Ruby surveyed the street, up and down, up and down. "Did you find my note?" she asked, her voice quiet.

"Yeah." Darrell followed her gaze and saw nothing moving. The two other figures had disappeared. If they had been there at all. Silent, dark cars lined both sides of the road, parked end to end. No one moved on the street. "Can we talk?"

"They're watching." Another cautious glance in both directions. "We want you to know the truth, but they will do anything to stop us." Her eyes were wide and her breathing labored. She looked like a scared kid, the long overcoat swallowing her small figure.

"Who's watching?" She didn't move and he asked, "Who wants me to know the truth? The Black Underground?"

She stole another glance in both directions and stepped off the curb. When she took two steps, Darrell heard it. He craned his neck at the sound. A black sedan, three cars down, pulled out from the curb, lights off. It accelerated quickly. Darrell had no time to react. No time to even yell. He hadn't heard the engine start.

Ruby must've heard it too. She turned, ready to bolt, but too late. The car stuck the young woman with an ugly thud. It threw her body in a blur past Darrell's open window. The sedan never slowed. It zoomed down the small street and around the corner.

Throwing the gear into park, Darrell leaped out. He left the door open, the engine running. Ruby's small figure lay sprawled on the asphalt. Her legs were bent at grotesque angles. Her body was sliced in several places, blood oozing onto the street. He bent down and touched her neck, checking for a pulse. It was there, faint but there. He stood and yelled, "Someone call 911." He stared into the shadows where he had seen the other two figures. Nothing.

"Darrell?" the voice so soft he almost didn't hear it.

He crouched next to her. He cradled her head and

lowered an ear. "I'm right here." Then he screamed, "Call 911."

"No time," she whispered and coughed up blood.

The metal tang of the fresh blood assailed his nostrils, and he held back a gag. "Wait here, and I'll run to Nick's and call for an ambulance."

When he tried to rise, she grabbed his arm, her grip thin but strong. He leaned in. "No time," she said. Red bubbled out the sides of her mouth. He wiped her lips gently with his hand. "Find...the diary," she whispered, more blood spilling from her mouth. Darrell's tears dripped onto her face. She grabbed his hand and stared at him, her eyes bulging wide. "Find...Kelly."

"Who's Kelly?" He got no answer and felt her fragile fingers release and fall away, flopping to the street. Her breathing stopped and her body lay there, motionless, pleading eyes still locked on his.

Chapter 21

This evil will not hesitate to kill.

He didn't know how long he sat there in the middle of the darkened street, crying over Ruby's limp body. Oh, God. He'd never seen anyone killed before. He hadn't even known this woman, but still. His lips trembled. He couldn't trust his legs to stand.

A car rolled down the small street, and its headlights ignited the strange tableau. The driver stopped, jumped out, and ran up to them. When he saw the girl lying there, a pool of blood in the street, he stopped short. "Are you hurt? Do you need an ambulance?" Darrell stared. Couldn't answer.

A few minutes later, the emergency vehicles arrived, their blue and red flashing lights strafing the fog over and over again like silent gunfire. Darrell glanced up and saw the familiar brown and tan cruiser of Officer Brown pull in alongside the ambulance. The EMTs ran over, their staccato steps pounding on the asphalt, and checked over Ruby. He watched as the lead EMT, an older woman with gray bangs, shook her head at her partner, who headed back to the ambulance. In a few seconds, he returned with a blue plastic body bag.

While the partner worked with the plastic, laying it open next to Ruby, the older one asked, "Sir, are you hurt?"

Darrell watched as the EMT—the name on her

uniform read *Frankie*—checked him over, using a flashlight to examine his arms, his torso and his eyes. Darrell shoved the light out of his eyes. "I'm okay."

"Let's get you to the hospital anyway," Frankie commanded. "Sir, can you walk?"

Darrell nodded, but his head started spinning. The second EMT left Ruby's body and came over, helping Frankie to lift Darrell to his feet. They walked him back to the ambulance and got him to lie on one of the cots. The last thing Darrell remembered was staring up at the white ceiling, following its long straight lines down the center and then losing consciousness.

When he awoke, Darrell took in the familiar confines of an emergency room. White sheet over cranked hospital bed, blue curtain pulled around the space, the smell of disinfectant hanging in the air.

A short, squat figure in a white lab coat stepped around the end of the curtain. "Coach Henshaw, are you all right?"

Darrell was surprised to see the surgeon and football booster. "Dr. Remington?" Then remembering the question, he said, "Yeah, I'm okay. Just shaken up. A little late for rounds, isn't it?"

Beneath a crop of close-cut black hair, Remington gave a small smile, but his eyes remained hard. Thumb and index finger stroked his small goatee. "I was called in for an emergency and heard you were here. Thought I'd check on you."

From somewhere in the hallway, a loudspeaker squawked, "Dr. Remington, you're needed for a consult in 6B."

"Now, they know I'm here. Duty calls. Glad to know you won't need my services." With that, the doctor left.

Darrell glanced down at his right hand and noticed the dried maroon stain on his fingers. Ruby's blood. He raised his left hand to his right, his fingers probing the stain. The ugly metal tang still hung in the back of his throat.

A calloused hand grabbed the curtain and yanked, the links clinking as they rounded the metal curve. "Well, good to see you're awake, Coach," called Officer Brown. He limped around the curtain and stood at the foot of the bed, wide-brimmed hat in hand barely covering his wide stomach. An unlit cigar drooped in his mouth. "Appears you had quite a night, son," he said, his "i" a little long again. "They tell me this black girl walked right in front of a car."

Darrell shifted on the bed and shook his head back and forth, the motion making him dizzy. "No. That's not what happened."

"Well, why don't you tell me what happened then?" The unlit cigar bounced in his mouth.

"Well, this girl stepped into the street, and this driver ran her over." Darrell explained he'd been leaving, and a car that was parked, idling probably—but he hadn't heard the engine—pulled out into the road and ran her down.

"Why'd she step into the street?"

"What?"

"You said she stepped into the street. She comin' to see you or something?"

Darrell picked up on the innuendo. "I don't know why she stepped into the street. It was deserted, I guess. Or she thought it was deserted, I don't know. Maybe she was headed into Nick's."

"Not likely. You get a look at this car that hit her?" Brown asked.

"No. A sedan. Couldn't tell the model and didn't get a license plate. It was too dark, and he never turned his lights on."

"You said this guy ran her over. You know it was a guy? Why would somebody go and run down this young black woman?"

"Hell if I know. I'm the new guy around here."

"Huh." Brown waited a bit and set the hat on the end of Darrell's bed. He drew a notebook from his pocket, opened it, and glancing down at one page. "Witnesses say you leaned down as if the woman was telling you somethin'. She tell you anything?"

"What?"

"Did the woman tell you somethin'?" Brown chewed on the cigar and then added, "You know anythin' that might help me catch the guy who did this?"

Darrell's head throbbed and his paranoia flared. *Tell no one.* "She tried to tell me something but never got it out. At least, I never heard it."

"Uh-huh." Brown put his notebook back in his shirt pocket, buttoning the flap.

"Where?" A small shriek erupted from behind Brown and a familiar nurse with flaming red hair jostled aside the officer. "Oh, God. You all right? Came out of delivery and they told me. What happened?" Erin checked Darrell over much as Frankie had done, anxiety etched in her features. Then she seemed to notice the cop. "Oh, sorry, Officer Brown. Were you finished?"

"Yep. Least fer now. Coach Henshaw, I'll check

back with you tomorrow. See if you remember anything else that might help."

"Sure," Darrell said, and the cop left, with a slight limp.

Erin closed the curtain and went over to the bed. Throwing her arms around him, she kissed Darrell so hard it hurt. A good hurt. "When I found out, I was so worried, couldn't even wait for the elevator. Ran down three flights of stairs. I'm so glad you're ok—" Her gaze landed on the blood on his hand.

"Not mine. Girl I saw get run down." Darrell's body shivered. "I watched this beautiful young girl killed right next to me. Deliberately run over." He wasn't sure who else might be listening in the ER, where there was no real privacy, so he whispered the next into Erin's ear. "I think I knew the girl, one of the subs from school."

Erin probably guessed there was more, and he was glad she trusted him enough not to push. Instead, she kissed him again, and that was the best he felt all night. The wonderful scent of her—perspiration, faint cologne, and flowers—helped to revive him, a little.

"Got to get back to OB. Two more girls ready to drop any minute." She looked into Darrell's face. "You sure you're okay? Have a way home or want me to try to get off to take you?"

"I'll be okay. I asked them to call Al, and they said he's on his way to pick me up." He glanced at his watch. 1:45? How long was he out? "Maybe get a few hours' sleep before I got to be at work."

Erin's hand touched his and held on. She flashed him a sad smile, then let go. She stepped around the curtain and turned back. "Doesn't let you out of our date this weekend, you know."

"Wouldn't dream of it," Darrell answered. "I'll call."

"See you then." She was gone, leaving him alone again, with his dread.

It took another hour before a nurse got to him, checked his vitals, and released him, and by then Al had arrived. Stray brown hairs still disheveled from sleep, Al gave the nurse—a thirty-some blonde he'd taught at Wilshire High—a hard time about the wait.

"Marion, you think it's okay I take this freeloader home? Coach, here, does have a game tomorrow."

The nurse patted Al on the shoulder. "He's good to go."

Al led Darrell out, and they made their way to the car. "You want me to take you home, or you want to swing over and pick up your car? Brown said since it wasn't involved in the hit and run, he simply pulled it back in the parking space. Left the keys with the nurse."

"I better get my car. Tomorrow's going to be crazy enough. I don't want to have to find a way to pick it up."

Once they were in his car, Al couldn't wait any longer. "You okay?"

Darrell shook his head.

"That had to be a little freaky. Seeing the girl get hit."

"Ruby."

"What?" Al threw a quick glance at Darrell.

"Yeah." Darrell's voice was weak.

"Who was she?"

Darrell shrugged.

After a few minutes of silence, Al asked,

"Everything go okay with Natalia?"

"Tomorrow. I'll fill you in tomorrow. I'm wiped and only want to get to bed."

Al pulled his sedan alongside the Corolla, and Darrell got out, thanking Al.

"Hey, that's what friends are for…even if you only coach football."

As Al drove away, Darrell clicked the key fob and the headlights of his car flashed once. He remembered doing the same earlier. The vision of Ruby being hit and hurtled past his window came back with startling clarity. He glanced at the space beyond the car and saw the sawdust over the oval, which looked black against the concrete.

Ruby's blood. That poor girl. *The evil will not hesitate to kill again.* What the hell had he gotten himself into?

He ran over to the sidewalk and vomited, retching over and over until his stomach was empty and all he tasted were his own bile and the metal taste of her blood.

He maneuvered his small car through the streets, on autopilot. He tried to tamp down his paranoia.

Where was he supposed to find this diary? And who was Kelly?

Chapter 22

Darrell couldn't shake the "accident." His sense of guilt about Ruby's murder followed him home like an ominous cloud, invading his sleep and plaguing his day.

When he got home late, he'd slept fitfully. Every time he drifted off, he jerked awake, gasping as the hideous thud echoed in his ears and he saw her body fly past him in slow motion. The next day, Friday, wasn't much better. Exhausted, dogged by what he thought was his part in Ruby's death, he slogged through the day's classes and stumbled through the game, losing by two touchdowns in a drenching rain.

He needed to get a hold of himself...and to recover. He desperately hoped his date with Erin could do that. He was glad he'd planned everything before...before all this.

Saturday, when he picked her up at three, she met him at the door in a stunning top, blue with a scattering of yellow sunflowers, and a pale blue sweater, over navy Capri pants and matching flats, her fiery red hair loose and free. The very sight of her helped dispel his gloom. Staring at the beautiful young woman on the seat beside him in the car, he decided, after the Carmen debacle, he wanted to get this right.

When they arrived, Darrell thought maybe his fortune had turned as the weather was near perfect, a few cumulus clouds skittering across a gorgeous azure sky. They boarded the small ancient ferry at Bellevue, one of only three cars this trip, and rode across the Tred Avon River to Oxford. He and Erin got out and weaved their way around the other cars to stand at the rear, watching the rippling waters.

Erin must have noticed him staring off across the water, distracted and quiet, because she asked, "Darrell, you okay? You want to talk about it?"

"Sorry, this is supposed to be our perfect date and…" He trailed off.

She looped one arm through his. "Yeah, but maybe you'll feel better if you talk about it. And I'm a good listener."

He checked to make sure no one else was around. They were alone. The others simply stayed in their car for the short ride. In the few minutes it took for the ferry to make the crossing, he told Erin what he couldn't say in the hospital. He told her about Ruby's messages, about him spotting her on the dock and then in town. Then he shared his nightmares about her death and how guilty he felt.

The murmuring vibration of the boat engines beneath their feet seemed to wrap them in the protection of a quiet cocoon. As he talked, Erin listened, stopping him a few times with an occasional question. Her patient, attentive response didn't change anything. Ruby was still dead, and Erin had no more clue than he about the diary. Or who Kelly might be.

But Darrell found simply sharing with her lightened his burden.

When he finished, she said, "But you weren't driving that car. Whoever was driving that car killed her, not you. You were trying to help, to do the right thing."

Her understanding released the tightness in his chest. He wrapped an arm around her, pulling her close. The metal floor trembled beneath them. Glancing behind the small ferry, they watched the waters churned up by the engine and witnessed a lone seagull dive into the froth and come up, a silver fish flopping in its beak.

The ferry made shore, its bumpers slamming into the dock, and the gate lowered. Darrell drove up the bank and parked on Morris Street, in front of the inn. Since they had arrived early—he'd planned it that way—they had time for a few tourist excursions in the historic town.

Not far from where they landed, Erin led the way to a tiny, white-sided building with green shingles. "Okay, teach, it's my turn to give *you* a little history lesson." Her eyes shone. "This," she flourished like a red-headed Vanna White, "is a replica of what they called a custom house from colonial times, a place where merchants would pay duty taxes." She pointed at a table inside the small structure, indicating an artifact under glass. "And *that* is an authentic custom book, complete with the original handwritten entries from the 1700s."

Darrell applauded lightly. "Impressive history lesson. I couldn't have done better myself." Maybe, she didn't think being a school geek was all that bad.

Hand in hand, they strolled down Strand Street, watching the waves lap at the shore. On the small sandy beach, they sat with their feet in the cool water, careful to avoid any swaying nettles.

At the end of the street, they arrived at the Oxford Yacht Club and Erin said, "Let me guess. You so enjoyed our sail together, you rented a yacht for the day."

He grinned. "Almost. Only a slightly different form of transportation."

He led her to the back where he rented bikes to tour the small town. Laughing like kids, they rode past quaint houses bordered by purple pansies and yellow mums, and they inhaled the homey scent of wood smoke from outdoor grills. They wheeled past the Mystery Loves Company Bookstore—only open from two to four—and checked out the antique collection at the Oxford Museum. Another couple helped them take a campy photo, complete with silly grins, beside the famous "Robert Morris Inn" sign.

A few minutes later, they were settled into a prearranged booth, staring into each other's eyes across a candle-lit, oaken table.

"Okay, what should we drink to?" Erin raised an antique wine glass toward Darrell.

"How about to, uh, a little romantic escape?" asked Darrell.

"Sounds wick-ed." They clinked again and sipped. She held the glass up. "This is really light. What is it?"

"It's a special Savennieres wine with a faint citrus and spice taste from the Loire Valley in France, recommended as a great pairing with crab cakes." He grinned. "That and the server suggested it."

Erin eyed the restaurant. "You did well." Darrell watched as her gaze roamed around the small room, hitting on the historic brick walls, the dark timber beams overhead and the uneven, ancient hardwood floor.

He was thrilled she liked the place. Complete with

old-style, coach light fixtures, white linen tablecloths and polished silver, the small restaurant created the ambiance Darrell hoped for. Both the food and surroundings took them to another place, another time.

After the winding bike tour, they were famished, and both ordered the seafood dish the restaurant was known for. The large crab cakes came loaded with blue crab, pan-fried only enough to seal in the flavors, delivered to their table sizzling and aromatic.

During the meal, the waitress said, "What a lovely couple you two make." A little later, when the server returned with the check, she asked, "Are you two staying at the Inn?"

Darrell's cheeks reddened, and Erin chuckled. Good thing he was sitting down.

The waitress put on her best patron smile and added, "I mean, did you want me to charge your check to your room?"

Darrell recovered enough to hand her a credit card, and the attendant disappeared.

"Don't want to charge it to *our room*?" Erin asked, eyes twinkling. "We could ask for the room used by Michener. Or even the George Washington room." She chuckled, taunting Darrell, but the server rescued him by returning.

When the waitress reached for the half full wine bottle, Darrell grabbed it. "Thanks, but I think we'll take this onto the porch. Erin, can you grab the glasses?"

She did, and they retreated to one of the tables on the brick portico, where they could enjoy the sunset. The bright orange ball hung above the trees lining the opposite shore. The temperature had dropped a few degrees, and Erin pulled on her sweater, while Darrell refilled their wine glasses. He went quiet again.

Erin said, "This has been great. You did well, especially for a school guy." When that didn't draw any reaction, she asked again, "You okay?"

He set down his wine glass, studying it. Deciding it was off center, he edged it over one inch. He examined his work and fought to keep his hands from realigning the glass. "I keep thinking about Ruby. I keep wondering if her death is my fault." He released a sigh.

Erin leaned over, so her face was in front of his. "Darrell, I know you care about her, but you did not run her down. I think that's how you're made. You care about your kids, other people. It's one thing that makes you...well, so loveable."

Darrell looked at her, the guilt spell broken again—for now.

"How about we change the subject." She put a finger to her red lips. "Hmm, maybe each share something about our past?"

"Okay, what would you like to know?"

"Well...why don't you tell me about this girl who almost dumped you at the altar?"

"Carmen." Darrell shook his head, a sad smile on his face. He turned back to Erin. "What to tell?"

"Like...What was she like?"

"What, was, she, like?" Darrell repeated. "Not much like you, if that's what you're thinking. Small, quiet and pretty."

"What?" Erin eyebrows arched.

"I don't mean you're not pretty." He searched her face. "You're beautiful."

"That's better." She smiled and Darrell figured she

was playing with him a little.

"I'd say she was more cute, you know perky." He checked to see if this got him in trouble. It didn't. "Oh and she had a great laugh. Black hair and nice curves," he teased. "Not as nice as yours, though," he added quickly.

"Good save."

"She was a teacher at the same school as me. Taught high school special ed kids. Tough job and she was pretty good at it, from what I knew."

"You date long?" Erin asked.

"About seven months. After the first month, we got pretty serious. Well, I guess I was the one who was serious."

"Were you in love?"

"I thought I loved her and thought she loved me." He sighed. "She told me she spent her days taking care of needy teens and wanted someone to take care of her. She said that was me."

"Sounds pretty high maintenance to me."

"Yeah, I guess you could say that." He paused, glancing out at the sunset again. "In the end, though, I don't think she was really ready to marry."

"Her breaking it off must've been hard."

He looked back at her. "She didn't break the engagement. I did."

Erin sat up in her chair. "What happened?" When Darrell didn't answer right away, she said, "If you'd rather not, that's okay."

"It's not that." She was going to think he was a wimp. "It's just damn embarrassing."

He moved the wine glass an inch to the right on the wrought iron tabletop. He couldn't help it. He'd been able to pretty much control his compulsion during dinner and now this. He hurried on. "The last month or so, while we were working on our wedding plans together, drawing up seating charts for the reception and the like, she was busy...uh, shall we say, shagging the head coach. My boss."

Erin stiffened in her chair and anger ignited in her eyes. "What a bitch."

"Yeah, they were doing it right there at school, in his office...as well as plenty of other places."

"They were what? Aren't there rules about that at school?" she asked.

"Oh, and it turned out pretty much everyone knew this was going on. Except me. None of my friends said a word. Said they didn't want to hurt me."

"Nice friends. *I* would've told you." Erin savored another slow drink then added, "Sorry. No wonder you wanted out of there."

"Yeah, but if it hadn't happened, I wouldn't've come here." Darrell refilled their glasses, emptying the bottle. They clinked, sipped, and sat in silence for a while, drinking in the incredible vista. "I wouldn't have had the chance to enjoy this...with you."

He let a few moments pass. "Your turn."

"Do I have to?"

He chuckled. "Hey, this was your idea, and you had me tell my tale. Time for you to spill some of your secrets."

Erin laughed. "My tale is *pretty bad*."

"Can't be much worse than your fiancée boffing your boss."

"Yeah, it can." Her cheeks reddened. "Afraid you might not think much of me."

"I promise that won't happen."

"Okay. Remember when I told you I wasn't very good at history?"

Darrell nodded.

"I didn't tell you the truth, at least not the whole truth. In school, wasn't very good in history, or anything else. A little wild in high school." She looked down, wouldn't meet his gaze. "Make that a lot wild. Booze, drugs, the whole package."

Darrell sat up, creaking the metal chair, but didn't say anything. Staring at the table, he moved to shift the cloth placemat to make it parallel with the table edge, but stopped himself. He realized Erin had gone quiet, and he moved his hand to her arm.

She dropped her gaze to the brick pattern of the porch floor. "Oh, yeah, *quite* the party girl. Drove Mom and Dad crazy. Wasted most of high school. Then, fall of senior year, my favorite aunt, Aunt Maureen, died from cancer." She looked up at Darrell. "You sure you want to hear all this?"

He moved his hand to her cheek. "I want to hear what you want to tell me."

She took a deep breath. "By the time they'd discovered it, it had eaten away most of her body and she only lasted six months. Watching her suffer really hit me. About the only good thing to come out of it was seeing how those nurses cared for her. I think they loved my aunt and cried almost as hard as I did when she died."

Her stare wandered out to the rippling, blue-green water and returned to Darrell, who said, "I'm so sorry, Erin. That had to be really hard."

"I haven't told you the hardest part." She took

another breath, and Darrell sat up straighter. "Anyway, right before she died, I was visiting Aunt Maureen. She was having one of those lucid moments, which didn't happen very often at the end. I was hung over and probably looked it. She grabbed my cheek and made me stare into her face and asked, 'Why are you wasting your life? Check me out. You never know how long you got and you, child, have so much potential. I want you to promise me you won't throw it all away.'" Erin swallowed once and teared up.

Darrell inched his chair closer and put an arm around her.

She glanced at the arm and gave him a weak smile. "Aunt Maureen wouldn't let up. She grabbed my arm— I was surprised how much strength she had." Erin gripped Darrell's arm to demonstrate. "She stared into my eyes and repeated, 'Promise me.'"

"What'd you do?"

"What could I do? I promised her. She died the next morning. In the days up to the funeral, I couldn't get that scene out of my head." Erin's green eyes, wet now, seemed to take on a new intensity. She released Darrell's arm, and he moved in a little closer. He wanted to let her know it was okay.

After a bit, she went on, "The day we buried her I quit the whole scene—the booze, drugs, and the meaningless sex. Hit the books and managed to pull out a decent senior year. Barely enough to get into nursing school at State. Then surprised everyone by getting straight A's there." A small smile pulled at her lips. "Well, almost everyone. Aunt Maureen probably wasn't surprised. And the rest, as you'd say, is history."

He wrapped his arm around her a little more

tightly, his gaze still on hers. "Wow, you're right. Your story tops mine."

"Gee, thanks." She managed a small grin.

Darrell added, "But everybody has their own baggage."

Erin nodded. He stood and extended his elbow. "Hey, I think we need some exercise after that meal and the wine. How about it?"

"Sounds great." She rose, laced her arm through his, and they headed for the shore.

He spied their bikes on the brick sidewalk. "Let's ride those back now, while we still have a little light." The sun had slipped below the tree line, leaving only a thin pink crease on the western sky.

"Race you." Erin ran to the first bicycle, knocked the kickstand back with her heel, and jumped on. She rolled thirty feet before Darrell caught up. They pedaled, side by side, down the deserted street to the Yacht Club, where they stowed the bikes. Holding hands, they strolled back Strand Street, heading toward his car and home, but in no hurry to get there.

"You've been out of college, what, two years now?" he asked after a bit.

"A little more. Why?"

He smiled. "Oh, I was simply wondering if the grown-up you had any romantic adventures?"

"Met this one guy—"

"Yeah?"

She turned and looked at him with a mischievous grin. "Kinda hot, in a Midwestern way."

"Uh-hum."

"He likes kids and is a kick ass coach, and he's got this cute dog."

"But?"

"Well, he's got this thing about ghosts—"

"And?"

"That I'm trying to get my head around."

Halfway down the deserted street, she stopped and turned. As the last of the sunlight leaked away, the first stars popped through the darkening canopy of sky and the lights from the Robert Morris Inn cast a soft yellow glow onto the street. There was no other movement on the road, no cars, no people. Only the swish of the waves and the chirp of an occasional insect. The near quiet and the almost dark engulfed them.

Darrell kissed her and enfolded her in his arms. He'd never told anyone the whole story of his personal haunting, not even his family. Anxiety rose in his throat. He swallowed. Could he tell her?

He glanced out at the river, seeing tiny whitecaps etched on the blue blackness of the water, and then looked into her face. When Erin gazed back, those green eyes catching the faint light from the Inn, he decided to take the chance.

Chapter 23

They strolled back to the porch of the Inn and sat at a corner table. The dark settled in around them, casting the perfect atmosphere. Two lamp fixtures emitted faint yellow rays and the subdued light from inside crawled through the windows. Darrell slid his metal chair around the table and edged closer to Erin. Away from the water now, the only sounds were the quiet voices and dish handling of the servers inside.

Darrell asked, "You sure you want to hear this story?"

"I'm sure." Erin set a hand on his.

"Okay, but remember you asked for it." He took a breath. "The Wilshire ghost, as you guys call him, isn't my first."

"What?" She leaned in closer. "You're kidding."

"Wish I was. My first 'encounter,' as they say, started with my favorite uncle, Uncle Ed, my dad's brother. He wasn't married and came by our place all the time, to play with us. At least, I thought that's why he came by. I loved tossing baseball with him. He used to play in college. Taught me how to throw a slider." Darrell demonstrated with his fingers.

"When I was about eight, he even built us a treehouse. Man, I loved that treehouse." Darrell got a faraway look in his eyes. "Oh, and he would drop by and give us rides in his sport car, a fire engine red

Camaro Z-28. Riding around with him was so cool."

"He sounds great."

"He was…at least that's what I thought." Darrell cleared his throat. "Dad called him the wild one of the family, and from what I learned later, Dad was right. Anyway, a few months after he taught me how to throw the slider, he was out cruising in the Camaro, hit the curve on Race Road too fast, and flipped the car. He wasn't wearing a seat belt—he said they made him feel hemmed in—and was thrown from the car and killed. My dad, and mom, were crushed. I cried for two days.

"About three months later, I was asleep in my bed. I woke up with a start when I thought I sensed something." He paused and stared at Erin. "You're going to think I'm crazy. I've never told anyone this story."

She placed her hand over his. "I want to hear it."

A dish fell inside and shattered. Darrell jerked. A long curse followed. He shot a look at the window and, after a bit, settled down. "I woke up that morning, and I could've sworn I saw my uncle Ed sitting on the foot of my bed." Darrell glanced around to make sure they were alone, then lowered his voice to a whisper. "I know it sounds crazy, but I *saw* him…or thought I did. He looked exactly like he did the last time he came around our house. He was wearing this crazy Hawaiian shirt he loved and worn jeans. Had holes in the right knee. Oh, and he had his sunglasses on top of his head, like he always wore them." Darrell patted his hair.

"You sure you weren't dreaming?"

"I thought so at first. But I sat up and noticed my bedroom had gotten really cold. I could see my breath. And Uncle Ed looked so real."

"Were you scared?" Erin asked.

"I guess. I didn't know. This ghost said, 'Hi ya, Champ' and that made me feel a little better. Uncle Ed always called me Champ. I said something like, uh, I thought you died. And he said, 'I did, but I had to come back to warn you.' I sat up in bed and said 'What do you mean, warn me?'

"He asked, 'Are you going snowmobiling with your brother tomorrow after school?' I said, 'Yeah, Craig's taking me with a bunch of guys over to Mason Woods.' That's when Uncle Ed, er, this ghost said, 'You can't go…and you can't let Craig go.' "

A bead of sweat dripped onto his forehead, and his voice went hoarse. "I said, 'What do you mean don't go? How do I stop Craig?' The ghost said, 'You're a smart kid. Hide his keys. Do something. Don't let him go.' Then he disappeared. One second, he was there talking to me, and the next he simply vanished."

Darrell stopped his narrative and Erin asked, "What'd you do?"

"I didn't do anything. I should've, but I didn't. I was scared everyone would laugh at me. Call me a baby. Hell, I was only thirteen. I told myself it was only a crazy dream." Darrell shrugged. "Anyway, I didn't want to believe him. After what I learned, I couldn't believe he'd really help me."

"Why? Thought you said he was your favorite uncle."

"He was…until the end." Seeing the puzzled look on Erin's face, he went on. "Look, the night he died, I went to the mall with my best friend. When we were heading out to go home, I thought I saw my uncle's '68 Camaro Z 28 at the top of the parking lot. So, I told my friend to hold on and ran up the row. Even though it was pretty foggy out, when I got close, I could tell it was his car. I came up alongside and saw the windows were steamed up. I was about to say something when I looked inside and saw my mom and Uncle Ed, both with their shirts off and arms around each other."

She slid her chair an inch closer. "What'd you do?"

"I backed away, ran back to my friend, said I was mistaken, and rode home with them. Later that night, Uncle Ed crashed his car and died. I never said anything, to anyone. I figured, what's the point. He was dead."

"I'm sorry, Darrell," Erin said. "Must've been terrible seeing them there...and then him dying right after."

"Yeah, I felt like he betrayed me. So when I got this...this visit, I refused to believe it."

Both went quiet for a bit, then Erin asked, "What happened with the snowmobiling?"

He didn't respond at first and only stared at the brick floor.

"Darrell?"

God, this was harder than he thought it would be. He sighed. "Well, that afternoon, I chickened out. Said I didn't feel good. Hedged my bets, I guess. The rest of the guys went joyriding through the woods and onto Mason Lake. The ice cracked and all three snowmobiles went under. The guys were trapped under the ice."

Erin's hand went to her mouth.

He continued, "The guys on the third, the one closest to the shore, were able to claw their way out, though one of the boys lost two fingers to frostbite."

"What about the kids on the other two snowmobiles?"

"Dave and his little brother Denny were on the first, out in front, farther out toward the middle of the lake. They didn't find their bodies until almost night. Their skin was nearly blue." He stopped.

"What about your brother?" she whispered.

"Craig was on the second snowmobile." Darrell's eyes teared up. "It took them seventeen damn minutes to pull him out. By the time they got him out of the water, he'd lost feeling in his right leg. Lost half his foot to hypothermia. Sports were out for good. He walks with a limp, still."

Erin wrapped both hands around his. "I'm so sorry. But it's not your fault, you know."

Darrell recalled Natalia's words. *You did not heed the spirit's warning.* "Yeah, it kinda was."

"You ever see your uncle Ed's ghost again?"

"No."

"Wow." Above them, a bug caught in the light fixture buzzed, banging its wings against the glass. Erin studied the insect for a while, her graceful fingers drumming the table. Then she looked at Darrell. "Okay, I think I get it."

"You do?"

"Sure. I'd be freaked too. You meet a ghost in one state, then travel six hundred miles and run into another one here. Man." She nodded. "Still, proves you're right."

"About what?"

"Everybody's got their own baggage." She grinned. "Only yours has traveled across the country."

He chuckled and kissed her.

"Okay, I'm in," she said.

"In?"

"Maybe our Wilshire ghost picked you. You know, because of this thing with your uncle's ghost."

"You might be right. A medium told me about the same thing."

"A medium?"

"Later. Anyway, I've decided to see what I can learn about the ghost. Maybe find a way to help him."

"How?"

"How else. A little research, history-style."

"Like a little company?" she asked.

Darrell smiled. "Misery *loves* company."

Chapter 24

"May have something here," Erin called from the booth next to Darrell, her voice excited.

After learning the U of M/Annapolis held the most extensive collection of area newspaper archives, Darrell had decided to research the Wilshire ghost there. When Erin said she wanted to come, he'd been thrilled. Now, *she* had made the first discovery.

He'd picked her up after church Sunday, and they grabbed a couple of crab rolls at the Crab Shack and headed out. They rode with the windows down, drinking in the aroma of dying fall leaves. Once they left the Eastern Shore, he drove Route 50 across the scenic Bay Bridge. As they rounded the curve out over the water and headed up the carefully-engineered grade, the sweeping vista of the sun-drenched water unfolded before them. Sleek, white-sailed boats plied the crested waves beneath the bridge and massive, gray container ships loomed on the horizon beyond. A brisk wind blew across the water. It rattled the supports, causing the bridge to sway a bit. Darrell tightened his grip on the steering wheel and shot a quick glance at Erin. Her gaze traveled both north and south of the span, and she grinned. He yanked his eyes back to the road and concentrated on maneuvering across the undulating metal and concrete structure. He merely wanted to get off the bridge. When they exited, tires hissing on asphalt, he released a loud breath. She grinned at him, eyes twinkling.

That had been two hours ago. After getting help from an attentive librarian, they'd settled into two adjacent carrels, sitting side-by-side. Pulling out some wet wipes, Darrell meticulously wiped down both carrels and readers before he'd let them start. He knew he wouldn't be able to work unless he made sure the spaces were sanitized.

As they settled in, Darrell thought they looked like two miscreant students in timeout. The high school used the same carrel arrangement for in-school suspension. He grinned. At least Erin was someone he wouldn't mind being stuck in timeout with.

The librarian retrieved the films they wanted from the archives and demonstrated how to use the microfilm viewer. Darrell already knew the drill but seized the chance to lean in close to Erin, inhaling the scent of her herbal shampoo as she watched.

But after they searched for what seemed like forever, any thought of romance was banished. Darrell's plan was to research past sightings of the apparition and begin to piece together the story of the ghost—and maybe make sense out of his own visions. But with no index for the newspapers, they had to crank the knobs of the reader, causing the images to blur and then refocus, time and again. They scanned the pages of newspapers, day after day, looking for any reference to "ghost" or "sightings" or "apparition." They started with spools of the *Wilshire Gazette,* Erin reviewing issues from the sixties and Darrell searching the papers from the early seventies. It was slow going and neither had any luck.

Maybe he'd been fooling himself? How could there have been no mention of any ghost in the paper in all these years? Could they have simply missed it?

Then, Erin—*not* the historical researcher—came up with an idea. Maybe they should check out the *Baltimore Enquirer,* since it often covered stories of the Shore. While he continued to search through more years of the *Gazette,* she started in on the *Enquirer* issues.

"Found it," she called.

When he peered around the wooden divider, he found her focused on the screen, the light from the computer reader reflected in her excited eyes. Darrell got up and peered over her shoulder.

"Listen to this," she said in a library whisper, her index finger following the text.

Ghost Still Haunts Area High School
Wilshire, MD by Kendrick Amos
Local police were called to what, in other towns might be a strange report, but in this Eastern Shore town, has become almost commonplace—a ghost sighting. Officer Larrick was called to the town high school early yesterday evening to investigate an "intruder and a disturbance." When the officer arrived on the scene, he found a couple of nervous teens, but no intruder.

According to the police report, two football players were walking down the main hall when they spotted an intruder, whom they described as "a large, scary black guy standing in the hall naked." One of the students, Jesse "Jumbo" Cranston was quoted in the report. "This black dude stood there naked like some dumb

N***r, with this crazy look in his eyes and didn't say anything. This was one big dude, so when he started toward us, we hustled back to the locker room to get the other guys. When we got back, he was gone." A second student, Joe Meyer, confirmed he also saw the intruder.

According to Officer Larrick, "the boys let their imaginations run away," but this reporter is not so sure. Wilshire High School has been the scene of a number of ghost sightings over the past years. According to one source, the ghost is rumored to be the spirit of a young black student who died under mysterious circumstances more than ten years ago. A review of police records turned up a several calls to the high school for similar unexplained disturbances in past years.

Darrell was bothered by the language of the athletes, but not that surprised. He'd heard as much last week in the halls and locker rooms. And he nailed the kids when he caught them but knew it didn't end there.

He peered down at the small computer screen. "When was this published?"

She scrolled up and read the date. "October 4, 1979." Erin turned and looked into Darrell's face, overhead fluorescent lights igniting her red hair. "Sound like who you saw?"

He nodded, leaned in, and kissed her, his hands caressing her cheek. She purred. "Thank you," he whispered.

"You're quite welcome." She kissed him back, and they sat together, heads touching.

He stared into her eyes. "Beauty and brains in the same package."

Before she could respond, he pulled away and snapped his fingers. "I have an idea. Print a copy." He hurried back to his own carrel.

Erin hit the print button, rose, and stretched her back. She stood behind Darrell, leaning over him, and her hands massaged his shoulders. Recalling a line from an old TV show, he said, "I'll give you twenty-five minutes to cut that out." He glanced up at her, and she smiled.

He wondered how he'd gotten so lucky after the fiasco with Carmen.

He returned his attention to the reader. "It should be around here," he said, pointing to the right side of the screen. He turned the knob and the facsimiles of newspaper pages scrolled slowly by. "Got it." He pointed and read.

Police Report
A cruiser was dispatched to Wilshire High School at 6:38 in response to a report of an intruder in the high school.

"And this was the day before the article in the *Enquirer,* October 3," he said. "The reports show up in the police blotter, but there's no mention of ghosts or sightings. See if you can find any more reports in the *Enquirer,* and I'll see if I can find more dispatches to the high school in the *Gazette.*"

"Sounds like a plan, teach." Erin did a small salute and returned to her stall.

For the next two hours, they searched and cross-checked both papers, going back fifteen years from 1979. They came up with five articles in the *Enquirer* about ghost sightings and at least eight different police roll outs to Wilshire High School to investigate "unexplained disturbances." They did the same for the years since 1979 and found six more articles on high school sightings, but all from the *Baltimore Enquirer*. Not one mention of ghost sightings in the *Wilshire Gazette*.

Erin grabbed the copies of the articles and police reports from the printer and returned to their carrels. With a yellow highlighter, she marked the dates of each page. "Darrell, all the reports come in either late September or October," she called across the divider.

"Huh?" He raised a finger. "I know it's late and I owe you a steak dinner, but I want to check one more thing."

She adopted a Mae West imitation. "You're going to owe me more than that, big boy."

Darrell slid another spool onto the sprocket and turned the knob. He sent the pages whirling past and then stopped and scanned again. After a bit, he repeated the process, his eyes searching the text. After several tries, he stopped and stared at the frozen screen. "I thought so."

Erin peered at his reader. "Did you find something else?"

"Yeah, an editorial about a haunting in the *Gazette*." Darrell indicated the screen and fiddled with the focus. "I figured if these sightings were all reported around October, it'd be too big of a temptation for a journalist to resist doing an editorial on ghosts for Halloween. Even in Wilshire. And I was right." He pointed to a line. "October 31, 1990. An editorial by Harmon McAllister." He read the piece aloud.

Frightful Haunting of Wilshire High

Many towns on the Eastern Shore can make their own claim for a piece of American history. St. Michaels is known as "The Town that fooled the British" in the War of 1812. Talbot County has the dubious distinction as home to the plantation where Frederick Douglas was born as a slave. And the town of Oxford was a port, which handled vessels from all over the world since 1683. Our town of Wilshire has its own historical notoriety as well, but you're not likely to find it on any town marker.

Wilshire is haunted. Or to be more precise, Wilshire High School is haunted. For more than two decades, students, janitors, and teachers have reported apparitions and strange occurrences in the classrooms and hallways of our high school. When called to the scene repeatedly, the police reported finding nothing, chalking the "appearances" up to overactive imaginations or Halloween pranks. However, the reports of the intruder are all strikingly similar—a large, imposing figure of a black man or student, always nude with desperate eyes. The ghostly apparition never speaks, but approaches others, arms outstretched as if pleading, and then disappears.

Who is this mysterious ghost? No one knows. Some townspeople claim he's the spirit of a slave who escaped from one of the nearby plantations and was caught and killed on the school site sometime last century. Others maintain he's the ghost of a black high school student who died there under mysterious circumstances in the mid-sixties.

Many residents of Wilshire shrug off these

paranormal claims, arguing ghosts only exist in the imagination of children and on Halloween costumes. But on this Halloween, I'm reminded of Shakespeare's line from Hamlet: "There's more in heaven and earth, Horatio, than is dreamt of in your philosophy."

My advice is, if you're wandering by the high school tonight and encounter a tall, naked black man, you might want to have some clothes with you. My guess is he's an extra large.

Happy Halloween, readers. Harmon McAllister, Editor

Darrell hit the print button. "*That's* the ghost I've seen. This guy, McAllister, is he still editor?"

"Naw." She paused and glanced up, as if trying to recall. "I remember him though. Tall guy with crazy, wiry black hair and a pockmarked face. Covered school activities when I attended Wilshire High."

"Is he still around? Maybe he knows more. I'd like to talk to him."

"No. Left before I graduated, I think. Heard he went to some town in Maine."

"Not long after this editorial, then." Darrell pointed to screen. "Do you remember why he left?"

"From what I remember, some falling out with some of the town heavies."

"Really?" Darrell mused and wondered who'd be in that group of town heavies. The bank president? The high school principal? Members of town council? An influential surgeon?

Chapter 25

Who was this ghost?
Why was he appearing to him?
What was Darrell *supposed to do?*

He was relieved he wasn't going crazy. Their research in Annapolis had confirmed what Darrell had seen but raised as many questions as they answered. The next day, Monday, his students had been so demanding, he hadn't had much time to ponder his situation. Now that classes were finished and football practice over, the questions nagged at him again and wouldn't let up.

Preoccupied, he headed down the hall and didn't notice the noise at first.

Ther-rupp. Ther-rupp. Squeech. Ther-rupp

It seemed to be coming from down the hallway and he headed that way. He thought he was alone in the old building, almost. He could hear Jesse, up somewhere on the second floor, his tenor voice crooning some oldie and his footsteps echoing through the stairwell. At least, he hoped it was Jesse. He peered up the empty stairs. "Jesse? You up there?" he hollered. No answer. Darrell figured the custodian was busy, his earphones on, and couldn't hear him or the noise. Probably.

But this clatter was coming from down the hall, on this floor.

THER-RUPP. THER-RUPP. SQUEECH. THER-

RUPP.

It was well past seven, and with the sun dipping low, the central corridor ahead of him was draped in shadow and bathed in the musty smells of pencil lead and discarded paper. He had sent the last of his players home thirty minutes ago and, though exhausted, had taken time to shower and dress. He only needed to stop by his classroom to pick up his manual, and when he stepped through the outside door, he heard it.

THER-RUPP. THER-RUPP. SQUEECH. THER-RUPP.

Darrell's paranoia erupted, amplified by the accounts of ghost appearances they discovered the day before. As he made his way down the hallway, the noise grew louder. He arrived at his classroom, halfway down the stretch, and confirmed the sound wasn't emanating from there, at least. It was coming from farther down the hall. He blew out a breath.

THER-RUPP. THER-RUPP. SQUEECH. THER-RUPP.

He remembered why he'd come. He unlocked and opened his classroom door. He scooped up the American Government manual off his desk, then headed back out the door. Back in the hall, as he turned the key in the old lock, he felt it. A rush of cold air flooded him. He shivered. He swiveled his head, his gaze sweeping up and down the corridor, searching the shadows for…what?

Someone was watching him.

"Hey, anybody there?" he called down the empty space. The only response was the echo of his voice and the unrelenting, pulsing sound, louder now. He licked his lips, twice.

THER-RUPP. THER-RUPP. SQUEECH. THER-RUPP.

Fear seized him, battled with intrigue.

He'd heard that sound before. He should know what it is. But he wasn't supposed to be here anyway. Let Jesse take care of it.

He wanted to bolt, to head out to the parking lot to the safety of his car. He'd burn rubber out of the lot and squeal his tires on the cracked asphalt. But his feet felt nailed to the floor and the sound seemed to draw him.

THER-RUPP. THER-RUPP. SQUEECH. THER-RUPP.

He took tentative steps down the dim corridor, toward the sound. No lights burned in any of the classrooms. He edged past their darkened doors, one after the other. The racket grew louder. The sound was coming from inside the final door, the teachers' workroom. He increased his pace, the sense of being watched intensifying with every step. He yanked open the last door. The noise became deafening.

THER-RUPP. THER-RUPP. SQUEECH. THER-RUPP.

The room was black. He groped for the light switch, first on the wall to the right—nothing there—and then the left. He found it. The room brightened.

"There," he said aloud, to hear something other than the unending racket. When he looked across the room, he released another loud breath. "It's only the damn copier."

Bathed in bright fluorescents sat the machine, chugging out copies and spitting out white papers onto a pile. The machine had ejected so many, they overfilled the tray, dumping them onto a messy pile on the floor.

Darrell hurried across the room. He scanned the machine's panel. He had to find the right button. He started pressing everything, but to no effect. Up close to the machine, with the gears rolling and the paper rocketing out of the copier, the clamor was ear-splitting. He couldn't think.

THER-RUPP. THER-RUPP. SQUEECH. THER RUPP.

THER-RUPP. THER-RUPP. SQUEECH. THER-RUPP.

His head pounded. He had to find a way to stop it. His gaze darted around, behind the machine. He ran over and yanked the plug from the wall.

The mechanical beast sat motionless. The silence was so complete, it only served to heighten his anxiety.

What idiot did this?

His neck began to prickle, and the room got colder. His gaze darted around the space. He saw no one, but he was *not* alone.

Someone, or something, was watching him.

He inspected every inch of the room—small blond Formica table and four folding chairs in the center, papers and supplies stacked in a rack against the right-side wall, and a counter with a small fridge and microwave on the left. The copier sat against the back wall, hulking, in front of him. The odor of greasy French fries flowed from the trash can next to the table.

He studied the pile of papers crowding out of the tray and spilling onto the floor in an unruly heap. He figured there must be almost five hundred sheets of paper, a whole ream maybe. He picked the first sheet from the mound and examined it. Completely blank.

What the hell?

He grabbed a second, and a third. The same. Darrell flipped through paper after paper in the overstuffed tray and found them all blank.

Someone pushed the copy button and simply left it? Who would do that?

Exhausted now, his adrenaline drained. He only wanted to go home and collapse in his recliner. Maybe catch a little Monday Night Football. He sure didn't want to stay here, clean up this mess, but the hairs on his neck still stood on edge. He *had* to do something.

Fumbling with the pages in the tray, he pulled them out and set them on the table, in something close to a stack. As he worked to straighten them, his fingers flipped through twenty sheets. He saw only white. They were *all* blank. Trying to figure out what might've been copied, he stepped back to the copier and lifted the lid. Nothing sat on the glass.

It must have been a stupid student prank. Damn, he'd have to report this to Douglass in the morning.

He stooped down to pick up papers off the floor. As he took them over in groups and added them to his pile on the table, he thumbed through these too. He found only more blank pages. There were so many spilled across the stained linoleum, it took several trips, but he got all the spewed papers off the floor and onto the table. Then, he couldn't help himself. He re-stacked the papers and hit their edges against the Formica tabletop until they were in a perfect, squared pile again.

He turned to go, ready to hit the lights and head out to his car, when he saw it. One sheet still lay on the floor.

Hadn't he gotten all the papers?

When he reached down to grab the last one, his fingertips tingled. He held the paper up and studied it. Blank, white, like all the others. Puzzled, he carried it over to the stack on the table. He flipped it over and, when he did, he saw it. The back side held one line of text typed across the middle of the sheet.

PLEASE HELP ME FIND JUSTICE.—H

Darrell let go of the paper as if stung. His head jerked around, searching the small room again. The piece fluttered onto the pile. His gaze returned to the top sheet and the single line of print, now screaming at him.

PLEASE HELP ME FIND JUSTICE.—H

He shot a glance back toward the closed door. He grabbed the sheet, folded it, and stuffed it inside the teacher's edition. He headed out and flipped the lights off. He hustled out of the room and down the hall, running. The echo of his steps chased him out the front door.

Chapter 26

"Do you remember anyone ever mentioning the ghost's name at school?" Darrell asked Erin at 11:30, as soon as she picked up the phone.

"What?"

He could hear her confusion and weariness etched into the single syllable. She had come off another twelve-hour shift thirty minutes earlier.

Man, he could be so stupid sometimes.

When he'd arrived at his apartment, he hadn't worked on his lesson plans or even reviewed videos for their next game. Instead, as soon as he'd fed Pogo and given him some water, Darrell scoured every article they'd printed yesterday, searching for any possible reference to a name for the ghost. A ghost name that started with H.

He came up with zilch.

He couldn't help himself. "Do you ever remember anyone calling the Wilshire ghost by a name? Maybe as a joke or something?" Embarrassed now, he fiddled with the glasses in the cupboard as he talked, rearranging them and aligning them in perfect rows. He couldn't keep the desperation out of his voice.

"Darrell, what are you talking about?"

He took a deep breath. Who else could he tell? Who else wouldn't think he was crazy? So he did.

"This was tonight? Anyone else see this?" asked

Erin.

"Of course not. I'm the *chosen* one. Jesse was working in the building, heard him singing up on the second floor, but I don't think he heard it. Probably plugged into his old cassette player." Darrell paused for a minute. "I should've gone and gotten him, shouldn't I?" He shook his head, even though she couldn't see him. "I was too freaked out."

"First of all, chill. Take a breath. Maybe it *is* only a student prank."

"Could be. So, do you ever remember anyone mentioning a name? Howie? Hal? Huck?"

Darrell listened to her breathing. She said, "I don't think so. I only remember them saying 'the ghost.' Nobody ever said more than that. Sorry."

Darrell wanted more than anything to see her, to hold her right now. He asked about her day.

"Delivered five little ones today, two preemies. One didn't make it. Hardly had time to sit down, much less eat. Wiped out would be too nice a description. Not a pretty sight tonight."

He knew he couldn't ask to see her and, after a bit, let her go. After all, he had work to do. Real work, not ghost hunting. Besides, he couldn't do anything about "H" right now. And the kids wouldn't teach themselves.

Darrell forced his attention back to his real world and tried to push his gnawing anxiety to the back.

H has been dead for decades. He can wait a few more days.

He went over to the couch and arranged his tasks. Atop the coffee table, he organized the student papers into three neat stacks, feigning some semblance of order. He set his grade book at a right angle to the assignments. He stowed the videotape in the player and sat in the center of the sofa. He concentrated on his breathing. Then he got busy.

****

Between teaching and coaching in the next few days, he found his mind fully occupied, almost. He spent pretty much every hour teaching, grading, practicing, and reviewing game films. And sleeping. Though he had managed a few brief late night calls to Erin. Thankfully, the week passed sans any more encounters.

But he hadn't forgotten about it. A couple times at school and at home at night, he slid the single 8.5 x 11 sheet out of his metal clipboard and re-read the one line.

PLEASE HELP ME FIND JUSTICE.—H

He even asked Al if he ever heard anyone mention the name of the ghost but had drawn a blank there as well. He didn't tell Al the whole story about the message because, the further he got from the "incident," the more ridiculous his paranoia seemed. Al, of course, took the opportunity to offer another one liner.

"Speaking of our ghost, did you hear about the gal who wanted to marry a ghost? They don't know what possessed her." Al had slapped him on the back and bounced down the hall, laughing.

He couldn't think of anyone else to ask—anyone who wouldn't think him crazy—so he kept his attention on his students all week.

****

"You remember, a few weeks ago, when we did the history lesson on the Holocaust survivors?" He offered the query Friday, right after the bell rang. The students had barely settled into the seats, their chairs making scraping sounds across the worn linoleum.

The first response came from Tiffany, who didn't bother to raise her hand and fingered the studs in her chin while she talked. "You mean, when we read what those old people wrote about the concentration camps and compared it with the textbook? That was boring— *not*."

Darrell recalled Tiffany's attempted rebellion the first day of school. Now, she had something *good* to say about history. Maybe *his* students wouldn't think history was their least favorite class. He smiled.

"Thanks, Tiffany. Shocking maybe, but certainly not boring. If you remember, each of the five excerpts I shared with you were firsthand accounts. One type of what we call *primary sources,* and that's what your project is going to be about. On your desks, I've placed a sheet with a list of possible types of primary sources you might want to use."

As the students studied their papers, Darrell exchanged glances with Molly McQuire, who sat in the last student chair in the first row. He was pleased to have her co-teaching the project with him.

"Because those people, Greta and Lev, for example, were actually there and went through the horror of the camps, their testimony is more accurate and complete than, say, our textbook or an encyclopedia or something you're going to get off the internet. Those other sources are likely to have been sanitized or compressed or sometimes, full of errors."

He got a few more nods and went on. "If you want to get the real history, it's usually better to study whatever primary sources you can find." Darrell searched the sea of faces for questions or confusion and, seeing none, continued.

"Okay, your assignment is to select some local or regional historical event and compare the historical account with primary sources about the event. You get to choose the event, though if you need help, Mrs. McQuire and I will be there for you." For the first time, Darrell pointed to the squat English teacher, glasses on a chain around her neck and corona of short black hair atop her head. She smiled as the students turned to notice her.

"You could choose to research the stories about Frederick Douglass' birthplace here in Talbot County. Or you could look into St. Michaels' claim as 'the town that fooled the British' in the War of 1812. Or you could choose to research the claims that pirates sunk ships in the Bay in the 1700s. The choice is pretty much up to you."

More nods from the students.

"Here's the history part. After you select your event, you'll have to get a documented historical account of the event from a legitimate source. We'll help you there if you need it, too. Next, you'll need to locate at least two primary sources about the event. Finally, like we did with the Holocaust survivors, you're going to compare the common version with what you learned from the primary sources. I'll let you get in your groups and brainstorm some ideas. Mrs. McQuire and I will circulate to answer questions."

Needing no more encouragement, the students slid their desks into semicircles and soon, the buzz of conversations filled the room. Darrell and Molly went from group to group, eavesdropping and answering student questions when asked. Mostly, they let students do what teenagers liked best—talk.

After several minutes of spirited discussions, Felissa, a black girl who had been defiant early on, raised a hand and asked, "What if we'd like to study somethin' more recent? Say somethin' only thirty years back?"

"That's an interesting question, Felissa." Darrell studied her, sitting back in her chair, arms crossed atop a very ample bosom, and flashed back to Tyler's crude reference to the young woman during their cheating discussion. "The short answer is yes. Did you have something in particular in mind?"

The student shifted in her seat and shot a quick glance around the room and then stared back. "Well, you was teachin' about some of the civil rights struggles in the sixties. I was thinkin' I might want to research some civil rights stuff here on the Bay, like how white folks tried to keep blacks from votin' back then."

For a few seconds, no one spoke. Darrell felt every eye on him. They all waited for the *white guy's* response.

"Sounds like an interesting topic," he said. "That ought to make the history real, don't you think? Write it up and we'll review it, okay?"

Before the student could respond, the bell rang, loud and obnoxious. "Think about what you'd like to research, and we'll pick this up on Monday. Have a good weekend."

He stayed up front as the students streamed by him. When the room emptied out, Molly lumbered up alongside him, carrying a clipboard.

"You think our students can do this?" Her chubby index finger tapped the assignment sheet.

Darrell smiled. "With our help, they can. Will they, is another question."

"Well, for what it's worth, I think you got the pumps primed today. But we'll see if they even remember it after the weekend." Molly grinned as she opened the door. "See you Monday. Oh, and good luck tonight, Coach."

Darrell moved back to his desk, needing to get to the football bus. As he stacked his books and clipboard, he noticed the paper sticking out of the pad, its corner turned down. He pulled it out to read it, again.

PLEASE HELP ME FIND JUSTICE.—H

Primary sources. What if he went back to the primary sources? There had to be a police report about the kid's death. At least, he might get a name.

Chapter 27

Darrell hammered his legs up the steps to his office. His players were assembled on the bus, pumped and ready to leave for the game, when he realized he didn't have his playbook. He could've sworn he had it earlier with his clipboard, thought he'd seen it when he went into the locker room to change. When he came out, it wasn't there.

He'd hassled his players about it—they claimed they hadn't touched it—then backtracked his way to his classroom. Again no luck. Even checked the teachers' workroom. Nothing. He *needed* that playbook, especially for tonight's game. Now he hustled back up to his office, the only other place he could think to look.

When he got to the door and had the key in the ancient lock, he felt it again, the hairs on his neck standing up. *Now?*

He shoved open the door and made a quick scan of the space, not expecting to have any luck. Then, he spied it. The blue playbook sat alone in the precise center of the pristine green blotter. How'd it get there? He let out a quick breath, scooped it up, and headed out.

Back in the hall, turning the key, he heard a *boing* from inside. He unlocked and opened the door just in time to see his prized basketball roll across the floor. It came to rest at the paneled wall, a few inches from the open door.

He knew he shouldn't. He had to get back downstairs. They were holding the bus for him. And he remembered his last weird encounter with the moving basketball.

Without thinking, he swung the door wide and stepped back inside. He reached down and grabbed the ball. He was relieved *and* disappointed he felt no tingle. No electricity. He spun the basketball and noticed nothing out of place, Jordan's signature right where it should be. He eased the basketball back into the holder on the shelf and, for only a second, ran his fingers across the cool, smooth leather.

He turned to go. Another shock streaked across his neck. He did a slow scan of the space—window, desk, bookcase, walls. Saw nothing out of place. He glanced out the window to the widow's perch. No one. Ready to convince himself he was imagining again, he caught sight of something on the linoleum. A piece of the baseboard molding had fallen to the floor.

The basketball must've knocked it loose.

In the small opening in the wall, he saw something sticking out. One corner protruded slightly, colors of pink and white barely visible. He leaned down and yanked at it, but it was stuck. He knelt and peered into the opening. The odors of damp and mildew hit him. He used both hands to maneuver the object out.

It was a book. He turned it over in his hand. It was the size of a paperback, but it looked like a small notebook, wire spiral down the left edge. The front was covered in stickers, one layered over the other, almost obscuring the pink paisley print. A circle with a peace symbol in the center. Three, six-petaled flowers in colors, now faded. The word "*Love*" filling a rectangle, with a heart for the O. Mold darkened some of the cover.

A narrow strap wrapped around the book with a tiny lock. But no key. He tugged at the leather strap, hoping age and rot might've weakened it. It wouldn't budge. He could force it open but was afraid that might damage it.

He stole a quick look at the clock. Already, his side trip had exhausted five precious minutes, and he had what he came up here for. He knew he should go, but the hairs on his neck still prickled. He stepped over to his desk. Opening the center drawer, he grabbed a pair of scissors and wedged them underneath the strap. He sawed and, after three tries, the leather broke free.

He flipped open the cover and found the first page inside almost completely blackened with mold and mildew. With two fingers, he edged another page over and noticed the second had a smaller stain. He could make out a date, written in a loopy feminine script and he could read

February 5, 1

but no more. Most of the rest of the page was blackened, At the bottom of the page, he could only make out a clump of letters in a swirling cursive

iary of ~~el~~

When he saw the name, he stopped breathing. "e-l-" and something. A squiggle, part of a curve. The vision of Ruby leaped into his head, bleeding and dying in his arms. He heard her desperate plea again. "Find the diary. Find Kelly."

Could this be the diary? Kelly's diary? Maybe—

Hoink. Hoink. Hoink. He heard from outside. The bus! They were blowing the horn on the bus. He

173

slammed the diary shut and placed it with his playbook. He locked the door and hustled down the stairs, taking them two at a time.

The diary had to wait. But not for long.

Chapter 28

Darrell stumbled into his apartment. The clock on the microwave read 1:47, and his body felt it.

God. What a night.

His last-minute trip to his office made the team late for the game, short circuiting their pregame routine. They started the game flat. By halftime, Wilshire had fallen behind ten points. It took all of Darrell's skill as a coach to rally his kids for the second half. They ended up pulling off the win with a game-ending, seventy-yard drive as the buzzer sounded. Relieved and delirious, he celebrated with the teens and volunteer coaches, getting high-fives all around.

Al trotted across the field to shake his hand. "Keep it up, and Wilshire's going to need to get you a trophy case almost as big as ours."

The Pirate faithful who made the trip to Cambridge came over to offer kudos, Bud Williams and Trevor Remington first in line. "That might be one for the record books, Coach," Williams said, placing a hand on Darrell's shoulder. "You had me worried for a while."

Remington engulfed Darrell's hand with his large paw and grinned. "Never doubted you, Coach."

The players were so excited, slamming into each other with such loving ferocity, Darrell found it a challenge to herd the group back onto the school bus. Then, on the boisterous trip back home, the bus broke down. At first, everyone took it in stride. But after the ninety minutes it took to get a new bus for the teens and arrange a tow for the wounded vehicle, Darrell's euphoria had evaporated.

When he crossed the threshold to his apartment, he was yawning, huge, jaw-stretching yawns. After letting Pogo out briefly and then corralling him, Darrell headed straight for the bedroom, though not before he folded his clothes and set them in the hamper. He set the briefcase next to the nightstand—he wasn't letting the diary out of his sight. He climbed into bed and pulled the mildewed book out of the satchel. So tired his eyes hurt, he still wanted to check out at least a few pages, before he lost consciousness.

He pulled it out and again read

iary of ~~el~~.

Carefully, he turned the next page.

Dear Diary,
Feb. 8
I'm glad I have you. I can write down my thoughts and dreams here and nobody will know. Jeez my mom is so square I can't talk with her, and there really is nobody else. Got friends but nobody I trust with my deepest feelings.
Feb 9
Watched the Beatles on the Ed Sullivan Show tonight. There great. I wish I had someone who could take me to see them. I mean wouldn't that be too cool?
Feb. 10
I found another zit on my chin today. I mean that

makes 8 but whose counting? Hah! 17 and still getting zits. When are they goin to stop? B told me the best way to stop zits is to go "all the way" with a guy cause your body knows to grow up, and it stops having zits. She's probly wrong, but I think it'd be cool to find out if these zits don't scare off everybody with pants.

Feb 15

Red took me out tonight. When he asked me yesterday, I couldn't believe it. Thank God my zits shruk a little. Cruised Main St in his cherry car and everyone was honking at us. It was Cool. I mean, his family has all kinds of bread, and he got this hot '63 red Corvette Stingray for his 16th birthday. Know what I got for my 16th birthday? A top, which mom got from the local five and dime and I don't like anyway cause it's so—

The next part was mildewed, the black obscuring the handwriting. Darrell slid his finger down to the next line he could read.

he took me to the passion pit where we made out. I think he wanted to Go All The Way. His hands were all over me. I got really excited. He wanted me to touch His Thing, but I got all embarest and said I wasn't ready yet. Boy, did I blow it cause right after that, we left and he dropped me at home.

Why'd I do that? He's fab and about the richest guy I know and now he probly won't ask me out again. Sometimes I can be so stupid. Anyway I gotta crash.

So do I, Darrell thought and rubbed his eyes. He flipped through the next few pages and saw more of the same, all teenage angst and rebellion. He got plenty at school.

How could this be the diary Ruby wanted him to find? That she died telling him about? Maybe, in the morning, when he could stay awake, he'd see something.

He surrendered, and sleep claimed his mind and body.

Deep in his slumber, he heard the first notes. They punctured his subconscious and crescendoed as the same song wafted over him, as if the record was spinning again on a player in the next room. Darrell started humming when he was interrupted.

A warm, smooth body slid into bed next to him. He felt the pleasant pressure as her nipples pressed against his chest. Immediately, he remembered their kiss last Sunday and the feel of Erin's breasts against him in the car.

When had she come over? He guessed he wasn't really *that* tired.

He felt her hot, naked skin press against his, drops of her perspiration sizzling his arms and chest, making his groin ache. As if she read his thoughts, her hand slid down his body.

The music surged again, intruding, making him smile…or maybe it was her fingers. He didn't want her to stop, so he leaned over and kissed her neck to encourage her. The hand still busy below, she kissed him, mouth open and tongue busy, like the other night.

Darrell closed his eyes. He surrendered to his other senses and drank her in, his mouth meeting hers, his hungry tongue finding hers. His hand fondled a very supple breast. At his touch, she broke the kiss and uttered a low groan of satisfaction. Her voice sounded different. Something was off. But he was hard and the kneading of her hand so delightful, he brushed off the warning.

The music stopped, strangling the room in silence. Darrell opened his eyes and peered into the gloom. The faint light from the outside framed three ghostly figures in the doorway to his bedroom, stacked one behind the other like parallel silhouettes. They strutted into the room, all three covered in white sheets with pointed hoods. The odor of stale beer floated in with them.

Oh, shit. In seconds, the three were on them. They ripped her away and dragged her across the room, screaming. When Darrell saw her by the door, he realized the girl was not...Erin. She was some other redhead, younger, *a teen.* He shut his eyes and shook his head back and forth.

This can't be real.

Rough hands hauled him from his bed and something—a bag or pillowcase—was yanked over his head. He could see nothing.

He flailed out, trying to find the intruders in his blindness. Powerful, chapped hands grabbed his arms. Jerked them behind him. A coarse rope was cinched around his neck. Tightened. Darrell tried to wrench his hands free, but couldn't. The hemp dug into his skin and constricted his neck, blocking off air. Darkness. He couldn't breathe, his chest suddenly heavy. *Oh, Jesus.*

"Yip. Yip, yip." Tongue slobber across his face dragged him back. Darrell bolted upright in bed, sending Pogo scrambling to the floor. His hands went to his neck, groping where the rope had tightened. *There's nothing there. Thank God.*

He exhaled quickly five times, sweat pouring down his face and chest, his breath in ragged gasps. His gaze searched the bedroom and beyond, the dim features of his apartment emerging in the low light. He was alone. No girl. No intruders.

No sound other than the panting of his pug beside his bed, eyes fixed on him. "Thanks, Pogo." He reached his hand out, and the dog licked it. "God. Only a damn dream. What the hell is going on?"

The bedside clock read 3:13. *The same time again?* He rose and checked out the rest of the small apartment. Nothing. Except Kelly's diary, lying open, waiting for him. Beckoning.

Chapter 29

Darrell awoke, feeling something on his wrist. He struggled to open his eyes. Dull morning light seeped through the window, casting everything in sepias and grays. Unmoving, he lay on his stomach, face to the wall. The temperature in the bedroom had dropped, as if a frigid wind blew into the space, and he wiggled a little farther under the covers.

His right arm lay above him, near the headboard, and he felt a pressure on the wrist again. He turned his head and saw a dark hand on his arm. He jerked. In the dim light, he could barely make out a large black hand wrapped around his wrist. His gaze followed the attached arm and took in a tall, naked, dark-skinned young man standing over him. Darrell couldn't breathe.

This could not be real. He had to be dreaming again.

He tried to call out, but his mouth was dry. Nothing came out. The visitor was huge with massive, broad shoulders and long powerful arms of ebony skin. And Darrell had seen him before.

The hand tugged, gently dragging him out of bed, the covers dropping to the floor. The chill flooded his half-exposed body. He trembled. Long, calloused black fingers pulled Darrell's wrist and guided him to the diary lying on the floor. Darrell bent down, picked it up, and turned to face his visitor.

The figure had vanished.

Darrell stood alone. Even the pug hadn't moved, curled up on his blanket at the foot of the bed. "Okay. I got it," he called out, to no one. Pogo jumped up and stared at him. "Another damn dream, Pogo." Seemingly satisfied, the dog settled back down onto his blanket. Darrell stared at the diary in his hand. "Could I at least get a shower first?"

Twenty minutes later, he sat at his small, blond kitchen table, hair still wet, but his mind a little clearer. He sipped his doctored coffee, the strong aroma helping to arouse him and the creamy liquid replacing the bitter taste in his mouth. Idly, he nibbled on an English muffin, careful to keep the crumbs over a plate. He tugged apart the pages of the diary and found where he'd stopped last night. His fingertips traced down the withered page to the next entry.

Feb 18

Big surprise Red hasn't even looked at me at school. I mean I know where he and his buddies hang out at lunch and I tried to hang around, you know, look cool. But for the last two days Red jus walked past actin like he dudnt even know me. I know he's a cool head

Mold obliterated a few lines of the script, leaving only

my face burped up another zit tonight.

Darrell took another bite, and some raspberry preserves plopped onto the table. "Damn. What's the matter with me?" he said. He edged the diary to the

182

side. Getting a paper towel to clean up the spill, he wiped the surface clean twice, before returning the notebook to the table. Standing over the sink, he finished the English muffin and then took the plate, rinsed it twice, and stacked it in the dishwasher. He drank some more of the coffee, also over the sink.

After washing his hands three times, he sat down again and carefully flipped through a few more entries. He found passages about a friend moving out of town, about a date with another boy, and about Kelly getting in trouble for passing a note. The teacher in him couldn't resist and he studied the entry.

Mar 1
God I hate school. Today, Mr. S caut me passing a note to B and grabbed it. He read it and sent me to Mr. A. He said the note was provoccative. All it said was what do you think I oughta do if he tries to cop a feel tonight? He called my Mom. *Shit was she pissed! She came in a little plaster. She grounded me for two weeks. When we got home she called me "worthless" and tried to beat me, but I wouldn't let her.* I Am Not Worthless!

Darrell couldn't help but feel the girl's pain. He'd seen the same thing happen a number of times. Kids get in trouble at school and parents overreact, saying things they didn't mean, but wounded anyway. Or maybe, did mean. All because their kids embarrassed them.

He wondered if he would have handled the situation any better. How many of his kids have been told they were worthless?

When his stare returned to the weathered pages, he noticed something he'd missed. Except for her mom and this Red, the writer—if it was Kelly—used no names, only initials. That gave him an idea. He picked up the diary and turned the pages, scanning the entries looking for any reference to "H." It was slow going as he flipped through March and April, catching glimpses of teen anxieties and dramas. The author tried smoking and choked on the fumes, had bad cramps with her period, professed her *Love* for the Beatle Paul.

He noticed the writer was prolific, recording entries almost every day. The mold and mildew complicated his examination, with large portions or entire entries blackened, making it hard to make sense of the writing. Frustrated, he downed another cup of coffee before it cooled. He rinsed and racked the mug in the dishwasher and stood there, stretching his neck in a circle to loosen it. He stared back at the diary.

What was he missing? What was so damn important about these old pages?

He went back to searching. In a May 23 entry, something caught his eye, right below a few blacked out lines.

dudn't like football but he loves basketball. He said his favorite player is Oscar Robertson (he calls him the Big O) and he wants to get his autograph.

Darrell stared at the line. *Oscar Robertson's autograph?* The first part of the passage was wiped out, so he turned the pages back, one by one, studying every line for some connection or reference to an "H." On an entry dated two weeks earlier, he found it scribbled in the beginning of a passage.

H saved my dumb brother today.

For a full minute, Darrell stared at the script *H,* trying to be certain he wasn't dreaming…or hallucinating. He closed and opened his eyes several times and found the *H* still there, at the start of the sentence. The same as his H?

PLEASE HELP ME FIND JUSTICE—H

He needed to see if he could find more entries referring to *H.* And he wanted to call Erin. His fingers turned pages, when a knock at his front door pulled his attention away.

"Coach?" called a male voice from outside.

Who in the world could that be on Saturday morning? He didn't want any visitors now.

Darrell grabbed a napkin he could use as a bookmark and closed the diary. "Coming." His glance darted around the apartment. Hurrying into the bedroom, he stuffed the book under his pillow. He went and opened the door.

On his small concrete porch, Jeff Jefferson bounced from one foot to the other, the brilliant sunlight framing his thin figure in the doorway and Darrel had to raise his arm to see. Jefferson stood there, with a crooked grin and those oversized ears, his arms holding an offering of two rectangular manila boxes.

Jefferson started in, "Good. I hoped I'd find ya home. Wanted to talk with you." He looked away.

When he didn't go on, Darrell pointed to the boxes. "You brought something?"

Jefferson grinned. "Yeah. Got delivery of the new uniforms and wanted to bring 'em right over," he rambled, blue eyes bright and, Darrell noticed, not red. "I know you can't use them till next Friday but thought you'd want to see 'em right away."

"Thanks, Jeff, but you could've waited till Monday." Darrell accepted the packages, and Jefferson fumbled with the top one and pulled out a jersey, the black and gold sparkling in the morning light.

"Do you like 'em?"

"Uh…yeah, Jeff. They look great. I'm sure the guys are going to love them."

Jefferson looked uncertain. "Well…w-well, good." He glanced back at the gravel driveway. Darrell looked beyond Jefferson and didn't see anyone else.

Jefferson said, "I have the rest in the car. I can leave 'em with you or if you want, I can bring 'em by the school on Monday."

"Monday'll be fine. Then all the players can get a look at them before practice."

"Um, okay." Jefferson kept the grin on his face. "Uh, could you let Bud know that you like the new uniforms?"

"Sure. I'll call Bud and tell him they came out nice."

Jefferson opened his mouth as if to say more, then stopped. He stepped to the car and said over his shoulder, "See you Monday at school."

Darrell closed the door, thinking what was that about?

Chapter 30

Darrell's stomach growled in protest. So, as soon as Jefferson left, Darrell headed over to the fridge and fumbled around for something else to eat. Behind four bottles of beer, he found leftover pasta from Leo's Pizza —he hoped it wasn't too old—and placed it in the microwave. He went into the bedroom and retrieved the diary and returned it to the table. Grabbing a cola from the fridge, he opened and downed half the can.

When the timer sounded, he brought the plate of warmed up spaghetti over to the table, the spicy aroma making his stomach grumble, and set it down a safe distance from the fragile pages. He stared at the items on the table and then arranged them, diary, pop can, and plate, into a perfect equilateral triangle with the notebook at the top. Using a napkin to open the diary to where he stopped, he scanned the lines until he found the entry with *H* again.

May 9
H saved my dumb brother Steve today. I haven't written about Steve cause he's a jerk. I mean he's 15 and his mouth is always getting him in trouble. Behind the school he must have been talking smartass to these big guys

A black, mildew stain covered the next two and a

half lines. Then—

him yelling over by the dumpster. These two big seniors—C and F—were punching Steve, over and over. When I got there, this big Negro was pulling them off Steve telling them to pick on somebody their own size. C charged this black kid who swung his arm and knocked him on his butt. Then C and F took off calling him a Fuckin N. *(Diary, I can't even bring myself to write the word they yelled.)*

I went over to make sure Steve was all right, he had some bruises on his face but he shoved me. He yelled at the guy who saved him. Why'd you do that, you stupid asshole? I didn't need your help. Thanks a lot. Now they're going to call me a N lover! My brother used the same word, then left.

No one else was around so I stood there and felt ackward. I mean, there are some Negroes in our school, but not in my classes and I never really talked to a colored kid before. I think they teach them in separate classes from us.

So he looked at me and I looked at him. He was really big. Had strong muscles in his arms. I didn't want to seem totally stupid, so I said thanks for helping my kid brother. Why'd you do that?

This Negro said, I don't know. Came around the side of the building and saw those guys whooping on your brother, I felt sorry for him. I know what that's like, so I stopped them.

I remember thinking this guy is so big who could whoop him?

He said his name was H and I told him mine.

Darrell took a careful bite of some spaghetti. He used a paper towel to wipe his hands and then use the napkin to edge the pages forward, one at a time, skimming the passages. Two entries later, Darrell found another passage with *H.*

May 12
I was down by the water, you know, in that spot at Bayside Park where I like to get away from everyone. Sitting there on the bench, staring out at the water feeling sorry for myself. I figure I had a right since nobody asked me out in almost a month. H walked up the shore and said hi and I was startled at first but said hi back. He just stood there, off to the side and didn't say any more. Right away I remembered him. I mean it would be hard to forget him he was so tall

A blackened streak covered the next several words, then—

believe, huh?) He said You look a little sad. Like some company? and I said sure. So he came over and sat on the next bench, across the walkway.
He asked me why I was sad and I Told Him *I mean, I don't know why I did that, but I did. He said as pretty as you are, it's hard to believe there wouldn't be a lot of guys who want to take you out. They must be crazy.*
I think I blushed but said thanks. No guy ever told me anything like that before. We sat on the benches for a while and watched the waves. I said they always make me feel better and he said he felt the same way. We talked a little more. We go to the same school but don't

have the same teachers.

You know it was really nice sitting there talking with him, even though he was sitting bout 6 feet away. I mean mom says you can't trust a N— (I won't write her word). I don't get it. H seems like regular people. No he seems nicer than most people.

May 14

Saw H again today. After school I was sitting on my bench in the park and guess who comes walking along the shore? H! I know I'm not supposed to but I was hoping I would see him and there he was. I think he was hoping to see me too. Me! Even with my zits!

We sat way apart on the two benches again and talked. It was colder with wind off the water but I bundled up in a sweatshirt and didn't mind. Nobody was there but us but he still sat 6 feet away. We just talked. He told me about his family and his mama and I told him about my mom. His mama sure sounds nicer than mine.

Darrell pondered the connection between Kelly and H—his H? He picked up the plate and finished the last of the pasta. Two more swallows drained the Coke and he tossed out the can. After he rinsed the plate, he stacked it in the dishwasher. Turning the water back on, he lathered up his hands and washed them in very hot water, scrubbing the tips of his fingers. Finished with his nails, he repeated the process till his hands were almost red and dried them with three paper towels.

Satisfied his hands were sanitized, he returned to the diary and skimmed the next few entries, turning several pages with the napkin. He found only more teenage drama. No further mention of *H.* Then, scanning an entry about an argument with her girlfriend, Darrell realized it was about *H*.

May 22

Me and B had a big one today. B is my best friend. Well, she used to be. I thought I could tell her anything. After school we went to hang out in her bedroom and we were talking like we do. You know, talking about school, our crappy parents and Guys. *She asked if Red asked me out again and I said I didn't want to go out with him.*

Anyway, I told her about H saving Steve and that he was kinda nice and we met and talked at the park. Me and B were whispering but when I told her who H was, she said Kelly, you can't have anything to do with those people. My mom says they ain't like us. They got these animal urges they can't control.

I told her H seems like everyone else, only nicer. She only got madder at me and hollered I didn't know what I talking about and if I was going to hang out with those people then we couldn't be friends anymore. I yelled that she couldn't tell me who to hang out with and left.

So caught up in the entry, Darrell almost missed the mention of the name. *Kelly.* It was the first time he found the author's name anywhere in the diary and confirmed the mildewed scribble in front. He ran the tip of his index finger over the word, *Kelly,* to make sure it wouldn't disappear. It didn't.

He paused for a minute, giving his eyes a rest from deciphering the cramped, feminine script. Her name there on the page removed any doubt.

He could see where this was going. White girl and black guy in 1964.

Despite the Wilshire legend about the ghost, Darrell was pretty certain the young black man—H—*didn't* commit suicide. Which means he was killed. Darrell touched his neck, where he could still feel the rope from the dream. Maybe lynched. Here in Wilshire?

PLEASE HELP ME FIND JUSTICE.—H

Justice, huh? Good luck getting anyone to admit that. Still, if Darrell was right about all this, he had to do something. He couldn't sit around and pretend.

He decided to run it by Erin tonight and see what she thought. He returned to his search and came to the entry he'd first noticed *H*. He skimmed a few paragraphs, stopping at the Oscar Robertson comment.

When he got to the bench and sat down panting—still not close to me, even though we were the only ones around—I could see grease on his face and hands. He said he'd jus come from the garage and had to work a few hours but hoped I'd still be here. He hoped I'd Be There!

He's planning to be on the basketball team and

The mildew made the next few lines unreadable. Then—

called him a gutless pansy but he wouldn't give in. He dudn't like football but loves basketball. His favorite player is Oscar Robertson (he calls him the Big O) and he wants to get his autograph.

Darrell stared at the name—Oscar Robertson. He could still see the autograph shift on the basketball in his office, right in front of him. Another wave of cold air hit him, and he glanced around looking for a draft...or something else.

This had to be it, but what was he supposed to see? What was in this diary?

He skimmed more entries, searching for any further details on *H*. The next several pages held Kelly's comments on teen fashions—something called coin bracelets and flip hairstyles—and her complaints that her mom wouldn't give her money to do anything. Red received another mention, this time for a new red Mustang. She saw an ad for the car on TV the night before when Ford announced the brand new line. The next day Red drove one to school.

God, this kid's parents must've had serious money.

He kept on, wading through more episodes of teen angst, acne and cramps before he found another passage with *H*.

June 1

School's out and I'm a senior! I can't believe it and I'm so glad. One more year and I'm out of here.

Uncle Ronnie—that's mom's Friend—*came over yesterday and he was showing us his new Polaroid camera, asking me to do a silly pose took my picture in color and gave the photo to me. That gave me an idea. Mom and Ronnie started drinking and both got plastered and past out. I used a little five finger discount and* borrowed *his camera. (Don't worry, I returned it.) Then I snuck out to our place at the Park. Isn't it interesting that I call it our place? and* He *was there! I showed him Ronnie's Polaroid and took a picture of him. I was so excited when the film came out the picture of his face and strong shoulders showed up great. He took my picture too and I had the biggest smile on my face in the photo. When I asked him if he wanted to keep it, he said no they'd beat him bad if he's caut with a picture of a white girl, especially a young, pretty one like you. So I agreed to keep both pictures secret and I hid them inside here since I don't know of any place safer. So I cut the*

The mold erased the next line and a half. Darrell stared at the black crease across the page, trying to decipher words, letters, anything. Further down, he read.

keep my thoughts and photos safe and secret, but at least I'll have a picture of Him.

Darrell studied the writing on the wrinkled paper. *I hid them inside here.*

Somewhere inside this diary, after all this time. Surely the pictures would darken, erode.

He flipped through the pages, one after the other, searching for the photos. About halfway into the notebook, he got to the final entry—dated October 21—checking every page, and came up empty. Carefully, he flipped through blank pages till he arrived at the back cover with no sign of the photos.

He turned the diary over and examined the back cover, inspecting the seam along the center, thinking, maybe, he saw a bulge he hadn't noticed before behind the flowered print. Darrell brought the notebook close to his face, so close the mold odor hit him, and studied the cover. Grabbing a small steak knife, he slid it along the seam to separate the cloth from the cardboard. Like the rest of the book, the material was blackened and mildewed, tattered in places. But as he pulled, the fabric came away, obvious it had been cut before. He gently peeled back the cloth and saw them.

He recognized the shapes, about three inches square. After freeing them from their hiding place, he peered at them in his palm and his heart plummeted. They were stuck together and appeared to be blank, white, the photos erased or faded over time. He grabbed another paper towel from above the sink and set the joined pair on it. Using his fingernails to exert gentle pressure, he tried to tug the squares apart. At first they wouldn't budge. Then, all at once, they popped apart and lay face up on the white paper towel.

He stared at the two photos and his pulsed raced. "Damn."

Chapter 31

Darrell couldn't believe his eyes. Both photos were in color. Faded, weak color. They were a little cloudy, and some of the film from each Polaroid had adhered to the other, leaving dark splotches on both pictures. But he could still make out the faces.

The first was a shot of a large, young black man in a T-shirt, his skin incredibly dark and his smile looking brighter because of it. Darrell had seen that face—in the window of his office, on the grainy game video, and a few hours earlier right here in his apartment. He would recognize those haunting, brown eyes anywhere. Kelly's *H* was clearly his ghostly visitor.

What unsettled him more was the second face. He slid his chair back from the table, the legs squeaking against the hard floor, and stared at the photo.

She was pretty, the shoulder straps of a yellow sundress visible beneath the bright young face, still obvious even through the faded color. Long, curling red hair framed an oval face with shining green eyes and a sprinkling of freckles on her cheeks—and he knew her. Rather, he recognized her and *almost* knew her, in the Biblical sense. He'd been entranced by her, in his wild, sensuous dreams. His mind conjured up the image of her naked, trim body, next to him. Then he saw a white-sheeted figure dragging her by her hair. He ran his fingers over the Polaroid, feeling the bumps where the film had rubbed off.

Kelly? He'd been dreaming about a student? My God.

The loud bleat of the phone jerked him. He jumped to grab the kitchen extension.

"Hey, Darrell."

"Oh, hi, Kelly...er, I mean Erin," he said quickly.

"Kelly?" she asked.

"Uh, yeah. She's...connected to our ghost, I think." Pause. "Uh, I'll explain when I see you."

"You okay? You sound, I don't know, a little strange."

"Yeah. No. I don't know. You're not going to believe the day I've had."

"Really? Realize what time it is?" Erin asked.

Darrell shot a quick glance at the clock radio. "Oh, Jeez, I was supposed to call you and come over. I'm sorry, but I have a good reason. I found *it*."

"Found what?"

"The diary I told you about. *Kelly's* diary. The one Ruby mentioned right before she died. Give me a few minutes to change, and I'll be over to pick you up. I can fill you in over dinner."

He made one of the quickest changes ever, swapping his sweats for a clean pair of khakis and a brightly colored polo, and stood ringing her bell less than half an hour later. To make up for his tardiness, he took her to her favorite place, the Town Dock in St. Michaels, with a table overlooking the harbor. They enjoyed a quiet sunset, the sun dropping behind the buildings to their right and sailboats bobbing at anchor, their tiny lights flickering on. Between bites of Crab Imperial, he told her of his discovery of the diary, about

Kelly and her *H*. By the time the server cleared away their dishes, he had covered everything he'd learned so far.

When Darrell got his wallet out to pay the check, he looked at his watch. "I know you really want to see the movie. If we hustle, we can still get there in time and probably only miss a preview or two."

"Got a better idea." Erin stared across the table, emerald eyes bright. "How about we put the movie off, and let's go see if we can make any more progress on this mystery of yours?"

"You sure you want to trade William Hurt and Meryl Steep for a moldy, thirty-five-year old teen diary?"

"William will have to wait for me." Erin's mouth curved up. "I've got my hands full with another guy…and his ghost." She leaned across the table and kissed him.

In forty-five minutes, they were back at his apartment, huddled together on the soft suede couch, the first domestic purchase he'd made when he came to town. Right now, one arm around Erin, inhaling the delightful herbal scent of her hair, it seemed like a very smart acquisition.

Pogo came over and snuggled between Erin's legs, and she rubbed his neck. "How's my second favorite guy, hey, boy?" He licked her hand and went to Darrell, who tossed him a doggie treat. The pug snatched it and padded back to the bedroom, his paws making tiny, clicking sounds on the old wood flooring.

Kelly's diary lay open in front of them, in the exact center of what passed for a coffee table, really a large piece of clear glass supported by a concrete block on each end.

"This is where I left off." Darrell pointed to the "June 1" entry and flipped the diary closed, indicating the crease. "And here's where I found the hidden photos."

Erin picked up the notebook. Her slender fingers ran over the flower petals, now faded, and traced the outline of the peace sign. She turned the book over and pulled out the old Polaroids, one by one, handling each by the edges, and laid them down on the glass. She pointed to the torso shot of the handsome, young black man. "So this, is our Wilshire ghost?"

"Well, he certainly looks like the...the...the apparition I've seen."

"I believe you, Coach." She smiled. "Too bad he can't play for your team. Look at those huge shoulders."

"He probably wouldn't have played football anyway."

"No?"

"According to Kelly, he didn't like football. He liked basketball and wanted to get Oscar Robertson's autograph."

Erin's eyes widened. "Same autograph you saw on your prize Jordan basketball?"

"The one and the same."

"And she's pretty, isn't she?" Erin picked up the photo of the teen girl and held it alongside her own face. "Looks a little like me, don't you think?"

"Yeah, I guess." Darrell swallowed twice. He did *not* want to tell her about his dreams, not yet anyway. How would he explain he'd been fantasizing about a student?

"How old is she, can you tell?"

"Don't know for sure. Seventeen, I think. Just finished junior year when I stopped. You want a beer before we start back in?"

"Sure."

Darrell went to the fridge and grabbed two Dogfish Head beers, the brown bottles cool against his fingers. He placed one on his forehead to settle himself down.

Chill, Darrell. Erin doesn't have to know everything.

Erin deposited her flats on the floor and sat cross-legged, the diary in her lap, but set the book on the glass when she accepted the beer. After they both took a pull, she said, "Want me to pick up where you left off?"

"Have at it," Darrell said, and she put down her bottle, pulled the book close, and started reading aloud.

June 4

I went out with Red again tonight, and boy was that a mistake.

"Catch me up here. Who's Red?"

"Some rich bad boy at school she went out with before. It didn't go well. She gives him a name, well a nickname. I don't know why. Pretty much everyone else only gets an initial."

Erin nodded and went back to her reading aloud.

But he rolled by me in town in this hot new Mustang with those whitewalls and asked if I wanted to go down to Betterton Beach. I mean, he has this bitchin car and I was hoping things would go better this time and they did, at first.

We did some cruising around town and headed over to the beach. Got there pretty late. Grabbed a blanket out of the trunk and we sat on the beach and watched the sun set and it felt kinda romantic. I mean, there was a bunch of old beer bottles and paper cups around but we found a clear spot. We were the only ones there, us and some seagulls. We weren't supposed to be on the beach cause it was almost dark and it was kinda exciting at first.

Red looked so cool in his shorts and white T-shirt with the cigarette pack rolled up in his sleeve. He put an arm around me and was smoking blowing smoke into the breeze and watching it float back over our heads. It was way cool. He leaned over and kissed me hard. I had on that yellow two-piece—mom wouldn't let me get a bikini—and he undid the clasp of my top in the back. He slid his hand under the straps and slid my top off. I was sitting there without my top

Caught by a black stain, Erin turned toward Darrell. He raised a palm. "Mildew and mold wipes out some lines on some pages, but not every page. Have to do the best you can to make sense of it."

She pulled the diary closer and read what she could.

cold some cause my nipples started to get hard. He started feeling me up. Wanted to tell him to stop, I know I should have but it felt good. He leaned closer and kissed me again and you know what he did next?

He reached his hand inside my bottoms! I backed a little away from him. He said what's the matter don't you like it? Don't you like me and what could I say but sure.

I heard a car and grabbed up my top cause I didn't want to get arrested for

Another black streak stopped Erin and she moved on to the next legible words.

friends, but I held my top against my chest. Red hollered up and T and C came over the dunes, both holding beer bottles and laughing. Red turned to me with this smirk on his face. You said you like me and I thought, now you're all hot, you might want to show all three of us a Good Time.

That's what he said. I couldn't believe it. I can be so stupid sometimes.

He grabbed my hand so my top would come off again but I swatted it. Still lost hold of the top. The other two boys kept staring. I grabbed the top and pulled it on but some sand got in it. All three guys took a step toward me and I backed up the sand dune. I told Red I wanted to go home and he just laughed and said I guess you'll have to

Erin halted again and moved her fingers down two more mildewed lines to where the writing was clear again.

heard Red say where's she going to go?

I was so mad grabbed my cover up from the car and starting walking. I knew I was a long way from home (found out it was 10 miles) but some grandpa saw me walking on the road and stopped and picked me up.

Told him my boyfriend had dumped me and he took me all the way home, even though he was heading to Easton.

I'm really mad, mad at Red, but mostly so mad at myself.

Erin set the diary down and picked up her beer, which had lain untouched, and drank. "Whew. Is it all like this?"

"Well, it's not usually this heavy," Darrell said.

"Who's this Red again?"

"Some jerk in her class." He indicated her beer. "You want another?" She shook her head and he carried his empty bottle over to the kitchen. "I've had enough for now, too. Don't want to miss anything."

Erin took another drink and pointed at the diary with the bottle. "Hell of an entry. If we believe her, it sounded like attempted rape."

He returned with a dish towel and wiped the sweat rings off the glass. "Today, yeah, but in the sixties, I'm not sure it would've gone like that. Her word against his, er, rather theirs."

"Probably right, but still?"

"I know." Folding the towel on the arm of the couch, Darrell settled in next to her again. "I'm glad to have the company for this, especially yours. You want to keep reading, or you want me to take over."

"I'm okay." She set her empty bottle on the glass with a little clinking sound, picked up the notebook, and started in again. The latest sweat ring left by her bottle mocked him, but he tried not to think about it. He leaned in, looking over her shoulder, and listened as Erin's narration gave voice to the scribbled words and they re-entered Kelly's world.

Chapter 32

June 8

We met again, me and H. We both showed up at the park about the same time. A few people were around a couple of kids and their mom and we sat on two different benches again. When they left we talked. That's all, talk.

I asked him if anyone knew he came, he said he dudn't think so and told me he can get out cause his mama works so much. I told him I could come cause my mom drinks so much.

His mama works to jobs. During the day she cleans white peoples' houses. And evenings, she works at this expensive restaurant in Oxford and cooks for them. Makes the best crab cakes anywhere and does a bunch of other cooking.

Then H stopped and looked around, making sure no one else could hear and said My mama can cook in that Fine *restaurant for all those white folks, but says if she brought me and my brothers in the front door, we'd all be thrown out.*

Erin looked up at Darrell. They'd eaten at just such a restaurant last week, maybe the same one. Thinking back, Darrell tried to recall how many black faces he'd seen on their dinner date. One, behind the bar.

Maybe some things hadn't changed that much.
Erin returned to her narration.

Here, his mom is working hard to take care of 5 kids. And my mom who likes to get blitzed all the time and is living off welfare and she's the one who says you can't trust them No Account N *word. Who do you think I believe?*

June 10

We met on Our *benches and H told me we can't meet there no more, because it's too public. His brother found out and is worried that us being seen together will cause trouble. Because we're talking, sitting on two different benches!*

H would like to keep seeing me and got a plan. He can pick me up in his car. Diary, did I tell you He Has A Car? *It's an old car he's fixing up, but its his. He knows a place where we can go where nobody will see. Then he got all serious and told me he was going into Baltimore tomorrow to hear Martin Luther King, Jr. Yeah, the Negro civil rights leader who's been arrested and been in the news! I asked if I could come. He looked surprised, but said yes. Tomorrow I'm going to ride in his car to Baltimore!*

June 12

God, me and H almost got arrested last night. He picked me up outside of town—where nobody would see us—and we rode into Baltimore, although it took us an hour. Pulled up at this church, and a bunch of Negroes were going in and we followed. I wasn't the only white girl but there were only a few others. People seemed nice, just nervous and excited. Up front behind the pulpit was this short handsome Negro man in a black suit and small mustache and I learned later he was this Martin Luther King, Jr. Oh,

Erin slid her fingers past two lines obliterated by mold and read the next words she could decipher.

went quiet and people called amen over and over again. Passed out a little pamphlet with some of his preaching in it and I brought it home even though H said I could get in trouble if someone saw me with it. I don't care. I read the whole thing twice—more than I do for school.

They were going to do a sit in at a "whites only" diner. Warned it could be dangerous. H wanted to go, but when Dr. King came down the aisle and saw us, he told H to take me home. On the ride back, we heard on the radio that Dr. King and the group didn't make it inside the diner. They were beaten and arrested on the steps outside.

June 14
We did it. No not that.

Erin stopped and exchanged glances with Darrell, her eyebrows raised, and then read on.

Left a message in our secret hiding place. H picked me up and drove down a side road to an old gravel driveway along the edge of the water where nobody would see us. We were surrounded by high weeds and there was only a small break ahead where we could see the water. So quiet and peaceful, all I could hear was some insects. So exciting I could hardly stand it. It was like we were spies or something.

But H didn't look excited he looked mad. I said at least this way we can stay friends and no one has to know about us. He said he didn't like it that way but that's the way it has to be for now.

We held hands and I said I was sorry about Dr. King and the others, but I was glad we didn't get arrested. He said he wasn't

The next few lines were blackened and her finger followed to the next readable words.

they were going to a sit in at the motel pool next to the diner and he asked me to go with him. I said yes and he kissed me. For The First Time!

June 19

You're never going to believe what happened. Me and H went back to the same church in Baltimore and listened to Dr. King—he'd gotten out of jail. A group of us walked over to this motel. Then Dr. King and a few others climbed into the pool with this "whites only" sign hanging on this fence. We stood around, watching and singing hymns.

This crazy white man—the owner—came running out to the pool yelling, You can't do that. Can't you read, you stupid savages? Get out. Nobody moved and we kept singing. He went inside and came back out in a few minutes with this big orange plastic bottle and started screaming, I told all you dumbasses to get out of my pool. If you don't get out, I'm going to dump this here acid into the water. This crazy guy dumped Acid *into the pool where these men were standing. It was going to burn their skin. The Negroes got out, but we didn't leave. Two cops were there and I thought they might arrest us, but they jus laughed. A bunch of whites yelled at us and threw stuff at us but the cops didn't do anything. It was scary.*

H was worried and he decided things might get worse so he took me home.

I don't get it. All these Negroes want is the same rights we have as whites, like swimming in the same pool or drinking from the same water fountain. Why is that so much to ask?

Erin stopped her reading and glanced up at Darrell. "Hey, couldn't you use this entry as an example for your class of a first person history account?"

"The seniors' project using primary sources?" Darrell scrunched his forehead. "I hadn't thought of that, but yeah, I guess I could. The students would probably be interested in it. Let me see." Darrell took the diary and reread the passage. "I'd need to check to make sure it's accurate, but yeah, sure."

"Sounded pretty accurate to me."

Darrell liked the idea—though he decided he wouldn't explain where he got this particular primary source—but his mind was elsewhere. He thought he figured out where the story was headed, and maybe, why Ruby had pressed him to find this diary.

He placed the notebook face down on the glass and, after studying it, moved it two inches to the right, so it sat in the exact center of the top. He turned to Erin. "Let me ask you a question about all this."

Leaning against the back of the couch, she stretched her neck and folded her long legs under her. She stared back, smiling. "Sure, shoot."

His throat was suddenly dry. He cleared it. "Uh-um. Do you think this kid, this H could've been lynched…here in Wilshire?"

Chapter 33

"What?" Erin's eyes got huge.

"Well, he was found hanging from the widow's walk."

"Yeah, it was a suicide." She shifted on the couch, pulling her legs out and dropping them to the floor. "Lynching in Wilshire? Come on. Lived here all my life and never heard anything like that. How could they keep something like that quiet?" She stopped and then asked, "Besides, didn't lynchings happen much earlier?"

"Lynchings were more common in the '20s and '30s," Darrell said, "but there's been documentation of lynchings of blacks up through the mid '60s. One of the most infamous was a few years earlier, in '55, Emmett Till, this black kid from Chicago who was visiting Mississippi. You might've heard of the case. He was lynched for supposedly whistling at a white girl. It looks like H is doing a whole lot more."

"Still, this isn't Mississippi. I can't believe anything like that would happen here."

"Well, did you know you had two lynchings, right here on the Eastern Shore?"

Erin sat up. "Somehow, they missed that in history class. Where?"

"In Salisbury, a little east of Cambridge. Two guys back in the thirties, I think."

"How'd you know about them?"

Darrell said, "To get ready for the primary sources project, I've spent time at the Local History Room at Easton Library. I was checking out some resources the students might want to use and stumbled across a mention of the lynchings."

"Still. I've never heard anything about any lynchings."

"I suspect it's because of what historians call a 'conspiracy of silence.' After a lynching, communities cover it up and make up some story people can live with." He paused a beat and added, "Like a suicide."

Erin took a slow breath. "You think the answer might be in there." She pointed to the diary.

"I don't know. Maybe something."

"Okay, let's get back at it then. You want the honors or you want me to continue?"

Darrell said, "You make her words come alive. Sounds better, more natural."

He settled in next to her so he could look over her shoulder. Erin picked up the old notebook and together they studied the lines as she thumbed slowly through, searching for the next passage about *H*. She saw it first and said, "Here," and continued her narration.

June 25

As soon as he turned off the car H said They killed them. I asked who but he wouldn't say anything. He jus kept hitting the steering wheel. He asked me if I heard about these three college kids who went down to Miss. to help register Negroes and were arrested and disappeared. One was a Negro from Miss. and the other two was white and from New York City. I jus know there dead, he kept saying over and over.

He said we can't get together so often. There looking to cause trouble and it's dangerous. I said I don't care I jus wanted to be with him.

He got mad and said I don't understand cause I'm white and I yelled that's not fair. I slid closer to him and whispered the message I had learned from Dr. King. Hatred can't overcome hate. Only love can do that. Put my arms around him and told him we were going to make it better. He kissed me again, longer this time.

Erin raised her gaze and then turned her attention back to the pages. She thumbed through the next several entries, the two of them skimming the writing together—complaints about her mom's latest boyfriend and about how hot and sticky the weather was, worries she was too skinny. Darrell caught the next reference to *H* and leaned across her to indicate the passage, his arm brushing her hair as he pointed. She read aloud again.

July 24
H and I got together today in his car of course. Its been a long time more than 3 weeks. Missed him so much. I asked him why its been so long and he said we got to be careful. I asked him if he was excited Pres Johnson signed the civil rights bill and he said nothing's ever going to change. I told him it has to change and we'll help it. I remembered what Dr. King said and repeated love can conquer hate.

He pulled me to him and turned the radio on. A song he liked was playing and he said he thought of me every time he heard it and he sang a little of it to me.

It's called My Girl and he said it's going to be Our Song! *I'm going to buy a 45 tomorrow.*

Darrell yanked his arm back, coughing. His hand pounded on his chest.

"What happened? You okay?" Erin put down the notebook and placed her hand on his chest.

Red-faced, he managed a strangled, "Yeah. Need a little water. You can continue." He got up and walked into the kitchen.

The same song as in the dream. Another coincidence, like hell.

He filled a glass from the tap, drank it down, and returned to the couch, nodding at Erin who returned to her reading.

Couldn't stand it any longer and slid next to him and took his hand and put it right on my breast. When his big hand pressed and squeezed he was gentle and I moaned a little, it was so-o-o good. Not at all like how Red felt me up. We kissed and he kept his hand there. We started breathing hard. My insides felt funny and I slid my hand down to the front of his pants where his jeans bulged. He was So *hard. He started breathing even harder. Then, all of a sudden he pulled away and said we got to stop before we go too far. He turned the car on and backed out through the weeds and took me back.*

Darrell touched Erin's hand, covering her long, delicate fingers, and encouraged her to set down the diary. She did. "We've been at this for quite a while. You want to keep going or you want a break?" he asked.

She brought both index fingers to her eyes and, lids closed, she massaged them, stretching the skin on both sides. "It's a challenge trying to decipher her script, especially reading around the mold." Dropping her arms, she opened her eyes and looked back at Darrell. She flashed a coy smile. "But quit now, when it's getting hot? Don't think so."

She leaned over and kissed him, the kiss warm and lingering. He wrapped her in his arms, and she snuggled into him, her subtle perfume filling his nostrils. He was enjoying this—sitting here listening to her bringing the story to life, her willingness to delve into this mystery with him. Oh, and the feel of her soft body next to him.

"How about I get us some tea and put a little music on?" Darrell asked, when they broke the embrace. "And then we can get back at it." He didn't say back to what.

"Sounds good."

When he headed for the kitchen, she got up too, stretching and bending forward. Darrell watched her out of the corner of his eye. He managed to fill the kettle and light the burner all while keeping her in his peripheral vision. His libido started to heat up along with the stove. He pushed the button on the radio, bringing it to life, a loud piano riff filling the apartment. He turned it down a bit. "In the tales about the Wilshire ghost, did you ever hear any talk about a white girl?"

"No, I don't think so," Erin said.

"Clearly, Kelly's involved in all this. If *H* died, what happened to her?"

Before she could answer, the song ended and the DJ announced, "All you lovebirds out there, thanks for tuning into WJDT. For Saturday night, we're serenading you with love songs from our oldies collection. Next up is a number one from the '60s I'm sure you'll remember. Here are the Temptations with 'My Girl.' "

A guitar strum repeated three times, followed by the signature finger snap, and the lead singer started in. Darrell dropped the two mugs he was carrying.

Chapter 34

"Be careful. Don't come in here." Darrell knelt on the floor, his fingers moving methodically to collect the ceramic shards that had been two coffee mugs seconds before. He glanced up to see Erin at the edge of the kitchen, her feet bare. "I don't want those lovely feet to get sliced. And besides, then I'd have to clean up all this blood as well."

Erin got down on her knees and started helping him corral scattered fragments. Opening the cupboard under the sink, Darrell pulled out a spotless, gray dustpan and set what he'd collected into it. He slid the dustpan over to Erin. The tea kettle screamed a long, piercing note and he got up, turned it off, and went back to cleaning up.

Without stopping her work, Erin asked, "Okay, what gives?"

"What?" Darrell focused his attention on a large, rectangular fragment along the baseboard.

"Before, when I read Kelly's line about H singing 'My Girl' to her, you got this coughing fit. Then, the DJ plays the same song on the radio, you get dropsy with two mugs. What's up? Something about that song?"

He placed the retrieved shard into the center of the dustpan and looked across, seeing concern etched on her features. He started to bluff her, but stopped.

She might think he was crazy, if she didn't already,

but he needed to tell someone. He watched her, crawling around his kitchen floor with him and picking up the broken pieces. It was so domestic and so intimate, he decided he *had* to come clean.

So, after they'd gotten every sliver collected and disposed of and he'd swept the floor twice with a small whisk broom, he sat down on his cold linoleum, his back against the cabinet. She joined him, leaning against the cupboard next to him. And he told her. About the dream of the naked, young girl in his bed, the dark skin of his hand in the dream, the three intruders and the song.

"You thought this girl was me?" She grinned.

"Well, she was beautiful, had gorgeous red hair and a delightful sprinkling of freckles down her—"

"You thought this girl was me?" Erin's grin got wider.

"Well, it was a very erotic dream…at first."

"Until those three guys came in and put a bag over your head."

"Yeah, there was that."

"And you're sure it was that song?" She gestured to the radio.

"It was 'My Girl' all right. It was playing all three times I had the dream."

"Now, you think it was Kelly in your dream?"

"No, when I saw the photo, I *knew* it was Kelly, although I only saw her face clearly in the third dream." Darrell saw the question mark on Erin's face. "Well, you're the one who said you looked alike. When I first had the dream, I didn't think much about it. We'd just met, and well, I figured I was fantasizing about you."

Erin's face lit up. "You were already fantasizing

about me right after we met?"

"I *thought* I was fantasizing about you. You, er, I mean Kelly was pretty hot in the dream."

Her eyebrows raised.

"You get the picture."

She chuckled. "Yeah, I get the picture." Erin leaned in to kiss him, and Darrell reached his hand behind her head, pulling her toward him and entangling his fingers in the long red hair. It was a sensual, drawn-out kiss and he tasted the strange combination of garlic and beer. He liked it.

This, she was what he wanted. What he needed. Right now, he'd be happy to forget about the ghost and the diary.

After the third kiss, when they came up for air, she released a long breath. She bit her lower lip and said, "Let's get back, or we won't finish the diary to see if there's any more clues." She tilted her head toward the couch.

"Damn. I can honestly say I've never made out on a kitchen floor before. You know what else I've never done on a kitchen floor?"

She shoved Darrell, who fell to the side, his shoulder landing on the cold linoleum, and she scuttled back to the couch. When he collected his dignity, such as it was, he brought the tea over, steaming in two new mugs. He set them down atop napkins, so they wouldn't leave rings on the glass.

They resumed their search through the diary. This time they had to skim more than twenty entries, all without a mention of *H*, if you didn't count the ten times she'd written, "Hadn't heard anything from *H*. Hope I get to see him again." At the end of August, they discovered another *H* entry and Erin read aloud.

August 29

I was so excited when he Finally *left a message. Picked me up and drove to our spot, but he didn't look happy and kept checking over his shoulder. He asked if I heard about a church burning this weekend. I said the one in Preston that had an electrical fire? He said weren't no electrical fire. They burned it down cause they were registering folks to vote there and my brother was one of the volunteers. Only now he's scared after the fire and those dead kids in Miss.*

H said he was scared of what they'll do if they catch us together. I said I don't care cause I loved him. I said I Love You *to him! He didn't say anything back, but he kissed me and put his hand on my breast. I took off my top and my bra and he stared at me. Then he started massaging my breast again and it felt* So Good. *I undid his belt and opened his zipper and he slid a hand underneath my skirt.*

Erin halted her reading and glanced across at Darrell. Before he could say anything, she cleared her throat and returned to her narration.

Before I knew it we had our clothes off and I can't write all the details here but we went All The Way! *We were a little clumsy in the car and it was the first time for both of us but* We Did It *and it hurt a little and felt wonderful at the same time!*

After, H kept looking around like he was expecting someone to come out of the woods. He said we can't keep doing this in the car cause it's too dangerous and

I kissed him and said we'd work something out.

Erin took a slow breath. Setting the diary down, she sipped the tea.

Darrell asked, "You want me to take over reading?"

She shook her head, returned the mug, and picked up the diary, flipping pages again. He took another drink, while he studied the entries.

Most of the passages were short now and they scanned them together, looking for any more clues to *H*'s fate. They skimmed entries about Kelly's arguments with her mom (she defended Negroes but never told her mom about *H*), about the boys who had graduated and got draft papers for Vietnam, about starting her senior year and how she became an aide for the athletic department. No mention of *H*. Then, near the end of September, a larger entry jumped out at them and both saw the initial at the same time. Erin gulped and started in.

Sept 28

I did it. H was too scart to meet in his car and I So wanted to be with him and figured out a place where we could be together. Been an AD aide for three weeks helping Coach with keeping books and cleaning up. Last week asked if I could have a key to the office, so he wouldn't have to wait while I took everything up to the office and he gave me his spare.

Friday after the game I made sure everyone had gone home and then let H in the back door, where its dark and nobody would see. We climbed up three floors to the office and closed and locked the door behind us.

There's even an old couch for us. It's small but it's better than his car. And we did it More Than Once. *He is* So *big you know what I mean? And he gets this huge smile when he you know.*

Erin stopped and slid back into the couch, crossing her legs. Grabbing her mug, she took another slow sip. She set it down and brought the diary up on her lap. Noting the flush on Erin's cheeks, Darrell leaned in closer. She raised her eyebrows, offered a bemused smile and continued reading.

God it feels so good to be with him. It is a little scary too but that makes it exciting and I don't care cause I love him. I asked about running away together but he said he promised his mama he'd finish high school. So for now we'll take what we can get and we're already planning on next week.

Erin kept her stare on the diary, but a blush betrayed her. To distract herself, Darrell thought, she went back to turning pages. When Erin got to the last handwritten passage, she turned back to Darrell. "Last entry is October 21?"

"Yeah, I noticed that when I went through the whole diary searching for those photos." Darrell pointed to the two smiling faces, still staring at them from the glass.

"Better check the rest," she said.

"Agreed." Darrell slid closer, so he could read over her shoulder again, her body's curves pressed against him. He savored the closeness. It felt domestic…and natural. Together they reviewed the brief entries on the last six sheets, but found nothing about *H*'s fate. Until the final one. Erin read it aloud, a slight tremor in her voice.

Oct. 21
Going to meet again tonight. Been so great to make love to H and we've been up in my Love Nest *(that's what he calls it) eight times already—but whose counting—always late at night and without anyone knowing.*

I'm so excited about tonight, my insides get weak thinking about him but I have to admit I'm worried too. H thought he saw some guys following him. Each time we get together it's still wonderful, but we're both tense like we're waiting for something to happen.

"That's it?" Erin's voice was quiet, disappointment evident in her words. "But it doesn't tell us what happened to H *or* Kelly. Why would Ruby use her dying breath to beg you to find this diary?" She set the notebook down and stared at it, lying open to Kelly's last written words.

Gently, Darrell turned her face so it met his, their eyes inches apart. "I'm not so sure. True, nothing in the diary *tells* us exactly what happened, but Kelly has left us plenty of clues."

"Like?"

"Like the attitudes of the whites around her toward blacks, like *H* being nervous and followed, like the threats of Red and the others—"

"That's not much," she said.

"True, but don't forget about the piece de resistance, evidence of the ultimate taboo, at least in the

'60s. Kelly and *H* were lovers. It doesn't take much imagination to predict some catastrophe."

Sadness filled Erin's eyes. "Those poor kids. But we don't even know when all this happened, and we don't have names for either Kelly or *H*, at least not full names."

"No, but I'm pretty sure how to figure out the rest."

"How?"

He took her hand. "Research, of course. A little more historical research. How do you feel about another field trip to Annapolis?"

"Do I get to pick the teacher?" She kissed Darrell, and he wrapped his arms around her. When they stopped, she added, "I promise to be a very good student."

Together, they eased back against the sofa, their foreheads touching. Darrell kissed her again and when they broke, said, "I think this teacher could learn as much from the student as the other way around."

She pushed him down into the cushions and leaned over him. "Won't it be fun to find out?"

Chapter 35

"I think I got it," Darrell called in a hoarse whisper over the carrel divider. "At least, I think this may be it."

Erin dragged her chair over and settled next to him, so she could read his monitor. She leaned in close, and Darrell caught the scent of her "Allure" perfume. He liked it and put an arm around her shoulder. Darrell began to read.

Police Blotter
A Wilshire High School student was reported missing this week. Kelly Halloran, a 17-year-old senior, did not show up at school or home. Her mother, Mrs. Sheila Halloran, told authorities she last saw her daughter Tuesday afternoon when she stormed out after an argument. According to the mother, Kelly is high strung and independent and has likely run away. Anyone with information on her whereabouts should contact the Wilshire Police Department.

"The date on this?" Erin asked.

He worked the knob to scroll up. "Thursday, October 23."

"Which would make Tuesday, October 21. The date of Kelly's last diary entry. Nice find, my handsome research hero." She glanced around, then kissed Darrell, lingering there a while and sliding her hand on his cheek. She asked, "How'd you narrow it down to that year?"

"I simply asked Jeeves."

"Who?"

Darrell chuckled. "Not who. What. Early this morning, while you were still sleeping with a smile, I used an internet search engine I like called 'Ask Jeeves' to search for when Martin Luther King led the sit in at the diner in Baltimore. Summer 1964. Then, to be sure, I checked when 'My Girl" by the Temptations was released, and it turned out to be 1964."

"Handsome *and* smart." She looked at him in the small space. "Find any mention of the death of our ghost fellow?"

"No luck so far. I've checked the issues starting with October 21 and have scrolled forward. Ran into this." He jabbed at the screen. "No mention in the local paper of the death, suicide or otherwise, of any Wilshire students. Of course, they have extensive coverage of the engagement of Sally Blackman to Hugh Stewart, complete with a photo of the happy couple. The happy, white couple. Maybe, in '64, the death of a black student didn't merit any ink in Wilshire."

"Even if they wanted to write it off as a suicide, wouldn't there be an entry, in the police blotter or somewhere?"

"I don't know. Remember what I told you about the conspiracy of silence that surrounds a lynching. If it's not documented, it didn't happen."

"Still, rumors have persisted, at least about his suicide," she said. "I recall hearing them even when I was in grade school."

"I'll keep checking the *Gazette* to see if something

surfaces in the next several days. Now that we have a definite date, why don't you scroll through the *Baltimore Enquirer* issues to see if there was a mention there?"

"Sounds like a plan, teach." Erin gave him a quick peck and scooted her chair back to her own carrel. She resumed adjusting her microfilm.

Darrell studied her for a moment, her head bent toward the glowing screen, intent on the task. Whatever else happened, at least he'd found her. Enough reason alone to be here.

Anyway, now they had Kelly's full name. Maybe their luck would hold and they could find a name for his spectral visitor. He returned his attention to his own machine.

A few minutes later, Erin announced, "Bingo. My turn."

Darrell slid his chair into her narrow carrel as she fine-tuned the focus. She pointed a pink fingernail at the bright monitor. "Remembered seeing a weekly roundup of area news in the Saturday *Enquirer* editions." The tip of her finger touched the glass. "This is it for Saturday, October 25th."

Darrell moved his face closer to read the small print. He could see the old newspaper photographed for the digital copy had been smudged, the ink smeared over a few lines, blurring some words. Pulling a handkerchief from his pocket, he wiped the screen.

Erin used the right dial to make the image clearer and then slid her finger down to the bottom of the screen. "Here are the Wilshire items for the week. And *here* is what we're looking for, I think." She leaned her head in next to Darrell and read aloud.

Wilshire Report

A dark green '59 Ford was reported stolen from the property at 823 Water Street, Wednesday of this week.

City Council approved the repaving of the stone walkway in Bayshore Park. The work is scheduled to be completed next spring.

A young colored man committed suicide by hanging himself from the widow's walk at Wilshire High School earlier this week. Local sources only gave his first name (Hank) and said he had been depressed recently.

The final sailboat race of the season, the Wilshire Regatta, will be held this Sunday, October 26.

Erin stopped reading, releasing a sigh. Both stared at the screen and Darrell said, "Hank." Pause. "H. They didn't even bother with a last name."

They leaned back, and she shook her head in disbelief. "Stuck the mention of his death between the city council's sidewalk and the final sailboat race. Incredible."

Turning away from the computer screen, they faced each other. Erin bit her bottom lip.

Darrell placed a hand on her cheek. "That's better than pretending nothing happened, like in the *Gazette*."

She released her lip. "What do we do now? All we have is a first name."

"Well, I think we've probably gotten what we can from these files, but we can check a little longer." Darrell indicated the microfilm. "Then I'm going to take you to Cantlers for lunch. How do crab cakes and

Maryland Crab Soup sound?"

This nudged a small smile from her. "Cantlers, huh? You know how I love crab cakes."

"Believe me you've earned them."

"Then what?"

"Then, my lovely student, *I* continue our research."

"You do? Where?"

"Why, where the rest of the answers lie. At Wilshire High School."

Chapter 36

Halfway into Monday's seventh period, Darrell found himself facing a dour Miss Meredith Merriweather. The veteran Wilshire librarian had barricaded herself on the other side of the wooden counter, buffed to a high sheen and redolent of furniture polish.

"The older school yearbooks are *not* for public examination. Too great a chance they would be defaced," she said in a high-pitched voice. "Those volumes are in the locked reference section. I would have to leave the desk to go into the back room to retrieve the yearbook, and I do not leave the front desk unattended."

Darrell glanced around the nearly empty school library and found only one student with his nose in a science book. "I think it'll be all right, Meredith. I'll defend the front desk for you while you're gone." He tried his most disarming smile.

"I prefer *Miss* Merriweather, Coach Henshaw."

"Please, *Miss* Merriweather. It's important."

The librarian heaved a huge sigh. "I'll be right back." She turned and disappeared into the back room.

Darrell checked his watch. He had only fifteen minutes before the bell, and he'd have to hustle down to the locker rooms to start practice. He'd planned on more time for this, but after his last class, a student had required some individual counseling, and Darrell had spent most of his free period trying to get the rebellious student to chill a little.

And he hadn't counted on Meredith Merriweather, the "Custodian of the Collections."

Used to the friendlier environs of his former high school media center, he'd been unprepared for the stern librarian when he arrived at Wilshire. She looked the part, as if she'd been sent from central casting. A tall, thin woman, she had gray hair pulled tight into a bun, a wrinkled face etched into a permanent scowl, and thick-lensed glasses perched on a beak nose. *Her* library was governed by her three rules. "1) The library is a place for learning, not for browsing. 2) If you are talking, you are not learning. 3) Treat the books with respect or get out." These commandments had been repeated so often, Wilshire students could deliver a near perfect parody, right down to the imitation of her shrill voice. The teens got the message. They were not welcome here.

Merriweather had been here so long she thought she owned the place. Could she have been here in the '60s?

Like the kids, Darrell didn't want to be here either, but he had to go through her to locate the next piece of the puzzle. After he and Al had talked at lunch today, bringing the band leader up-to-date, Al had confirmed Darrell's speculation. The student information he was looking for could most likely be found in the old school yearbooks.

Merriweather bustled back to the front desk, dusty volume in hand. "Coach Henshaw, have you washed your hands?" She did not hold the book out.

Like some guilty student, Darrell glanced down at

his hands, embarrassed for a moment he'd forgotten to wash them, twice. He hadn't, of course. "They're quite clean. I washed them after changing the oil in my car." He grinned.

Miss Merriweather did not. "We cannot be too careful. These books are old. They require special care." She extended her arm, the volume in hand.

Darrell took the old yearbook and turned to leave.

"Oh, that book cannot leave the library. It is part of our vintage collection, and library rules state those volumes cannot leave the premises."

"Right," Darrell mumbled and slid into an uncomfortable, wooden chair at the second table. After he used his handkerchief to wipe off the book, he examined it, briefly fingering the raised letters and numbers on the tan cover, "Wilshire High School, The Wave, 1964." He opened the volume, thumbing through until he found the table of contents. Scanning the headings, his index finger stopped at the third listing. "Juniors...page 42."

He flipped through the pages, some of which were stuck together. When he got to the section he wanted, he studied the layout. Two pages of tiny black and white photos—little more than head shots with names beneath—stacked eight across, eight neat rows per page. An occasional candid shot of students at a dance or on the basketball court interrupted the spread.

Darrell thought it best not to bring the Polaroids, but figured he'd be able to recognize both Kelly and Hank from their school photos.

When he glanced up, he noticed Merriweather glaring at him, and he turned so he could study the yearbook without her seeing what he was looking for.

He also took the opportunity to align the bottom of the yearbook exactly with the table's edge.

The students were listed only by first initial and last name, the photos of guys and girls intermixed on the page. He followed the alphabetical order of the pictures to the H's, about a third of the way down. The fourth H in, he found her, K. Halloran. Hair in the swoop style of the time, looking somewhere between brown and red in the photo. Bright eyes and same smile he'd seen on the Polaroid. And in his dreams. When he saw her there, staring back at him, crammed in between S. Hall (male) and B. Hart (female), it made the whole thing more real.

He stole another glance up and caught the librarian still watching him, like a suspect he thought. He looked up and met her hard stare until she turned away, busying herself with some returned books.

Was she simply nosy, or was she taking special interest in what he was doing?

To make sure she couldn't make out anything, he turned so his body would block her view. Studying the photo arrays, he noticed something else. On the first page he saw no black faces. He moved his finger faster over the images, searching for any "coloreds" as they would've called them. At the bottom of the second page, he found them. There were only twenty-two and they were in a separate section, cordoned off from the whites by some text and a candid photo of a white couple at prom. The segregation, even without the heading *Colored Juniors*, spoke volumes. But he realized this separation made his job easier. Since he didn't have a last name for Hank, he'd have to check males and try to match one with the first initial H. After a quick glance at his watch, he moved his finger atop each photo and name. He found him in the final photo. Handsome, young, black man, his face so large it almost filled the frame with the name beneath, H. Young.

Darrell simply stared at the picture. Details of the strong face came back from both the Polaroid and his visions. He smiled. Under his breath, he said, "Good to meet you, Hank Young."

Ghost or not, he was a real person.

He wanted to make a copy of each photo to show Erin and stole a glance back to the front desk. The counter stood empty. He heard movement next to him. Turning, he found Merriweather huddled at the library stack behind him, pretending to be re-shelving some books. As soon as Darrell caught her, she turned away, her attention back to the biography shelf.

When she walked to the back wall, he returned his attention to the final photo, held his finger on it, and flipped the page back to Kelly's picture. He glanced from one to the other, studying them as if to make sure neither would disappear like his basketball autograph. They didn't.

Now, he knew they went to school together. They were real kids.

The bell rang, and Merriweather strode over next to where he sat. As soon as the clanging stopped, she said, "I will take the yearbook now. I have to leave early and I need to lock it up before I go."

Darrell's gaze moved from the volume now closed in front of him to her. The dour librarian stood over his chair, glasses almost at the end of her beak nose and wrinkled hand thrust in his face. He rose till he was standing over her, very close, close enough to smell her sweat. He returned her glare.

"Thanks so much for *all* your help." He handed her the *1964 Wave* and headed for the door.

"Did you find what you were looking for?" the librarian asked, the words sounding more like an interrogation than a question.

At the open door, Darrell stopped and smiled. "Yeah. The photos were right there."

"Whose photos?" Merriweather—who had to leave—stood rooted to the spot next to where he'd been sitting.

His paranoia kicking in, Darrell decided he needed a plausible lie. He kept his smile plastered. "Oh, a couple of my kids told me about their parents who were students here, and I thought I'd have a look at their old photos." He stepped through the door into the hallway congested with teens.

As the door closed, Merriweather called, "Which students?"

Darrell kept walking.

Chapter 37

"According to the news coverage, you're probably right, Tanya. The beating of Matthew Shephard is being called a hate crime," Darrell explained to his government class. "No one's disputing that. The question I'm asking is, what gives the government the right to prosecute the two men who beat Matthew Shephard differently because they committed a hate crime?"

"Well, this Matthew guy was gay," offered Tanya.

Another student snickered.

"That's enough," Darrell chided the class and then to Tanya, "Agreed, but where does the *authority* come from to prosecute these men differently for the crime?"

"The constitution?" the female student tried.

"Can anyone else help her?" Darrell's eyes swept the class.

Justin, a dark-haired athlete with intelligent, blue eyes raised a hand and Darrell nodded. The student said, "The federal government could only prosecute these men if Congress passed a law—"

A light knock at the door interrupted him. "Hold that thought." Darrell went to the door, opening it.

A student office aide, Britney, a pretty blonde from another of his classes, was standing in the doorway. "Mrs. Sinclair asked me to give you a message." Her eyes glanced around the teacher into the classroom and she gave a short wave.

"Okay, Britney, what's the message?"

"Oh, sorry, Mr. Henshaw. She asked if you could stop by after classes. She has something for you." Her gaze migrated from the teacher to the students again.

"Don't worry. I'll tell him you said hi." Darrell saw her cheeks flush before he closed the door and turned back to the class. "Justin, your pretty girl says hi. Now, you can finish."

"Uh…oh, yeah." Justin blushed. "Congress passed a law authorizing federal law enforcement authorities with this power."

The young man continued his answer, but Darrell only half listened. He knew Justin, being the great student he was, probably knew the law about as well as his teacher. Nervous, Darrell had fought all day to stay focused on his teaching. Now, Britney had delivered the message he'd been waiting on.

Harriet Sinclair had found something. Early this morning before classes, he had stopped by to seek the school secretary's help. Checking to make sure they were alone in the small office, he'd asked her if she could find the school record of Kelly Halloran, a senior in 1964-65.

"Hum, '64. That'll be back in the archives." Harriet continued processing the pile of excuse slips. "With moving to the new building, we've been packing up the old files."

"Can you still get to the old files?"

Harriet looked up at him. She wore her usual gray, this time in slacks, blouse, and jacket. The blazer sported a little color, one lapel with a brightly painted pin in the shape of an old school building and the other with a "GO PIRATES!" button in gold and black. "If the file's there, I can probably find it. I labeled all the boxes myself. It'll take some time to go through them."

"If it's there?"

"Sometimes, files go missing. Especially over time, old files disappear."

Darrell thought, particularly if *they* wanted it to go missing. "I appreciate your help. I know how busy you are. I mean, since you practically run this place."

That elicited a grin from the secretary. "Don't let Mr. Douglass hear you say that. I'll see what I can find. Graduating class of '65 then?"

"I don't know if she graduated, but I know she was in the '64 yearbook as a junior and would have been a senior in '64-'65."

"This important to you, Coach?"

Darrell hadn't been prepared to give a reason, so he improvised. "Going through some of the old stuff in my office, I found a diary of hers and thought she might like it back."

"Some thirty years later?" The gray eyebrows raised.

"Never can tell. May be important to her."

"What information are you looking for?" she asked.

"You know, what I need to reach her. Phone, address, parents."

"I'll see what I can do. Now, go teach our kids what a great country we have."

"Yes, ma'am, and thanks."

From her reaction, he wasn't sure what to expect. That had been six hours earlier. Now, she had something for him. What?

"Coach? Coach, is that right?" he heard Justin ask.

"I couldn't have explained it much better myself. Thank you. I'd like everyone else to review chapter twenty-seven, pages 155-160 for tomorrow."

The bell clamored and the students reacted, slapping their books closed and filing out, headed to their last period. Done with classes for the day, Darrell collected his teacher editions and gradebook and hurried down the hall to the office, and Harriet.

When he arrived, the secretary was on the phone, and she waved him to come around the counter. He did and stood next to her desk, waiting. He glanced around. The door to the rear office, Douglass' office, stood open, and Darrell could see in and noticed it was empty.

She hung up the phone. "Mr. Douglass asked me to remind you he's scheduled to observe your class tomorrow." She glanced at a calendar on her desk. "No, Thursday, sixth period."

Darrell's face dropped. Not what he was hoping for. Maybe he made a mistake coming to her. "Uh, yeah, I, I've got him down." He turned to leave. "Did you have any luck—"

Harriet interrupted him by extending a scrap of paper. "I think that's what you asked for, but don't know if it will be any help. The information's more than thirty years old."

"Still, it's something."

"Oh, and you were right. According to the file, Kelly never graduated. Said she dropped out October, 1964."

"Thanks, Harriet, I owe you."

When Darrell turned to go, the secretary put a hand on his arm. Her eyes focused on his. "October '64.

Wasn't that around the time that poor black kid hanged himself?"

His paranoia on alert, Darrell wasn't sure what her question meant. "Harriet, were you here then?"

She grinned at him. "Not that old, kid. We didn't move to the shore till 1970. Been here since."

Her answer was so direct and disarming, Darrell decided to level with her. "Yeah, from what I've been able to find out, she went missing about the same time the kid died."

"Good luck then. Hope you can find her." Harriet returned her attention to handling money from the latest fundraiser. Darrell heard her counting the bills aloud. He headed out, but when he got to the door, Harriet called, mid-count, "Thirty-five. I hope you can help our ghost find some peace. Forty. Forty-five."

Chapter 38

"Think Kelly's mom still lives there?" Erin asked as Darrell drove.

As they headed away from the shore, they watched as the neighborhoods deteriorated and houses became more rundown. As soon as Darrell got the name and address from Harriet, he called Erin, who had the day off, and explained he was going to try to see the mom after practice. Erin asked to come along, so he'd picked her up.

"We'll see," Darrell said. "Before practice, I called information and asked for the number and address for Sheila Halloran, the name I got for Kelly's mom. The computer voice spit out the same info I got from Harriet, S. Halloran. 8547 Homesteader Court."

Turning, Erin petted the brown pug who sat in the back seat next to the open window, tongue lolling to one side. Evening had fallen, and the weather had darkened, clouding up and chilling the temperature. Cool air streamed in the lowered window next to the dog, and both Erin and Darrell were wrapped in sweatshirts. Erin scratched the dog behind the ears. "Glad you brought Pogo."

"I've been so busy lately I haven't had much time for him, so I thought he'd like a little excursion."

"He's glad to be here, aren't you, boy?" The pug turned from the window and licked Erin's hand.

"You said you know about Homesteader Court?" Darrell asked as he stopped at a light, glancing down at a map in his lap.

"Here, let me have that." She snatched up the map. "If it's the same Homesteader I remember, it's a trailer court, and *not* a nice one. I haven't been there for years, but it had a rep for drugs and prostitution, among other things. Was there in my, uh, wild years." She watched the street signs and studied the map. "Take the second right here."

"And Kelly grew up here." Darrell turned down the shadowed street.

"Don't know what it was like back then, but probably not good." She pointed at a weathered wooden sign, with several carved letters missing. "There it is."

As Darrell turned the car into the gravel driveway, the tires bumped over the uneven ground and jostled the dog. Pogo emitted a low growl. "Sorry, guy," Darrell said and slowed the car, eyeing the sign.

HOM ST AD R LUX RY HO ES

The trailer court had no lights, and the dark seemed to close in around the dilapidated mobile homes, each one looking more forlorn and wretched than the last. As they rolled down the row, searching for house numbers, they studied the trailers and patches of dirt that passed for yards on both sides of the pot-holed lane. Broken down cars sprawled in front of trailers, worn spare tires and rusted car parts littering the yards. Two barren lawns even sprouted discarded porcelain toilets with rust stains crawling down the sides.

"The number again?" Erin asked.

Darrell pulled the slip out of his shirt pocket. "8547." He lowered his window to peer out, and the stench of mold hit him. As he studied the trailers passing on the left like collapsing, derelict ships washed up on the shore, he noticed a name over a door on one, "Manhower." He had a student in the third period with that name, Amber Manhower, he remembered. This was her home? God, what it must be like to grow up here. To come home to this, every day.

"Okay, that one is 8533." Erin pointed to a leaning mobile home on her side with faded green siding peeling off, numbers barely visible under a yellowed porch light. The structure looked like it could cave in at the next brisk wind. "Should be on this side and a few houses down."

Darrell rolled the car past the next two lots and strained to look. "There's 8543. Got to be the next one."

He steered the car into the next driveway, a gutted dirt path with a few remaining pebbles scattered around, and examined the narrow metal building illuminated by the car's high beams. A small wooden porch clung precariously beneath the only door of the trailer, the once-white metal supports rusted brown in long, vertical streaks. Cigarette butts, beer cans, and booze bottles lay discarded along the wooden floorboards of the porch. When the bright headlights struck it, the siding appeared a dirty gray, patches of darkened rust consuming the metal edges.

Darrell doused the lights, casting the space in near blackness, and Erin let Pogo out. Together, they approached the porch, the pug at their heels. From inside the trailer, a faint light oozed from a window to the left of the door. They stepped onto the wooden deck, warped boards creaking under their weight.

Darrell moved forward and searched for a doorbell. Finding none, he knocked twice on the door, the hollow thumps echoing and dying away. Nothing stirred.

Not sure they had the right trailer, or anyone was home, Darrell figured he had nothing to lose. He knocked and called, "Mrs. Halloran?"

No response.

He tried again, a little louder, "Sheila Halloran?"

Silence. He glanced at Erin, who shrugged. The Pug shuffled forward and pawed the door. Darrell said, "Okay, Pogo, let's go. Maybe, we'll check at a neighbor's."

Erin and Darrell turned to step off the rickety porch, the dog following.

"Who wants to know?" a gravelly voice called from behind the closed door.

The pug reversed his direction and scampered to the door, pawing the rotting wood, Darrell right behind. "Mrs. Halloran, my name is Darrell Henshaw. I'm a teacher at Wilshire High School, and I'd like to ask you a few questions about your daughter, Kelly."

"She ain't here," the woman's voice started and then erupted in a fit of coughing. "That bitch ain't been around for years."

Darrell glanced over at Erin and said, "Could we come in? We only have a few questions. It won't take long."

"We?" The voice behind the door coughed again.

"I have a friend with me, Erin Caveny."

"Well, I guess it's okay, if you leave the mutt out there." Three more hacks.

Darrell tried the door handle, and it turned in his hand. "Pogo, you stay here."

The dog sat on the wood, and Darrell held the door open, following Erin through. Inside, they found a scene as gloomy as outside, the space enveloped in shadows. The only illumination came from a small flickering television across the room. Supermarket magazines lay sprawled on the floor, open to some lurid story. Scattered among the tabloids sat crumbled-up bags from fast food joints splotched with congealed grease. As he examined the mess, Darrell felt the compulsion to clean it up, to organize everything into some kind of order.

How can anyone live like this?

The place was sweltering, and cigarette smoke hung thick in the air, so thick Darrell could almost feel it clinging to his clothes. When he opened his mouth to speak, he could taste it. *Damn.* He'd have to shed all his clothes before he went into his apartment, or it would reek for weeks.

Across the room, he could barely make out a figure slumped in a recliner, beer bottle in one hand.

Another spasm of coughing erupted from the woman. "Well, don't stand there," she called. "Come over here where I can see ya."

Darrell and Erin stepped around the debris. The woman's face was more wrinkled than any Darrell had seen, and her greasy, white hair hung in uneven tufts around her face. She was wearing an oversized jogging suit, her thin frame swallowed up in the folds.

"Mrs. Halloran?" Darrell asked again.

"Yeah, yeah." The woman brought the footrest down. She eyed her visitors up and down. "Okay. Had to make sure you weren't no N—" She looked up and must have noticed Darrell's expression because she finished, "those people. You know you can't tell by their voices anymore."

Darrell and Erin exchanged glances, but neither said anything.

"What are ya asking bout Kelly for?" Sheila Halloran snapped.

Erin said, "We're trying to locate her."

Darrell added, "I'm a new coach at Wilshire, and I was cleaning out some things at the athletic office and came across something of hers. From when she was in school. Thought I'd try to return it to—"

"Don't know. Don't care." The woman started coughing again, long strings of hacks that made her thin body shudder. The fit went on for half a minute, and Darrell waited. Before the last hack erupted from her mouth, she snagged a cigarette from a pack on the table next to her and lit it. She inhaled and blew smoke out. "Yeah-h-h."

Darrell did some quick calculations in his head. If this woman was, say sixteen when she had Kelly, she'd be almost seventy now. He studied her. She looked every bit of it, and he couldn't figure out how she made it this long.

Halloran put the cigarette in an overflowing ashtray and took a long pull on the beer. She belched.

"You are Kelly Halloran's mother?" Darrell asked.

"Yep, for what it's worth. That bitch ain't been around here for thirty years. Good riddance. What a tramp." She put her elbows on her knees and stared up at her visitors, cigarette in her right hand, bottle in her left. "Did ya know she had this thing for this big black N...guy." She pointed with the neck of the bottle. "When word got around, I couldn't go anywhere without people laughing at me and pointing fingers."

Erin looked across and must've read Darrell's face because she broke in, "Do you have any idea where we could find Kelly?"

Halloran cranked up the footrest and lay back in the chair again. "Hell if I know. Last I heard, she was up in Philly."

"Would you have an address or phone number for her?" Erin pressed.

"Got a number over there on the fridge." She gestured with the beer. "Some dive she worked in. Someplace in Philly. Number's a few years old. Don't know if she's still there."

Darrell walked over to the refrigerator. Take-out menus from area restaurants and carry-outs littered the entire front. Studying the collection of flyers, he couldn't see anything else so he lifted each one up and searched underneath. He didn't find any number. He turned to ask and saw it. On the side of the fridge hung a small yellowed post-it, the edges curling up. He pulled it off and read it, only a name and a number.

Kelly 215-934-3768

From his shirt pocket, Darrell retrieved the note he'd gotten from Harriet and wrote the number down. He put the faded post-it back, making sure to secure it under a magnet, though he doubted this woman would have much use for it. He walked over to where Erin still stood, watching Halloran lying back in the chair.

"Thank you, Mrs. Halloran. We'll see ourselves out." He glanced down at the prone woman and noticed she was asleep, her eyes shut and her mouth open. The beer bottle sat in her lap and the burning cigarette in an overflowing ashtray. Darrell reached down and snuffed out the cigarette.

This was what Kelly was dealing with more than thirty years ago.

Darrell and Erin turned and hurried outside, not caring if the slammed door woke her. "I need to try this number," he said, as soon as they were outside, "and hope Kelly's nothing like her mother."

Chapter 39

"How *old* was the writer of this diary?" asked Tiffany, the studded girl who had challenged Darrell the first day of class. He'd been coaxing her ever since, trying to draw her out of her self-imposed, anti-academic shell. Sometimes, it was working, like now.

"Around your age, seventeen or eighteen," he answered. "And she lived around here about thirty years ago."

Darrell had decided to pull two excerpts from Kelly's diary, the one about her meeting Martin Luther King and a second about the sit-in at the pool. He hoped Kelly's words might hook them. He was right.

"You think that stuff about acid is on the level?" asked Robert, a wiry, blond-haired youth, one of the few in his class who didn't come from poverty and whose dress screamed that fact. "They did all that merely to keep some blacks out of a motel pool? Hard to believe."

"Hey, don't even go there, white boy," challenged Tyler, his brown head gleaming in the fluorescent light. He sat two rows across from Robert and turned to face him. "In the sixties, it wouldn't surprise me. Not at all."

Robert raised both palms in surrender.

Tyler turned his gaze back to the front and held the two stapled pages over his head. "Hey, teach, where'd you get this?"

Darrell looked at the student and then to the rear of the room. In the last desk sat Principal Jeb Douglass, completing Darrell's official fall observation. Darrell smiled at both Tyler and his boss. At least, the lesson wasn't crashing and burning.

Darrell returned his attention to the students. "A local heard about our 'primary source' project and thought you might be interested in the diary, since it was from around here. They lent me a copy, and I pulled a couple of the entries from it."

"How do we know this really happened?" asked Tiffany. "I mean the girl could've made this stuff up for her diary. Some girls do that, you know."

"Good question, Tiffany," answered Darrell. "Of course, we know she's writing about things as *she* sees them, which may, or may not, be accurate. So, with primary sources like this, we need to cross check to see if we can confirm the details."

"And?" Tyler dangled his handout in the air.

"And that's what I did. I checked the *Baltimore Enquirer* for the date of Dr. King's protest at the pool and found an article with pretty much the same details."

"*Pretty much* the same?" asked Tiffany.

With her question, Darrell knew he'd hooked her and, glancing at the rest of the students, most of the class. He loved watching the light bulb go on and stole a quick look at Douglass. He released a breath. Thanks, guys.

"Well, the editors of the *Baltimore Enquirer* didn't quite see Dr. King in the enlightened manner the diary author did." He held up his copy of the front page article from the newspaper. "They confirmed the details about the acid in the pool but called Dr. King a rabble rouser and agitator—"

The bell clanged, cutting him off. As the students got up and headed out with papers in hand, Darrell called, "More tomorrow."

When the last of the teens exited, the principal extricated himself from the old-style student desk. "I'll be damn glad to get into the new building and replace these ancient desks with new tables and chairs." He strode to the front and closed the door.

Darrell retreated to behind his teacher desk and straightened the sets of student papers, using the top surface to make three near-perfect stacks aligned along the right side of the desk.

Douglass glanced at his watch. "This is your plan time, right? You have any place you need to be right now? If not, I'll give ya a few impressions while they're fresh."

Darrell realized his boss wasn't really asking, so he indicated the open chair beside his desk. He sat, too. Nervous about the evaluation, he simply wanted it over. The lesson had gone well, but he figured Douglass would pick at something.

More than anything else, though, he wanted to get back to a phone.

When he and Erin had arrived at her apartment last night after their visit with Sheila Halloran, he asked about going inside, but Erin turned him down. She had to be at the hospital by six a.m. Grinning, she claimed if they went inside, they might not get much sleep. Instead, they'd heated up his car.

By the time he got back to his place, he decided it was too late to try to reach Kelly, so he waited till today. He'd called the number twice during lunch and got nothing. No Kelly. No voicemail. Nothing. When he dialed the Philadelphia exchange, the phone rang and rang. The second time, he counted fifteen rings before he hung up. He wanted to try again before he had to leave for their game.

"First of all, pretty good class," Douglass started. "Nice to see you got Tyler and Tiffany involved. Not an easy task. You know those two got quite a reputation in the office."

"Thanks. I've been working with them. Sometimes, it pays off."

Douglass raised his eyebrows. "I got to tell ya. When I heard about your 'primary source' project, I doubted it would work with *these* kids." One bony hand gestured to the empty desks. "But it looks like you might've found a way."

"We'll see. Still a long way to go yet, but they seem to be into it."

"You need to work more on classroom protocol, though," said the principal.

"Protocol?" Darrell felt a bead of perspiration roll down the side of his face.

"You know, like making kids raise their hands before answering."

Darrell nodded, holding his breath again, waiting. He knew there'd be more.

"The class was a little slow getting started, but overall pretty good. I liked most of what I saw. I'll complete the eval form and get it to you tomorrow." Douglass stood up and leaned over the desk, the pungent odor of nicotine fouling the air between them. Darrell tried not to wince.

The principal continued, "Oh, and before I forget,

the team is doing great. Four n' two already. Long time since the Pirates had that kind of record. The kids' new uniforms look sharp, don't they?" Douglass looked at Darrell. "You send a proper thank you to Williams, Remington, and Jefferson yet?"

Darrell felt his face flush. "Sorry. Been a little busy."

"Yeah, I heard. Heard you been asking about some student from back in the sixties. Something to do with this diary lesson?"

Darrell managed, "Yeah," but when he saw Douglass' face, he didn't think the principal believed him.

Douglass took three steps to the door. Hand on the door knob, he turned back. "Son, ya might want to stick to teaching and coaching. I don't know where you're headed with, uh…your primary sources project. You be careful. Sometimes, it's better to let sleepin' dogs lie." He pulled the door and stepped into the opening, twisting his head around. "Oh, and good luck tonight."

Chapter 40

When Douglass disappeared through the doorway, Darrell was up and moving, the principal's warning echoing in his ears. The team was scheduled to leave in forty minutes, but he wanted to try the number for Kelly again, before they left. He hit the stairs, taking them two at a time, figuring if he used the phone in his office, he'd at least have privacy. By the time he got to the top floor, his breath came in ragged gasps.

He'd better do a few extra miles along with the players next week.

Atop the stairs he approached his office, pulling the key ring out of his pocket and flipping through to find the right one. When he was six feet from the door, it opened slowly in front of him, as if some unseen hand held it wide.

He'd locked the door earlier. He knew it.

Staring ahead, he stopped breathing and jammed the keys back in his pocket. He stepped into the office and exhaled, his breath becoming a tiny white puff in front of his face. A chill wrapped around him. He shivered, the hairs on his neck prickling again. Eyes darting left and right in the small room, he saw no one. But he was not alone.

He shut the door and whispered, "Hank, is that you? Are you here?" He waited, for something. For an answer, for the chill to leave, for the hairs on his neck to relax. Nothing happened. He stared at the closed door and spoke again, only slightly louder. "Hank, I think I'm piecing together what happened." He turned and checked the whole space, his gaze searching the room and returning to the door. Nothing.

The old casement window slammed shut. Darrell spun around. He ran over and fumbled with the rusty latch and, with a little effort, got it locked in place. He was positive it had been closed and locked when he left. Looking out at the widow's walk, he half-expected to see Hank's apparition. Of course, the walk was empty. The green copper top of the cupola gleamed in the sunlight. As he stood there staring, he realized the cold had...vanished. He turned and studied the office. He glared at the basketball, as if willing *it* to jump off the shelf. Again.

He checked his watch and realized he'd lost...fifteen minutes? Then he remembered why he came up and went to the phone. Pulling the slip out of his shirt pocket, he punched the numbers again. "Come on, Kelly. Pick up," he said, more to himself than to the phone, but all he heard was an endless series of hollow rings. No answer. He replaced the receiver.

Maybe the number was a bust. Sheila Halloran said it had been years since she used it. Maybe Kelly changed her number, didn't want her mom to have the new one. He wouldn't blame her.

He shot another glance at his watch and decided he'd better get moving, if he was going to make it. He'd try Kelly's number later tonight. Reaching into his pocket, he retrieved his keys and, looking around, asked aloud, "Should I even bother to lock up?" No answer came, of course, and he twisted the key in the lock, listening to the tumblers click in the ancient mechanism.

"Hey, Mr. Henshaw," called a reedy voice from behind. He jumped.

He turned to find Jesse standing in the third floor hallway, leaning on his broom.

"Jesus, Jesse, you scared me."

"Sorry, Mr. Henshaw." The custodian gave a sheepish grin.

"Darrell's fine."

"I'm glad I caught you." Jesse shot a quick glance around. His left hand slid down the broom handle and his right held up a sheet of paper. "I got something for you."

"You do? What is it?"

"I gotta tell you a story first."

Darrell pulled his sleeve back and pointed to his watch. "Can you make it quick? The team bus leaves in twelve minutes." He couldn't afford to make it late again.

"It's about our ghost."

"What about him?"

"I've been seeing and hearing things again...at night."

"What things?"

"Every night this week, while I'm sweeping," the custodian said, leaning closer, "I hear the copy machine. Running like crazy."

Darrell's eyes got wide. "The copy machine? In the teachers' lounge?"

"Yeah, 'cept when I get down there to turn it off, I don't see nothing. No copies, nothing."

"The copier was running, but not making copies?"

Darrell fought to keep the lump out of his throat.

"Yeah and then I seen him."

"Him?"

"Yep, I seen the ghost again," Jesse said.

"When?"

"Most every night this week when I'm making my final rounds."

"What'd you see?"

"I seen the ghost go into one of the classrooms," Jesse rattled on. "Sometimes on the first floor, sometimes the second. Well, he didn't exactly go into a classroom. I mean, the door was closed and locked. I make sure myself every door is locked when I'm finished. Part of my job. But I saw this big figure kinda float through the door. I see him and run down the hall to the room. Well, not run exactly. These old legs don't carry me too fast anymore." He stuck out one stick leg to demonstrate.

"Jesse, what'd you find?"

"Nothing, at first. I mean, I turned the light on and looked around. And every time, no ghost. I'd walk the room, checking. Couldn't find anything. Then I walk over and happen to look down in the trashcan. Every time I find one white sheet of paper in the can. Jus' one."

"Well, you probably forgot it when you emptied the can. Like it got stuck inside."

Jesse smiled. "That's what I thought too, at first. So the next night I made extra sure I got everything out of those cans. I mean everything. Then I saw the ghost again, going in to room 212. I followed him in, a little faster, you know thought maybe I could catch him, but he was gone, disappeared er something. I went over and found a single piece of paper in the trashcan. You want to know what it said?"

"What?"

"Two words. *HELP ME.*"

"Really? Okay." Darrell nodded. Shot another glance at his watch. "Okay, thanks for letting me know. Glad you told me." When he started to move past the custodian, Jesse reached out and stopped him.

"That's not all."

"What else?"

"Last night I saw *him* again. Same thing. Saw him in the hallway and watched him float through a door. Went in and found a single sheet of paper in the trashcan. You want to know where?"

"Where?"

"In your office."

Darrell's head shot up. "Where?"

The custodian pointed at the closed office door. "Right inside there. Found another paper in your trashcan. The one I'd *emptied* an hour earlier."

"Did it have the two words on it?"

"See for yourself." Jesse handed him a paper. "I figured maybe the ghost meant it for you."

Darrell stared down at the white sheet. Not two words.

DON'T LET THEM GO UNPUNISHED.
HELP ME FIND JUSTICE.
IT'S ALMOST TOO LATE.

Chapter 41

Saturday morning, the only thing on Darrell's groggy mind was hearing back from Kelly. *Diary Kelly.* He still couldn't believe he'd finally gotten through. Kind of.

As he sped through the rain-soaked streets, trying to avoid hydroplaning, he had trouble concentrating on his driving. After losing the game last night in a torrential downpour, he returned to his apartment drenched, exhausted, and pissed. Even though it was 11:30, he was so desperate he'd tried the number for Kelly anyway. Only this time, someone answered. Not Kelly, but another waitress at this bar. Said Kelly was there, but couldn't talk and would call him back. He was still waiting, nine hours later.

He *had* gotten another call, at midnight no less, but not from Kelly. From Jeff Jefferson, the squirrelly salesman who supplied the team with the new jerseys. Jefferson wanted to meet for a "private conversation" some place away from Wilshire. Darrell tried to put him off, but Jefferson insisted and offered the Robert Morris Inn, so Darrell conceded. Besides, he figured with the guy's connection to Douglass and Williams, it was hardly political to blow him off. And at least he'd get breakfast.

The rain had let up, leaving an ominous, gray-shrouded sky and slick roads. And Darrell was on his way to Oxford, late. He'd slept badly all night. Three times during the night, he jerked awake, certain he'd heard the phone ring, but each time discovered only a silent bedroom inside and an angry storm raging outside. So, of course he overslept.

A shrill horn blared, wrenching Darrell's attention back to the road, and he slammed on the brakes. The little Corolla skidded to the left and stuttered to a stop, just in time. He'd missed the stop sign. Nearly ran into a crossing truck. Shit. He willed his respiration to return to normal.

When he got his heart rate back under control, he made the final turn onto Route 33 which took him to the Inn and Jefferson. As he crossed the threshold of the old restaurant, the smells of the place—the odor of old wood and fresh coffee and the tempting aromas of bacon and maple syrup—drew him in and made his stomach growl. An arm heralded him from across the room, and Darrell waved back.

"Thanks so much for coming." Jeff Jefferson was up out of his seat, hand extended. "I really appreciate you meetin' me." He gestured Darrell to the seat opposite. "I ordered some coffee for you. Thought you might need it."

Darrell slid in. "You got that right." He glanced around as he poured from the carafe. The restaurant looked practically deserted, with two couples the only other customers. The brick-lined booth Jefferson had chosen was tucked into a private corner of the dark, wood-paneled room.

"Sorry about the late call last night," Jefferson continued. "I know I shouldn't have, but it was an impulse and by the time I realized how late it was, you were answering and…well, you know the rest."

A server came over, a petite girl dressed in a starched white shirt and black tie, brown hair in a tight bun. She asked for their orders. Darrell studied the options while Jefferson ordered eggs over easy and hash browns. When his turn came, Darrell rattled off a Western omelet with a side of bacon. Then, remembering his host was paying, he added a stack of pancakes.

After the waitress disappeared, Darrell took a sip of his coffee, letting it revive him. "Okay, Jeff, what's so important? Though, I'm certainly not complaining about the breakfast." He tipped the cup. "Great coffee."

Jefferson nodded. "I apologize for the intrigue, but some of what I've got to tell you is, well, embarrassing, and I didn't want to have to worry about other ears." Jefferson leaned out of the booth, glancing around and checking the restaurant before going on. "You probably know I've had a drinking problem. The truth is I've been an alcoholic since my teens, what they call a high-functioning alcoholic for much of that time. Able to get things done, but never able *or* willing to stop drinking."

To Darrell, the man appeared quite sober now, his usual turtleneck and slacks neat and wrinkle-free. Darrell said, "I got a cousin with a serious drinking problem. Cost him his job and his wife. Nearly cost him his life."

Jefferson nodded harder. "Yeah, I've been there. My wife left me years ago when I refused to stop, and if it hadn't been for Bud, who's bailed me out more times than I can remember, I wouldn't have a job now."

The server returned with their breakfast plates. Darrell started in, eating with vigor, while his host picked at his food. After a few minutes of quiet, Jefferson continued, "A few weeks ago, twenty-five days to be exact, I hit bottom. Ran off the road, struck a guardrail, could've killed myself."

Darrell paused between bites. "I didn't hear. I'm sorry."

"I was driving drunk, and it was a couple counties over. Bud helped me out and kept it quiet." Jefferson took a sip of coffee. "Wasn't the first time. This time, though, something snapped. After I dried out in the hospital, I went to my first AA meeting the next day and have been sober twenty-four days. Been to twenty-two AA meetings. That's where I was last night." He paused. "Instead of the game."

"Good for you. Didn't miss much anyway." Darrel grimaced. "Game was a sloppy mess."

"I heard about it. Sorry." Jefferson took another sip. "Anyway, in AA, they tell ya, you have to work the program. You know, one day at a time."

Darrell said, "Not a bad philosophy for life."

Jefferson leaned forward and his voice got quieter. "In the program, for one of the steps, step nine, you're supposed to make amends for past wrongs." Jefferson's gaze searched the small restaurant again. "God, this is hard." His focus returned to Darrell. "I tried to do this once before but couldn't get up the courage. Remember, couple weeks back, I came to your house Saturday morning. Said I was there to show you the new uniforms?"

"Yeah."

"I had decided to tell you then, but when I got there…well, I guess I wasn't strong enough yet. Only a few days sober."

"Tell me what? Why do you need to make amends to *me*?"

"Not you, exactly." Jefferson pulled out a handkerchief and blotted a stream of sweat on his brow. "I heard you've been asking about two students I knew when I was in school, Hank Young and Kelly Halloran."

Darrell's hand stopped in the air, two triangles of pancakes suspended midway between plate and mouth. He set the utensil on the plate. "Who?"

"You know, Coach, the black kid who's supposed to have killed himself. His name was Hank Young. You know, the guy kids say haunts the high school. I heard you've been asking about him. And about a girl named Kelly Halloran."

"Where'd you hear that?" Darrell's throat went dry. He reached for the water glass.

"Not important."

"Uh-huh." Darrell stared at Jefferson. "You said you knew these kids?"

"Yeah, they were in my class at Wilshire, class of sixty-five." Jefferson met Darrell's eyes. "I know you heard the story Hank committed suicide. That's not true. At least, I think it's not. It's all pretty hazy now. It's been thirty-four years, and I was blitzed and don't remember much." Jefferson's face reddened. "Well, I don't know if Hank killed himself, but…I, I think I'm responsible for what happened. According to AA, I'm supposed to make amends for wrongs I've done, so I'm here, telling you. I didn't know who else to tell."

Stunned, Darrell asked, "Can you tell me what you do remember?"

"We found them, you know, together, on the

couch."

"Who?"

"Hank Young and Kelly Halloran, a white girl."

"Where was this?"

"In the athletic office. Right there on the couch in your office. Back then, black and white weren't supposed to, you know. In fact, most people 'round here still ain't too great with that." Jefferson seemed to ease into his telling, his words tumbling faster. "Anyway, back then, we heard Kelly and Hank had a thing going on, and we couldn't stand it. I mean with that long red hair and those big tits, all the guys wanted Kelly, and we find out she's with this N—, I mean black. We went ape. Said we was going to teach 'em a lesson. We yanked them apart and managed to knock Hank out. Man, he was one big dude. And Kelly ran off. No one ever heard what happened to her after that."

Without thinking, Darrell said, "I might have found her, in Philly."

"Oh, good. Then maybe I'll get a chance to make amends to her."

Darrell stared across. "You were wearing white robes, kind of Klu Klux Klan, weren't you?"

Jefferson blue eyes got wide. "Where'd you hear that?" When Darrell didn't answer, Jefferson shrugged again. "Not my idea anyway."

"And you killed Hank."

"No. No, at least I don't think I did, but I'm still responsible for his death."

"What do you mean, you don't think so?"

"I couldn't have killed him. Look at me." He indicated his puny upper body, where the turtleneck sweater hung loose. "It's all pretty hazy."

"But you still feel responsible?"

"Well yeah, I knocked him out, with a trophy or something. After, I got out of there. Don't know what happened, but he ended up…dead."

Jefferson said the last word so soft, Darrell strained to hear it. After a bit, he looked Jefferson in the eyes. "You said 'we.' There were three of you, weren't there?"

Fear ignited in Jefferson's features and his large ears turned red. "How'd you know that?"

Darrell fumbled for an answer. "I-I-I have my sources. Look, Jeff, if you didn't kill him and you want to make amends, who did?"

Jefferson started shaking his head. "No. No, no, no, I'm not doing that, I'm not. I want to make amends for my part in the kid's death, but I'm not going to rat on anyone else. That's on them. But I wanted someone to know. Now I've told you." Jefferson stood. He yanked out his wallet and tossed a few bills on the table, leaving his breakfast untouched. "Thanks for meeting me and hearing me out."

Darrell watched him disappear through the doorway. So someone *had* lynched Hank. And Jefferson was one of the three guys, but not the one who killed Hank.

Who were the other two?

Chapter 42

When Darrell walked through the door, Pogo crashed into him, tail wagging, and jumped up onto his legs.

"Hey, boy." Darrell reached down and scratched the fluffy skin on the dog's neck. He walked over to check his answering machine. Nothing. No message from Kelly. He glanced at his watch. 11:25. Erin wouldn't be up yet, either.

The pug's short stubby legs scratched on the door.

"Okay. Okay, I get it." Darrell opened the front door and let the dog out. At least the rain had stopped.

After hearing Jefferson's admission, Darrell was even more anxious about Kelly's call and couldn't sit still. He stripped the bed and remade it, stretching the sheets so straight the creases disappeared in the deep crimson. As he examined his work, he located a wrinkle near the headboard and leaned across the bed to smooth it out. When he crawled off the bed, his elbow glanced the phone on the nightstand. He stared at the phone, but that didn't make it ring.

He dialed the number and listened to it ring, over and over again. In disgust, he set the receiver back down and moved into the front room, slumping on the couch.

At least now, he'd have something big to share with Kelly, if she didn't already know Jefferson was one of the three attackers. But she had to call back first.

Trying to figure out what to do next, Darrell rubbed a hand over his chin stubble and realized he hadn't shaved or showered. He didn't want to face Erin scraggly like this, still reeking from last night's soggy failure. Other guys could pull off the day-old beard thing, but every time he tried, he simply looked like a homeless bum.

After running the shaver over his face, he stepped into the shower, all the while keeping an ear out for the phone. He hurried and soaped himself from head to toe. As he was rinsing, he heard it.

Ring.

Of course.

He shut off the water and yanked back the shower curtain. Ring. Snatching a towel, he wrapped his body and hurried to the phone. Ring. He grabbed up the receiver with a wet hand.

"Darrell Henshaw," he said, breathless into the phone.

"Hey, Darrell. It's me, Erin." She yawned. "Just got up."

"Oh."

"Well, that's a great way to greet your hard-working girl."

"Sorry." Darrell straightened up and saw he dribbled more water onto the carpet. "I was in the shower and heard the phone. Ran out soaking wet to get it."

"Shouldn't have done that. Would've left a message on your machine. You could've called me back."

"I didn't think it was you."

"Oh?"

"I thought it was Kelly."

"Really?"

"Late last night I finally got through and left a message. Asked her to call back."

"Wanna hear everything," Erin said, excitement in her voice.

"Can I tell you in a bit? I'm waiting for her to call. Besides, I just got out of the shower, and I'm standing here dripping on the floor."

"Standing there, *naked*?"

Darrell found himself getting hard, right there alongside his perfectly re-made bed. "Naked and wet."

"Maybe I should come over now?"

Darrell pictured them entwined on the fresh sheets and grinned, making sure she could hear it. "I'm game."

"Down, boy. Only kidding. Came home from work this morning and literally fell into bed. Woke up a few minutes ago and probably look a mess."

"I doubt it, but you're missing it," Darrell said, drying his back. "But seriously, I need you to come over here, so I can catch you up. I have a lot to tell you, but I don't want to tie up the line in case Kelly calls. And I need to be here, for her call."

Erin chuckled. "You know how to tempt a girl. I'll pull myself together and be over."

By the time he wiped up the water and finished dressing, he heard Pogo pawing the front door. He hurried and let the dog back in. When the pug tried to bound through the opening, Darrell grabbed him by the neck. "Hold on there, boy. Not so fast." He carried the pug over to the sink and cleaned off the dog's muddy paws. "That's better. Now, no brown footprints all over the apartment." Pogo licked Darrell's hand.

Picking up the phone, he was busy placing an order to the local pizza place when he heard a knock on the door. He hollered, "It's open."

Erin came through, looking fresh in a white knit sweater, stone-washed jeans, and black boots, hair still wet from a shower. He smiled at her as he finished, "See you in a bit, then." He turned to Erin. "Thought you'd probably be hungry, so I ordered us a pizza—onions, mushroom, and sausage."

"You know what I like." Erin walked into the kitchen, Pogo close on her heels. Reaching into the bottom drawer, she pulled out a doggie treat and tossed it to the pug. The dog grabbed the snack and went over to his corner, gnawing on it. She moved next to Darrell, put her arms around his neck, and kissed him.

He leaned into her, savoring the kiss. "Yum. Not a bad appetizer." His arms circled her waist and pulled her to him.

After a few deep kisses, she eyed him up and down. "And to think, if I'd been here a little earlier, I could've had all this *au naturel.*"

"Well, for you, I'd do a command performance." Darrell grinned, and his hands crawled lower.

Erin slipped from his grasp. "Hold your horses, Romeo. Tell me everything first." She grabbed his hand and tugged him over to the sofa. Pogo, done with his nibbling, came over and settled at their feet.

Darrell started with Jefferson's confession this morning, adding his confirmation about the three assailants in KKK gowns.

"Jeff Jefferson?" she asked, clearly perplexed.

"I know. Hard to take in." After he finished about

Jefferson, he went on to explain about his late night call to Kelly's number, the "McAllisters" answer and the message he left for Kelly.

"McAllisters?" Erin asked.

"I don't know. From the sound of it, probably a bar."

Working backward, he caught her up on the disastrous game last night, told her about the "haunting" in his office before, and ended with Jesse seeing the ghost leave a paper in the athletic office.

"Do you have it?"

A knock on the door interrupted them.

"It looks like our nourishment has arrived."

While Darrell went to the door followed by Pogo, Erin headed into the kitchen. By the time he paid the delivery guy and brought the pizza in, she had dishes, silverware, and sodas on the small kitchen table. Glancing at the arrangement, he set the box down and placed the forks and knives exactly parallel to both plates and moved the pop cans to the two o'clock positions.

If Erin noticed, she didn't say anything, instead opening the carton and serving up slices on both plates. The aroma of garlic and tomato sauce was so pungent, it made his stomach growl—even though he had eaten only two hours earlier—and he joined her in wolfing down the pizza.

"Don't let this get on the floor." He tossed a bit of sausage to Pogo, who scarfed it up.

Erin wiped her lips with a napkin. "So wrapped up in your story, forgot how hungry I was. Thanks." She took a drink. "Can I see the paper Jesse found now?"

"Sure." Darrell got up and washed his hands at the

sink, twice, drying them with three paper towels. He went into his bedroom and returned with his satchel. Taking out his clipboard, he opened it, found what he wanted, and set the sheet on the table in front of her.

Erin stared at the paper and, without touching it, read the message. She glanced up, a puzzled look on her face. "What do you think it means, it is almost too late?"

Careful with the edge of the paper, Darrell picked it up and replaced it inside his clipboard. "I'm not sure, but I may know someone who might."

"You do? Who?"

He pulled a business card from a pocket in the satchel and handed it to Erin, who took it and studied it. The card had an image of a purple hand with an eye in the palm and a few printed words to the right.

Erin read, "Natalia Pavlenco, Psychic Medium with other talents." She glanced up at Darrell. "This the girl Al introduced you to?"

Darrell gave a quick nod.

"You said she was this weird medium who lived in this sleazy place. What other talents?"

Chapter 43

It required major negotiations to arrive at a resolution.

For a while, Darrell thought it would have been easier to mediate the Israeli-Palestinian conflict. But in the end, Erin had come up with a compromise, and only if she drove. After extracting a few more details about Natalia—what did she look like, how did she act toward him, how old was she—Erin would not hear of Darrell meeting the medium alone.

"But I need you to man the phone, in case Kelly calls," Darrell had said. "The girl who answered at McAllister's said Kelly worked late last night, so I figured she'd sleep in and maybe call when she got up. She could call anytime."

Erin scanned Darrell up and down. "If you think I'm going to let you meet up alone with a hot looking harlot, even if she moonlights as a medium, you're crazy." She shook her head. "But you're right. Someone needs to stay by the phone."

She put her finger to her mouth, and Darrell thought how much he liked those lips. He needed Natalia's help, but it felt *really* nice that Erin was so protective of him. And jealous.

Erin went over to the phone. "I'll see if Sara can come over, in case Kelly calls while we're gone." Snatching up the receiver, she called their friend, gave a brief explanation, and hung up. "She's on her way over and will hold the fort down for us."

"Okay, let me check if Natalia can see me." Darrell glanced at Erin. "Er, I mean see us." He grabbed the business card off the table and called. It took him even less time. "She's open for the next two hours." He looked at Erin. "Said she has a busy night scheduled."

Erin threw a piece of pizza at him, which he caught.

A few minutes later, Sara arrived, wearing a faded sweatshirt and jeans, and a tired smile, and Darrell and Erin passed her in the doorway, both thanking her. In twenty minutes, they made it across town, found a parking space on a shadowed side street, and climbed the rickety stairs to the medium's apartment.

While Darrell knocked, he noticed Erin's gaze roaming the cracked and damaged walls and ceiling, much as he had on his first visit. "Can't believe Al brought you here—" she whispered. The handle turning cut her off.

When the door opened, Natalia slouched against the wood frame. Her small, shapely figure was encased in a black mini dress, revealing plenty of thigh and, Darrell guessed, even more. Twin spaghetti straps looped over bronze shoulders, allowing the plunging neckline to reveal a generous view of breasts. The red and blue scarf he'd seen on his earlier visit was cinched around her slim waist, causing the dress to ride up even higher.

"Darrell Henshaw, you came back so soon. Have you returned to teach me some *history*?" Her brown eyebrows raised and her mouth creased into a leer. "Perhaps you have returned to sample my other talents?" Her gaze flicked to Erin. "And you brought a friend. *This* could be interesting." A manicured hand made a flourish, inviting them inside.

As they walked through the doorway, Darrell started, "Natalia, this is my friend—"

"Ahem," Erin cleared her throat.

Darrell corrected, "This is my girl, Erin Caveny."

Natalia shut the door and came around Darrell. The two women faced each other, Erin tall, lithe, and athletic, Natalia short, dark, and curvy. The medium stood her ground and glared at Erin. This only emboldened Erin, who edged close enough to tower over the smaller woman. Neither said a word and, as he stood by helpless, their eyes shot daggers at each other.

He really needed Natalia's help, but he didn't want to screw up what he had with Erin.

Natalia's smirk never faltered. She kept her gaze focused on Erin, even though she spoke to him. "I don't normally do a threesome, but for Darrell Henshaw, I will make exception. I can help this one reach great feats in pleasuring you."

Erin spoke through barely gritted teeth. "Don't need any help in that department. I know all about the body. After all, I'm a nurse."

"Still—" Natalia began.

"Natalia, I told you on the phone. I need your help as a *medium*." Darrell placed a hand on her arm.

"Oh, all right." The medium gave a long sigh. "Come, sit at the table as before." She untied the scarf from her waist and fastened it as a bandana cinching her long black hair. Her head jerked toward Erin. "She will have to leave—"

"Not going anywhere," Erin said.

"Then you can stay over there." Natalia pointed to the side of the small apartment that held a queen bed, with ruffled sheets.

Erin stepped past the disheveled bed, went over to the wall, and leaned her back against it. She crossed her arms, and her glare remained focused on Darrell. He swallowed and stepped over to the small round table, taking in the rest of the room. The apartment was spotless, no dishes in the sink, no food left out, garbage can empty.

Did Natalia clean this place up for him?

By the time he settled into the chair, Natalia had again turned out the lights and lit several candles, the last being a tall, green taper on the table. The room darkened and the fragrance of incense drifted into the air. Darrell turned to look where Erin stood and noticed she was almost obscured in the artificial darkness.

"Give me your hands." Natalia's voice mutated to the deep, creamy tenor it had on his earlier visit. He placed his hands in hers and immediately felt the heat radiating from her fingers and up his arms. When he stared down to where their hands joined, he saw only the flickering shadows created by the candles.

"Someone you know has already met her fate," Natalia said.

He said, "Ruby."

"I told you a shroud of malevolence surrounds this spirit. It has already claimed one victim. It vill claim more."

"What? Are you saying more will die?"

Natalia tilted her head back as her gaze drifted to the ceiling. When she brought it down again, her eyes were white orbs. He stared, unable to look away.

Natalia said, "It is unclear but, yes, this evil vill claim more victims. I am not sure how many."

Darrell glanced over at Erin. He could *not* let anything happen to her. "Then I need to stop. I don't want anyone else to get hurt, much less die."

"That is no longer your decision, Darrell Henshaw. Your presence here has opened a portal to the other side. There are those who do not vant this conduit and vill do anything to stop you."

"Oh my God."

Natalia's eyes returned to normal. She gave his fingers a squeeze and unleashed another bolt of heat up his arms. Darrell squirmed, but she didn't let go. "That is not vhy you have come. You have received a message from the ghost, and you need my help with it."

He withdrew two papers from his clipboard he'd placed alongside his chair. "The first is simple. It says 'Help me,' and I found it in the copier. Oh, and I think we found out who the ghost is, er was. His name, I think, was Hank Young, and I believe he was lynched at the school some thirty years ago."

Natalia's glance went from the paper to Darrell. "That is good. If you are correct, it vill please the spirit that someone remembers and perhaps he vill be more open in contacting you."

Darrell laid the second sheet on the table between them. "This was left in my office. It's why I came. What does it mean?" When the medium didn't respond, he asked, "Is it almost too late because of this evil?"

Natalia moved her head slowly, back and forth. "I do not think so. It is…the building."

"What? The high school? What about it?"

"The building is scheduled to be demolished, is it

not, vhen the new high school is finished?"

"Yeah, sometime next summer, I think."

"We believe spirits, like Hank's spirit, are tied to physical buildings, the place of their deaths. His lynching, if you are right. If you are not able to help him take care of his unfinished business, then he vill not be able to cross over and will be trapped forever between vorlds." She looked at Darrell. "He vill become a lost spirit."

"A lost spirit," he repeated.

"Do you know vhat his unfinished business is?" The medium's narrowed eyes held his gaze.

Darrell broke eye contact and looked down at the sheet between them. "It says 'Help me find justice.'"

"Then, that's vhat you must do. Only then can this evil be vanquished and Hank's spirit released."

Chapter 44

Damn. Darrell wished he was driving. He needed to do something with his hands. Other than drum his fingers on the clipboard. Erin was a good enough driver, but he wanted to be behind the wheel. And in control. He watched as she maneuvered the Jeep through the narrow streets of the ugly side of Wilshire back onto Shore Drive. He stared out the window at the rolling waves.

After her bit about "vanquishing evil," Natalia had squeezed his hands again, spending a final bolt of heat up his arms. She'd stood up and, in one smooth motion, transferred the colored scarf from her head to her waist and knotted it. By the time Darrell got himself together and followed, she was at the door, hand extended. "Fifty dollars."

Erin came off the wall. "What?"

Intent to head off another confrontation, Darrell extracted the cash from his wallet and placed it in the outstretched palm.

Natalia's fingers closed around the bills, and the money disappeared inside the black dress between her two large breasts. "Whenever you need more help with the spirit world, Darrell Henshaw," she stopped and eyed him up and down, "or if you'd like to sample my other talents, let me know. I think you'd be...yum."

Erin announced, "We're done here." She yanked

Darrell's arm and propelled him out the door. They hurried down the creaking stairs, onto the sidewalk, and around the corner to their parked car. Neither spoke until they had pulled out of the parking space.

"Do you think she could be right?" he asked, fear edged in his question.

"I think she's weird." Erin never took her gaze off the road. "What is it the thing with the eyeballs? And her voice?"

"Strange, I know. But she knows stuff."

"She seems to." Erin sounded skeptical. "Don't get why guys would want that woman." She chuckled. "Take that back. Of course I do. Reminds me of something Sara once told me. Over the years working in the OB, she's heard pretty much every story you can imagine about how the girls got pregnant."

"Yeah?" Darrell asked, glad for a break in the tension.

"She says a stiff peter has no conscience." She glanced over at Darrell and laughed. "It also explains men's attraction to *Natalia*." She uttered the name in a perfect imitation of the medium's deep voice.

Darrell chuckled. "I can't argue with that. She's over the top, but I still prefer you."

"You better." Erin's glance was stern, but a grin followed it.

Darrell pressed, "What do you think? What if she's right about this evil? About more people dying?" His question hung in the air. Only the hiss of the tires on asphalt broke the silence.

Erin asked, "She predicted Ruby's death? Before?"

"Sort of. She told me 'the malevolence' that took the ghost's life would kill again and that night Ruby was run down." He stared at Erin. "I couldn't live with myself if something happened to you."

"Don't worry about me. I can take care of myself." She shot a quick glance at Darrell, then back to the road. "What she said about the ghost having to find resolution before the building's torn down kinda makes sense."

"Yeah," Darrell agreed. "And what Natalia said maybe explains why Hank has been so desperate to contact me."

"Yeah, maybe the ghost feels you're his last—"

"Look out," Darrel screamed. A truck raced straight toward them. A silver pickup with tinted windows had crossed the centerline and veered into their lane.

Erin spun the steering wheel as the pick up's massive front grill rushed straight at them. The Jeep swung wildly to the right. Its fat tires bounced over the curb. But Erin's maneuvering wasn't fast enough. The truck clipped the rear corner of the Jeep. They skidded sideways across the shoulder. Darrell's gaze darted from the road ahead toward his side window. They were hurtling right at a telephone pole. He let go of the clipboard and raised his hands to brace himself. Heard the sickening crunch of wood against metal. The dash rushed toward his head. Everything went black.

****

When he came to, his senses returned slowly. The bent sheet metal creaking. The waves slapping at the rocks in a slow rhythm. The odor of burnt rubber. A metallic taste in his mouth. An insane throbbing in his temple. Through blurred vision, he saw the hood of the Jeep, bent and bowed. Then he spied a red blotch on the dash. He patted the spot, and his finger came away wet with blood. He touched his forehead and felt more blood. Pulling a handkerchief from his back pocket, he wiped his forehead and stained the cloth crimson. He pressed hard to stop the bleeding, taking three deep breaths.

Darrell had no idea how long he'd been out and, when he glanced at the street, didn't see the silver pick up or any other cars. He turned to tell Erin the coast was clear and realized…she wasn't there.

"Erin?" His gaze darted left and right. "Erin!" Left hand on his temple, he used his right to pull the door handle. It didn't work. The mechanism unlatched, but the door wouldn't budge. He rammed his shoulder into the door. Once, twice, three times, but couldn't move it. Now his shoulder ached, and his head hurt worse.

There were no cracks in the windshield and the driver's door was closed, but he didn't see her anywhere. "Erin?" he screamed.

Darrell's panic grew. His fingers fumbled and unzipped the window frame. He crawled out through the opening and landed clumsily in the dirt. Darrell had to use both hands to right himself, dropping the handkerchief. A trickle of blood ran down the bridge of his nose. He ignored it. No cars came from either direction.

Making a small megaphone with his hands, he called, "Erin, can you hear me?"

The only sound he heard was the swish of the water, a few feet away. He stepped toward the shore and scanned the water and sand. He didn't see her. When he glanced over the top of the Jeep, he saw only an empty field, irregular stubbles of corn stalks sticking out of the ground like a miniature skyline. No Erin. Head hazy, he stumbled to the front of the car. Saw nothing. He hurried around the car on the road side. No Erin. He completed the circle at the rear of the car and stopped.

"Oh, God."

He saw her, lying face down on the pavement behind the car.

Not her. What had he done?

His heart stopped. She wasn't moving.

"Erin." In a flash, he realized he'd found Ruby exactly like this, behind *his* car. He stopped breathing. "No." He knelt next to her and grabbed her arm.

Oh, God, please. She was warm. She was warm.

He turned her over gently and called her name. "Erin?" She was breathing, eyes closed.

Oh, thank you, God, thank you. Please, she has to be okay.

Crying, he hugged her. His arms encircled her. Drops of blood rolled into his eye. He heard her cough.

"Darrell?" She opened her eyes.

Darrell sniffled, his response coming through tear-soaked words. "You're okay. You're okay."

Her hand went to his forehead. "What happened? You're bleeding."

Darrell pulled back, his fingers touching his head. "I'm okay. I've got a small cut and a killer headache—" He stopped and gaped at Erin's chest. Pinned to her muddied sweater was a crumpled sheet of paper. "What the hell?"

Erin, still dazed, stared down at the paper.

With shaky hands, Darrell unfastened the pin and removed it. He laid it on the asphalt next to them. It was the sheet Jesse found in the athletic office, the one Darrell had showed Natalia minutes earlier. But beneath the typed message from the ghost a sentence had been scribbled.

Quit now or next time you'll find this on her corpse.

Chapter 45

"Darrell, now hold still," Sara scolded, as she applied a butterfly bandage to his temple. "I'll have this on in a second, and it should stop the bleeding." She examined her work. "That ought to do it. Though I'd feel better if you'd go to the hospital and have it looked at. You could have a concussion."

"I'm fine." Darrell fingered the bandage, feeling the bump on his forehead. His head hurt like hell and the antiseptic stung, but his gash proved to be their only lasting injury.

When they made it back to the apartment, Sara had taken one look at them and started fussing. Darrell had her check out Erin first. After making sure Erin was okay, Sara tended to him, hovering over him like an overprotective mother. As Sara cleaned and prepped the wound, Erin jabbered on.

"After we hit the pole, I remember seeing Darrell on the seat next to me, his head bleeding. He was out and I leaned over to check him when a car door slammed behind us. Opened my door to call for help and a hand reached in and put a cloth over my nose and mouth. Next thing I remember, I'm waking up and Darrell is holding me crying, his head bleeding on me." She touched the dried blood on her sweater.

"Not any more, I think," Sara said, as her fingers smoothed the edge of Darrell's bandage, making him wince. "I'd guess you were drugged. Chloroform, probably. And you never saw who it was?"

"Never saw a face, only heard a male voice." Erin took the next chair.

"And *you* didn't see anybody, Dashman?" Sara smiled at Darrell.

"Funny." He touched his forehead again. "I don't remember anything till I came to and couldn't find Erin. Then my heart stopped when I saw the message." He glanced at the crinkled paper on the counter. "I don't know how long we would've stayed there if Remington hadn't come by."

Sara washed her hands in the sink. "Trevor Remington? Dr. Remington?"

Erin said, "Yeah, a little after I came to, his Mercedes rolled up." She squeezed Darrell's hand. "He said he was driving to his office to see a patient, saw my car next to the pole, and came to see if he could help. We told him what happened, and he checked us out. He wanted us to go to the emergency room, but I told him we were heading back to see you and he said, 'Sara will take care of you.'"

"See anyone else?" Sara asked.

"Not right after the accident," Darrell said. "A few cars passed us on our way here, but not many. Only person we recognized on our way home was Bud Williams."

"Williams?"

"Yeah, we missed the light by the bank just as Bud was crossing the street. He stopped and looked at the car and asked me if we were all right."

"Like he would care," Erin snarled.

"Anyway, I told him we had a little accident."

"And then we came straight here," Erin added.

Sara pointed to the message on the counter. "Well, somebody wants you to stop asking questions." She turned with her back against the small counter and faced the couple. "Maybe it's time you guys got out of this ghost business."

Erin spoke up first. "I'm not letting some jerk scare me off. This is my town, too. And I hate to admit I agree with that weird medium, but if she's right, someone's got to get to the bottom of all this. Especially, if this kid *was* lynched. Besides, I'm going to get whoever did *that* to my Jeep."

Darrell smiled at Erin. "I'm with Ms. Fearless, here."

Sara eyed them both. "Whatever you do, be careful." She looked at her watch. "Yikes. I've got to get home." She headed toward the door.

Darrell met her there and held it open for her. "No phone calls here?"

"Sorry, quiet and peaceful. Got some reading done." She clutched a paperback and placed a hand on Darrell's arm. "You take care of her, Coach, you hear me?"

"Count on it," Darrell said. "Thanks for everything."

After he closed the door, he walked over to the sink and washed his hands with care, counting to twenty while he kept them under the warm water. He glanced at the digital clock on the microwave. "It's after five already. I'm going to call the number again."

He turned off the water and dried his hands, using his usual three paper towels. When he finished, he picked up the phone and punched in the ten digits he'd memorized. Holding the handset to his ear, he slouched against the counter.

"McAllisters?" came out of the receiver.

Darrell stood up straight. "Yes, hi. Uh, can I speak to Kelly, please? Yes, I'll hold."

Erin got up off the couch and came over next to Darrell. She leaned her head in and he cradled the receiver, so they both could hear.

"This is Kelly," barked a raspy voice over loud country music.

"Hello, is this Kelly Halloran?"

The voice laughed. "No one's called me that for years. I go by Kelly Young."

Darrell thought *Hank Young* and nodded to Erin.

"Ms. Young...Kelly, you don't know me, but my name is Darrell Henshaw, and I'm a new coach at Wilshire High School." He stopped and when she didn't respond, he continued. "Wilshire, Maryland, on the Chesapeake Bay. I think you went to high school here in the sixties?"

"Son, that was a long time ago."

"Yeah, I know." Darrell swallowed. "I was cleaning up the athletic office and found an old diary I think belongs to you."

"Oh, that," the voice on the phone said, followed by a bark. "I'd forgotten about that."

"I'd like to return it to you, if that would be okay?"

"Son, I wrote that when I was a teenager. I appreciate your offer, but you don't have to. It's a long way to Philly."

Darrell heard the music subsiding in the background and used the relative quiet to plunge on. "Ma'am, I'd also like to ask you a few questions about

Hank Young."

The woman sighed and said, "Best man I ever met."

"And Red?"

"Worthless piece of shit."

Darrell heard a gruff man's voice yelling in the background. Kelly yelled back, "Manny, hold your horses. Sorry, the mean boss man says I got to get off the phone."

"Could I come up there? Bring you your diary and maybe talk about what happened to Hank? It's important."

"I'll be there in a minute," Kelly screamed away from the phone, then said in a quieter voice. "I don't see how it can be important. That was a long time ago." There was a pause, and Darrell held his breath, waiting. Finally, she asked, "What did you say your name was?"

"Darrell. Darrell Henshaw."

"Darrell, why don't you come by, say tomorrow around three. I ought to be awake and clear-headed by then." She rattled off an address. "I got to go."

The line went dead, and both Darrell and Erin stared at the phone until the receiver emitted a piercing bleat. He replaced the handset and said, "Kelly Young."

"Alive and well in Philly." Erin flashed him a crooked smile. "Supposed to be a great day for a drive into Philadelphia tomorrow. But we have to take your car."

He kissed her. "Thanks for hanging in there with me."

"I got your back." She kissed him this time, leaning into him, loose strands of her red hair across his cheeks. She hung her arms around his neck. "Man, you feel tense. Have a seat and let me work on you." She led him over to the sofa. She sat next to him, turned him slightly so he faced away and began massaging his shoulders.

"Oh, thanks. That feels better." Darrell released a sigh. "Since we found her, I don't want to wait. I have a feeling we ought to jump in the car right now and go up and see Kelly. Get the whole story."

"Wouldn't do any good. You heard what she said. She's working tonight. Couldn't talk to her anyway." Her fingers worked his skin. "The questions can wait till tomorrow."

"I hope so." Darrell prayed she was right, but even as Erin's fingers kneaded his muscles, he felt the hairs on his neck start to rise. Again.

Chapter 46

Darrell gunned the accelerator, revving the engine, and watched the needle slide past 80. He *needed* to get there. He knew it. He felt sure Kelly had some answers. The skin at the back of his neck still prickled.

Last night he and Erin had checked out the map and figured it would take almost three hours to get to the Philly neighborhood. They wanted to be there by three. In the morning, he let Erin sleep in a bit and made a trip to school to set up the video equipment, so his two assistant coaches could review the game tapes without him. By the time he got to her place, Erin was up, dressed—looking great as always—and ready to roll. Grabbing a sandwich on the way, they headed out of town by 11:30.

Darrell, unable to relax as he twisted and turned the car through the back roads, concentrated on following Erin's directions. Only when he drove onto the entrance ramp for I-95 was he able to take a few deep breaths and settle back. He maneuvered the Corolla into the crush of speeding cars heading into the "City of Brotherly Love" and studied the ten-lane expressway. He had checked—the Eagles were out of town this weekend—and was grateful he didn't have to fight the football traffic.

He caught sight of the fading colors of the trees framing both sides of the highway, the picturesque natural view scarred in places by huge billboards for chain restaurants and hotels. He could be anywhere, he thought, even back home on I-75 in southern Michigan. It didn't look much like the Bay anymore.

Maybe today he'd find some answers. He stole a sideways glance at Erin, next to him with the map in her lap. She must've sensed him looking, because her gaze came up, eyes sparkling, and she grinned at him.

"Another exciting adventure," she said. "Thank you, Mr. Henshaw."

"What for?" Darrell pulled his eyes back to the road as another car squeezed into the lane in front of him.

She chuckled. "Life wasn't near as interesting before you."

Erin wore a simple white blouse topped with a light cardigan sweater with broad red and white horizontal stripes. Designer jeans completed her outfit. He'd chosen a navy polo shirt over khaki Dockers. He figured they looked fine for their visit.

"You know, she probably doesn't look much like this now." Erin held up the Polaroid from the diary. "How old would she be?"

"According to her diary, she had the picture taken when she was seventeen. So, she'd be fifty-one or fifty-two."

The skyline of the city slid by on the left, highway signs indicating the exit for the historical district. All this history only three hours away. He definitely needed to check out Independence Hall and the Liberty Bell soon. Hopefully with Erin.

Traffic was thicker now, with cars zig-zagging from one lane to the other, and it took Darrell more than a mile to negotiate to the inside lane and exit. He followed the street signs and Erin's directions. Unfamiliar with the area, they went down one road, only to discover a dead end. They had to make a couple of right turns to get them back to the correct street and, with each wrong turn, Darrell's anxiety rose. He didn't like being lost…and wanted to get to Kelly. When they got close and found a parking spot, he backed in.

They walked through a neighborhood that was dirty, noisy—even on a Sunday—and congested. The roar of cars and the rumble of engines rained down from the highway above, and the smell of diesel fuel hung heavy in the air. The area, called Kensington Kelly had told them last night, was a mix of abandoned commercial sites and ancient brick brownstones with crumbling porches. Fast food wrappers and crushed beer cans were wedged into almost every crevice. In places, they had to step around the debris and tried not to inhale the stench of alcohol and vomit.

On one stoop they passed, a gang of black teen boys crowded together, scowling. Darrell, watching for tattoos or bandanas, kept a tight hold on Erin's arm and hurried them down I Street. Once past the kids and around the corner, Erin stopped and re-checked the map. "The address she gave us is 1806 E. Russell." Her index finger pointed to a spot on the map. "Should be one more over."

They headed that way and, in a few minutes, found the street. As they rounded the corner, they ran into a crowd of people blocking the sidewalk. Darrell and Erin worked their way through the gaggle of onlookers and saw the house number "1806" on a building three structures down. Yellow police tape cordoned off a space in front of the building, one end fluttering in the light breeze.

Darrell turned to one of the bystanders. "What happened here?"

"Some woman done got kilt," said an older, black man in a torn sweatshirt and stained Phillies ball cap. Darrell noticed a dark wad in the stranger's mouth, a mouth with only a few teeth. "She came out this morning, er, I guess it was this afternoon, to get the paper and got mugged, right here on the street. Damn cops came, put that damn tape up, and took her body an hour ago. Won't do nothin' though."

"Do you know who it was?" Darrell asked.

"Damned if I know. I's jus' visitin' my daughter across the street."

Darrell turned toward Erin and saw dread ignite in her eyes.

Hell of a coincidence.

"Her name was Kelly Young."

They jerked around, and Darrell dropped the diary. When he reached down and picked it up, he saw the edge of the old Polaroid sticking out. He pulled it out and gaped from the photo to the woman who had spoken. The speaker could've been an older sister of the teen in the picture, though the woman's skin was dark. Same penetrating eyes, now wet.

She said, "I'm Kelsie Young, her daughter."

Chapter 47

"Damn. She lived here more than twenty years." Kelsie wiped away some tears. "A few neighbors have had some problems, but never Mom. Then today, this. I can't believe it."

Erin and Darrell sat on a worn sofa in the front room of 1806 Russell—after he'd first inspected the covering. On the sidewalk, they'd introduced themselves, and Kelsie invited them in. She perched herself in an overstuffed chair opposite them and folded long legs beneath.

Darrell had a hard time not staring at her.

She was tall, even taller than Erin, with an athletic build, strong arms and legs. Little flab. She wore a faded gray tee shirt with the word *Eagles* stretched across an ample chest and matching gray sweat pants with identical lettering down the side. Her face bore the same features—burning green eyes, high cheekbones sans freckles and long graceful neck—as the face in his dream and the Polaroid, though Kelsie's skin was a creamy sienna and her hair a russet color. He'd guess her age to be thirty something, then he did the math. Thirty-three.

Not wanting to gawk at the woman, Darrell's gaze wandered to the map lying open on the coffee table. While his fingers busied with it and worked it back into its original folded pattern, he asked, "What happened?"

Kelsie massaged her cheekbones and eyes, as if doing so would keep her from crying. "Cops say she was mugged. Some damn junkie, they guessed. They didn't catch him. Been telling her for years she ought to move out of here. She said her place had *character*." She let her eyes roam around the space.

Darrell followed her gaze. Overall, the place looked comfortable and clean, but shabby, with a slight musty smell. Like the couch, the gray carpet was threadbare, with holes in places, dull wood showing through.

"The cops know what happened?" Erin asked.

"Uh, well, they said when she came down the steps to get the Sunday paper, some guy jumped her and bashed her head in. Old man Grimes from across the street yelled, and the guy took off. Grimes called 911." Kelsie's deep voice caught again and she sniffed. "She loved looking at the Sunday paper. Said it gave her a window to the rest of the world. Been following the stupid Monica/Bill affair."

Above a boarded-up fireplace, a blond, wooden mantel held three picture frames, each containing photos of the same two people. A much older Kelly than the one in his Polaroid and a near identical, younger and darker "twin," Kelsie, in each. Both women aged in the three photos, though Kelsie more noticeably, from child to teen to young woman. The center picture held a tall, adolescent Kelsie, whose resemblance to the young woman in his Polaroid was so close, Darrell was drawn to it. Sliding the old, faded picture out of his pocket, he held it alongside the one on the mantel.

It could be the same woman, except for the skin

color.

Darrell returned to the sofa and asked, "Did she have money or a purse with her?"

Kelsie sniffled. "What?"

Erin said, "The cops said she was mugged. Did your mom usually take money or a purse with her when she went down her steps to get her paper?"

"I don't know." Kelsie shook her head. "The cops guessed the guy was probably headed inside to steal what he could when Grimes scared him off. He didn't get much of a description, though. His eyesight ain't too good." She stopped and looked at her visitors. "What else could it be?" Her long arm swept toward the window and beyond. "Hell, look where she lives. Not exactly the burbs here."

Outside, a diesel engine thundered past.

"We noticed," said Erin.

Kelsie used her right forearm to wipe her tears. "Mom called me and said you were bringing something of hers you found. Some *notebook* from when she was in high school? She wouldn't tell me what it was. Wanted it to be a surprise."

When Kelsie raised her arm, Darrell noticed the tattoo, visible below her sleeve. A drawing of an arm with a closed fist wrapped around her skin. He remembered the image, the symbol for black power. Popular in the eighties.

"Did you bring it?" Kelsie asked, her tone somber.

"We did, but there's a bit of a story attached to it," Erin broke in and glanced at Darrell. "And before we start, could we have some water?"

While Kelsie went to get drinks, Darrell and Erin conferred. When the hostess returned with three glasses of water, they told her as much of the whole story as they dared. Darrell supplied most of the details, while Erin jumped in from time to time. He ended with the death of Ruby. He pulled out the diary, and after using his handkerchief to wipe the water rings off the table, he set the mildewed notebook down.

"And this Ruby told you to find my mom?" Kelsie asked, as she stared at the diary.

"Right before she died, she begged me to find that diary and talk to Kelly," Darrell said.

"And you come to see my mom and before she can talk to you, somebody kills her? What the hell is going on?"

Darrell studied her face, trying to figure if her grief would explode into anger against them, against the death they may have brought. Kelsie picked up the diary and flipped through the pages, glancing at the entries. After a while, she dropped it back on the table. She pointed to the notebook. "I'm grateful for this, especially after losing her. Might give me a window into her as a teen." She cleared her throat, then asked in a low whisper, "Why do I get the feeling there's something you're not telling me?"

Darrell and Erin exchanged glances. She nodded and he took the lead. "How much did your mom tell you about, uh, your father?" He handed Kelsie the Polaroid of her mom.

She studied the photo. "Wow. Could be me a few years ago."

Then Darrell pulled out the photo of Hank and gave it to her. Kelsie's gaze went from her mom's picture to Hank's. She laid both on the table beside the diary. "So that's what he looked like. You know, my mom never had a picture of him? She would've loved this." Her eyes misted over.

"Did your mom tell you much about your dad?" Darrell tried again.

"The famous Hank Young." Kelsie kept her eyes on the photos. "Hell, looking at me, it's no secret. Mom used to talk about him all the time when I was growing up. About him being brave. About how she loved him. About how he risked everything to be with her. Always said he was the best man she ever knew. You know, like he was some mythical person, too good to be true. This photo makes it seem more…real."

"On the phone last night, she said the same thing about your dad," Darrell said. "Did she tell you about how Hank died?"

"Yeah, she told me." Kelsie's face grew dark. "When I was little, I asked about it a lot, but she refused to say much. Till I was sixteen. On my birthday she told me how those three racists attacked Mom and Hank, and how he almost beat all three before they hit him with something and killed him." She finished in a throaty whisper, "When Mom told the story, in the end she blamed herself. She said if she stayed, Hank might not have died."

"Not surprised," Erin said. "Sounds like the strong, independent woman we met in the words of her diary. We could tell, even as teens, Hank and your mom had something special."

"She told me my dad was so strong, so powerful, she couldn't believe that night was the end of him. She loved him so much, she couldn't believe he was *really* gone. I think that's why she tried to keep him alive for me all these years." Tears dripped from her eyes and she slid one finger across her lips. "And now, now she's gone, too."

"Maybe it wasn't…the end of him?" Darrell posed.

"What?" Kelsie turned. "You mean my father wasn't killed that night?"

Darrell and Erin exchanged glances again. He said, "No, your dad was killed in 1964. He was lynched by three cowards in white sheets and hoods, and then the story was put out in town that he committed suicide."

"How do you know that?" Kelsie jerked her gaze from Darrell to Erin and back. "My mom told me about the three jerks in the white robes when she told me about his murder. Said she never told anyone else." She stared at the diary, still lying open on the table. "Did she write about his death in there?" She picked it up and flipped to the final entries.

Darrell placed a hand on hers. "No, it's not in her diary. We think she made her last entry the afternoon *before* your dad was murdered."

"I don't understand. Then, who told you about how my dad was killed? About the three assholes in white sheets?"

Darrell looked to Erin, who nodded again. He said, "I think your dad did."

Chapter 48

"That's not possible." Kelsie barked a short laugh.
"How old are you? Twenty-five? If my dad's been dead
for more than thirty years, how could he tell you?"

Darrell's eyes went to the coffee table. He picked
up the map and turned it over in his hands, fingering the
square edges. Now that he was here, he wasn't sure
how to explain it.

Erin jumped in. "Look. The story's a little
complicated. Is there someplace we can get a drink?
And maybe something to eat?"

"Sure. I could use a *drink*." Kelsie closed up the
apartment and led them a few blocks over to a place
called Byrne's Tavern. On their walk, she pointed out
McAlisters, down the street one block, having to yell
over the blaring horns. "I don't want to go in there right
now. Can't face her friends yet. And besides, way too
noisy for any conversation."

After they settled into a booth in the darkened
interior of the tavern and ordered beers, Darrell did his
best to explain, the story taking a while. The presence
in his office, the rolling autographed basketball, the
vision on the TV, the printed pleas on paper, and,
finally, the crazy nightmares with the details of the
lynching.

"That's pretty much how Mom told me it
happened, but come on. You expect me not only to

believe in ghosts, but believe my dad *is* this ghost." Kelsie's voice caught.

"I know it's a bit much. Believe me, it was for me, too," Darrell said. "At first, I didn't know what to make of the visions. I'd heard about the Wilshire ghost and started getting these visits, but I wasn't sure. A medium gave me a hint and your mom's diary helped me,"—he glanced at Erin sitting next to him—"helped us put it together." He picked up his beer, took another pull, and noticed it left a wet ring on the wooden table top. He used his napkin to wipe the spot clean. Again.

Kelsie shook her head. "Still. How did you go from these, these visits to murder?"

Darrell said, "I know. I know, but when I began asking about the kid who'd died, I got hints to leave it alone. When Ruby tried to help me, she got run over right in front of me. Her pleas led me to your mom and look what happened to her."

Erin put down her Dogfish Head beer. "Then yesterday, somebody ran into my car. Drugged me, knocked him unconscious, and left this." She pulled the folded sheet from her purse and passed it over.

For a few moments, no one spoke, their eyes on the crinkled paper, silent on the scarred wooden table between them.

DON'T LET THEM GO UNPUNISHED
PLEASE HELP ME FIND JUSTICE.
IT'S ALMOST TOO LATE.

Quit now or next time you'll find this on her corpse.

Kelsie stared at the sheet. "Do you know who did this?"

"Can't be sure," said Erin, "but my guess is the

same people who killed your dad. And now, maybe your mom."

The noises in the tavern—murmurs of quiet conversation, glasses sliding on the long bar, and the TV sound on low—surrounded them. His paranoia on alert, Darrell scanned the interior and searched for anyone appearing interested in them. He found nothing.

The waitress must've seen Darrell looking around, and she came over to ask if they wanted another round. Darrell snatched the paper off the table and glanced at his watch. It was almost five. He held his palm up to the waitress and turned to his companions. "How about we get something to eat? Kelsie, what's good here?"

"They do a mean burger," Kelsie offered.

"Could eat something," Erin said.

The waitress leaned across the table and pulled the menus from the stand at the back of the booth. "The Philly Burger is the most popular item. We also have chicken strips and a good fish sandwich." She laid the menus open.

Darrell's fingers held the sticky plastic card by the edges and he glanced over it. "Burger and fries sound good to me. Erin? Kelsie?"

"Sure," both echoed and the waitress headed back to the bar.

When they had privacy again, he asked, "Did your mom ever say if she figured out who the three guys were who killed your dad?"

Kelsie shook her head. "She said the night they attacked her and Hank, she was so scared, she simply ran. Hitchhiked to Philly and heard about Hank's *suicide* along the way. She never looked back." She stared off into the distance, sniffled once. She turned back to face them. "She did tell me one of the attackers called himself 'Red'."

"Red? You sure?" Darrell asked.

"Yeah." Kelsie nodded once. "When she told me about the attack, she said she saw his red hair when his hood slipped in the fight with my dad. Course, this was more than sixteen years after it happened." She looked from Darrell to Erin. "Is that important?"

Erin answered, "Red was this guy at school who tried to gang rape your mom with his buddies."

"What?" Kelsie's eyes got huge. "You mean—"

Erin's hand on her arm interrupted her. "Your mom stopped him. Read about it in the diary. He's one of the only people your mom gave a name to, well, a nickname. Pretty much everyone else in there only got an initial."

Kelsie had carried her mom's diary with her, and she brought it up from the bench. She began paging through it, her gaze intent. After a bit, she set the notebook back down. "Even if you could, how'd you ever identify these guys, after all this time? They'd be in their fifties now, like my mom. I don't know how you'd ever track them down, much less bring them to justice. They could be anywhere."

Darrell said, "I know who one is."

"You do?" Kelsie's head jerked up.

"Yeah, a guy named Jeff Jefferson. Salesman in town, who said he went to school with your dad and mom." When he saw the question in Kelsie's eyes, he went on. "He's a recovering alcoholic and came to me because I'd been asking about Hank. Said he wanted to make amends. He admitted he was there that night, drunk, and said they only wanted to *scare* your mom and dad. He insisted he didn't kill Hank, only knocked him out and left. Didn't know what happened after."

"Maybe he's Red," Kelsie said.

"Don't think so." Darrell shook his head. "His hair is thinning but definitely brown. Besides, this guy is a real follower. Can't believe he'd have enough balls to lead a gang rape, much less a lynching."

"Well then, he can tell us who the other two were." Kelsie's voice was indignant.

"I already tried. He said he wasn't going to rat on anyone else." When Darrell saw the disappointment on her face, he added, "When we get back, I can try again. Maybe ask him about Red and push a little. But he can simply clam up and deny he ever told me anything."

The waitress returned with their meals, the burgers still sizzling when she set the plates down. She asked after drinks, took orders, and left. The aroma of the fried beef and potatoes filled the booth, and busy with their food, no one spoke for a while. The server returned with another round of drinks, deposited them, and left.

Darrell picked up a fry and pointed it at Kelsie. "I'm not going to drop it. Though I'm not sure where to go next. Talk to Jefferson again and maybe ask around. See if anybody knew a kid nicknamed Red." He dunked the fry in a perfect circle of ketchup and ate it. "I'll see what I can find out. Your dad's waited a long time for justice."

Kelsie set down her burger. "Be careful." She looked from Darrell to Erin, suddenly appearing older, more mature. "If you're right, these guys have already killed Ruby and maybe my mom to keep their secret. Who knows what they'll do, if you get too close."

"I'll make sure he doesn't take too many chances," Erin said.

"And I'll go through my mom's things to see if I can turn up anything else. If I do, I'll let you know. You do the same for me?"

Darrell nodded, and when they finished their meals, they exchanged numbers. He waved the server over and grabbed the bill. Handing her two twenties, he told her to keep the change. She turned and left, a smile on her face.

"We got to start back soon. The drive to the shore will take more than three hours," he said.

"So sorry about your mom," Erin said. "Let us know about the funeral arrangements, please?"

"There won't be any. Mom didn't want anything. She wanted to be cremated. No ceremony." She started to tear up again.

Erin reached across the table and set her hand on Kelsie's, the pale skin a sharp contrast to the dark. "You have our numbers."

"Thanks." She tugged at Erin's hand. "Oh, if you do find out and I can help *with anything*, call me. I'd love to help nail those bastards."

Chapter 49

"You know he was shot jus' because he was black. Ain't much changed round here."

Monday's classes had been over hours ago and practice was finished, but as Darrell sat, drenched and exhausted, on the bench in the locker room, Tyler's comments in class replayed in his head. They'd haunted him all day.

His seniors had spent the day working on their independent projects, and Tyler had reported on his research into discrimination on the Eastern Shore, his shaved brown head gleaming under the lights. He'd read from a *Baltimore Enquirer* article about the hearing for the alleged shooter, the white shooter. Three months earlier, a white off-duty officer shot and killed a black off-duty officer at a D.C. nightclub.

"They were both cops," Tyler had argued to the class. "Didn't matter much. The dude is dead because he's black. Some things ain't changed."

Ain't changed much since the Wilshire ghost, Darrell thought.

Al trounced into the locker room, interrupting Darrell's musings. "What's the matter? Erin wore you out over the weekend?" He leered at his friend.

"Get your mind out of the gutter. I did spend most of the weekend with Erin, but it was hardly romantic." Darrell took a few moments to fill him in on their trip to

Philly.

Al sat down next to him on the bench. "Jeesh, kid, you seem to attract trouble the way road kill draws turkey vultures."

"Thanks."

"You said this daughter, Kelsie, looks like her mom?"

"Al, except for the skin color, she could pass for an older sister of the woman in the photo. It was uncanny."

"Well, take a deep breath, kid." Al placed a sweaty palm on his friend's shoulder. "You're back in the bosom of the Bay."

"Hey, do you know of a guy around here with the nickname 'Red'?"

"A student?" asked Al.

"No. An adult. Would've been in class with Hank, and Kelly. Be in his fifties, now."

Al scrunched his features. "Can't think of anyone right off. Why?"

"Kelsie said her mom told her one of the attackers was a guy named Red."

"Nobody comes to mind." Al paused. "He could've moved away. That was a long time ago. After the lynching, I'd suspect he might want to put some distance between himself and this town."

"Maybe...but from what I've read, guys like that have a different mentality. Anyway, tonight I can't worry about all that. I've got a few normal things to take care. I promised Douglass I'd get thank you notes out to Williams, Remington, and Jefferson." When he saw the puzzled glance from Al, he explained. "For the new uniforms."

Al got up off the bench. "I'd hold off on the one to

Jefferson."

"Why?"

"Jefferson is dead."

"What?" Darrell's mouth dropped open. "How?"

"He committed suicide late Saturday night. Apparently he got drunk at home and got into his car. Kept the garage door down and started the engine. Let carbon monoxide do the rest."

"Suicide? They're sure?"

"Found a note on his home computer. A little rambling, but according to Sara's EMT friend, the note said he couldn't handle it anymore."

"Oh, God, another one. That makes three," said Darrell.

Who's next? Erin? Him?

"What do you mean, three?" Al asked.

Darrell stole a quick glance around the locker room again and lowered his voice. "I met with Jefferson Saturday morning, out of town, in Oxford. Over breakfast, he told me *he* was one of the guys who attacked Hank all those years ago."

"He what?" Al collapsed back on the bench.

"Yeah, he told me he was twenty-three days sober and was working the steps. He wanted to make amends and came to me because *I* was asking about Hank. He looked great, seemed fine. Relieved, even." Darrell shook his head. "I can't believe he killed himself."

They sat in heavy silence for a bit, then Al asked, "I still don't get the three?"

"First, Ruby tries to give me information about the lynching, and she gets run over. Then I reach Kelly and we're set to meet and she gets her head bashed in." Darrell's voice quavered.

"I thought the cops said it was a mugging?"

"Hell of a coincidence. Now, Jefferson comes to see me about the lynching and conveniently kills himself. What are the odds?"

"Did Jefferson admit he killed Hank?" Al asked.

"No. He claimed he and a couple of guys only wanted to scare them, and things got out of hand. He said he knocked Hank unconscious and left the other two there with Hank."

"Did he say who the other two were?"

"No, he said he wasn't going to rat on anyone else. I was giving him a few days before I tried again," Darrell said.

"And now *he's* dead."

"Yeah, he won't be telling me anything."

Al got back up. "Think I better get going. Looks like it's dangerous simply being around you."

"Thanks, you really know how to make a guy feel better."

"Only kidding, kid." He flashed a crooked smile. "Take care of yourself. I'll mention Red to Sara, and she'll ask around. Discreetly. See if anyone in hospital circles recognizes that nickname. If I were you, though, I'd keep my head down."

Keep his head down? Then he wouldn't be able to see what was coming.

Chapter 50

"What do you mean I can't look at it?" Darrell asked. "I checked out that yearbook last week. You had to get it from the special collection in the back." Darrell's voice rose a level and the few students in the library turned to watch.

Merriweather's gaze dropped, eyes and thick lenses disappearing beneath the edge of her gray bun. She refused to look up at first, but her shrill voice didn't lose any of its arrogance. "I'm sorry, but someone walked off with the yearbook. It's come up missing."

"I thought you kept them in a special locked cabinet in the back. How could someone *walk off with it* without you knowing about it?"

"I can't explain it. It must've been some student."

Merriweather knew every student and wouldn't let one near the old yearbooks. She was lying. "And you simply *let* a student waltz out of here with one of the old yearbooks?"

She harrumphed. "I did not *let* him do anything. He must have snuck it out of here. You know how students are."

Darrell scowled. "Okay, then let me look at the '65 annual then."

Merriweather straightened, but remained stone-faced. "I've been given orders not to let any other editions out."

Orders? Ordered by whom?

And on it went. The bottom line was Darrell had to leave without being able to re-examine *The 1964 Wave*. Or *The 1965 Wave*. Or *The 1963 Wave*.

Despite his efforts to focus on his classes and on prepping his team, he'd spent the better part of the last three days obsessing about "Red." With Kelly gone, he thought, or rather felt, the nickname was the key to unlocking the rest. When he'd asked a few experienced staff members about the nickname, he tried to appear casual, but it did no good. He came up empty. No one could remember a student or an adult who'd once gone by that. The only reaction he got was from Jeb Douglass. Not a good one.

"Heard you been askin' about someone named 'Red'." The principal had stopped him in the hallway between classes.

"Uh…yeah," Darrell answered, clearing his throat, not sure what to say. "Did you know him?"

"Naw. Simply wondering why you wanted to know? Something about this research project?"

"Yeah—" Darrell started when a misbehaving student saved him from having to produce a further explanation. Darrell turned his head and called into his classroom, "Mr. Bookwalter, you know better than that. Pick up her books and apologize." Then back to Douglass, "I've got to take care of this." He stepped inside the classroom and closed the door, as the bell echoed down the hallway.

Even Sara's questions around the hospital had gotten the same response. No one knew anyone in Wilshire named "Red," or was willing to admit it. In desperation, he came up with the idea of scanning the photos in the old yearbooks to see if he could locate a picture captioned with "Red." Now that looked like a dead end as well.

He might be going paranoid, but this sure felt like a damned conspiracy.

He'd still been grumbling to himself when, after his futile visit to the library, he arrived back at his classroom.

"Problems, partner?"

He jerked his head up to see Molly McQuire in the teacher's chair behind his desk. "Shit," he muttered under his breath. So intent on uncovering Red's identity, he'd forgotten about meeting with his teaching partner. "Sorry, our planning session slipped my mind."

Molly stood, and her black-framed glasses swung on the chain around her neck. From where Darrell stood at the door, her short, plump figure appeared to emerge right out of the desktop. She wore a navy top with black slacks, and a kind smile. "Everything okay? Do you still want to meet?"

Darrell sighed, crossing the room. "Might as well. Sure. Need to think about something else."

"Anything I can do?"

Darrell explained he wanted to look up a former student in some old yearbooks, but Merriweather said the edition had come up "missing," and she'd been given orders not to let any others out.

"Missing?" Molly raised both eyebrows. "That old battle axe doesn't let anything out of her library. My students say she has them sign in blood to check out books for their term papers."

"Yeah, I've heard that."

"Doing more research on our resident ghost?"

Molly asked.

"Yeah."

"Which years you looking for?"

"Early sixties. '63, '64 and '65," said Darrell.

"I think I might have those editions in my room."

"Really?"

"Yeah, we keep a decent collection of past editions of *The Wave* for the yearbook staff. I think our volumes go back that far. We can check as soon as we're done here."

Darrell wanted to get to the yearbooks right then but did his best to focus on their planning for next week's lessons. Thirty minutes later, they finished and headed down the hall to McQuire's classroom.

Molly strode to the rear and, using a set of keys, opened the doors of a tall, gray, metal cabinet. She levered her bulk to the floor and knelt. Reaching inside the bottom shelf, she pulled out tabbed file folders, dog-eared teacher manuals, and boxes of used novels and set the assorted materials around her on the linoleum. Her head and squat torso disappeared inside the cabinet, and Darrell heard her bump her head into a shelf followed by a brief squeal.

A few moments later, she backed out, three yearbooks in her hands. When Darrell saw the name across the one on top, *The 1964 Wave,* he blew out a breath and thanked her profusely.

Now that he had the yearbooks, he wanted to ditch practice and begin his search but knew he couldn't. Tomorrow was important, since it was the final game. So he stored the three editions of *The Wave* in his office and tended to his players. Three hours later, he had showered, dressed, and was back at his desk. He knew he should be tired. Hell, he should be exhausted, but he could feel the adrenaline pumping through his body. He was close, he knew it.

He stared at the top yearbook, *The 1964 Wave*. He didn't really have a plan, so he started with the junior page—where he'd found Kelly and Hank—and scanned the names under each photo. The process took only a few minutes, but produced no results, though he ran his fingers over the pictures of Hank and Kelly again. From what they'd read in the diary, he was pretty certain Red was a member of the junior class, but he checked the names under the photos for the other classes as well. Except for the seniors, it came to naught. As for underclassmen, they listed only first initial and last name and, of course, all in black and white. After that, he went through the annual, page by page, examining every candid shot for a caption that included "Red." He came up empty.

Undaunted, he moved on to the next two,'65 then '63. Two more hours of scanning and checking yielded only a throbbing headache and a grumbling stomach, but no Red. He had been so certain *this* was the answer, now this.

If he came up with nothing, what the hell did he do now?

He turned and glanced around the room, but felt nothing. No presence, no prickle on his neck. "Okay, Hank," he whispered, "where do I go from here?" His tired gaze crisscrossed the room. He saw nothing. Spent from poring over hundreds of photos, he felt weariness invade every part of his body.

He decided to head to the bathroom to throw water on his face. Maybe, wake himself up. Have another look. Picking up the three books, he went over to the file cabinet and pulled out the bottom drawer. He placed the yearbooks behind some old textbooks, closed the drawer, and locked it. He pocketed the key. Then he locked the door to his office.

He was taking *no* chances.

The restroom was one floor down, and the round trip took about five minutes. Head down, he staggered back up the stairs, searching for something he might've missed. When he got just outside the office, he stopped short. The door was wide open.

The yearbooks? Somebody got to the yearbooks.

He approached the office, and as he crossed the threshold, a wave of cold struck him. He looked at the file cabinet, and his heart sank. The bottom drawer was open. His gaze went to his desk. It was empty.

"Hank?" His voice sounded hollow and uncertain. No response.

He scanned the office desperately, and when he got around his desk, he saw them. A loud breath rushed out. Underneath the picture window, in the middle of the couch, the three yearbooks rested in a clumsy pile, *The 1964 Wave* on top, open to a page near the end.

He went over, sat on the couch, and picked up the yearbook. He studied the open double-page spread and his hand traced each photo, searching every caption. On the second to the last picture, he found it. "Red." In his fatigue, he must've glossed over it before. The photo captured two couples mid pose, dancing at a spring "Sock Hop." He stopped and stared at the last name that followed "Red."

"Oh, shit."

Chapter 51

"Can we stay a few minutes more? We've got some um, important info to share," Darrell asked Al and Sara. "And we could use some advice."

"Sure, kid." Al levered down the foot piece of his recliner and sat up, still balancing his drink—his third—in his other hand.

The rest of the gang had exited the McClure postgame party a few minutes earlier, leaving Darrell and Erin alone with their hosts. And party, it was. The Pirates had won the final game and posted a seven and three record, the best in three decades. They had all been celebrating for the past two hours and had the inebriated conditions to show for it. Except Darrell and Erin, who were too preoccupied to be in total party mode.

"Al, put down your rum and Coke, before you spill it." Sara moved to the couch, across from Darrell and Erin. "How can we help?"

Darrell picked Erin's bottle off the hearth and placed it on a coaster. With his handkerchief, he wiped up the moisture ring. "After the game tonight, Williams and Remington came over to congratulate me."

"Yeah, I saw that. Happy man, Williams, from the look of it," Al said. "All kidding aside, it *was* a great win. The flea-flicker in the fourth quarter caught the Mariners napping. Great call, by the way."

"Thanks. Williams came up to me, put a hand on my shoulder, and told me my coaching skills were 'exemplary'." Darrell made air quotes. "Then he said he was disappointed my brilliance didn't extend beyond the football field."

"What'd you say?" Sara asked.

Darrell continued, "I didn't know what to say. Before I had a chance to answer, Remington said 'Bud's only kidding, Coach.' Then he added, 'Don't worry about it. If you're a winning football coach in this town, you can get away with anything.' Then both Bud and Remington laughed and Bud said, 'Well, almost anything'."

"You deserve the congrats and should be thrilled," Sara said. "I wonder where Bud's comment came from."

Al moved onto the couch next to his wife. "Maybe I've had one too many, but I don't get it. You ought to be delighted the school board president thinks you're *brilliant* at anything. I've been leading the music program for twenty years and have never gotten anything like that from him."

Darrell shot another glance at Erin, who laced her arm through his. He said, "Maybe I'm paranoid, but Bud's comment got to me. And there was something in how Remington looked at me."

Sara said, "I realize Bud Williams is no prince among men."

"No, that would be me." Al grinned.

Sara gave him a peck on the cheek. "Sure, you keep thinking that, honey." She turned back to Darrell and Erin. "Whatever his shortcomings—and I grant you there are many—Bud Williams is one of the richest and most influential men in Wilshire. He and his family own half this town and are bankrolling the new high school. I don't think it'll hurt you one bit to have him think you're the next Mike Ditka."

"All that might not help, if he finds out I know about his past," Darrell said. "If he doesn't already."

Al asked, "Kid, what are you talking about?"

Erin jumped in. "What if we told you 'Bud' is not his real nickname? Or at least not his original nickname?"

Al's eyes widened. "You don't mean—"

Erin finished, "Darrell found Williams' original nickname, the nickname he went by in school was 'Red.' *The* 'Red'."

"It took some searching, but I found the nickname in *The 1964 Wave*," Darrell said. He reached into a bag Erin had brought and pulled out the yearbook. Opening it to a page he'd tabbed, he handed it to Al, who laid it out on the coffee table. "I marked the photo with a Post-it."

Al lifted the yellow square, and he and Sara studied the picture, heads together. She read the caption aloud. "Sophomores Red Williams and Trevor Remington at the Sock Hop, twisting the night away with their dates." She looked at Darrell and Erin. "Williams is the 'Red' from Kelly's diary? The one who tried to rape her?"

Erin said, "Won't surprise my mom. Said when she worked for good ol' Bud, he was all about control. Control over everything and everyone."

Al pointed to the yearbook photo. "Are you sure this is Bud? I mean, we're talking thirty-some years ago. Besides, they could've put the wrong last name under the picture."

Darrell nodded. "I thought of that, so I cross checked it with another photo." He handed them a second yearbook, opened to another Post-it. "Check out what I found in *The '65 Wave*."

Sara read, "Red Williams, Athlete of the Year." She placed the one open yearbook next to the other. "That's definitely Bud."

Sara and Al studied the two photos and the family room got quiet, deathly quiet, Darrell thought. He stowed the handkerchief and said, "When we talked to Kelsie, she told us her mom said Red was one of the guys who lynched Hank. The only one her mom could identify, because of his red hair. *He* was the reason her mom ran away from Wilshire that night. Kelly was worried Red would come after her, since she recognized him."

"Holy shit." Al grabbed up his drink from the end table. "Bud Williams, '97 Chamber Man of the Year, is one of the guys who lynched Hank all those years ago." He started to take a drink and stopped. "Who's the third one?"

"What?" asked Darrell.

Sara explained, "Jefferson told you he was one of the attackers. You're pretty sure Williams was the second one. Who's the third?"

"Maybe Remington or Douglass."

"Douglass?" Al was incredulous.

"I don't know. Maybe somebody not even around anymore. Could be anybody from back then. Your guess is as good as mine," Darrell said.

Sara scowled. "Now that you know, what are you going to do about Bud, er Red?"

"Do?" Darrell and Erin replied together.

"Yeah." Al got up and paced the room. "All you have on Bud is Kelly's account told to her daughter. And this from a woman who fled Wilshire more than thirty years ago. Even if Kelly had come back, I'm not sure anyone would've taken her word against a Williams, anyway. And now she's dead." He pointed his almost empty glass at Darrell. "How do you propose to prove Bud was one of those who lynched Hank?"

Darrell stared at his two hosts. "I have absolutely no idea."

Setting his glass back on the table, Al glanced around the room and whispered, "You want some advice. Be damn careful who you share this *supposition* with."

Chapter 52

Darrell could not get Al's warning out of his head.

After leaving the McClures, he dropped Erin off at her place since she had an early morning charter with her dad. They made plans to meet up together after, to figure out what to do next. Actually, Darrell would be thrilled simply to *be* with her, even if they couldn't figure out anything. She was the best thing that had happened to him in this whole mess. One thing he knew—he would not, could not take any chance that might endanger her. No matter what.

He'd told Erin he was heading to his apartment to crash. He was exhausted, but when he pulled the car out of her driveway, he found he was too keyed up to sleep. Instead, he drove to Wilshire High School and climbed the dark, creaking steps up to his office, in search of inspiration.

Standing there next to his old metal desk, he looked out the window and studied the widow's walk. Its brass cupola reflected green as intermittent streams of moonlight struck it. He stepped out onto the walk and paced all the way around the square space twice, peering in every direction. The second time around, he stopped at the front, hands on the railing, and stared into the darkness at the black Bay ahead. Sporadic wafts of sea air drifted past, and his eyes could barely make out small white crests of waves on the water. He glanced down at the cracked wooden railing in his hand and thought, *this* was where they did it.

But what did he think *he* could do about it?

Frustrated, he stepped back inside the building and returned to his office. He resumed his pacing, this time across the worn linoleum, between the window and the couch and back again, his rigid foot pattern only underscoring his sense of futility. He was getting nowhere. No matter how he looked at his *ghost situation*, he saw no way to resolve it.

He stared at the paper on his desktop, the one with the plea from Hank *and* the scrawled warning about Erin. Recognizing it was off center, his fingers edged it over until it was in the exact center of the desk.

PLEASE HELP ME FIND JUSTICE.

What the hell. Who was he kidding? Why did he think *he* could remedy injustice? All he had to do was look around, and he could see injustice and bigotry in Wilshire hadn't died with Hank. He'd done everything he knew to do and look where it got him. All his investigation had managed so far was to get people killed. Ruby. Kelly. Jeff Jefferson. *And* targeted Erin. What if something happened to her? He could not keep this up if it put her life in danger.

He glanced back at the paper.

IT'S ALMOST TOO LATE.

That might be true, but what was he supposed to do? Sure, Kelsie's story from her mom confirmed his *dreams,* but Al was right. No one in Wilshire would take his word—and Kelsie's—over Bud Williams'. Who else was left to tell the story?

He looked around the small office, trying to *sense* something. Nothing. He tried to will his neck hairs to prickle, but they lay relaxed and undisturbed. Moving to the bookcase, he grabbed his basketball off the stand, balancing it in his fingers, and struggled to pick up any vibes. Nothing. Sure, now when he needed a message, he got zilch.

Finally, he let out a scream. "Okay, Hank, I'm sorry about what happened to you, but that was a long time ago," he yelled out the open door. "I don't know what else to do. I'm done." The echo of his words down the stairs seemed to laugh at him and die away. Just like his resolve.

He collapsed onto the old couch, the ancient upholstery releasing dust and mold into the air. Darrell stretched his legs out as best he could and closed his eyes, hoping more for inspiration than sleep.

When he opened them again, he felt...different.

Snuggled next to him now lay a beautiful young woman with long red hair. A beautiful, naked young woman. Kelly. Instead of the anxiety he'd experienced in his dreams, he felt contentment...even delight. He watched her chest, two perfectly round breasts, rise and fall in peaceful slumber. Looking at her like this, studying her, he thought, she was so...gorgeous.

He examined the sprinkling of freckles across her cheek and neck that looked to him like a comet's tail. When he raised his hand to caress her soft skin, he noticed his hand was...black. He stared down at himself and realized he too now was nude and his huge body was ebony. Only then did it dawn on him that he was channeling Hank. Darrell had a momentary hesitation. He wasn't sure he wanted to go there. Then, he heard...no, he felt Hank's request, urgent and desperate. He surrendered to it.

Hank had never met anyone like Kelly. He hadn't talked with that many whites, much less white girls, but he found he was more comfortable with her than anyone else. She wasn't afraid of him and, once they got started, they talked about everything. Unlike every other white he had known, she had no prejudice. She was as dedicated to justice as he was. Hell, she was fearless. She'd been brave enough to go the demonstrations with him, sometimes the only white face there. Not many white guys had the courage to do that. She'd even met Dr. King.

He loved her...and would do *anything* for her. To protect her.

When his fingertips brushed her freckles, she stirred, burrowing her warm body closer into him. She stared up at him, joy in those stunning green orbs. She exhaled, her breath warm upon his skin. Using one elbow, she leaned up and kissed him, her lips moist and sweet. She whispered, "You know I love you." Her face broke into a huge smile. "And I love this as well." Her gaze roamed across his naked body. "Remember, Dr. King said only love can conquer hate."

Hank chuckled, pulled her a little tighter against him, and returned the kiss. After, he said, "I don't think it's quite that simple," but couldn't help smiling a little. He found it hard *not* to smile around her. She made you believe *anything* was possible.

But eyeing the two of them together, he knew deep down he shouldn't. They shouldn't. Even though it felt good, felt natural. Last night his brother told him *they* were out looking for Negroes to mess with. Only they didn't say Negroes. With Kelly close like this, he thought, this sure as hell fits. His chest tightened.

"I'd run away with you tonight," she said. "Now, if you say the word."

"As much as I'd love that, you know I promised my mom I'd finish high school."

"Just saying." She grinned at him and brought her hand to his face.

He glanced over her lovely shoulder and read the time on the clock, almost quarter past three. They'd have to leave soon. If they wanted to be safe.

He lifted her chin and held it in his hand, the flawless pink against his black. She gave him a little pout and wrinkled her nose. So he kissed her, first her nose, then her lips, this one long and sensual, both of them breathing hard afterward. Foreheads together, they stared into each other's eyes, sparkling greens into deep, dark browns.

So intent, it took a moment for Hank to register that the lock turned. Or the door opened.

Hank saw them first. Three white-clad figures emerged from the darkness like ugly ghosts. He gaped at the covered forms, the adrenalin already rushing through his body. He assessed the invaders. Each wore an old sheet, a rough opening cut out for the head, and a small white tented pillowcase with eye slits. Dirty blue jeans and muddied leather boots jutted from beneath the ragged, soiled edges of the sheets. The first two through the door looked tall, skinny almost, under the bleached linens. The third was short and squat.

His brother had been right.

Hank grabbed Kelly and started to shove her behind him.

"What?" she gasped.

Before she finished the single syllable, the short

figure lunged forward. He grabbed Kelly by the hair and yanked her off the couch. The other two intruders pounced, like a choreographed move on the football field, and grabbed Hank. They dragged him off the couch. Hank slammed an elbow into one and knocked him to the floor. The third grabbed Hank's other arm, twisting it behind his back. With his free arm, Hank thumped a huge fist into the stomach of the attacker.

Kelly screamed, "Get your hands off me." She swung a wild arm into her captor's side.

The covered head yelled, "Ow-w-w."

She stood, feet planted and sweat running down her face and between her breasts. She squirmed in his grasp, twisting and turning. "Get 'em, Hank." She swung her knee.

The white figure holding her jumped back, the sheet billowing in the move. He wrenched her hair. She yelped. He slapped her across the mouth. "Shut up, bitch."

Hank turned to see Kelly grab her reddening cheek, tears welling in her eyes. Something inside him cracked, his fury boiling over, and he started toward her. The attacker Hank had knocked to the ground struggled to get to his feet. He stumbled in the folds of the sheet and his headpiece shifted, revealing a tuft of red hair and sideburns.

Hank's gaze darted from his attacker getting up to the one torturing Kelly. From the side, the third figure charged and threw a hard kick at his groin. Hank collapsed to the floor and grabbed himself, writhing in pain.

The tallest attacker, now upright again, yelled, "Asshole!" His partner said, "Goddamn asshole!"

Both attackers kicked Hank in the side. The metal toes of their boots struck his ribs with ugly thuds. They laughed hard, gasping between laughs. Hank groaned, curling to avoid the next assault.

Kelly yelled, "Leave him alone, Red."

They stopped kicking. "Red" turned back toward Kelly and growled, "Shut her up."

The guy holding Kelly slapped her again. She yelled and then opened her mouth and bit the arm gripping her. Her captor bellowed, but held on. He yanked her hair again, making her shriek.

Hank used the distraction to wrench the leg of the closest attacker. Red went down. His body slammed the floor, the air knocked out. Hank scuttled across the stained linoleum, wincing with each movement. He placed one massive hand on Red's neck. Stared into dazed olive eyes. Beer-belched fumes erupted through the headpiece. Hank shoved his oversized palm down and squeezed. The costumed face made gurgling, choking sounds. Hank's anger at these cruel bigots— and others like them who burned down his church— exploded. He pressed harder.

The third intruder struck Hank's torso with his fists. He tried to drag Hank off his buddy, but his efforts had little effect. Hank tightened his iron grip. On the floor, Red clawed at Hank's fingers. Red squirmed, but it did no good. Beneath the ragged holes in the sheet, his eyes got wide, then hazy.

From the corner of his eye, Hank saw the third assailant stop his futile assault. He made jittery moves around the small office. Plucked something shiny from a shelf.

"Watch out," Kelly cried, as the assailant swung

some trophy like a club.

Hank saw the blur of the metal edge coming at him, but too late. The trophy smashed into his forehead. He collapsed onto the floor. Blood oozed down the side of his head onto the linoleum.

Released from Hank's grasp, Red began to cough. His breathing in tortured spurts, he staggered to his feet. He directed several more vicious kicks into Hank's side. "Shit." He spat on him. "My grandpa taught me what to do to you people who rape our women." He glared at Kelly. "Even a whore like you."

Kelly screamed.

Hank turned to tell her to—a bag or something was dragged over his head and everything went dark. Then he felt a rope cinched around his neck. Dazed, he tried to work his hands free, but one of the intruders sat on him, pinning his arms under. He struggled to breathe. Hank tried to buck, to throw off his assailant, but the other landed another vicious kick and knocked all the breath out. Something hit the back of his head, and the pain exploded.

Everything went black.

Darrell jerked up off the old sofa, gasping for air. He leaned on the armrest, his chest heaving in and out. He couldn't catch his breath. As his eyes adjusted, he noticed he was alone again, the only light in the office from the small lamp on his desk. As he forced himself to breathe deep, he discovered the ribs on both sides of his body ached...as if someone had kicked him there. Beads of sweat slid down both sides of his head. He staggered to his feet and limped over to the window.

He peered out at the nearly dark widow's walk. "Okay, Hank, I get it," he said in a hoarse whisper, recalling the ghost's message. *DON'T LET THEM GO UNPUNISHED*. "I still don't know what I'll do, but I'll figure out some way to expose these bastards."

Chapter 53

All that night and into the next day, the only thing Darrell could think about was the horrific vision of Hank's murder. He'd been so focused on the lynching, he was afraid he may have been made a really stupid decision. At least, that's what he thought as he stood on the deck of Williams' yacht. He stared at the angry whitecaps surrounding the boat, as if ready to swallow it. Darrell swayed, trying to keep his balance, and cinched the life jacket a little tighter.

Damn. Maybe coming aboard was not such a great idea.

Earlier this afternoon he'd headed down to the dock, Pogo at his heels, to try to catch up with Erin. Anxious to share last night's vision, Darrell planned to be there, waiting, when she returned with her dad's charter. He still couldn't believe anyone wanted to sail in this ugly weather. As he strode along the pier, the pug keeping pace, he searched the water for any sign of *Second Wind's* white-and-gold billowed sails.

"Ahoy, there."

The voice startled him. It took him a second to recognize the board president, decked out in a stylish sailing jacket, navy khakis with razor creases and white Docksiders. An image from his vision—red sideburns beneath the tented white cap—leaped into Darrell's mind. His heart hammered in his chest and his answer got strangled in his throat.

"Hey, Coach, *you* may be the answer to my prayers," Bud Williams called from deck of his boat.

"I-I-I am?" Darrell managed. Could he possibly know that Darrell knew?

Williams stepped down onto the dock. "This morning my first mate came down with that stomach flu, and the Wilshire Sloop Rush is today."

Darrell's students had talked all week about the end-of-season sailboat regatta *and* the attendant parties. Even the prediction of nasty conditions on the water hadn't dampened their enthusiasm. No doubt, due to the lure of after-race parties and alcohol.

Williams said, "I need a two-man crew to compete, and I have already donated a *sizable* entry fee. Would you be willing to help out a board member and serve as my second today?"

Sailing with Bud? After what he witnessed last night, that was the last thing he wanted to do.

Darrell stuttered. "L-l-look, Bud, I-I-I don't know much about sailing. I don't think I'd be a very good second."

Williams chuckled and placed a firm hand on Darrell's shoulder, which sent a twinge down his back. "Not to worry. I will teach you anything you need to know. And it can hardly hurt my chances when I cross the finish line with the winning coach as my mate."

Darrell studied the skies, gray with dark, brooding clouds crowding the horizon and the roiling waves beneath. He turned back to Williams. "You're going out in this?"

"Certainly," Williams crowed, "the race goes on, rain or shine. Besides, it is all for a noble cause, the

Domestic Shelter. Will you help me out?"

Darrell stared at the ugly waters and considered the request. The vision of the red-haired figure kicking Hank and screaming the "N" word came back, and Darrell could almost still feel the bruised ribs. Maybe, if he could get Williams alone, he could get something out of him. Darrell figured he'd be safe enough. They'd be in the middle of the other boats. Besides, he figured he could take Williams, if Bud tried something.

And it might give Darrell a chance to ask a few tough questions, without any other ears around.

Williams held out his hand and Darrell took it. He turned toward his dog, panting on the dock. "Pogo, you stay here and wait for Erin." He scratched the pug's head and the dog gave a short yelp.

Darrell started untying the lines from the cleats, his fingers pulling on the slick nylon rope. As he worked his way down the side of the boat, he noticed the sailboat was larger and grander than the other crafts in the harbor. He gestured to the painted name on the side, *Without Pier*.

"Oh, that," Williams said, as he climbed back aboard and went through his preparations. "It is an inside joke. I enjoy being out on the water so, to me, a pier is hardly necessary. Only the boat."

"I was thinking of the other spelling," Darrell said.

"Of course, that as well." Williams smirked.

Darrell stepped onto the deck of the boat and moved to a seat in the stern. He grabbed the railing and scanned the water for any sign of Erin. He was glad for a chance at Williams but still hoped he'd see Erin returning and use her as an excuse to get off. He'd caught no sign of *Second Wind*.

That had been more than twenty minutes ago.

Williams powered his boat away from the dock and out into the channel. As soon as they were in open water, he pressed a button on the high tech control panel beside the helm, which released the rigging and unfurled the two pale blue sails. Immediately, the winds inflated the sails, and they surged ahead. As he directed the boat out into the Bay, Williams bragged on the craft, which he insisted on calling a yacht.

"This beauty is a Beneteau Oceanic 36.5. Brand new and built by the French. They truly know how to design these." He tossed a life jacket at Darrell. "You, son, are sitting on the edge of a 12.5-foot beam, so *Without Pier* can take some major waves and keep on plowing." Williams pointed to the water. "That may prove to be fortuitous today."

Darrell noticed the affected speech again, but said nothing. He studied the waves heading at the boat. As they moved farther out into the harbor, the waves grew larger, three- to four-foot swells at least. He fingered the Velcro straps on the front of his life vest, opening the closure, readjusting the straps, and tightening them again. He repeated the process three times before he looked up and caught Williams watching him. Darrell stopped.

"We might get a little wet today, but we are certainly going to have some fun," Williams called over the rising wind. "You hold onto your life jacket." Then he laughed and spun the wheel, which turned the sail, driving the boat farther west.

To distract himself from the heaving waters surrounding them, Darrell studied what he could of the craft. Like the Caveny sailboat, the teak and brass of the boat was highly polished, though Darrell had trouble believing Williams used his own elbow grease to keep it that way. Like *Second Wind,* the steering wheel was at the rear or stern, but here a captain's chair sat behind the helm.

Darrell didn't want to budge from his seat, but he leaned and peered inside the cabin. He could see the polished wood interior, a sink at the end and teal-colored benches running down the length of the space, their color matching the flapping sails. A table sat in the center. He said, "Beautiful cabin."

Williams smiled. "*That* is an understatement, son." He indicated the interior of the cabin. "That table comes out, and those benches fold down and make a *very* comfortable bed. Comfortable for a lot more than sleeping, *if* you get my drift." His grin morphed into a leer. "The rocking of the water adds a whole new dimension of pleasure, and I have found women truly enjoy the ride."

He was bragging about his conquests, Darrell thought. Maybe, he has no idea what Darrell knew.

Hearing the lewd boasts reminded Darrell of the diary entry about Red's attempted gang rape of Kelly years earlier. Of his unwanted "advances" to Erin's mom. It made Darrell's skin crawl. "I'm sure they do." Darrell did his best to hide his reaction. He turned his attention back to the boat.

The console, nestled just inside the cabin interior, looked like a collection of high tech toys. A depth finder, a nautical clock, a radio, and a ship-to-shore phone sat within easy reach. When he saw the equipment, Darrell breathed a little easier.

At least he could call for help, if he needed it.

Before he realized it, they'd caught up with the rest of the sailboats in the mouth of the Bay. Everywhere he looked, he saw white and brightly colored sails around them, all billowing above sloops and sailboats of different sizes, the crafts bobbing in the water. None of them bearing the white and gold colors of *Second Wind,* though. Several of their fellow sailors scurried from stem to stern, adjusting the sails.

In the few months he'd been on the Eastern Shore, he noticed the pace aboard sailboats on the Bay was usually relaxed, almost languid. Today, the action in every boat seemed hurried, frantic, as if the angry waters dictated the mood. That, he figured, and this crazy contest. As Williams leaned back in his chair, Darrell studied the other sailboats and noticed many seemed to be manned by only one person.

What gives? Bud said he needed two guys.

He shot a glance at Williams, but before he could say something, Bud yelled, "It appears we made it right on time. Would you go forward and check on the jib? Yesterday, the rope kept getting caught and wouldn't let the sail open all the way." He pointed to the starboard side, and Darrell's gaze followed. From Erin's tutoring, Darrell remembered the jib was the smaller sail nearer the front of the boat.

What was Bud up to? Darrell needed to be careful and not underestimate this guy.

While he kept one eye on Williams, Darrell grabbed the cold, slick rail to balance himself in the swaying boat and edged up along the side. He examined the sail, which billowed in the wind and noticed the rope was taut. "Everything looks fine," he yelled back.

Williams eyed the second sail. "Okay, thanks."

Darrell used the handrail to pull himself back to his seat, and as soon as he sat again, a horn blasted in the distance.

"And the fun begins," Williams called, and he pushed the button on his control panel, opening the sails further.

Williams maneuvered *Without Pier* between the smaller crafts, and the yacht glided easily toward the head of the group. Out in the open Bay, under ominous, darkening clouds, the waves deepened and the swells lashed at the boat. The waters splashed up the sides and soaked Darrell. Shivering, he glanced over at Williams, who sat in his Henri Lloydsailing jacket, calm, confident and dry. The jacket was red across the front with a stripe of white down each sleeve and high blue collar, which fastened across the front. Darrell knew it was a custom-made, waterproof jacket, designed for Ben Ainslie, the famous Olympic sailor, because Williams had taken pains to tell him. Nothing like Darrell's black sweatpants and Pirate sweatshirt. Which were now soaked.

Darrell peered at Williams, perched in the captain's chair like some aristocrat, and contemplated what he'd done. Done to Hank as Darrell himself experienced in last night's vision. And what Williams had done to Erin's mom, and who knows how many more.

Someone has to stand up to this guy. Why not Darrell?

Memories of his earlier sail with Erin flooded back, when everything from the weather to the company to the atmosphere had been the opposite of today. With Erin, the Bay had seemed enchanting, mysterious, and serene. Today, the brooding, vengeful waters collided with the hull, sending the brackish scent into the air. Darrell stared out at the endless, watery expanse with equal measures of humility and fear. The knuckles of his fingers around the railing turned white, while his other hand opened and tightened the straps on the front of his life jacket again and again. His confidence faltered.

What the hell had he gotten himself into?

The noise of the waters in his ears, he didn't hear something Williams had said. "Sorry, I didn't catch that."

Williams turned so he faced him. "I said, how goes your ghost hunting?"

Chapter 54

"What?" Darrell called, hoping he misheard.

Williams smirked down from the captain's chair. "I merely asked how the great ghost hunt was proceeding?"

Darrell choked. "Uh, okay. Didn't realize you knew much about it."

Williams bellowed a huge laugh. "Coach, Wilshire is a *very* small town. I have found it hard *not* to know pretty much everything about everyone."

Everything about everyone? Hope not.

Darrell focused back on the water and, watching *Without Pier* pull in front of the other boats, asked, "How far out does the race go?"

"Eight miles into the Bay and back. It should not take long with this wind, though." He gestured to the mainsail, stretched to the limit. "By the way, I hear you have been spending time with young Erin Caveny. How is she?"

"She's great," Darrell said, fighting to keep his face passive. He sure as hell didn't want to discuss Erin with Bud.

"I would wager she is a real spitfire, like her mother. You know, she used to work for me. Her mother, Beverly, not Erin."

"I heard. And yes, Erin is a very spirited woman."

Williams released a guffaw. "Spirited. I like that,

Coach. The Caveny women are certainly *spirited*."

As the yacht plowed ahead, Darrell watched the shores recede farther away, the houses appearing like tiny white and green Monopoly pieces, vehicles like mini-matchbox cars. The docks from the houses grew shorter as *Without Pier* slipped farther into the Bay, and he figured the waters here must be not so shallow.

It was deeper out here. Great. He recalled an image from last night—he, er Hank, being kicked and spat on—and tried to build up his courage.

His fingers opened and closed the straps again.

"I heard you even had a few visits from our resident ghost," Williams yelled, jolting Darrell.

How did he know? He'd only told Al, Sara, and Erin. A bad feeling gnawed at his stomach. Maybe, he'd miscalculated.

Darrell did an exaggerated shrug. "I think I've seen him once or twice. Heard I'm not alone. They tell me ghost appearances are pretty common at the high school. How about you, Bud? Ever met our ghost face to face?"

"I have never had the privilege. I choose not to believe in ghosts. You are right, though. Others claim to have seen him." Williams' thumb edged the small scar on his chin. "What can I say? Wilshire is an old building. Lots of years and lots of stories. It will be good to put all those behind, when we get the new school built."

"What's your opinion on who the Wilshire ghost might be?"

"A very good question," Williams said. "If I did believe in ghosts, I would venture he was some unfortunate slave from the 1800s still wandering the area. You know, the Eastern Shore is famous for our slaves. They tell me the Williams land used to be a thriving plantation." Perched in the captain's chair, Williams' attention seemed focused on the waters ahead. As if he were surveying his realm.

Darrell scanned the horizon but couldn't see anything in the waves forward of the boat. He glanced behind and noticed they had now outdistanced all the other sailboats. They had moved so far out in front, Darrell could only see the tips of a few sails behind them. As he watched the yacht sliding ahead, even these disappeared behind his view.

Damn. He hadn't thought of that. No witnesses now.

When he glanced to each side, he searched for the coastlines but couldn't locate either now. All he saw was water, the whitecaps seeming to go on forever in every direction.

Shit. Maybe this wasn't such a brilliant idea.

His clothes now soaked, Darrell shivered. He gripped the hand hold even more tightly and stared. If something happened to him out here... He took a deep breath, trying to assure himself. People saw him on this boat. Bud wouldn't try anything.

But Williams killed Hank. And maybe Jefferson and Kelly. What the hell should I do now? Darrell wondered.

As he studied Williams smug in his chair, Darrell's anger flared, and he figured he was stuck here now. Besides, what did he have to lose? Maybe keep Bud off balance. "Hey, heard you had a different nickname in school? Read somewhere you went by Red."

"Red?" Williams threw his head back and chortled,

the whoop getting swallowed by the wind. "Oh, that." He brushed back his hair sticking out the edge of his cap. "Believe it or not, this was not always white. Red, huh. I hadn't heard that in a long time."

Darrell smiled, going along. "What do you think about the theory that the ghost is a student from the sixties who hanged himself?"

"I have heard that as well," Williams said, "but I like the slave story better."

Bet you do. Darrell's hand went to his throat, and he felt the rope around his neck from last night. He coughed. "Wasn't there a student in your class who hanged himself?"

Williams said nothing, and Darrell waited, the flapping of the sails loud. After a bit, Darrell pressed, "Heard his name was Hank Young. Did you know him?"

Williams called from his perch, "I heard you were checking out some old yearbooks. Were you trying to track down his name?"

Darrell figured Merriweather had reported to Williams. Or talked to Douglass, who reported to the board president. And he calculated why the yearbook had come up "missing" and now off limits. He stayed silent and stared at Williams.

"Oh, Coach, that was more than thirty years ago." Williams chuckled. "I am not sure I remember much from back then. And that may be a good thing."

Darrell shuddered in the biting wind and pulled the tabs tight on his life jacket again. "Really? I'd thought it'd be pretty hard to forget a black kid messing with a white girl, especially back then." He struggled to keep his voice from cracking. Though he was freezing cold in his soaked clothes, he was now sweating inside. And his throat was raw.

"Where did you hear that?" Williams asked.

Darrell swallowed a lump. "Uh... some of the students said their parents told them."

"I do not recall anything about some black kid with a white girl back then. What did you say his name was?"

"Hank. Hank Young." When Darrell got no response, he added, "He was a kid in your class at Wilshire, according to the '64 yearbook."

"Rings no bells." Williams shifted in his chair. "Back then, they kept blacks pretty much separate from the white kids. We had very little to do with them. Not like today."

Except when you ganged up on one to beat and kill him. "Probably easier back then?" Darrell offered.

"Damn right it was. Everyone knew what they were supposed to do." He pointed out to the water. "See the buoy out there. That's the marker. We only need to round it and head back."

At least, they'd be headed back. "Hey, where're the rest of the boats?" Darrell pointed to the stern. "I haven't seen any for a while."

"Hell, Coach, you are the first mate on the fastest sailboat in the harbor. But no worries, we will be passing them in short order."

Darrell peered behind toward the horizon, now empty of boats. God, they were out in the middle of nowhere. He glanced back at Williams and could feel his courage ebbing. He needed to keep an eye on him. Make sure he didn't try anything.

Williams tilted his head toward the approaching

marker. "Now, as we pass the buoy, we need to grab that flag." He pointed to a small red and white flag flapping wildly atop the flashing marker. "If you could help out again?"

Darrell said, "I'm pretty unsteady on my feet, and you want me to grab it as we go by?"

"Well, we need to collect that flag to win. It proves we rounded this point." Williams, snug in his chair, shrugged his shoulders. "Someone's got to steer this baby."

Darrell stood and took an unsteady step in the shifting boat. He watched as the bright orange buoy approached on the port side, its red light blinking a warning, the flag flapping back and forth. The bell clanged as the marker was tossed about by the rolling waves. He faced the water, and with one hand grasping the railing, he stretched out his other arm to grab the flag, but it was just beyond his reach. He had no choice but to release his grip on the rail and lean over the railing to reach the fluttering flag.

Too late, he heard it. Whipped by the wind, the huge mainsail shifted abruptly. It veered from port to starboard. The boom swung straight across the deck. The hard frame of the sail slammed into his back. Hands no longer on the rail and off-balance, Darrell lost his footing. He went over the edge.

The angry waves reached up and swallowed him.

Chapter 55

Darrell didn't even have time to yell. Or close his mouth. The salty liquid rushed down his throat. The entire world went silent. The wake of the boat dragged him under. The craft's rudder, huge and menacing, came within inches of his head. His arms windmilled furiously to avoid the blade. It sliced through the water like some mute reaper. He stared up, dumbfounded, as it passed overhead, so close his hair tugged up and then forward in its wake. The vest dragged him back to the surface. His ears popped.

He spat out what he could. The heavy boom had shoved the air out of him. And bruised his back. Now his ribs and back ached. He heaved.

Coming from the deadly quiet beneath, the gurgling waters sounded so loud, Darrell couldn't hear anything else. He hacked over and over. His sides ached. He tried to inhale, but before he could take a breath, another angry swell slammed into him. Barely in time, he shut his mouth.

The Bay washed over him, and the eerie silence wrapped around him like a shroud. Lungs bursting, he flapped his arms. He broke through the surface again and exhaled. Drew a quick breath and breathed out. The waves gurgled. He shook his head, trying to make sense of the cacophony. He drew a long, ragged breath. He scanned the surface, searching for *Without Pier,* and blew out. Doing a clumsy dog paddle, he rotated. Halfway around, another surge rolled over him. He submerged again. Came back up, sputtering. Stared. He saw the boat through dripping eyes.

Amazed at how far the yacht had sailed, Darrell yelled, "Hey," but it came out as only a weak croak. The water filling his ears, he hardly heard it himself. He knew, with the howling wind and surging water, his voice wouldn't carry. Williams couldn't hear him. Darrell flailed his arms in huge circles and yelled anyway. "Come back."

He didn't know how long it had been. Couldn't be more than half a minute. A minute maybe. By now, Williams would realize he'd gone over the side. Darrell stared at the yacht, sails full and billowing, as it cut through the water. Away from him. Through chattering teeth, he yelled, "Turn the damn thing around!" His useless words were whipped away by the wind and drowned by the water. Relentless, the boat continued on.

Williams had left him here. Darrell wasn't brave—he was merely stupid.

His whole body shuddered.

Oh, God. Oh, God. Oh, God. Oh, God.

Swell after swell tossed him about. He fought to keep his gaze focused on that slice of the horizon. The slap of the water echoed in his brain. The sailboat was still there, but it had shrunk. Sails and hull together, it was a tiny blue-and-white smudge on a canvas of ugly, swirling grays. As he clutched the life vest, he tried to use it to ride the swells. As he watched, the yacht disappeared.

He remembered hearing the Bay weather report for

the day. Recalled the announcer saying "The water temperature would be sixty-five degrees." Not too cold, Darrell told himself even as his body shivered. His fingertips tingled and were going numb. One at a time, he pulled each hand from its iron grip on the vest collar and shook it to try to keep life in the fingers and keep blood flowing. His hands returned to their frenzied grasp.

His feet rose in the wake, and he saw the tops bob up ahead of him in the water. He stared at them. He was no swimmer, but he knew enough to recognize his shoes were now only dead weights on his feet. He'd spent a small fortune on those damn things. He needed to get them off.

One hand clenched the collar of the vest, the knuckles white. He would not let go. His other hand slipped into the water and pulled at the Jordan Nikes. Got the right one off. He watched the red and white stripes descend in a strange dance below him. He tugged at the other shoe, but the angle was wrong. It wouldn't budge. He tried to use his free foot to nudge the heel of his other shoe, but his toes wouldn't cooperate. He switched hands, left now clutching the life vest, and felt it. Or thought he did. Another cruel surge dragged at the life vest and the straps gave a little. He remembered sitting in the sailboat, opening and closing the straps. Maybe he weakened them.

His condition threatened to paralyze him, the panic trying to seize him like the cold slicing through his body. He fought it. He could not let *it* take over. He moved his right hand down the length of his body and twisted his frame under the water. It took three yanks, but the sneaker came free and spiraled down. He rushed his hand back to the vest collar. Held on and bounced. He waited. He stared at the endless march of white caps and, because he had to do *something*, started to count them.

"One, two, three, four, five, six." Breath. "Seven, eight, nine, ten, eleven, twelve." Another roller struck him in the face, and he swallowed, the briny taste stronger now. He choked again on the burning bile in his throat. He spat it out and kept his mouth shut, except for quick breaths. The counting didn't help, didn't accomplish anything.

God, there were so many waves.

But he had to do something. He strained to hear the sounds of a surge rolling up on him. He focused. It took several tries, but he was able to use the noise of an onrushing wave to ready himself, mouth closed and breath taken.

As he looked around, he could see only water, the waves slapping across the Bay, most of them in angry, white-capped rows. He tried to recall what Erin had taught him about how most of the Bay was shallow, six feet deep or less. Out here? He guessed it was worth a try. He *had* to do something. He stretched his legs down, but felt nothing. Nothing but wet, cold emptiness.

The ragged ebb and flow of the Bay had tossed him so, he couldn't tell where he was and which way was east, the closest shore, he guessed. Dark, brooding clouds covered the sky, obliterating any sun, so that was no help. Darrell hadn't forgotten which way Williams' yacht sailed and figured he had to move perpendicular, if he wanted to see a shoreline.

One hand clutching the life vest, he used his other

and his legs to try to navigate. It was hard going. Every few seconds, another wave slammed him, the sound deafening in his ears, and shoved him back. The hand gripping the vest started going numb. He switched hands, shook the other and paddled with it, trying to keep the blood flowing and the numbness at bay.

It wasn't working.

The tingling had spread to the toes on both feet. He knew it would only get worse. For a moment, he flashed back to the sight of his brother's friends, years ago, limbs stiff and cold, bodies blue from the frozen water. He shuddered to realize the same numbness was now invading his body. As he recalled last night's vision, he gasped through chattering teeth, "Why the hell did you get me into this, Hank?"

Chapter 56

He wasn't dead yet.

He thought it. Repeated it out loud, his voice in creaky syllables. Or maybe, the voice was in his head.

Not. Dead. Yet.

The cold slithered deeper into his skin.

Erin.

He would not give up. Not yet.

Darrell kept at his plan. His only plan. One arm clutching the vest collar, his other stroked and his legs paddled. Moving him east. To the shore. He hoped. His head twisted and turned between the assaults of the breakers, but he still couldn't see any sign of land. Nothing but water.

Wave after wave after wave.

Desperate to navigate, to make any progress, he freed up his second hand and used both to paddle. The straps loosened more, the life jacket going slack. He jerked one hand back to the collar. Held on for dear life.

He wished he'd learn to swim better, when he had the chance. When his life didn't depend on it. Although, with the angry waters surging around him, he wasn't sure it would make much difference. He knew the basics. Use the hands to pull through the water. Kick with the legs. But he'd never been very good at it, and he was losing feeling in his limbs. The numbness was worse. The tips of his fingers tingled—he had almost no feeling in his index and pinkie on both hands. It was spreading across his toes.

After a while, he started counting again, to keep his mind occupied. With the sound of his hand slapping the surface, he struggled to do twenty sets of strokes and kicks. He concentrated on keeping his mouth shut. Worked to time his breathing between the endless waves, to keep feeling in his fingers and toes. Then he stopped, allowing his legs to dangle, and switched hands. He extended his feet down and tried to find a shoal or sandbar. Anything. All his feet touched was more nothing. He cursed. Started over.

This time he could barely make fifteen before he had to stop and rest. Stretched down one more time, feet feeling nothing. Took three slow breaths. His head throbbed. Again, he urged himself. He managed fifteen more. His breathing now so labored and fast, he feared he might go into shock. In and out, his ragged breaths huffed. He stopped moving and concentrated on reining in his panic.

Tried to.

He stared where he thought the shore should be, but only saw more water, more swells marching across him as if they wanted to pummel him.

It was working.

He struggled to say, "Erin," but all he heard was a two-syllable croak.

He'd never see her again.

It's better to have loved and lost, he recalled the old Shakespearean line. No. It was not. It made the loss even greater, the hurt deeper.

As he floated, body curled in the water now and both hands grasping the life jacket, he closed his eyes.

He pictured her face—the brilliant green eyes, the shimmering red hair, the sprinkling of freckles. And that incredible smile. Saw her sleek figure running, remembered her huddled in the library carrel, felt the touch of her skin next to him on his couch. He smiled and used one arm to wipe the snot from his nose. Realizing he would die here, wet and cold, he cried. She wouldn't even know what happened to him.

A loud clap surprised him and he jerked open his eyes. His gaze darted around and he saw…water. More waves with more raging whitecaps, everywhere he looked. Maybe he had imagined it. Didn't he read somewhere that hypothermia affected the brain as well?

He watched, waiting. A streak of white ripped the ugly grays of the sky and sea. Then another, followed by two thundering booms. His ears hurt and the pounding in his brain worsened. The first drops struck his forehead. As he watched, the rain hit the waves around him, sending tiny jets into the surging waters.

Tilting his head up, his open mouth caught a few drops, their moisture feeling cool against his rough throat. He opened his mouth to catch more rain and another swell rolled over him. The salt water rushed down his throat. Darrell broke the surface and coughed. He tried to look around. The rain pelted the surface surrounding him. It looked like bullets were striking the water. The sheets of rain slicing into the Bay darkened the gray, obscuring everything.

He stopped paddling. Stretching his legs down, his numb toes searched for something, anything other than water. Found nothing. He curled up and attempted to ride the waves. The rain reduced his vision and the waves tossed him so, he had no idea which way to paddle now, even if he had the strength. He let the Bay rock him and waited.

When he thought he'd have enough time between rollers, Darrell tilted his head up and caught some raindrops. A few drops. Not enough to wash the salt from his tongue. How long had he been in the water? It felt like hours. His whole body shivered. He couldn't see anything now, with the rain emptying into the Bay wherever he looked. Gray upon gray upon gray. His gaze clouded, he zoned out. He half expected to see his life flow past him like a movie, but he saw nothing. Weariness tugged at his eyelids and it felt good to close them, if only for a minute.

From behind, a towering wave struck him. It slapped him hard and wrenched him awake. He tugged at the life vest. He felt the vest loosen more, pulling away from him. Both hands clutched at the collar, knuckles white with effort. Another fierce breaker hit. The vest gave way from around his body. He saw the straps floating ahead in the water, the blue padded sections dragged with the current. He held tighter. Both hands still grasped the collar as another wave yanked at the jacket. He knew he couldn't continue like this. He released his right hand and grabbed the floating strap. He wrapped it around his palm, once, twice, three times. He closed his numbing fingers, pulling the device closer to his body. Both hands clutched the broken pieces and held on.

He knew he couldn't last much longer. His whole body chilled, his teeth chattering. All feeling was leaving his fingers and he was barely holding on by a death grip.

I'm sorry, Erin. Mom, Dad, Craig, I love you.

He wanted to be somewhere else, anywhere else, and returned to his reverie about Erin. He would not let his last thoughts be of this Godforsaken, endless stretch of angry water. He conjured her up, this time at the helm of her father's sailboat, red tresses gleaming wet in the rain. As he watched, he could've sworn he saw her handling the craft, the sail, white with the long gold stripe, being battered by wind and rain. He thought he heard her call his name.

Then, he let go.

Chapter 57

No matter what he did, Darrell could not get warm. He hunched in the armchair in front of the fireplace and huddled underneath a quilt. He couldn't stop shivering.

But, at least he was alive. He still couldn't believe it. He'd pinch himself if he could make his fingers do his bidding.

Earlier, when he'd first awakened, foggy and disoriented, he saw two faces hovering close to him. A blonde and a redhead. Sara and Erin. They were such a welcome sight he wanted to scream with joy. He opened his mouth, but his throat wouldn't work.

"You're okay," Erin had whispered, her hand warm on his cheek. "I found you. You're safe now."

His brain wouldn't function, as if it had been frozen in the cold water as well. But it dawned on him that Erin had somehow saved him.

He'd tried to move but had trouble making his body respond and could only watch as Sara and Erin pulled off his cold, sodden clothes. They helped him stand and, speaking in urgent, hushed voices, led him into a bed and piled a mound of covers over him. He drifted in and out, remembering Erin's beautiful green eyes on the pillow next to him. He reached out to touch her face—to make sure she was real—and her hand met his. It felt so warm. As her fingers touched his skin, massaged his hand, he thought, I'm alive. With her.

In the water he hadn't merely conjured up her image.

He tried to concentrate but found himself losing consciousness. When he came to again, mostly awake, Erin helped him into some of Al's old clothes. Darrell was still chilled, and as she guided his limbs into the sweats, her touch felt comforting and so *real* on his bare skin. Then she'd wrapped a huge quilt around him and escorted him down to the family room next to the roaring fire.

He fell asleep again there in the chair, and when he awoke, he stared up at the mantel clock. Twenty minutes past six? Almost seven hours since he climbed aboard Williams' yacht?

God, how long was he in the water? How long had he been out?

After the life jacket had come apart, he didn't remember much. Just his body tossed helplessly by the waves. He'd drifted in and out, imagining Erin above him? And Pogo? Darrell shivered and wrapped an arm around his body, trying to stop the shaking. And he wanted to make sure this was real. That he was on dry land.

As he stared at the mug quivering in his other hand, he watched steam rising from the swaying liquid. The numbing began to ease, releasing some sensitivity into his fingers as he flexed them. In the hearth, the fire crackled and a half-burnt log dropped through the grate, sending sparks flying and releasing the aroma of burning pine. He inhaled the smell, glad for anything to replace the brackish odor from the Bay stuck in his nostrils.

With a bang, Pogo bounded through the door and

rocketed across the room, colliding into Darrell's legs. He reached down and stroked the dog's neck, savoring the soft feel of his fur. The pug snuggled tightly against his master.

"Thanks, boy. I'm pretty sure I'm still among the living," Darrell croaked, his throat sore.

"When I first saw you in the water, I wasn't so sure." Erin came into the family room and knelt next to him. She wrapped both arms around him and kissed him urgently. Her lips were soft and moist on his chapped lips and her embrace radiated warmth through his body. The realness of her assured him he wasn't dreaming.

She continued, "When I found you, you were clinging to that torn up life jacket with your eyes closed and I thought…" Her eyes brimmed with tears and her chin quivered.

Darrell didn't want to see her cry. He put on a brave face on and managed a weak smile. "Nope. I had my eyes closed and was dreaming of you."

Erin kissed him again softly, and he savored the feel, almost able to taste her.

When they finished, he took another sip of tea and let the warm liquid slide down and soothe his scratchy throat. He stared at her. She looked disheveled, long red hair tangled, tears and black mascara streaming from bloodshot eyes. The faded, gray sweats hung loose on her. And Darrell had never seen a more beautiful sight.

As her hip bounced open the door, Sara entered, cradling a bright yellow bowl, its contents steaming. "How's my favorite drowned sailor?" Wearing an apron with the words, *"Women—like wine—get better with age,"* she took Darrell's mug and handed him the bowl and a spoon. "If my world famous chili can't get your engine heated up, nothing can."

The rich, spicy aroma of the soup wafted in the air. "Thanks," he croaked. He took several spoonfuls, slurping the meaty liquid. "Ah, that tastes great."

Up on all fours, the pug rubbed against Darrell's legs.

"Pogo, leave your master alone for now," Sara said. "Don't worry. I'll get you some in a bit." With a forlorn look, the dog settled back down.

From the other end of the house, the clanking of the garage door opener sounded, followed by Al's booming voice. "Sara, I hope you're sitting down. I've got some terrible news." His tone subdued, the voice held none of its usual glibness. "You're not going to believe what I heard at Danny's." The door into the kitchen banged shut. "A bunch of the guys just returned from a search mission on the water. Oh, God! Sara?" Without waiting for an answer, he went on, "Apparently, during the race, Darrell fell over the side of Williams' boat." Soles slapped across the linoleum floor and Al's voice got louder. "Sara? Did you hear me?"

"Al—" Sara began, but he cut her off.

"Anyway, by the time Williams noticed it and went back, he couldn't find any sign of Coach. So Williams sailed ahead and got the other sailors to help him. They broke off the race and went back hunting for him. He told them Darrell was wearing a vest when he went over, so he had a chance, but they were out for three hours and never found him. They think he's—"

Al pushed open the door to the family room and stopped. Taking in the three by the fireplace, his eyes went wide. "I guess he's right here." He strode across the room and slapped Darrell's back, making him wince. "Glad to see you're still with us, kid," he said, the glibness back.

"Not as glad as I am," Darrell squawked.

Chapter 58

A bemused grin on his face, Al flopped into the recliner. "I guess the news of your death has been greatly exaggerated. Thank God. I mean, where will I find a coach I can torment as much as you?" He levered up the foot piece, and Sara came over and sat next to him on the sofa. "Now, will someone please tell *me* what happened?"

Darrell finished another spoon of chili before starting. "About 11:00 this morning, I was down at the dock to catch up with Erin when she got back from her charter. Only, Williams tricked me into helping him in the race."

"Tricked you. How?" Erin's eyebrows scrunched together.

Darrell continued, his voice a hoarse whisper, "Well, he said his first mate came down with the flu, and he needed a second for the race. I didn't realize until we were out on the water it was a ruse." He shrugged and went on. "Besides, once aboard his yacht, I thought with all the sailboats around, he wouldn't try anything, *and* I might be able to have a little private conversation with him. I guess I was so focused on catching him, I let my macho get the best of me."

Erin said, "That didn't quite go the way you planned." She pulled a chair next to Darrell and sat. "So what happened on the boat? While you were delirious, you mumbled some, but nothing made much sense."

"We started the race along with everyone else and then, with that yacht of his, we got way ahead of the rest. When it all happened, I looked for the other boats behind us but couldn't see anyone. He knocked me overboard and then sailed off and left me."

"What?" both women said in unison, leaning forward.

"Knocked you overboard? On purpose?" Al stared at his friend. "You're sure?"

"Pretty damn sure," Darrell croaked. "When we were ready to come about, he had me lean over the side to capture the flag off the buoy."

"The flag?" Erin interjected. "You're not that steady a sailor. Why didn't he get it himself?"

"That's what I said, but Williams said someone had to steer the boat. Anyway, when I was reaching over and off-balance, he swung the boom around and slammed me overboard. Hit me so hard, it bruised my ribs and almost knocked me out." Darrell touched his back and winced.

Al nodded. "Okay, so, if you were in the middle of the Bay, how'd you end up in front of my fireplace? I know you can't swim worth a damn."

Erin placed an arm around Darrell's shoulders. "I found him out there, floating and unconscious."

Al said, "Wait a minute. How'd you even know where he was?"

From her seat on the couch, Sara placed a hand on her husband's knee. "Al, take a breath and let her tell the story."

Erin said, "I didn't know where he went. Not at first. When I got back in from Dad's charter, I saw

Pogo alone, prancing back and forth across the dock."
She reached down and brushed the dog's neck. "When I
couldn't find Darrell, I asked Brad, the harbormaster, if
he'd seen him. He told me Darrell went with Williams.
That worried me, so I took Pogo out on *Second Wind*. I
followed the race course and saw some of the boats
pretty far out in the Bay on the return leg. I tried to
signal to them, but I guess they were so intent on this
stupid race, they didn't notice. Finally, I got alongside
of Chuck Menton's boat and asked about *Without Pier*.
Chuck said Williams had been way ahead, but he hadn't
seen him at the turn."

Putting down the leg rest, Al sat up in the chair.

Erin went on. "I didn't know what else to do. I had
a bad feeling about it, so I kept heading south toward
the Little Choptak, in hopes of catching sight of
Williams' boat. By then, the rain had started coming
down hard and cut visibility way down." She put her
hand on her forehead. "I was getting really desperate
when I caught sight of those blue sails of his. Williams
was on the other side of the Bay heading back north."

She turned toward Darrell. "I started to head across
the Bay to try to catch *Without Pier* when a strange
thing happened."

Darrell looked at her and said, "You had a
little...help?"

Al looked from Erin to Darrell. "What help? What
are you talking about?"

Erin continued, "I figured I had to come about, so I
went to the adjust the jib to swing *Second Wind* around.
I untied the rigging from the starboard cleat, swung the
sail around, and fixed it to the port side. As I was
making my way back to the helm, I felt the boat sway

and turned back around." She turned toward Al. "You're not going to believe what I saw."

"What?" Al's voice carried his exasperation and he stared at his wife. Sara pointed to Erin and smiled.

Erin hurried on. "I saw the rigging which I'd just attached with a cleat hitch come *untied* and get loose. All by itself."

Al said, "Maybe you didn't tie it right. You were in a hurry."

Erin stared at Al. "I've tied maybe a thousand cleat hitches and this is the first one that came loose. But, yeah, I thought the same thing. Until what happened next."

"What?" Al cried.

"The jib swung back, and I watched the rigging get wrapped around the starboard cleat again and tied in a perfect cleat hitch." Erin's hands tied a knot in the air and finished, "As if invisible hands were maneuvering the halyard."

"Hank," Darrell said.

"That kept us heading south." Erin glanced down at the dog, now settled on the carpet. "Then Pogo here ran forward and stopped next to the starboard cleat and yelped twice. At something or someone. Then he trotted into the bow and stared south into the Bay."

"Weren't you freaked? What'd you do then?" Al asked.

Sara said, "I was pretty weirded out, but all I could think about was finding Darrell. I *sensed* he was out in the Bay somewhere. Maybe Hank was telling me, I don't know." She glanced over at Darrell. "So I sailed on, searching, and started calling your name."

She shook her head. "I didn't know what I was

doing, but I couldn't quit. I was scared and kept sailing back and forth, fighting the wind, staring through the pouring rain." She indicated the pug. "It was Pogo who saw you first. He yelped, turned, and looked at me and then stared straight ahead, into the water. Then I saw a flash of blue in the roll of the waves—turned out to be the damaged life vest you were clinging to."

Darrell set down his empty bowl and picked up the small dog, hugging him. "Thanks, boy."

Erin got up and walked over to the front door and snatched up a soggy, tattered blue life jacket and tossed it to Al. "Darrell was unconscious. I had to really work to get him aboard. Wrapped him up as best I could and got us back as quick as I could. I knew he was in hypothermia, and I needed to get him warm. He was turning blue, and I was terrified I was too late."

Al asked, "Why didn't you take him to the hospital?"

Erin glanced at Sara. "I was going to, but after what happened, I wasn't sure what I should do, so I came here to ask Sara."

Sara interrupted. "Darrell was delirious, and I could tell his core temperature had dropped, but his hypothermia wasn't severe. Thank heaven Erin found him when she did." She paused a bit. "And after Erin told me her story, I thought it might be better to keep Darrell under wraps."

Darrell noticed his throat was feeling better and cleared it. "Erin saved my life." He smiled at Sara. "Erin and this chili. I'm starting to feel human again."

Sara got up from the couch. "You're welcome. That reminds me. It looks like Pogo's out but would either of you like some?" When Al and Erin nodded,

Sara headed into the kitchen.

Al examined the life vest and turned it over in his hand. "I'm no expert on these things." He held a piece of the strap. "This belt doesn't look like it ripped. I think it's been cut." He pinched the edge between his fingers. "Sliced through."

"That's what I thought," Erin said, eyebrows raising, "but I hadn't said anything to Darrell."

"That son of a bitch," Darrell said. "He knocked me overboard *and* made sure I had a damaged life vest."

"Kid," Al said, "Williams must really want you dead."

Sara came through the door carrying two bowls. As she handed them off, she said, "So right now everyone thinks Darrell is dead."

Al took a loud slurp of chili. "That was the prevailing theory at Danny's."

Darrell said, "God, my kids will be going crazy. I need to get word to them I'm okay."

Erin shook her head. "Don't think that's such a good idea."

Sara agreed. "She's right. Williams tried to kill you once. And you suspect he's behind the deaths of Jefferson and Kelly." She returned to the couch. "What makes you think he won't try again?"

Darrell set his empty bowl on the hearth, went over, and grabbed the mangled life vest. "Maybe I should go public and let everyone know what Bud did." He held up the vest. "After all, I've got the proof right here."

Al pointed his spoon at Darrell. "I don't think that'll fly. By the time you get to town, Bud will've spun the story so your death was a great tragedy and he's the hero. Hell, if I know Bud Williams, he's probably down at Danny's, drinking toasts to his lost friend and colleague, Coach Henshaw."

"But what about this?" Darrell held up the tattered strap.

"Bud will come up with some story to explain it." Sara crossed her arms in front of her. "Right now, you're better off dead. I mean, Williams thinking you're dead." She turned to Erin. "Did anyone see Darrell with you when you came off the boat?"

"Don't think so. It was really pouring when we got to the dock, and I didn't see anyone else around."

Sara glanced back at Darrell. "So Williams must be convinced you didn't make it." Then to Erin, "But he also knows you were looking into things with Darrell, so he might come after you."

Eyes wide, Darrell stared at Erin. "I can't let anything happen to you. I will not."

Erin asked, "If we can't go public, and we can't prove he did it, what are we going to do? We can't hole up here forever. I'll make sure my mom and dad know I'm okay, but if we go anywhere, somebody will recognize us."

No one spoke for a while, Al's slurps of chili loud in the silence. Darrell closed his eyes and rubbed his lids with his index fingers. When he opened them, his eyes shone. "Do you still have the clothes I had on in the water?"

Sara said, "Yeah, they're in the utility tub, dripping. Why?"

"I'm going to need them." He saw the questions on their faces. "I think it's time to make Bud Williams a *believer*. We're going to arrange for his own personal encounter with a ghost." A smirk tugged at the corners of Darrell's mouth. "Maybe...two."

Chapter 59

It took them most of the evening to work out the plan.

By the end, after they realized Darrell and Erin would need some other clothes, the McClures waited till after midnight and Sara picked up a few things from her friend's apartment and Al did the same for Darrell. No stalkers appeared at either location.

Al said, "Looks like, with you out of the way, all's quiet."

Taking the clothes, Darrell deadpanned, "The Coach is dead. Long live the Coach."

They spent much of Sunday making calls, collecting information, and assembling what they would need, the four of them working on different tasks. Darrell and Erin stayed inside and collaborated on the details of the plan. Sara spent most of the day on the phone, collecting information on Williams' habits, including some juicy gossip on his latest indiscretions. Al got food and supplies. On a trip to the store, he swung by the school.

"It seems everyone thinks you've gone to Davy Jones' locker." Al deposited the groceries on the counter. "The kids have started a memorial shrine for you at the corner of the football field. They left notes, flowers, and even teddy bears next to a sign that says 'We'll miss you, Coach'."

367

Darrell said, "Well, at least we won't maintain the lie for very long. Whatever occurs tomorrow, everybody will know what really happened."

Al pointed a finger gun at his friend. "Or you'll really be dead."

Darrell swallowed hard, as he realized Al's joke could become reality.

Hanging up the phone, Sara smacked Al on the arm. "Don't even say that, Alan Raymond McClure."

Unwilling to let up, Al said, "Darrell, since you're no longer swallowing Bay water, you can appreciate this. How do you save a drowning lawyer?"

Darrell sighed. "I don't know."

"Take your foot off his head, of course." That earned him another swat from his wife, but Al chuckled at his own joke anyway. Still, as they worked through the weekend, Darrell came to appreciate his friend's humorous efforts to break the tension.

Saturday evening, Darrell had decided to enlist the help of one more co-conspirator, this one from Philadelphia. Sunday evening, Darrell, Erin, Al, and Sarah were reassembling in the McClure family room to work out the final logistics of their plan when Kelsie arrived. Darrell did the introductions.

Kelsie stopped in the middle of the family room, glancing at the others, maybe a little awkward, Darrell guessed. Over gray cargo pants, she wore a clean, white top with a choker of green and blue glass stones. The necklace seemed to reflect her deep emerald eyes and contrast with her long, russet hair, which curled around one shoulder. Recalling the girl in his crazy dream and in the Polaroid, he thought again—in a dark room she really *could* pass for the young Kelly.

"Glad to meet you," Kelsie said, her deep voice faltering a bit.

Sara stepped forward and took Kelsie's hand in both of hers. "I'm so sorry to hear about what happened to your mom."

"Thank you." Kelsie took the seat next to Sara and gathered her long legs under her. "I haven't met this guy, except through my mom's diary, but he must be some piece of work. I'm on board with anything that will nail the bastard who tried to gang rape my mom and then probably had her killed." Looking at Darrell, her voice got hard as steel. "And after you told me what he did to you...tell me how I can help."

"What about your job?" Erin asked. Then to Al and Sara, "Kelsie's a personal trainer in Philly at this big health club."

"No problem. I had some vacation coming and took a few days. They figured I needed some time." Kelsie stared at Darrell. "So what's the plan?"

Darrell eyed the others and said, "We're going to *help* Mr. Bud Williams experience a few personal visits from the spirit world."

"And how will you arrange that?" Kelsie asked. "Do you mean Hank's ghost?"

Al grinned. "No, our coach here has a plan that relies more on flesh and blood...and a little deception. You see, Williams—and most of Wilshire—thinks Darrell here is dead."

Erin jumped in, "And if we're right about Williams being behind your mom's mugging, then he knows she's dead as well."

Kelsie's eyes narrowed. "She *is* dead."

On the sofa, Sara slid closer to their guest and

placed a hand on her arm. "I'm sorry. We're not trying to be insensitive, but you look an awful lot like your mom. At least, the pictures we've seen of her when she was young." Sara looked into Kelsie's face. "Did they used to tell you looked like her?"

Kelsie nodded. "They did, all the time, except for one big thing. I got my *tan* from my dad. Mom was quite fair skinned."

Darrell said, "Makes it a little tricky, but I think it can still work."

Sara started, "You see, the plan is—"

The doorbell sounded and cut her off mid-sentence. They all glanced at each other, eyes wide.

Al whispered to his wife, "You expecting someone?"

Sara started to respond when the voice on the other side of the door yelled, "Pizza delivery."

Darrell and Erin exhaled, and Al got up from his chair. "Don't anyone else get up. I'll pay for it."

Darrell whispered, "I can't. I'm dead."

He pointed at Darrell, then went to door and came back in with two large pizza boxes with *"Howies"* in big red letters across the top. He set them on the coffee table.

"Hey, Kelsie, you're new here." Al pointed to the boxes. "You know why Howie went into the pizza business?"

Returning from the kitchen with plates and napkins in hand, Sara said, "Don't humor him, Kelsie."

Al finished, "Because he really wanted to make some dough."

Kelsie released a short bark. "I like that, Al." She accepted a plate from her hostess. "Thanks, I'm starved.

370

I haven't eaten since this morning."

The aroma of tomato sauce, garlic, and onions filled the room. After getting drinks from the kitchen, they all clustered around the coffee table. For a few minutes, no one spoke, each busy eating, and, from time to time, blotting the corners of their mouths for stray red sauce and strings of mozzarella.

Used to eating quickly, Darrell finished first and pushed his paper plate aside. He rose, went into the kitchen, and went through his ritual of washing his hands, twice and dried them with three paper towels Then he returned and began reviewing the plan for Kelsie, the others happy to add their parts in between bites. All the while, Kelsie listened, even as she put away three slices herself. "You think that will be enough to lure him to this widow's walk?"

Sara added, "After Williams catches a glimpse of you a couple times throughout the day, he's going to be awfully curious."

Kelsie asked, "You sure you can set up these encounters without him getting close enough to realize I'm *not* Mom's ghost? And what about this?" Kelsie pointed to the skin on her arm.

Darrell said, "There is that, but we're hoping we can pull it off, *if* we keep you at a distance and in the shadows. Williams' imagination will do the rest." He looked over at Sara. "And with her help, we even got some clothes from the sixties to enhance the illusion."

Sara studied Kelsie. "I had fun going through the attic. I think what I found might fit you, though the skirt may be a little short." She got up and walked over to the coat closet, taking out two hangers with clothes. When she pulled off the plastic bags, she revealed a top in a vibrant yellow-and-black check pattern along with a matching bright yellow skirt. "I remember I called this my bumble bee outfit."

Kelsie broken into a small smile. "That looks like a classic."

Sara said, "Yeah, and if we do your hair up a little different, and add a little make up, I think you'll look so much like your mom looked. It might work."

Kelsie still didn't look convinced. "Yeah, but this guy knew my mom was old. Won't it throw him off, if she looks young again?"

Erin said, "We're counting on it throwing him." Then she pointed to Sara. "Oh, and thanks to our friend here, we got a bead on Bud's plans for the day. She has quite the network of phone contacts."

Sara said, "Williams starts every day with coffee at Fine Grounds. It's this little coffee shop down by the water. It's a ritual for him. You're going to be in a dark corner booth. The plan is to make sure he sees you and then whisk you out before he gets more than a glimpse."

Al added, "Then, my resourceful wife learned good ol' Bud takes the first floor office duty at the bank during the noon hour. See, Stella's off for lunch, and he keeps an eye on the tellers' counters."

Polishing off her second slice, Erin licked her fingertips. "We think we can set it up so you kind of *float* through the lobby, giving Williams just enough time to notice you, and then exit."

Kelsie raised one finger. "Not sure that will be enough."

Sara set down her plate and smiled. "Tomorrow is the board meeting night, and Bud has dinner every board night with a couple of board members at Chester's. It's this fancy place over on Second Street, and I have some friends there. Anyway, during his meal, we're going to arrange it so he sees you across the room—again in the dark. After the waitresses cluster around his table, we're going to whisk you out, so it looks like you disappeared."

Kelsie shook her head. "I still don't see what that gets us."

"We saved the best for last," Darrell said, "When he gets up to leave for the board meeting, Sara's arranged to have her server friend slip Bud an envelope with a message inside. She'll say the woman that was here left it for him. Take a look for yourself."

Kelsie took the sheet from Darrell and read, "We must all pay for our misdeeds. Darrell uncovered your crimes and so will others. You may have drowned Darrell, but he left the evidence for others to find. Your time is almost up."

Kelsie said, "You think this will do it?"

Darrell said, "He'll figure the only place Darrell would have this evidence is in his, er, I mean my office. When he comes up there to check, we'll lure him out onto the widow's walk and get him talking."

"You're sure he'll come." Kelsie still seemed unconvinced. "He won't be worried it's a trap."

Settling back in his recliner, Al said, "Oh, he'll be worried—we're counting on that. We think your *apparitions* will really rattle him. As soon as he can get away from the board meeting, he'll come. Bud's big into control, and he'll believe he can *manage* the whole thing."

As he studied the others, Darrell marveled at his

luck. *With these guys' help, this might actually work.* He said, "Then, when we get Bud out on the widow's walk, he's going to come face to face with two ghosts. The ghost of Kelly and the ghost of Darrell. We're hoping, between the two of us, we can spook him into blurting out what happened. I'm going to have a recorder hidden and hope to get it all on tape."

No one spoke for a bit. Kelsie raised a finger to her lips and then pointed it. "Nobody wants to get this guy more than me." She glanced across at Darrell. "Well, maybe you do. But have you realized this could get dangerous? What if he brings a gun?"

"You're right, it could be dangerous," Darrell said. "He might bring a gun, but I doubt it. After all, he'll come straight from the board meeting and will want to search for evidence. But he's coming to meet with a ghost. What good is a gun against a ghost?" He raised one hand, palm out. "But to play it safe, Erin's going to a local cop her family knows and get him to the high school about this time, as a little added protection."

Al said, "Pretty ambitious plan, kid. But you still don't know who's the third guy who attacked Hank." He counted off three fingers. "Jefferson, Williams, and?"

Darrell said, "One step at a time. We'll get Williams up on the widow's walk and see where it leads. Maybe he'll give us the third."

Al looked back. "Okay. While you're up there, try *not* to do a flying leap off the walk."

Chapter 60

"Oh, God! You scared me," hissed Kelsie, as she whirled around to face Darrell, who'd just slid in through the door. "What happened to *you*?"

After he was sure the school building was dark and empty, Darrell had brought her in through the back entrance, up the dim stairwell, and into the athletic office. As they climbed the two flights and he unlocked his office door, he had the uncanny sense they were walking in the footsteps of Kelly and Hank, some thirty-four years earlier. He said, "I wonder how many times Hank and your mom sneaked up these same stairs."

He'd left to change in the restroom and returned, a few minutes later, on silent, bare feet. Seeing Kelsie's astonished look, he glanced down at his clothes. He wore the pants and sweatshirt he'd had on when he went over the side. The fabric was discolored and stretched with rips in the sleeves and pant legs. He also dripped water. With the help of some makeup from Sara, he had black circles around his eyes and a blue tint to his face. "Oh, this get up. We figured it would enhance my ghostly appearance if I looked like I just came out of the Bay."

Kelsie eyed him up and down. "Well, it works."

Darrell glanced down at the old watch Al had lent him. "It's almost time, and we need to be in place before Williams gets here."

He led her through the short hallway and opened the door that led outside. As they stepped onto the narrow ramp, fog from the Bay rolled and curled around their legs. The mist ebbed across, obscuring the ramp and the floor of the widow's walk. Only the top white rail surrounding the space was visible above the fog, as well as the four posts supporting the cupola in the center.

It's almost as if the Bay was their accomplice. Or maybe Hank was helping out.

Darrell guided Kelsie to the far corner of the walk behind one post, where she stood in the shadows. He returned to the doorway and studied her, now only a silhouette, partially hidden by the support.

"If you're there facing him when he comes through here,"—Darrell pointed to the door behind him—"all he'll be able to make out is your silhouette. His imagination will fill in the rest." He turned and indicated the darkened window to the right. "I'll be in my office, off to the side, watching. After he gets out here, I'll turn on the cassette recorder and join you." He placed one hand on her arm. "You okay?"

Kelsie gave a quick nod. "I'm fine."

As he stood beside the post nearest to the door, Darrell glanced out where he could hear the waters of the Bay, but he could make out little in the dark and fog. The smell of the Bay he'd grown accustomed to over the past few months floated in on a breeze. Clouds blotted out the stars, and the moon had taken the night off, transforming the sky into a dark mantle. Darrell thought, nature seemed to be conspiring with them to create the perfect stage. He turned to see Kelsie across the walk, studying him.

"I've really loved coming out here, taking in this incredible view of the Bay." He pointed out at the water. "But that doesn't mean I ever forgot what happened to your dad up here."

Kelsie's gaze went from Darrell to the white railing around the walk, now almost completely wrapped in the shroud of fog. "Maybe we'll get some justice tonight," she said in a murmur.

The clang of footsteps echoing up the stairwell interrupted them. Darrell whispered, "Showtime."

As the steps got louder, he crept back through the opening, around the corner and into his office. At the open window, he gave Kelsie a quick wave. He positioned the tape player on the ledge and hit the record button. Then he squeezed himself into the corner, barely left of the window frame, where he could watch, but couldn't be seen.

He waited. It didn't take long.

The footfalls grew louder as the tunnel effect of the old staircase carried the sound up to the third floor. Darrell concentrated as the steps halted. From the sound of them, Williams had stopped at the entrance onto the top floor. Darrell held his breath and listened. For several seconds he heard nothing, the silence deafening. He glanced toward the hall, at his office door. It was open a crack.

Williams was coming into the office to search, but they wanted him out on the walk.

He focused on the tape player, whose small red recording light blinked. Panic spiking, he strained to listen. Footsteps sounded in the hallway. Outside his office. Manicured fingers came around the door edge.

When the door opened, he was pretty sure Williams couldn't see him in the darkened room, but he couldn't miss the flickering light of the recorder.

"Red. Red, it's me." Kelsie's raspy whisper came through the open window. "I'm here on the widow's walk. Waiting for you."

Darrell listened as the footsteps hurried away from the office and over to the open doorway. He exhaled and inhaled slowly, quietly, he hoped. He watched as Williams emerged onto the widow's walk, dressed in a white shirt and one of his dark suits, the tie hanging loose. He stopped at the nearest post, catty-corner from Kelsie.

Williams called, "What are you trying to pull here? Do you know who I am?" His tone was sharp, but Darrell thought he heard it cracking around the edges.

Kelsie kept her voice low—a hoarse, almost sultry whisper. "Oh, I know you, better than a lot of others. Like, I know you took me out to Betterton Beach one night…"—she stopped, waited a beat, then finished—"and then tried to gang rape me."

"Who told you that?" Williams' response was quick. "How do you know about that? That was a long time ago. Who *are* you?" He took one step forward and peered around the post.

"I think you know who I am. Think hard, *Red*."

"Red? No one calls me Red anymore." He ran one hand through his graying hair. "Kelly?" Williams croaked out. "It *was* you I saw today. At Fine Grounds. And the bank. And you were *there* at Chester's. I thought I was imagining things." He spoke aloud, almost to himself, then stared at Kelsie. "But that can't be. You're dead. Killed last week by a mugger in

Philly."

Kelsie stretched out the next words in another stern whisper. "Dead...but not...forgotten."

Williams took two more steps toward the center of the space and edged closer to Kelsie. He stopped again, still several feet from her, his back now to the office window. The move gave Darrell the opening he needed. In a few seconds, he crept out of the office, through the short hallway and onto the walk.

"Good to see you again, Bud," Darrell croaked.

Williams whirled around, and when he turned, shock and fear exploded in his wide eyes. "B-b-but, that's not possible." Williams turned his head hard from side to side. "You're dead, too. Goddamn, I must be hallucinating."

Darrell chortled, "Huh, you can't get off that easy. We're a lot more than mere *hallucinations*." Both Darrell and Kelsie took a step toward him.

Williams recoiled. His head swiveled from Darrell to Kelsie and back again. "W-w-what do ya want?"

Darrell smirked, hoping the grin was apparent even in the dark. "Oh, we're merely getting started. Now that you've sent us to the other side, we've decided to hang around. You'll be seeing us everywhere. At home, at work, even at that motel in Easton you like to sneak off to. With the cute little thing in accounting."

Williams closed his eyes. "N-n-no. Goddamn no, no, no." He shook his head again and then jerked them open.

Darrell took another staggering step along the office side, in a shambling gait. At the same time, Kelsie edged farther out of the shadows along the rear of the walk. Williams backpedaled onto the Bay side of the walk. His eyes grew huge. He huddled back against the white railing. Jerking his head from side to side, he stared at the two figures. "W-w-what do ya want from me?"

Kelsie spoke, her voice low. "Red, the truth. We simply want the truth."

Williams shrunk lower, his body pinned against the railing. His gaze darted from one "ghost" to the other. "W-w-what truth?"

Darrell said, "The truth about Hank's death, for starters."

"Who?" asked Williams.

"You know, the kid you *lynched* all those years ago," Darrell yelled.

"Oh, that stupid fuckin' kid." Williams frowned. "We didn't mean it."

"You didn't *mean* to lynch a black kid?" Kelsie hissed between clenched teeth.

"No, it was a dumb accident. Hell, we were just a couple of kids," Williams rambled. "We only wanted to teach him a lesson. I mean he was messing with this white girl. You can understand that."

Darrell saw Kelsie flinch at that word. "You mean messing with *me*?" she asked, her voice edged in steel.

Williams rattled on. "Only, when we were fighting, Jeff hit him and killed him, by accident." He looked desperate. "Hell, we were all drunk. He was just a stupid ass wipe. Nobody gave a damn. We figured if we hanged him, people'd think he committed suicide."

Darrell glanced over to the open office window, checking on the recorder.

"For once in your life, Bud, shut up," called a phlegmy voice from inside the doorway. "Ya always did talk too much. Good thing I got here. You pretty much told them ever'thing."

Darrell glanced back at the door to see a bulky figure with a Smokey Bear hat step through the opening. The gun in his hand swung toward Darrell.

Chapter 61

While one hand aimed the gun at Darrell's chest, Brown yanked forward Erin with the other. Erin dragged her feet, struggling in the grasp, and said, "I'm sorry, Darrell. Had no idea."

Darrell's gaze went from her flushed face to the pistol. He had never seen such a large handgun before, not for real. And up close. Even in the murky dark, it looked huge. Brown's fleshy hand clutched the fat wooden stock and aimed the hideous black barrel at him. He glanced back and saw Erin's eyes darting left and right. Afraid she might try something, he decided he needed to buy some time. Maybe figure something out.

Darrell edged back toward the office window. He wanted to put a little space between Kelsie and him, and block the light on the recorder. "Well, if it isn't Officer Cameron Brown." His tone casual, Darrell turned toward Kelsie. "He is what passes for the law around here, though I don't believe he's here in that capacity. Right, *Officer*?"

Brown lumbered around the corner post, his left leg dragging. His eyes bloodshot, he waved the gun a little but kept it pointed at Darrell. "Shut up, Henshaw. You know, you're one stupid Yankee, stickin' your damn nose in where it don't belong."

Though his heart was thudding, Darrell feigned a

relaxed pose and leaned back. He shot a quick glance over at the recorder, light still blinking, and looked back at the cop. "Erin, meet the third member of the gang who lynched Hank."

Erin turned to her captor. "You lynched that kid?"

Brown waved the gun. "Hell, jus' some asshole. He was a brute. An animal."

Darrell prodded, "What about it, Cam? Couldn't take him on, one on one like a man, so you ganged up on him?"

Brown released a loud belch. "Shut up. You know that punk beat me up after school, when me and another guy was wailing on this white kid." Brown shook his head, the broad hat shimmying in the movement. "He stepped in where it weren't no business of his and beat on *me*. Besides, he was rapin' a white girl. He got what he deserved."

Darrell recalled the passage in Kelly's diary where Hank had saved her ungrateful brother. He had a hunch and decided to push his luck. "And what about Jefferson, huh? Afraid he'd spill his guts, so you took care of him?"

Williams gasped, "What?"—the first sound he'd made since Brown showed up. "Cam, he was our friend."

Brown waved the pistol in the air. "He was a drunk. When I found out he was talking to this Yankee,"—the barrel aimed back at Darrell—"I figured he had to be shut up."

Darrell glanced from Williams to Brown and thought he saw something he might be able to exploit. "I got news for you, Officer Brown, Jefferson told me he was one of a group who lynched Hank, but he refused to give you guys up. He said it was all an accident, and he didn't want to get anyone else in trouble."

"Jeez, Cam. Jeff?" cried Williams.

"Shut up, Bud," Brown barked. "It's my job to clean up this damn town, same as you had me take care of the old broad in Philly." He turned to Darrell. "Enough of your damn questions, Coach. You might've found out all this shit, but it won't do you no good dead."

Williams waved his hands. "You don't get it, Cam. They're already dead. You're talking to, to...*ghosts.*" He stumbled over the last word. "Darrell drowned in the Bay. I saw that myself." He pointed to Kelsie across the walk. "You had her killed in Philly."

Brown said, "For a bank president, you can be pretty stupid, ya know. They're flesh and blood like us." Brown released Erin and made a swift move over to Darrell. He seized him by the hair and yanked. Darrell yelped. Just as quickly, Brown stepped back and grabbed Erin's arm before she could react. "There ain't no such things as ghosts."

"What?" Williams rubbed the scar on his chin.

Brown pointed the pistol at Darrell. "Okay, Coach, where's the recording?"

"What recording?" Darrell asked.

Brown brought the gun up to Erin's temple. "Don't be cute. She told me *all* about it on the way over here. Where is it?" He cocked the hammer.

"All right, all right," Darrell said, "it's in the office." He pointed to the open window behind him.

Brown ordered Erin, "Go in there and bring me that tape. Don't try anything, or I'll put a very large hole in your boyfriend." He pushed her toward the open doorway. "And hurry."

Erin stumbled and then caught herself and stepped into the building. As they all watched, she appeared in the office, went over to the window ledge, and picked up the recorder. She pushed a button and ejected the cassette. In a few more seconds, she reappeared on the landing, tape in hand.

"You, coach boy, get over there with her." Brown pointed his gun at Kelsie. "Get on that side of the walk."

Darrell joined Kelsie by the far post. "Sorry," he whispered.

When Erin came out, Brown growled, "Hand me the tape and go join 'em." He kept the gun leveled at Erin.

She extended the tape toward Brown, but right before he grabbed it, she let go and the cassette clattered to the floor of the walk.

Brown glared from her to the tape, clear plastic cassette against the weathered wood. "Very funny." His right foot came down on the tape, the heel of his boot crushing the plastic case. After he stomped on it several times, he kicked the remains with his toe. The cassette flew over the edge of the widow's walk and disappeared. On the way down, it banged against the side of the building.

Stunned, Erin hadn't moved. Brown grabbed her arm and propelled her toward the front railing. Erin stumbled hard into the short fence. Her feet slipped out from under her. The fencing splintered, and she screamed, windmilling for balance. Darrell lunged for her. He caught her arm as she teetered on the edge and wrestled her back. They collapsed on the floor, him on top of her.

"Oh ain't this cute," Brown growled. "Erin, get up and move over with the other broad." He gestured with the gun. "Bud, git over here and take the gun, while I handcuff Yankee Boy."

Erin stood and slid around the walk on unsteady feet, hand gripping the undamaged rail all the way. Darrell got to all fours, panting and acting as if he had to catch his breath.

Williams took the gun and asked, "What do ya want to do, Cam?"

"They ain't dead yet, but that can be easily remedied," Brown said. "These two,"—he pointed to Darrell on the floor and Kelsie in the corner— "everyone thinks they're dead already. We'll simply got to come up some excuse for Erin, here."

"You got your cruiser? Oh, duh, that's a stupid question. Where's it parked?" Williams asked.

Brown edged along the front railing. "'Round back."

Williams said, "Good. Damn good." He nodded up and down. "After you get 'em handcuffed, we'll take 'em down the back stairs. It's late, so nobody's going to see us. Then we can get them over to my yacht. We'll take them out and drop 'em deep, where no one will ever find the bodies."

Brown kept both hands on the railing and smirked at Williams. "Didn't work so well the first time."

Williams waved the gun. "Oh, shut the fuck up and get the cuffs on 'em." He glanced around. "I don't like being up here. It gives me the creeps."

Brown halted over the top of a still gasping Darrell,

his back toward Williams and the door. "Hey, coach boy, you need to get in better shape." Brown laughed, unleashing beer-drenched breath. "Put your hands behind your back."

When Darrell turned his head to look up, he could see the cuffs in Brown's fleshy hands, the steel glinting. Beyond Brown, he saw the moon, full and round now, had fought its way from behind the cloud cover. The moon seemed to shine directly onto the officer, outlining the wide Smokey hat. On all fours, Darrell's gaze went from the paunchy figure looming over him to Williams holding the gun.

Then a deep voice from the doorway called, "Hello again, Red."

Chapter 62

Williams jerked his head around. A huge, dark figure filled the entire doorway, head almost brushing the top of the frame, and stepped onto the walk.

Williams turned around and screamed, "No, no, no. It can't be." He jerked the gun back and forth. "You're d-d-dead. You can't be real. I know. I know you're Goddamn dead."

Darrell stared at the sight. As the figure moved into the light of the bright moon, Darrell recognized the same youth from his visions. Same huge shoulders, same massive arms, entire body naked.

It was…Hank. It was really Hank.

The ghost glanced toward Darrell and Brown and then back to Williams. He took a step toward Williams.

Wide-eyed, Williams howled, "It can't be." He brought the gun up and pulled the trigger. The bullets passed through the apparition and struck the building. Shards of brick and wood flew in all directions, pelting them. The women scrambled to the floor. Darrell raised his hand to shield his eyes.

Brown yelled, "What the hell?" His hand released Darrell and flew to his thigh. A piece of wood stuck out through the fabric of his pants, and a trickle of blood coursed between his fat fingers. He hissed, "Shit," and stared toward the doorway.

Darrell knew this might be his only chance. Using

a move he taught his linemen to ward off a defender, he pushed up on all four limbs, hard.

He knocked Brown off-balance and to the side. Brown's bad leg faltered, and he stumbled back against the railing. His massive bulk fractured the slats. With a loud crack, the wood split. Brown tumbled through the opening. Without thinking, Darrell reached out his hand to catch him. His fingers closed on air. The cop's screams lasted all the way down and were cut off by a sickening thud. Darrell crab-walked away from the gaping hole and back to the two women.

Williams jerked back around. He peered over the railing. Shock exploded on his face. Hank moved toward Williams—slow, long strides. Williams turned back. He saw the ghost almost upon him. Williams tried to take a step backward, but his foot slipped. He yanked the gun up and fired twice. His aim went wild. Bullets pinged off the brass cupola and the bricks, sending shrapnel everywhere.

Darrell dove for the floor and dragged Erin and Kelsie under him. He used his body to shield the women, as tiny pieces of rock tore at his flesh.

"No, no. Keep away from me," shrieked Williams.

Darrell glanced up to see Williams shake his head and back up. He fired the gun once more. The bullet passed through the ghost and struck the office window. The glass exploded into a shower of fragments.

Williams aimed and pulled the trigger again. The cylinder clicked empty. He stumbled back against the split railing. Two more pieces broke away. They clattered to the floor of the walk and slid off the top of the building. Williams refused to let go of the gun and reached out with his left hand to grab another slat of fencing. That wood piece cracked too. He tore his stunned gaze from the ghost, but too late. The chunk of wood he clutched came away in his hand.

Hank took another step toward Williams, who backed into the open hole. Williams disappeared through the split but never cried out. One second he was there, and the next he was gone. The only sound was another dreadful thump on the asphalt below.

Hank stood hunched over the splintered opening and glared down after the two dead men.

Scrambling to his feet, Darrell helped the women stand on shaky legs. The three of them stood, shocked at the deaths, but mesmerized by the sight of the huge black man. They took a few uncertain steps across the walk, toward him.

As if he realized he was being watched, Hank turned around and looked back, huge brown eyes steady. Darrell turned to see Kelsie beside him, tears streaming down both cheeks. Hank's and Kelsie's gazes met, and after a beat, the ghost nodded. Kelsie sniffed once and nodded back, using her arm to wipe her face. The tears rolled down and glistened the "Black Power" tattoo on her bicep.

The ghost took a step toward the doorway and stopped. He turned and looked at Darrell and the broad, black face broke into a huge, white smile. Darrell could've sworn he heard the young man say "Thanks," though he never saw the ghost's lips move.

Then, the hulking figure turned and stepped from the widow's walk into the doorway, the massive body disappearing as if swallowed up by the once again swirling fog.

Epilogue
Six Months Later

Knuckles white, Darrell grabbed the brass railing.

He couldn't believe he was back here again.

The *Second Wind* plowed through another wave that slapped the front of the sailboat, making it bounce. Erin, hands around the helm and hair streaming behind her in the breeze, looked calm and pleased with herself. She glanced over and grinned at him.

For the past two months, at every break in the weather, Erin had been trying to get him out on the Bay again, but Darrell had refused. Each time he thought about it, he'd find himself back here, swallowing brackish water, fingers clutching the torn life jacket, entire body shivering. Erin had been gentle, coaxing and encouraging him. She even offered some seductive enticements. She'd insisted he needed to get back "on the horse," but Darrell had *not* given in.

Over time, he and Erin had continued to grow close. Things were going so well, he didn't want to mess it up. They'd been through so much together, and she had stayed there beside him, supporting him every step of the way. If she hadn't been quick enough that night, he didn't know what would have happened.

When Erin called late this morning and said she'd swing by and pick him up for an outdoor getaway, Darrell envisioned a trip to the Maritime Museum in St.

Michael's or maybe a picnic at the Blackwater Wildlife Refuge. Not a sail on the same damn Bay he'd nearly drowned in.

But when she pulled up to the marina, she made quiet entreaties, using earnest, green eyes. She'd again hinted at other inducements. "You know, it's warm for this early in the season. Since there's not yet much traffic out there on the Bay,"—she pointed to the calm waters—"never know what could happen." Across the car seat, she flashed that great smile and arched her eyebrows. Darrell couldn't help himself. He'd let his libido lead, and here he sat. On a sailboat. Wrapped in a life jacket. Gripping the hand hold so hard he was afraid he might pull out the grommets fastening it to the port side.

He tore his gaze away from the railing and looked around. Even he had to admit the weather today was gorgeous. Though only the end of April, temperatures were unusually warm, predicted to reach eighty by midday. A few stray clouds chased each other across an azure sky which turned the water of the Bay a sparkling aquamarine. A light breeze filled the two gold and white sails and stirred the water, creating only small waves that rocked the sloop gently. Across the horizon, a few white sails punctured the beautiful blue that wrapped around them. The boulders lining the shores looked like pebbles from where they sailed.

A small breaker thumped the side of the boat and reignited his anxiety, reminding Darrell of the ugly sounds months before. Sometimes, when he closed his eyes at night, he still heard the hideous whomp of the bodies striking the pavement. That night, after Hank disappeared, Kelsie, Erin, and he had approached the split railing, peering over the side. Even now, six months later, he could still remember staring down the side of the building and watching the fog part below, revealing the smashed, bloodied bodies of Brown and Williams. Both women turned away from the grisly scene and buried their heads in his shoulders, while he fought back an urge to vomit.

As they stood there on the widow's walk and the adrenaline drained from their bodies, reality struck. Erin captured their situation. "What the hell do we say happened?"

"Nobody's going to believe my dad's ghost saved us," Kelsie said. Erin and Darrell agreed. Instead, together, they decided to say Darrell struggled with Brown first and then Williams and both men fell through the railing to their deaths. Darrell agreed to take the heat.

And heat it was.

When they were ready, Darrell called 911 from his office. After the bodies were discovered and statements taken, detectives from neighboring towns came to investigate. The three of them spent the entire night answering some difficult questions. *No one in town remembers anything about any lynching, so how did they figure out Williams and Brown lynched Hank? How did they know the name of the victim? Why were Darrell and Kelsie dressed the way they were? Did they lure Brown and Williams up to the widow's walk to kill them? How was Darrell able to overpower both Williams and Brown?* One by one, the three of them were called back for questioning over the next several days, as the authorities tried to sort it all out.

What saved them was the cassette.

That night Erin had thought quickly and switched tapes, sliding the original into a drawer. When she came out onto the walk, she'd handed a blank cassette to Brown, the one he destroyed. Later, she turned the original tape over to the police. The recording, though far from perfect, held both Williams' confession about the lynching and Brown's admission of killing Kelly and Jefferson.

Once the tape's details became known, the townspeople were stunned into disbelief. "Williams and his family have done so much for Wilshire," the locals argued, "and Brown has been our chief for twenty years." In the end, though, most in Wilshire merely wanted the whole thing over and, if possible, forgotten.

However, some would not let up. A few local cops, who had worked with Cameron, thought something was wrong with Darrell's story and simply couldn't believe *he* could get the best of their fellow officer *and* Williams. They circulated rumors—amazingly close to the truth—that Darrell and Erin had lured both the board president and the cop to the widow's walk and then they tripped each one over the railing to their deaths. They even accused Darrell of faking the "confessions" on the tape. They refused to quit until an investigator from the Highway Patrol sent the cassette to the lab where it was confirmed as original and accurate.

This drew out the investigation for three uncomfortable weeks and settled the case legally, but it didn't squelch the rumors. And, along the way, the editor at the *Wilshire Gazette* had a field day playing up the headlines, even though he eventually got the story right. He was not alone. Reporters from the *Baltimore*

Enquirer and cable and network news crews descended on the small town, interviewing anyone who'd speak with them.

Many Wilshire residents took time to thank Darrell for exposing such a terrible stain on their town, but he also received some furtive glances when he and Erin made their runs through the streets. The word was many locals were not happy with him, a Yankee, for exposing the skeletons in their closet. "After all, this is the Eastern Shore. Those things don't happen here," they'd repeated in bars and hair salons and the stands at basketball games.

In the midst of the worst of the media coverage, a small groups of football boosters—cronies of Williams, Darrell figured—even petitioned the board to terminate his teaching and coaching contracts. They threatened, unless the board took action, this "bad publicity" would cost the school district the coveted Williams money promised for the new school. In the end, the board realized they had no legal basis and let it drop.

It made for three challenging weeks, and through it all, Erin stood by her man, as she loved to say. That was reason enough for him to be here, out on the water, with her.

"See, I told you it would be great today," Erin said, bringing Darrell out of his trance.

Darrell blinked at her. The sun shone behind Erin and gave her a halo of shimmering red. It was great, he rationalized, to be here with her. His gaze went to the water surrounding the boat and then back, seeing her grin at him. He fought his fears.

Erin asked, "You've still never seen our ghost since?"

"Hasn't even raised one hair on my neck." Darrell's hand went to the back of his head. "I've watched for him in the office and nothing. Jesse told me he hadn't found a single message left behind either."

Erin set the line on the helm. "I guess Natalia was right about one thing. Hank had unfinished business."

"Yeah, that business ended up splattered on the parking lot."

Moving from behind the helm, Erin crouched into the cabin and re-emerged with a picnic basket. "Want to eat, or you going to stay glued to that railing for the whole trip?"

When she opened the basket, he could smell the tantalizing aroma. "Is that your mom's special fried chicken?"

Erin made her eyebrows dance. "Sure is. Plus some fresh French bread and a bottle of Pinot. Hope I don't have to *indulge* in all this alone."

"You do *not* play fair." Darrell checked the ties on his life jacket with his free hand. His other released the railing, and when he wasn't sent plunging over the side, he got up and sidled to the bench in the center of the boat. She handed him a plate of food and poured some wine into a paper cup. After a few bites and a little wine, his fears receded a bit. He mumbled, "Delicious."

About halfway through their picnic, Erin said, "Hey, tell me about the school assembly this week."

Darrell figured she was trying to distract him, but appreciated it. "Now that *was* a surprise. At the end of the day Friday, they called all the teachers and students to the gym. Said they had major news. When we arrived, the Superintendent Holtzman and Principal Douglass were on stage along with Bud's father,

William Williams II."

"How did Williams, Sr. look?" Erin took another sip of wine.

"Not very good. Disheartened and physically emaciated. To the whole school he apologized for his son's actions. He claimed he had no idea about the whole thing and only wanted to believe the best about Bud, like any father would. He said he was sorry for the shame this has brought the town and the lives it had cost."

"Pretty amazing admission from a man of his stature."

"You haven't heard the best part. Douglass brought out two guests. As soon as the woman came from the wing, I recognized Kelsie, who saw me in the first row and waved."

"You didn't tell me Kelsie was back in town," Erin chided.

"I didn't know till right then. The second was an older black man I didn't recognize. Turned out to be Marcus Young, Hank's older brother. Then, Williams, Sr., announced that he had met with the board in special session the night before and asked them to change the name of the new high school. He said the Williams family would continue to fund the building, but he wanted it be called the Young-Halloran High School."

"That's incredible. All because *you* saw Hank."

"Between you and me," Darrell said, "I'd be okay if I never saw Hank again…or any other ghosts for that matter."

"But Natalia said you have the *gift*." Erin's voice did a perfect parody of the medium's deep alto.

"Yeah, the gift that keeps on giving." He released a

dry chuckle. "The first ghost gave me a doozy of a case of OCD and two dead friends, and the second almost got me drowned and murdered. I don't want to see what the next one has in store for me."

Erin smiled and patted his arm. "Well, I know everyone isn't thrilled with what we uncovered, but I'm proud of you." She wrapped her arms around him, and they kissed, easing his anxiety a bit more.

After they parted, she returned her plate and cup to the basket and took Darrell's as well. She re-corked the bottle. "Might want to save the rest of this for a little later."

She rose, moved to the helm, and released the line on the wheel. She steered the sailboat south.

Farther out into the bay.

Darrell gulped. As the bow sliced through the waters, he glanced around and noticed they had left the few other sloops behind. All Darrell could see, when he looked in every direction, was the Bay.

Same as before.

He felt his nervousness resurging, and he re-checked the bindings on his life jacket and inched closer to the railing.

Either Erin didn't seem to notice or pretended not to. Once out in the middle of the Bay, she reapplied the line to the helm, then stepped forward, checked the rigging, and dropped the mainsail and jib. She hit a switch, and Darrell heard the anchor release and drop to the bottom, a very short trip. At least it wasn't too deep here. As the waves flowed past, the sailboat rocked with the motion but held its position.

When she came back aft, the corners of her smile came up. "What we need to do is help you get comfortable again being out on the water."

Darrel's gaze darted to the waves and back to her. "How do you propose to do that?"

"I love sailing the waters with the mainsail full and billowing, and *The Second Wind*'s bouncing across the waves. But I also enjoy days like this. When you're out in the middle of the Bay, and it feels like you're all alone in the world. And the waves rock the boat gently."

Darrell felt himself swaying with the easy motion of the sloop. He loved being with Erin anytime but would have much preferred his own suede couch. On dry land.

Erin raised her eyebrows and flashed a rakish grin. "Don't have any personal experience *yet*, but I've been told this state can be quite conducive to,"—she paused and let her gaze travel up and down his body—"uh, let's say, helping you regain your sea legs."

"I don't get it."

Erin squeezed his hand and stood up. "Did you like our repast?" she asked with a twinkle in her eye.

"Yeah sure. It was great, but—"

She put a finger to his lips. "Did you realize something was missing?"

"Something missing?"

She helped him to his feet and without releasing his hand, stepped down into the small cabin below. She ducked her head into the opening and turned back, a leer on her face. Only a few inches from Darrell's, she said in a breathy whisper, "Yeah...dessert." She released Darrell's hand and undid the buttons of her blouse, one at a time. She let go of the final button, and Darrell watched as the fabric flapped open. Her hand patted a tie of the life jacket wrapped tight around his torso. "Oh, and you might have to take that off."

She disappeared inside the small cabin, and, as Darrell followed her, fingers fumbling with the straps, he found his fear of the water subsiding.

For some inexplicable reason.

A word about the author...

Dr. Randy Overbeck is a veteran educator who has served children for more than three decades as a teacher and school leader. Over that time, he has worked many of the roles depicted in his writing with responsibilities ranging from coach and yearbook advisor to principal and superintendent. An accomplished writer, he has been published in trade journals, professional texts, and newspapers. His first novel, Leave No Child Behind, won the 2011 Silver Award for Thriller of the Year from ReadersFavorite.com. Dr. Overbeck is a member of the Mystery Writers of America and an active member of the literary community.

You can follow him on Twitter @OverbeckRandy, friend him on Facebook at Author Randy Overbeck or check out his webpage, authorrandyoverbeck.com.

Thank you for purchasing
this publication of The Wild Rose Press, Inc.

For questions or more information
contact us at
info@thewildrosepress.com.

The Wild Rose Press, Inc.
www.thewildrosepress.com

To visit with authors of
The Wild Rose Press, Inc.
join our yahoo loop at
http://groups.yahoo.com/group/thewildrosepress/